DEATH AND THE VISITORS

Also by Heather Redmond

The Mary Shelley Mysteries

Death and the Sisters
Death and the Visitors

A Dickens of a Crime Mystery Series

A Tale of Two Murders
Grave Expectations
A Christmas Carol Murder
The Pickwick Murders
A Twist of Murder

Heather Redmond

Death and the Visitors

www.kensingtonbooks.com

KENSINGTON BOOKS are published by

Kensington Publishing Corp.
900 Third Avenue
New York, NY 10022

All Kensington titles, imprints, and distributed lines are available at special quantity discounts for bulk purchases for sales promotion, premiums, fund-raising, educational, or institutional use. Special book excerpts or customized printings can also be created to fit specific needs. For details, write or phone the office of the Kensington Special Sales Manager: Attn. Special Sales Department. Kensington Publishing Corp, 900 Third Avenue, New York, NY 10022. Phone: 1-800-221-2647.

Library of Congress Card Catalogue Number: 2024936518

The K with book logo Reg. US Pat & TM Off.

ISBN: 978-1-4967-4903-1
First Kensington Hardcover Edition: September 2024

ISBN: 978-1-4967-4905-5 (ebook)

10 9 8 7 6 5 4 3 2 1

Printed in the United States of America

The royal parade
You go, love. I will flee to
A dark, quiet glade

Cast of Characters

Mary Godwin*	16	Child of fame, a writer
Jane Clairmont*	16	Mary's stepsister
William Godwin*	58	Mary's father, a philosopher
Mary Jane Godwin*	48	Mary's stepmother
Percy Bysshe Shelley*	21	Atheist. Lover of humanity. Democrat
Robert Baxter*	17	Mary's Scottish suitor
Eliza Westbrook*	29	Shelley's sister-in-law
Rev. B. Doone	24	A clergyman
Maria Naryshkina*	35	A Polish princess
Dmitry Naryshkin*	56	Maria's hofmeister husband
Pavel Naryshkin	54	Dmitry's brother
Alexander Fedorov	30	A footman
Michael Karamzin	50	A secretary
Viktor Hesse	35	A king's aide
John Cannon	48	A moneylender

John Williams*	33	A Welsh man of business
William Godwin the Younger*	11	Mary's half brother
Fanny Godwin*	20	Mary's half sister
Charles Clairmont*	18	Mary's stepbrother
Thérèse de Saint-Lary	34	The Godwins' French cook

*Real-life people

I was born in the right time, in whole,
Only this time is one that is blessed,
But great God did not let my poor soul
Live without deceit on this earth.
—Anna Akhmatova, “I Was Born in the Right Time,”
translated by Yevgeny Bonver

Am I a mere instrument to be played upon by endless hopes and fears and tormenting wishes? Am I to be the sport of events, the fool of promise, always agitated with near approaching good, yet always deluded?
—William Godwin, *St. Leon*

’Tis time, my friend, ’tis time!
For rest the heart is aching;
Days follow days in flight,
and every day is taking
Fragments of being,
while together you and I
Make plans to live.
Look, all is dust,
and we shall die.
—Alexander Pushkin, “ ’Tis Time, My Friend”

Chapter 1

London, Saturday, May 28, 1814

Jane

"How wonderful to know Mother's work has made it all the way to Russia," my stepsister Mary Godwin exclaimed, an expression of awed pleasure on her lovely fairy face.

As pretty as Mary was, the Polish princess sitting across from us at the dining table outshone her, despite her maturity versus Mary's fresh-faced sixteen years. Heavy eyelids over large, dark eyes gave Princess Maria an undeniably sensual air. The rest of her features were enshrined in a perfect rosy cream complexion, which continued down to her low-cut, tight bodice of blue velvet, necessary against the unusual May chill.

I fancied I had something similar to her looks, though with darker hair and no finery. She wore no necklace, the better to display her bosom, but a number of bracelets and rings adorned her wrists and fingers. Her ears, visible under an elaborate braided topknot hairstyle, sported pearl drops from which hung delicate gold chain and pearl loops. I might have been jealous, except that in the household of William Godwin, my stepfather, we were raised not to want such things.

Intellectual accomplishments were everything, and after all, that is what had brought such distinguished guests to the first floor of our listing, creaking, damp house on Skinner Street. The house was imposing enough to impress visitors, if one ignored the condition of it. Due to a dispute in ownership, Papa didn't pay rent but couldn't demand repairs.

The two men with her, Princess Maria's Russian husband and his brother, also cut fine figures, despite being considerably older, and their extravagant manes of gray and dark hair put Papa's balding head to shame. Little differentiated them, other than a faint white scar line stretching along the brother's jaw.

"I do hope the publisher of the Russian edition has paid for the privilege of selling *A Vindication of the Rights of Woman,*" my mother said acidly.

Papa spoke over Mamma, his second wife and my mother, drowning out the end of the title. "Either way, the volumes have brought fascinating guests to our table. I am curious to hear your opinions on the current situation in France."

"Why are so many foreign diplomats descending on London?" I asked.

"We come in advance of the Congress of Vienna meetings," Count Dmitry Naryshkin said in a heavy accent. "The servants of many royal persons are already arriving to ensure their masters' future comforts."

"I am sure the upper classes are preparing to celebrate with visiting leaders and statesmen," Mamma said. "We have had our fair share of such dinner guests over the years, like Aaron Burr, the former vice president of the United States."

"Why are all of your children not here?" Pavel Naryshkin asked, in an even thicker accent. "There is a daughter of the household missing, no?"

"The eldest, Fanny, is in Wales presently," Papa said. "She is interested in educational matters, like her late mother, and has taken the offerings of our Juvenile Library to a community there."

I watched Mary's eyelids flutter and her mouth work. I remembered my stepsister Fanny's tears as she was sent away for loving a married poet. The man in question, Percy Bysshe Shelley, a disciple of Papa's, had affected us all in curious ways.

"I see you live over your shop," Pavel Naryshkin said. "Is that common in London?"

"It makes life simpler," Papa said. "We are not proud people. However, the business continues into the next building. We publish many educational works as well as sell them here."

"There was a murder in the bookshop recently," Mary said, a malicious gleam coming into her eyes as she glanced at me.

"How dreadful," the princess murmured, but her husband spoke over her, changing the subject.

"When will Miss Fanny return?" he asked.

"We do enjoy traveling in this family," Mamma said with a vapid flutter of her fingers for emphasis.

"The air is terrible here," Mary said in a flat tone. "There are prisons all around us, and a slaughterhouse. Often, there are hangings." She pointed an accusatory finger toward the window.

"Mary," I chided. "It's not as if you can see the gibbet from the house. They build it a bit down the street when it is needed."

Mamma's face had gone florid. "Well."

Mary jumped in her seat. Mamma had probably pinched her with those strong, sausage-like fingers. Her pinches left bruises.

"Does she tend to illness?" Dmitry Naryshkin asked.

"Fanny?" I asked. "No, not of the physical kind."

"Jane," Papa barked. "Fanny is in excellent health, and we all enjoy traveling. Mary returned from a long trip to Scotland at the end of winter."

Fanny and Mary both tended to depression. Though they

had different fathers, the Wollstonecraft blood came with a heavy mental burden, it seemed. I only knew my father had been Swiss, but I must have inherited my cheerful temperament from him.

"Miss Fanny should be with her family," Count Naryshkin said. "She should be brought home to London where she belongs."

His tone, not to mention his opinion, confused me. Perhaps he believed that daughters of the household should be kept at home, minding their needlework. Unlike Mary and me, though, Fanny was old enough to be out in the world, married or even working. But these visitors were upper-class, after all, and their women were much more decorative than useful, as we had to be.

"I am very excited you are here, even if dear Fanny cannot be," Mary said.

"How sweet of you to say," the princess cooed.

"Oh, yes." Mary leaned forward. "You see, I am writing a novel called *Isabella, the Penitent; or, The Bandit Novice of Dundee.* My heroine is, as expected, in a most modest situation at the start of the book, but when she is kidnapped, she will be dressed by the wealthy villain. I must store away the details of your wardrobe and jewels for Isabella."

The princess smiled and saluted Mary with her wineglass. "Do you write with a message, as your dear mother and father did?"

"I think a well-educated girl can overcome just about any difficulty," Mary said, her words tumbling faster as she warmed to her subject. "Why should any girl be helpless? Papa and Mamma have always said they did not have time to educate us to my mother's standards, but I have a terrible fascination for natural philosophy and any kind of book, really."

"Do your ideas come from the natural world, then?" the princess asked.

"From dreams," Mary said, leaning forward until the bodice

of her black silk dress nearly dipped into her buttery potatoes. "I read too much, or see something in the neighborhood, and it is all twisted into dreams. Why, I—"

Papa cleared his throat. "At my age, we have many young people around us, carrying the torch for our principles. One of the best, Percy Bysshe Shelley, has just assured me he will be staying in London under my tutelage, instead of returning to Wales."

I wondered what that would mean for poor Shelley's disastrous marriage. I half thought he should return to Wales with his cheating wife and horrid sister, abandon them there, then flee back to London. Mary's eyes had widened, though the rest of her expression remained serene. Papa might have at least let her finish answering the princess's question.

I noticed the princess had not touched anything on her plate after the first couple of bites. Our French cook, the poor dear, had burned the potatoes again and boiled the cabbage down to an unappealing mush. "Do you hire many Frenchwomen in Russia?" I asked, setting down my knife. "Are they all as difficult to train as our cook?"

"Jane!" Mamma whisper-roared, then pushed her chair back so quickly it fell over, dropping with a dull thud onto the threadbare carpet. "Why don't we leave the men to their libations? I am sure Her Royal Highness would like to see the portrait of the first Mrs. Godwin that hangs in Mr. Godwin's study."

She had captured all three of our guests' attention.

"I would like that most excessively," Princess Maria said, daintily rearranging her place setting. "To see an image of our Mary painted from life is an inestimable privilege."

I had the feeling Mamma shouldn't have risen before our royal guest, but the princess didn't show obvious displeasure. Possibly she never ate much anyway, to maintain her stunning figure.

My half brother Charles, a bit younger than Fanny, smirked at me. "Someone should take Willy upstairs."

"Yes, take Willy up, then you can join us," Mamma said to me. When his tutor was not in the house, we often had to take charge of our shared half brother. What an interesting tangle we were, five young people, none of whom had the same set of parents.

Mary and I rose after the princess did. We followed Mamma out of the dining room. The door would not close into the warped frame as she tried to push it. I turned my back to the door and, ignoring the grinding and squeaking sounds of the wood, forced it shut.

Mamma's lips tightened, but she turned away, fingering the dark curl that lay against her throat, and marched down the passage to the study, holding a candle high to illuminate the passage.

I hauled eleven-year-old Willy upstairs, then ordered him to wash the sauce off his face and trotted back downstairs, unwilling to miss any of the conversation.

The study still had illumination from the street at this time of year. When I came in, Mamma was droning on about Papa's extravagant collection of books. They filled untidy bookcases all around us, nearly to the ceiling. I wondered if she hoped to sell some of the titles to our guests. Papa would be dreadfully angry if she managed it, but I was on Mamma's side. We needed to raise money somehow.

However, Princess Maria did not take the bait. After a significant pause, Mamma left the bookcases and stepped around Papa's chair behind his desk. She set the candlestick on the table underneath the portrait of Mary Wollstonecraft, illuminating it. The princess gasped theatrically and clasped her hands together over her heart.

"She contemplates eternity, this sweet lady," the princess said.

When I glanced at Mary, she had her hand over her abdomen, as if reminding herself that her mother had been carrying her at the time the portrait was created, just a few months before her death.

The painting showed a mature lady who possessed few to none of her daughter's features. Her nose might have been similar, except that I knew Mary's nose to be an exact copy of Papa's. Her brown hair had a bit of the flyaway quality of Mary's, but the color was not a match. I recognized the serenity of her expression, however. Had Mary come by her peaceful demeanor, regardless of the inner workings of her mind, naturally, or had she cultivated her looks after long hours contemplating her mother's visage?

As if I had spoken out loud, the princess turned to Mary and took a long look at her, then gazed at the portrait again.

"Is Miss Fanny Godwin a good likeness of her mother?" she asked.

Mary's stiffening told me she felt the slight. "She is my mother's exact size and can wear her clothing."

"And her face?"

"Fanny is very quiet," I volunteered.

"A peaceful and plain creature," Mary added.

"Her father, is he still living?" asked the princess, not looking away from the portrait. Indeed, she lifted the candle to examine some detail.

"Mr. Imlay, if that is who you mean, had no interest in her once Mother was dead, I'm told," Mary said. "Papa has always been her father."

"I have read Mr. Godwin's biography of your mother." The princess set the candle down. "It is tragic. I am happy to have married as I did."

"Do you have children?" Mary asked.

"Do they look like you?" I added.

The princess smiled at us, but Mamma interrupted before

she could respond. "Go downstairs, Mary, and make us a pot of tea. Jane, light the parlor fire. We will descend in a moment, Your Royal Highness."

Mary and I left the room together after a joined glance at Mamma's steely face, hugging the wall along the staircase to reduce the groaning of the tired steps.

"I do wish someone would take a hammer and nails to this riser," Mary grumbled, kicking a piece back into place.

"With ownership in dispute, there is no one to maintain it," I pointed out.

"And all of the rent money Papa doesn't need to pay goes to feeding distinguished visitors." Mary dropped to the bottom step and put her head in her hands. "Can you imagine? A real princess in Skinner Street?"

"It is desperately exciting," I agreed.

"There will be many such people coming into London now," Mary said. "We should get a look at as many of them as possible, to store up in our imaginations."

"Pulling yourself away from natural philosophy for a few months?" I teased.

"My education must be well-rounded," Mary said. "I have often thought that Mother didn't write until she was nearly thirty because she needed to bank enough experience first."

I wondered how Mary thought she would do that. At heart, I thought her a more conventional sort than her mother. I had the spirit of a philosopher much more than Mary did. She wasn't even an atheist like me. "You will have to do the same."

"I am conscious of the issue," Mary said. "I will stuff my brain like a Christmas pudding and hope it all spills out again long before I'm middle-aged."

"There is only so much you can fit into such a tiny carapace," I said, reaching through the fluff to knock gently on her skull. "But you will try, poor thing."

"At least I have six months more learning than you." She batted my hand away. "I suppose I should fetch the tea."

"I should light the fire," I said agreeably.

We didn't move. The windows were set rather high in the walls and door, so we couldn't see out, but torches flashed as people passed by in the growing dark. We had sat quite late at dinner, given our fascination for our guests and theirs for us.

"Why do you suppose they were interested in Fanny?" I asked.

"She is the oldest, and they seem far more interested in Mother's fame than Papa's."

"I suppose his was far greater in those years."

"He is a man." Mary sighed. "You can see by the number of portraits painted of him as a young man that he was well-respected."

I smelled the mold and mildew always wafting through the air. "He has lived long enough to be forgotten."

"We are lucky to have Shelley to shore us up, or at least he will do, when the loans come through." Mary reached for the banister and hoisted herself. It listed but held under her slight weight.

I didn't risk it, being a more robust specimen.

A half hour later, we were gathered around the parlor fire, teacups in hand. Considering she was a princess and possessed almost unworldly beauty, Her Royal Highness was friendly and pleasant. She told us about her children in surprisingly good English. I didn't mind giving up the more comfortable chair for a stool.

She shared a charming story about her eldest daughter, Marina, who was just a little older than us and loved dogs. They had a number of them, and she counted off their names on her fingers. She also had a baby, left behind in Russia with his nurse, and a daughter who was still a young child. After each birth—not all of which had resulted in a child who lived to grow up, sadly—she'd been gifted with a ring, and she wore three on each hand, all gold. She and Mamma traded tales about her daughter Sophia compared to Willy, just a few years older. Mamma was positively jovial, and I could see she was making a good impression, which was not always the case.

Mary had pulled a stump of a pencil and piece of paper from somewhere and was making notes as they spoke, hidden in a squashy corner armchair in the gloom. Mamma didn't notice.

Papa came in with the Naryshkin men. The women quieted so that the men could discourse. I amused myself by making responses no one cared to hear in my head with their thick accents. Occasionally, a question was directed at Mary. She had to put away her pencil, even though Mamma answered most of the questions before she could.

After a while, my back began to ache from sitting on the stool. Mamma took the princess out of the room to refresh herself, and when they returned, that seemed to be the signal to leave.

Some ten minutes more were passed praising pretty Mary and suggesting Fanny be brought home so they could meet her before they returned to Russia in a few months. No one paid me any notice.

At least not until Mamma bleated, "Tidy up in here," into my ear, as everyone else returned to the front hall. Mary had already been sent downstairs with the teacups.

Charles smirked and tweaked one of my curls as he passed. I shut the door behind him, to conserve the heat, then flopped down on the sofa. Body heat had warmed the fabric and my aching back relaxed into it.

I felt something poking into my bottom as my senses calmed. Frowning, I rearranged my skirts. A small item pressed against my finger. In the front hall, the only door into the house and bookshop opened and closed. A horse whinnied, and I imagined the Russians helping their beautiful princess into the carriage, then riding off into the night. I stood when I could no longer tolerate the pressure. I ran my fingers along the sofa until I found the small object, probably one of Willy's marbles, then took it over to the fire so I could see what it was.

A gemstone winked at me, catching the fire. I lifted it to the candelabra on the mantelpiece. The mirror reflected my fine dark eyes and wild curls back to myself. I checked my hand. A gold ring with a red stone was in my palm! The princess must have dropped it. I'd noticed how expressive she was with her hands.

I ran to the window. The carriage had gone, taking the owner of the ring with it. I returned to the fire and examined the ring with my fingers and eyes. It had no markings. I could tell the stone wasn't a garnet. It seemed to have a deeper color. Could it be something truly valuable?

My first instinct was to tell Mamma, but what if she kept the ring for herself? Money was hard to come by in this household. Why could I not be as dishonest as she?

Chortling to myself, I closed my fist around the ring and ran upstairs. My private chamber was one long space, stretching the length of the house. I had no lock on the door but plenty of space, if not perfect privacy. I glanced around, then settled on my trunk. We had washed and put away most of our winter things at the start of this week.

I unlocked the trunk and pulled out a thick woolen sock, then dropped the ring in. It would do. My vanity desired that I put the ring on and parade in front of my little mirror, but Mary might come in at any moment to prattle about our guests. I closed and relocked the trunk, then turned around and sat on it, exhausted by my subterfuge. The ring would do me no good if I could not turn it into coin, but that was a matter for another day, another month even, when the Russians had returned to their frozen lands.

* * *

Washing day nearly trumped bookshop duties on Monday. Mamma forced Charles to mind the bookshop along with our porter and hauled Mary and me into the back garden to do the heavy work along with Polly, the maid. When she'd started with us, she'd thought our household a step up from the orange merchant's house where she'd been a maid-of-all-work, but after a few days of listening to Thérèse, Polly had lost her self-satisfied smile at the improvement in her lot. Now she was nearly as sullen as Mary and Charles.

I was stirring the kettle with the white clothing when a window opened in the schoolroom. Willy peeked out and waved at me. I blew curls out of my eyes and waved back, then felt a rush of dizziness. Blinking hard, I steadied myself on the stirring stick. A cracking sound caught my attention, then the stick broke in half, nearly launching me into the boiling water. I stumbled back.

"Jane!" Mother growled around a mouth full of clothes-pegs.

I put my hand to my head. After a moment, my nerves steadied, and I fished out the broken stick with tongs.

"What is wrong with you?" Mary asked from the wash-board, where she was scrubbing blood out of rags.

"I didn't sleep well." My voice didn't sound right to me. Surely my tossing and turning hadn't been over my theft of the princess's ring. Mary would say I had done worse things than that and slept like I was cradled by angel's wings.

She looked down at her bucket of rags, then back at me. "Go into the house to cool down, and come back with another stick," she advised.

"There are some in the scullery." I walked off, my back stiffened against Mamma's yell, but she didn't argue.

I felt a wave of dizziness again when I went inside, and then I needed my chamber pot. Instead of going down to the scullery, I rounded the staircase to go up. The first floor was silent, a bad sign which meant no customers in the bookshop, but I heard voices on the second, coming from the study.

My vision swayed. Had the Russians returned to retrieve the ring? I dumped out the wildflowers I'd placed in my listening glass, then took the glass to the door, ignoring the pain in my midsection.

"You have nothing to worry about." I heard Papa's rumble loud and clear. My fingers convulsed around the glass as I thought about how to sneak the ring downstairs to the sofa. I'd better do it now, while Mamma's and Mary's watchful gazes were safely outside.

"You owe me a great deal," said an English voice. "How can I possibly have nothing to worry about?"

After a moment's confusion, I recognized the voice. The moneylender John Cannon, who had been treated to a nice meal and the presence of the entire family about once a month since Papa had borrowed a thousand pounds from him late last year. He called regularly, which was a source of great stress on the household.

"We had a visit from part of the Russian delegation," Papa said.

"What does that have to do with our arrangement?" John Cannon said in a steely tone.

"Pavel Naryshkin, the brother of the tsar's hofmeister, has promised one thousand guineas worth of diamonds in pledge to the Juvenile Library," Papa said, the words ringing in my incredulous ears.

"Does he know they will go to nothing but paying down your impressive debt?" asked the moneylender.

"It is no business of his what I do with the money. Those in need are entitled to funds from those who have them."

"What does he think the money is going for?" Mr. Cannon persisted.

"My pressing money problems will be solved with this gift," Papa said, ignoring the question.

"Will they?" asked the acid-voiced moneylender.

I heard Papa's hand come down on his desk. "Very well, I can see your patience is at an end. I will repay you, sir, my loan balance in full."

"I think you owe more than a thousand guineas," said Mr. Cannon.

"I do not," Papa said. "I will pay you nothing at all if you do not agree. I will even hand you the diamonds myself, and if you can get a better price for them, then all the better for you."

"And if the price is less?"

"That is your failing, sir."

"I will see these diamonds before I agree to this," Mr. Cannon said. "I know better than to trust you, sir."

"What a thing to say to an honest family man. When I was only responsible for myself, I never owed any man a penny. Now it is different, with five children to feed, but I am still a man of honor."

"I understand you have sent one of your mouths away, and three of the remaining four work in your business, so you don't need employees. I wonder how you have quite this much trouble feeding them." I heard the sneer, and a chair pushing back.

Tiptoeing away, I set the glass on the plate and tossed the flowers back in before running upstairs, hugging the wall. I agreed with Mr. Cannon. Surely the Russians meant for their diamonds to go to Mary Wollstonecraft's daughters and not her widower's loans. Poor Fanny, sent away to be an unpaid governess. She asked for no dignity and received none either. Mary, I knew, was too resourceful not to find a way to escape. She'd been gone to Scotland most of the past year, and she'd find a way to leave again. I did not know how to hold onto her and was loath to try. I needed to make my own way, even if a bit of larceny came into play. At least the ring didn't contain a diamond, so it couldn't be a part of what Mr. Naryshkin had promised.

I tossed my head when I reached the top of the stairs, feeling sweaty ringlets flow around the back of my neck. I needn't feel guilty about keeping it in my possession. No one cared about Mary Jane Godwin's children.

On Tuesday, I had the bookshop counter in my charge while Mary was meant to be dusting. Mamma said she didn't trust Polly to dust the parlor, since it had to be fit for royalty and Polly had slovenly tendencies. I'd seen Mary tuck her paper and pencil into her pocket, and I suspected she'd clean out the coal clinkers from the fireplace and ignore the rest in favor of working on *Isabella, the Penitent*, or some maudlin work of poetry.

I wondered why she couldn't finish her novel. I'd reminded her that her mother's first novel, *Mary*, was quite short, but she'd pointed out that Papa's first novel, *Caleb Williams*, was quite long and had been much more successful.

She'd also said she might not have quite enough life experience yet to finish a novel, but Mary Wollstonecraft had been naught but a governess when she wrote *Mary*, so I didn't see the problem. I did see the danger, though, implicit in gathering more life experience.

The inner door into Mamma's office opened. She stomped through the bookshop muttering to herself, passed through the shop door, and had not returned by the time an anemic young tutor came in to pick up copybooks and *Aesop*.

Papa came in as church bells struck eleven, with a collection of pencils he wanted me to sharpen. I noticed his right hand had a bit of a tremble to it and knew that was why he hadn't wanted to wield the penknife himself.

"Why are you and Mamma dour?" I asked, innocently.

"Have any messages been delivered?" was his brusque reply.

I wished, as I often did, that Fanny had been here. Normally, she was given all of Papa's little tasks. They had the sweet relationship of chosen family, and Fanny could have soothed him.

"No messages, sir," I said promptly. "Am I looking for someone special?"

The door to the house opened, and then the shop. This time a middle-aged mother in muslin and a paisley wrap, towing a sulky boy in a cut-down coat, entered. Papa made himself scarce behind a bookshelf as she asked for *Tales from Shakespeare*.

After they left, I deposited the coins into the money box and pulled a penknife from the shelf under the counter. Mamma reentered and began to chide Papa as he appeared, leafing through a copy of Lord Byron's *The Corsair*.

She snatched the book out of his hands. "I will not have you leaving fingerprints on the books, Mr. Godwin."

He lowered his chin and said coldly, "I will do what I like in my own house, madam."

"We will not be able to pay for Jane's singing lessons much longer," she said in equal tones of ice. "Where are the funds you were promised?"

My stomach clenched around the remains of the porridge I'd eaten for breakfast. Surely, we were not so poor as that, when we were prominent enough to come to the attention of royalty? My unseeing gaze drifted around the bookshop. I suddenly felt all of Mary's despair descending upon me. Was this all we had, now?

Papa turned, lips pressed down into a half-moon, aging his face dreadfully. "No tears in the bookshop, Jane." He snatched the half-sharpened pencil out of my lifeless hand and walked out.

Mamma rushed toward me and slapped my cheek. "There, that will snap the tears right out of you." She whirled toward the office, raising the leaves of the *Morning Chronicle* a customer had left on the bookshelf.

I put my hand to my cheek and knew despair afresh. Pushing the pencils and knife aside, I lowered my cheek to the counter. The coolness of the polished wood soothed the heat in my flesh, even as hot tears trickled down.

After some time, the door opened again. I lifted my face and attempted to school it into something less than an image of misery.

A hand plucked the book Papa had left off the counter. "Ah, *The Corsair*," said a delighted, rather high-pitched male voice.

> *O'er the glad waters of the dark blue sea, our thoughts as boundless, and our souls as free, far as the breeze can bear, the billows foam, survey our empire and behold our home!*

"I am not in the mood for poetry, Shelley," I growled, knowing Papa's future benefactor instantly.

Shelley was much too goodhearted and handsome not to be welcomed whenever and wherever he appeared. "You are indeed a tonic for all enthusiasm, Jane Clairmont. What troubles you?"

I pointed to my cheek, and he peered at it, then shrugged. "I guess the counter worked," I said grumpily.

Mary came in softly, for Shelley had left the door wide open. He turned to her with a grin, then leapt to her side with a balletic pose and whispered in her ear.

"A walk?" she whispered. "Oh, do let's."

"They'll never let us go," I said. "Mamma and Papa are in foul moods over some money matter."

"Has a man come to call on Godwin today?" Shelley asked, brushing his light brown curls out of his eyes. As usual, he'd forgotten his hat.

I shook my head and lowered my voice. "About diamonds?"

Shelley wagged his finger at me. "Listening at doors again, Jane?"

I wrinkled my nose at him in response while Mary gazed at us, confused.

"If he has not come, then your father is at risk of defaulting on a loan." He sniffed. "The air is much too close in here, and I have an errand in mind that even your mamma will approve."

"She's in the office," I said.

He bounced away, as happy as a puppy being let into a back garden.

"Not going to Wales agrees with him," Mary said, picking up the book. "I wonder why I have not read *The Corsair* yet?"

I'd fallen asleep with it next to me on the pillow back in February, right when we'd received the first copies. "You were still in Dundee when it came out."

She tucked flyaway strands of hair behind her ears. "That makes sense. We did not see many new books there."

"Did you finish dusting?" I asked, all false innocence.

"I did, and rinsed out the dust cloths in the scullery," Mary said unexpectedly. "I'm as eager as anyone to have the parlor sparkling for distinguished guests. This summer we should see quite a few of them, if Papa and Mother are properly remembered throughout Europe."

I heard Mamma's office door open a couple of minutes later, just after the porter returned from taking an order to Grosvenor Square. Shelley quirked his fingers at us, and we followed like a pair of well-trained pups ourselves.

"Who is going to watch the bookshop?" I asked as Mary stopped at the pegs beside the front door and handed me a bonnet and pelisse before putting on her own.

"The porter is there, and your mamma can listen for the bell from the office," Shelley said carelessly.

I pulled on my gloves in record time and followed them out of the door, before Mamma could change her mind and come bellowing. She was generally very respectful to Shelley, but I didn't like to chance it.

We started up the street, which meant walking past a succession of warehouses that stocked a variety of products, from cloth to oranges. Small shops took up additional storefronts.

A man was smoking a thin cigar in front of the warehouse next door to the one we used for the publishing firm, where my brother spent most of his time. The man—someone's footman from the look of his fancy, dark blue coat and knee breeches—must have been an ex-soldier, judging from the thick line of raised flesh that marred his skin from his left eye to his chin, cutting into the flesh at one side of his mouth. His tricorn hat shadowed his upper face, and I did not recognize the livery as belonging to a well-known aristocratic family.

"Not a Londoner," Mary said. "I wonder what he is doing in this part of town?"

"All sorts of strange folk around, with these statesmen arriving in London," Shelley said.

I put my hands into the pockets of the pelisse. I felt something and pulled it out. Fanny must have worn the garment last, for I recognized the small reticule worked in lace over pink silk as her work. It had been many months since the air had been warm enough to don the unlined pelisse. I tucked the purse as deep as I could into my pocket, for fear of thieves.

Shelley continued. "They are bringing their troubles, and troublemakers, with them."

Mary put her hand on Shelley's arm. I daresay she took any opportunity to touch him, naughty thing. "What do you know?"

Shelley reached for me, then pulled us both across the street. I batted at flies, distracted from my pleasure at him not allowing Mary to monopolize him. We were moving toward Smithfield Market, where animals were killed and sold every day.

"A Russian corpse was pulled out of the Thames River this morning," he reported.

Mary stopped, looking very pale. "Oh, no."

Shelley frowned and released both of us. "What does that have to do with you?"

"It might be Pavel Naryshkin," I said. A cart rolled by, stirring up a cloud of effluvious dust from the side of the street. I rubbed my eyes as Mary sneezed. "Papa is very upset that he didn't keep his promise to come. Not that he's told us anything."

"Explain," Shelley demanded.

"I listened at the door when the moneylender came," I said triumphantly. "Papa said Mr. Naryshkin had promised him diamonds."

Shelley wiped dust out of his eyes and lowered his voice. "Why?"

"The visitors are obsessed with Wollstonecraft. Do you think he was killed by a robber? I'm sure he's never come back, or even sent word, since they went away on Saturday night."

"He must have been coming with the diamonds," Mary whispered. "And someone knew and followed him."

I started to nod, then stopped, puzzled. "Why was he near the river? It isn't close to Skinner Street."

"Do we even know where the Naryshkin party was staying?" Mary asked. "Maybe they are lodged near the river."

"I believe the distinguished families are staying with our own local aristocrats," Shelley said. "Likely in Mayfair somewhere."

"The Thames is south of there," Mary said. "No reason to go south before coming to Skinner Street. Whereabouts was the body found, exactly?"

"In the worksite where the Strand Bridge is going up," Shelley said. "Maybe he went for a bit of sightseeing, since that *is* in between Mayfair and here."

Mary's voice was hollow. "He was followed until no one watched, then discarded in the river."

I moaned. "We are as good as killers. Mr. Naryshkin was trying to help Papa, and now this!" Was Mary's God punishing me for stealing the ring, by taking the rest of the Russian treasure away from us? No, I could not think such a silly thing.

"Jane, what's wrong?" Shelley asked.

"It's just dreadful. We were at dinner with him this past Saturday." I sniffed and put my hand to my cheek. Should I give Papa the ring I found to pay off John Cannon, or even take it to him myself? No, that would expose me as a thief, and it wasn't worth the risk. I was sure the ring wasn't worth a thousand guineas. It would not do much good.

Chapter 2

Mary

Mary knew Shelley was leading her and Jane toward Charterhouse to walk in the cool gardens there. While it would be peaceful, she didn't think she could stand any more flies, not to mention she couldn't endure the stench of Smithfield Market.

She stopped, tugging on Shelley's arm. "We need to see the Naryshkins, don't you think? To find out what is going on?"

"How would we do that?" Jane asked. "We'd never be welcomed into a house in Mayfair without an explicit invitation."

"Shelley would be allowed entrance," Mary said, looking at the handsome young man next to her. A baronet's grandson, so grand that she was often amazed he spent time with them.

"That is true, but it would take me a day at least to learn where they are lodged." He scratched his long-tipped nose, dislodging a fly.

"Papa might know," Jane said. "But he has not been evident much these past few days, and might not tell us anyway."

"He won't let us interfere," Mary agreed. "We shall have to

lean on Shelley. We should give up our walk and return to the bookshop so he can pay calls and learn where they are lodged."

He snapped his fingers, surprising her. "I know a way we can both avoid your bookshop duties and get the answers we need."

"How?" Jane asked.

"We'll walk down to St. James's Palace to get viewing tickets for the Thursday royal drawing room. It's at two p.m. that day, less than forty-eight hours from now."

Mary's thoughts flew lightning quick. "The Naryshkins won't be the only rich foreigners about. There are likely to be people like them from all the courts of Europe."

"Could we meet more foreigners with money to hold off Papa's creditors there?" Jane asked.

"We can't get into the drawing room itself," Shelley said. "But we can watch them enter, which will help us learn who is in town."

"We might find someone who can aid us until you can finalize those loans on your future prospects," Jane said. "Though I do think it dreadful that these diamonds go to pay debts, when they ought to go to Mary and Fanny, as the Wollstonecraft heirs."

"Your papa was an extraordinary celebrity years before Mary Wollstonecraft," Shelley said. "He merits much in his own right, which is why I pledged himself on my honor to support him in his old age, once I discovered he wasn't already dead. You girls are laurels on his wreath. It does me good to know he kept Fanny, given her unfortunate circumstances."

"They say her father still lives, somewhere," Mary said. "We've never heard anything from him."

"Poor Fanny," Jane said. "Though I know nothing at all of my own father. Isn't that even worse than knowing he didn't want you?"

"I thought Mr. Clairmont was dead," Shelley said.

"I have my doubts," Mary told him.

"You see a story in everything," Jane said, starting to sniff.

Mary batted three flies out of her eyes. "We can't trust a thing your mother says, and you know it. Besides, Papa has been an excellent father to you and Charles. You couldn't want for better."

Shelley's look at her was quite intense. She felt the implied criticism and bristled. "You never see your father at all. You have to hide from him to sneak visits with the rest of your family."

"I would rather he wasn't such a Tory," Shelley said agreeably. "Come, girls, let's turn around and make our way to St. James."

The two-mile walk became much more interesting as they reached Fleet Street and turned west to head to the palace. Shouting over the noise in the road, Shelley regaled them with facts about the 1530s-built structure. Mary hid her blushes under a mask of polite interest as he told them about the royal mistresses who had been kept there by earlier King Georges. The palace had seen Queen Elizabeth await the fate of the Spanish Armada and had housed Charles I the night before his execution.

When the red brick façade of the palace came into sight, Shelley stepped between them and said, "It was built on the former site of a leprosy hospital. Odd choice."

Two women with a male servant frowned and passed by them.

"It's haunted, I'm sure of it," Jane said.

Shelley laughed and nodded. "We have to see the lord chamberlain's servants to try to get viewing tickets. I believe the privy chamber is the best spot because you can actually see the royals passing, but there are two other rooms to stand in as well."

They joined a line of fellow Londoners outside the lord

chamberlain's office, just behind the two women. Rather long, it snaked into the palace.

"I don't think we'll be able to get the best tickets," Jane opined, "but we aren't here to see the queen."

"We want to see the people being presented," Mary agreed.

"Good point. Then the guard chamber or royal presence chamber will be fine," Shelley said.

Mary heard the word *Thames* coming from a couple of people ahead of them and shushed her companions. She held out her hand and turned her palm down.

Shelley listened for a moment, then stepped out of line. "I say, are you talking about that body they fished out of the river this morning?"

The two men, both dressed like merchants, turned to him. "Yes, what have you heard?" one asked, huddling into a fine winter greatcoat, too warm for most people that day. His cheeks were sunken, like he'd had many teeth pulled, and he looked like someone on a milk and toast diet due to an inability to chew properly.

"Russian, they say," Shelley said.

"A nobleman's brother," agreed the man.

"A name something like narwhal?" queried the second man, rounder than the first, with a watch chain that stretched across a waistcoat that strained at the buttons.

"Naryshkin?" Shelley asked.

The second man poked Shelley in the chest. "That is it, exactly, sir."

The line shuffled forward. Shelley kept up with the men, asking more detailed questions, but they had nothing more to offer but comments about foreigners in general.

"How can we learn more?" Jane asked when Shelley stepped back into the line. "This is terrible."

"Your papa should go to the inquest to learn what happened, but he'll never see the diamonds."

"Shelley," Mary hissed, then faked a laugh when the women in front of them turned around. What was he thinking, to bring up diamonds?

He looked at her, then shook his head as if startling it back into order. "We really should stop rehearsing this play in public. People will get notions."

Jane trilled a very high-pitched laugh, then sang a couple of lines about a milkmaid. The cadaverous merchant stepped out of line to glare at her, but then up ahead, someone exited and a few more people stepped over the threshold. Everyone turned around to move forward.

"I'm not thinking about them," Mary said in a very low voice, as her trio was restored. "Another murder, attached to our name?"

"Papa's name is already mud in certain circles." Jane crossed her arms over her pelisse. "I'd rather just have the, you know, special items."

Shelley patted her shoulder, though his words weren't comforting. "If they weren't stolen, or can be retrieved, the Prince Regent will get them somehow."

"I'm not going to let this be the end of it," Mary said. "We can still investigate. Maybe we can get a reward if we learn valuable information about Mr. Naryshkin's death."

Jane shuffled from side to side. "If we can never retrieve the special items, what is the point of upsetting Mamma? It's better to stay home and mind the bookshop."

"When the weather is finally better?" Mary scoffed. "I'm spending as little time in Skinner Street as I can."

"Mamma will be furious," Jane warned.

"Her moods shift with the wind anyway," Mary said. "What does it matter? Her abuse will continue even if we are the most perfect daughters who ever lived."

"Like Fanny," Jane said.

"Exactly."

"We really need those diamonds," Jane whispered.

"We didn't know they existed a week ago," Mary said into her ear. "Let us turn them into some other sort of opportunity."

Jane pressed her lips together and looked away, her eyes glistening.

Mary met Shelley's gaze. She thought he suspected what she did. Jane knew something more. She was acting too strange for it to be otherwise. Jane would never want to tie herself to the bookshop, ordinarily.

Mary jolted as someone poked her in the back. She turned around and was assaulted with a barrage of questions about what she had overheard. By the time she'd lied her way out of the conversation, they were through the door and Shelley had successfully obtained three tickets for the guard chamber on Thursday.

"My feet hurt," Jane announced as they walked out of the door into the courtyard. "I want to go home."

Other than a quick stop at a public fountain to refresh themselves, they made it home in good time, though Jane was limping slightly by the time Mary divested herself of her outerwear in the front hall.

"I'm going to take my shoes upstairs and take a look at the leather," Jane said.

Shelley shook his head in the direction of the staircase as she went up. "Can your father afford a pair of new shoes?"

"It depends on how many books we can sell, I suppose. More children need to be born so we can improve the customer base for the shop," Mary joked.

Shelley raised his eyebrows.

Mary blushed as she realized what she'd said and hoped her bonnet hid her cheeks. "I'm not wrong."

"No, you are not," he said softly. "Though the children conceived today will be of no value to the shop for years."

Mary put her hands to her cheeks to cool them as she changed the subject to the weather. Jane rattled down with the force of an elephant on the stairs, distracting both of them.

A loud screech erupted from below them as soon as Mary removed her bonnet. The floor shook under her feet. "What was that?"

"Mamma," Jane said grimly, straightening her skirt. She'd taken off her pelisse and bonnet upstairs, along with her shoes. Her stockings were at risk on the rough floorboards. "Shelley, you had better go."

The floor shook again. "Something is going on in the kitchen," Mary said. "Oh, I do wish Fanny was here to smooth things over."

"It's only us," Jane said. She pulled on slippers.

Shelley sketched a bow and slid gracefully through the front door and back into the street. He moved with unearthly grace, the fascinating creature.

Mary peeked into the bookshop. The porter snoozed on his stool, and no customers were in sight. She'd have to go downstairs with Jane. If only she could have left with Shelley.

When they reached the top of the steps, the sounds of Mamma's fury became even more audible. Mary heard, "How dare you! You slovenly beast! Betrayer! Fool!" as well as a number of even worse things in French.

She stopped at the last basement step. Jane, ahead of her, had pressed herself into the wall. Mamma ran past, already out of breath, holding a broom, straw up. Thérèse was a couple of feet ahead of her. Instead of wearing her usual black, she was in an old gray dress that belonged to Fanny. Mary recognized the navy band decorating the bottom of the skirt.

"Why is she wearing that dress?" Mary asked Polly, who

was standing at the head of the table where all the food was prepared, looking paralyzed.

"Mrs. Godwin caught Thérèse stealing a dress from Fanny's room."

"Where is her dress?" Mary asked. The cook's bombazine dress had been secondhand mourning but was good quality silk and wool, even if a bit shiny around the elbows. She had saved up her holiday and birthday gifts from the Godwins to buy it shortly before Mary had returned to Scotland the last time.

Polly shrugged. "She ruined it somehow."

"I bet it was worth more than Fanny's old muslin," Mary said.

The cook screamed as Mamma caught up to her and battered her around the head. Her cap went askew as her pins shifted, and it fell over one eye.

Mary judged her chances and realized she couldn't let the cook be hurt. It wasn't her fault she was a silly old thing, with a mind half-broken by the Terror. She ran into the fray and snatched the broom away. Mamma was startled enough to let it go.

"If she wants to wear Fanny's old rag, let her," Mary said. "She's good with a needle and can do something with the bombazine."

Mamma fisted her hands on her hips. "It's old but still worth a pound."

"Thérèse paid good money for the bombazine," Mary argued.

"It's ruined," the cook sobbed.

"She's a thief," Mamma said, huffing with each word. She turned around, clutching her chest. "Polly, you girl. Go quick and fetch a parish constable."

"No," cried Mary.

"Mamma, please," Jane begged, finally leaving her post at the wall. "We don't need any more trouble."

"I had nothing to wear," Thérèse cried. "Would you have me be naked? Oh, the shame!" She pulled her apron over her head, her sobs increasing in volume. Mary attempted to put her arm around the older woman, but it did not console her.

"Stuff and nonsense," Mamma replied with a cough. "A thief is a thief no matter the circumstances, and I won't have it. Go, girl, do as I say."

Polly, looking hunted, ran for the stairs.

The four women remaining stared at each other. Mamma stuck her nose into the air, then threw up her hands to match.

"Tie her to a chair until the constable comes," she said.

"Don't be rash," Jane begged. "She's not well."

"Ten to one she'll poison us next, if she has a chance to," Mamma told them. "I won't eat another bite made by this Jezebel's hand." She marched to the stairs and took them up to the first floor, leaning on the banister heavily.

"I'll make you a cup of tea, Thérèse," Mary said, running for the kettle.

"Tyrant," the cook spat, then dropped her face into her hands.

Mary tossed the drying tea leaves from this morning's breakfast table into the teapot. "She is, you have spoken truth. How are we going to eat now? Papa will be furious."

Thérèse laughed maliciously. "I would have poisoned her, too. The tyrant knows where the rat poison is kept, and so do I."

Mary used a rag to take the kettle from the hook and poured hot water into the brown, large-bellied teapot the servants used. "Don't say such things. You could be hanged."

"I am a decent woman," the cook declared.

"You can't threaten to murder Mamma," Jane told her. "No matter the provocation. Why, Mary is always furious with her, and she doesn't threaten murder."

Mary raised an eyebrow in Jane's direction. "Let's sit down

and have a nice hot cup. The heat of the day hasn't made it down here, even with the fire going."

"It will be blazing in June," the cook said.

"June is tomorrow."

"I won't see it here." The cook stared into the reflection the fire cast onto the teapot. "I always knew I'd have a bad end."

She said nothing more in English. Mary's written French was vastly better than her command of spoken French, so she didn't understand the cook's mutterings.

Ten minutes later, Mamma shrieked for them to come and mind the bookshop. Mary and Jane were forced to leave the cook by herself. It seemed inadvisable with all of the knives below, but half an hour later, they heard the parish men taking her out of the front door without protest. Poor Thérèse was all emotion and no vengeance.

Behind the bookshop counter, Jane pushed herself against Mary and put her dark head on her shoulder. Curls brushed Mary's cheek. "First Fanny and now Thérèse. Who will be next to face Mamma's wrath?"

Mary's mouth twisted. "Me. It's usually me." She pressed her arm against her body. It wasn't giving her trouble yet, but history had shown that was where the stress would be felt. She'd feel the itching, then the welts would come, and then Papa would have to let her leave again.

Mary rolled over in her bed, something rousing her into half consciousness.

The harsh whisper came again. "Mary."

Mary's eyes opened. Her vision blurred around a candle flame. "What?" She sat up in bed.

Mamma pulled off her covers. "Go downstairs and kick Polly awake, then start breakfast for the family."

"What?" Mary repeated. Pitch black surrounded her, other

than the candle flame. Her nose picked up the scent of fancy lavender soap. *Mamma*.

"I will not repeat myself. Get moving, girl." Mamma walked out of Mary's small bedroom, half the size of Jane's, and kicked the door shut behind her so that the wall rattled.

Mary shivered in the chilly predawn. The news from the previous afternoon slowly came back to her. Pavel Naryshkin, fished lifeless out of the Thames. No rescuer had been able to save him, unlike when Mother had tried to drown herself after the unfortunate business with her faithless lover, Fanny's father. Mamma had Thérèse arrested, so now the Godwin household had no cook.

Mary's eyes opened completely. Did the ghastly bitch think to make her, Mary Wollstonecraft Godwin, the cook? How bloody dare she?

She dressed, unwilling to open herself to the physical abuse Mamma had proven herself capable of, and went to Jane's room, feeling her way in the black passage. She put her ear to Jane's door. No sign of her stepsister rustling. No, Mamma had chosen Mary to be the family drudge.

She considered waking Jane as well, but if Mamma had decided to let Jane sleep, there would be hell to pay if Mary woke her.

Mary went downstairs, her mood darkening with each step. Fanny, the only early riser. Charles, the petted son, treated like an adult, unlike Fanny. Charles and Jane, the only children of the household any money was spent on. Well, Willy had a tutor. Fanny and Mary were left out. Fanny, an unpaid governess; Mary, an unpaid drudge. What would Mother think? She'd paid dearly for her romantic fantasies, even past the grave, thanks to Papa's unfortunate biography of her. Now Fanny had cost herself her home due to her own unfortunate romantic fantasies about Shelley. And Mamma's foolishness had cost them all the early riser who liked to be helpful.

Now she would cost the world a talented future writer, the heir to Wollstonecraft and Godwin. What might Mary be able to accomplish if her prospects were not ruined by this beastly second wife? How was she to escape a servant's duties in her father's house?

Her fervent ruminations kept her going, loudly tramping on stairs and floorboards, until she reached the basement kitchen. She could see Polly rolled into her blanket in front of the banked fire. One edge of the blanket was visible, so she pulled it back until the girl stirred.

"Get up and clean out the fire," Mary said. "It's a new day."

Blinking, the girl came to a sitting position. "What are you doing here?"

"I'm the cook now," Mary said.

"You don't know how." Polly yawned.

"I know enough to see that there isn't enough coal on the fire to make porridge."

"You can't just serve porridge in this house. They want sausages and toast and tea," Polly said.

"What did Thérèse make in the mornings?"

"Tea and sausages. I did the toast and stirred the porridge."

"What do I do first?" Mary asked, still sullen.

"Fetch water."

"Isn't that your job?"

"No, I have to do the fire." Polly licked her lips. "Are they going to make you sleep down here? Thérèse has a little bed at the end of the passage next to the scullery."

"Of course not. I'm still a daughter of the house."

"Such a house," Polly mocked. "All pretension. I suppose Mrs. Godwin can't afford a new cook. What she paid Thérèse wouldn't get anyone nowadays."

"Is that why she couldn't afford a new dress?"

Polly shrugged and wiped her eyes. "It's nothing to me. I'm not stupid enough to steal."

Mary went into the scullery and fetched the water bucket. It had enough in it to put in the porridge pot, then she braved the cold morning to refill the bucket from the water butt in the back garden. At least she didn't have to break ice off it.

She stood in the back, looking at the faint haze on the horizon. The first of June. She pledged to herself not to be here on the next first of June, whatever it cost her.

Chapter 3

Jane

I opened the Skinner Street door just after the St. Sepulchre church bells tolled eleven. It had been so quiet in the bookshop that I heard the knock. Usually people just came in, since we were a business establishment.

Outside, I found a footman in the livery of the Pulteney Hotel in Piccadilly.

"Is Mrs. Godwin available to receive Her Royal Highness, Princess Maria Naryshkina?" he asked.

I noted the elegant carriage behind him, and the beautiful woman in profile behind the glass.

"Y-yes, my mother is at home," I said. Why had the princess not sent a note? Perhaps she'd called for a carriage on a whim, wanting to talk about her brother-in-law with someone who had met him. At least we now knew where the family was staying.

Mary had found a mention in the newspaper saying that Catherine Pavlovna, Duchess of Oldenburg, sister of the Tsar, was staying at the same hotel at great expense. It made sense that the Naryshkins were lodging there as well.

The footman bowed, then returned to the carriage and helped Princess Maria down. I stood paralyzed in the doorway. I couldn't run for Mamma with the royal personage coming quickly.

My mouth dropped open in admiration as she walked toward me. The Polish beauty wore a black gown trimmed in French lace, even at the bottom edge of the skirt. It wouldn't last long in London streets. French lace on a dust ruffle? Why, that was simply decadent.

I felt quite self-conscious in my plain muslin, straining at the bosom as I had continued expanding in the torso since Fanny had finished sewing the dress last spring. I didn't care about such things, but the princess made me unusually self-aware.

I greeted her with a curtsy and the most grace I possessed, then installed her in the parlor, knowing full well she wouldn't be able to find her ring if she hunted for it while I ran pell-mell for Mamma. For once, I wanted her overwhelming presence to hide my own. I would be a better liar in her shadow.

Mamma came out of her office with me, plucking self-consciously at her own black dress. I reached for her shawl, which was a nice piece of Fanny's domestic accomplishment, and wrapped it around her to hide the butter stain over her clavicle.

At the door to the parlor, she hesitated, then said, "Go tell Polly to bring tea. Don't you do it. Give the order and come back here to sit with me."

"What about Mary?"

"Make certain that she stays in the kitchen to prepare some luncheon for Mr. Godwin."

I sped down the passage as Mamma opened the door, a strong sense of wrongness starting to weigh down my feet. The Naryshkins were after Wollstonecraft lore and had an interest in her daughters, not the second Mrs. Godwin. Why was the princess even visiting Mamma? She never knew Mary Wollstonecraft.

Downstairs, the scent of roasting chicken filled the kitchen as Polly turned the spit in front of the fire. Mary stood at the table, kneading dough while chanting another of her Scottish recitations.

> *"Bannocks o' bear meal,*
> *Bannocks o' barley,*
> *Here's to the Highlandman's bannocks o' barley.*
> *Wha, in his wae days, were loyal to Charlie?*
> *Wha but the lads wi' the bannocks o' barley!"*

"Bannocks and chicken for lunch?" I said dryly. I didn't mind the Scottish flat bread.

Mary nodded.

"You'll have to stop that and watch the chicken. Polly, you're to bring tea to the parlor. Use the good pot. Mamma has a distinguished guest." I flounced off before Mary could get the name out of me. I didn't want to miss the conversation anyway, for fear that the princess knew she'd lost the ring here.

Upstairs, as I came through the doorway, the conversation was flowing politely. The carriage passed by the windows as the driver walked the horses. The tight circuit must mean that the princess intended to pay only a short call. To retrieve her ring?

Mamma's chin lifted when she, too, saw the carriage. "Sit, Jane, you're making me nervous."

I pulled up a chair and sat next to her, not sure if I should be speaking or not.

"How are you finding the Pulteney Hotel, ma'am?" Mamma asked.

"Very loud, I'm afraid. I prefer staying in our dacha in the countryside to city living, especially when I have a young baby." The princess smiled wanly, her eyelids drooping.

"Much more healthful," Mamma agreed. "Do you know, Mr. Godwin was expecting a call from the junior Mr. Naryshkin on Monday, but I don't believe he ever arrived."

"I am looking for him." The princess set a finger against her lips. "He has not been seen for days. At first, we thought he was preoccupied with business, but now we are rather concerned. Do you know if Mr. Godwin saw him on Sunday?"

"No, I believe their conversation all took place on Saturday. Your gentlemen had that private conversation in the dining room," Mamma replied.

The princess tapped her cheek very charmingly, displaying her slender, manicured fingers and an entirely different set of rings. I began to relax. If she had so many rings, she'd never miss just one little red-stone adornment. "I wonder if Pavel shared any special plans with Mr. Godwin."

"I don't imagine they exchanged a single word without your husband present, ma'am," Mamma said. "Surely Count Naryshkin remembers the conversation."

The princess glanced away and turned one of her rings. "He did not tell me that Pavel had an appointment with Mr. Godwin on Monday."

"Did you know the subject of the appointment?" Mamma asked baldly. "That he had promised my husband a thousand guineas in diamonds to continue the work of our beloved and necessary Juvenile Library?"

Her Royal Highness slowly returned her gaze to Mamma. "This is indeed interesting, but I knew nothing of it."

The tension was broken by Polly, suspiciously cheerful as she delivered a tray with the good tea service. I wondered if she disliked Burns, or at least Mary's recitation choices.

Mamma unlocked the tea caddy with the key she kept at her waist and spooned tea into the pot. She added the hot water that Polly had brought and let the mixture brew. We also had cream in a pretty pink pot, though never sugar, for my mother had stopped taking it when she was young, because of the abolitionists, and had never resumed the habit.

"Did Mary Wollstonecraft live in this house?" the princess asked.

"No, we moved here some six years ago. The Juvenile Library was so successful that we had to move to a larger place of business. We left the Polygon and took this establishment for both home and the business." Mamma smiled.

"It seems an unusual part of London for a bookshop," the princess commented.

Jane wanted to nod in agreement. "There are others in the vicinity."

Mamma cleared her throat and poured the tea for the three of us. After she had taken a sip, she returned to the subject of Pavel. "If I may ask, ma'am, these diamonds that your family promised the Juvenile Library, do they exist?"

"What an unusual question," the princess commented.

I could see Mamma visibly settling herself. "Ma'am, I am simply trying to determine what we need to report to the authorities. If Mr. Naryshkin was murdered on the way here, it will matter to the coroner if you can verify that the diamonds were in his possession. Diamonds are easily portable. A thousand guineas of them are, what, contained in a small pouch?"

The princess's eyes had taken on a rather distant stare, but her smile became even more charming. "I know nothing about the business of the gentlemen. I am afraid I am not like you, Mrs. Godwin. I have no head for such matters."

I knew the difference between a real smile and a false one. The princess was lying when she claimed not to know about

Pavel's business dealings, though I could not discern the extent of her diamond knowledge. Why had she even called at Skinner Street?

"Jane," Mamma said suddenly. "Why don't you check on the bookshop? I see some gentlemen in the street."

As she spoke, the front door opened. I drained my teacup, not wanting to waste a drop of the expensive brew that I didn't normally drink at this time of day. I was afraid my mother would collude with the princess to get money for her own purposes as she had done in the past, but I had to go. Mary couldn't watch the bookshop right now.

I went out, greeting the men in the hall, then led them into the bookshop. As I stepped behind the counter to wait on them, a smile as false as the princess's on my lips, I wondered if I was becoming as dishonest as Mamma and the princess. Perhaps, but no one was looking out for my interests. This might be the fate of all women, to wear a false mask while we schemed for whatever piece of stability we could get. Newly sixteen, I was learning fast.

I heard the rattle of a carriage in the street some forty-five minutes later. Was the princess finally leaving? I wanted to find out from Mamma why she had stayed so long. I dropped the quill pen I was sharpening and dashed to the bow windows that formed the only charming piece of the shop, for all that we'd found a body on the floor in front of them not long ago. The large, homemade rag rug was still on the floor to cover the dark remains of the blood, soaked into the wood boards.

Confusion filled me when another carriage from the Pulteney Hotel drove up and stopped behind the first. When the first man exited, I recognized Dmitry Naryshkin. Had he come to collect his wife, since she had stayed so long with Mamma? A social call could be as little as fifteen minutes, but she'd been here for over an hour. Perhaps she had been waiting for him to arrive.

When a second man climbed from the carriage, for a moment I thought it was Pavel Naryshkin, and he wasn't dead after all. Instead, I recognized a different man, the individual with the scar from the day before, dressed in his livery. Were the Russians spying on us? I couldn't think of why. What were they after?

I drummed my fingers on the top of the bookshelf. They would not have gone to all this effort of befriending the household just to, for instance, steal the painting of Mary Wollstonecraft.

I frowned. They must have written to Papa to request an interview when they arrived in London. Probably, they wrote several such requests, to any famed sorts of people they had the once-in-a-lifetime opportunity to meet. Papa offered a family dinner. Then, at the meal, they evidenced their tremendous regard for the fame of Mary's mother, to the extent of worshipping her painting. In a private conference, Pavel either offered, or Papa somehow enticed, a promise of a thousand guineas worth of diamonds. What the diamonds had precisely been marked for by the Russians, I could not say for certain. Papa had made it clear to John Cannon that it would go straight to paying off the one large debt.

Then Pavel never showed up that day. Had he learned that the money would not go to any specific purpose, such as new editions of Wollstonecraft works or for the care of her daughters? Or had he been coming in good faith and been killed before he could arrive at Skinner Street?

As far as I knew, they hadn't offered to buy the painting, nor examined the bookshop and offered the jewels in exchange for the contents, for instance. Regardless, here were the other two Naryshkins and their scarred servant, circling around Skinner

Street. I had to confess that I didn't like it. They made me uneasy. Any unknown purpose did.

I watched as the princess departed with her husband, her head bowed as he spoke to her. Even if I could have heard them over the noise of the street, I would not have understood the language they spoke in intimate moments. As a girl with secrets, I recognized my fellows who carried them as well.

"I do love the freedom we have at this time of year to dash about," Mary said as she buttoned her pelisse at three p.m. that afternoon.

Mamma had given me permission to seek some fresh air, since the porter didn't have any more deliveries, but I doubted Mary had the freedom she claimed.

"What about dinner? Shouldn't you be preparing it?"

"We're having fish and potatoes. Even Polly can manage that. I set the dining room table."

"You can't only serve fish and potatoes. Mamma will box your ears." I tugged my bonnet over my hair and tied the ribbon under my chin.

"We already prepared a white soup, and I boiled asparagus as well," Mary said grumpily. Her cheeks were very red from working in the heat of the kitchen all day. It would have been pleasant last month, with the unseasonal cold, but now the weather had turned.

"I suppose that is barely sufficient. Another meat course would be nice."

"As far as I know," she said, interrupting my chain of thought, "it is just the family to dine. But if Shelley were to come, he would only eat the asparagus and potatoes anyway. I don't think anyone else would simply turn up."

"The Naryshkins did," I reported. "I'll tell you what I know as we walk to the Bow Street lockup."

"I do hope Thérèse isn't having difficulties there," Mary said, picking up a basket that smelled like potatoes. "I have often been concerned about her mental state as it is."

I heard heavy footsteps in the bookshop. Mamma must be coming out of the inner office. I grabbed Mary's arm and we dashed into the street, then ran around the corner, away from the windows. Mary guarded her basket of foodstuffs. The nicest route avoided the prisons, but I'd rather escape than not. I rarely pitied Mary despite her constant claims that I was treated the best of us three sisters, but she'd proven her point today. If Mamma forced her to stay her in the kitchen, she wouldn't keep her fresh prettiness long.

"We'll know about Thérèse soon enough," I said. "The lockup is only a mile from here. What about you, having to do her duties?"

"I long for some sort of writing device," she said. "I wouldn't mind peeling potatoes and such if I could create my stories out loud and have a pen writing away for me."

"Your words going into the air and coming back through some automatic writing device?" I asked.

"Why not?" She pulled down the brim of her bonnet. "If I was wealthy, I could hire a secretary to do the writing for me. It is not such a leap of the imagination to consider some sort of machine that could do it. I wonder how spoken words could be made material."

"Well," I joked. "If anyone offers you a writing machine in exchange for you signing something in your own blood, don't do it."

She grinned at me, then nearly tripped over a crate that had dropped onto the road. I grabbed her arm and steadied her. "It's kind of you to bring food for Thérèse. You don't want to lose any of it."

"My good angel," she said airily. "Thank you for the rescue.

I'm not trying to be damned, just find a way to do what Mamma demands and still lead the life of a writer. Mother managed it."

"Not until she was much older than us," I pointed out. "She was a dozen years older than you before she fit in her first writings around her work as a governess."

"When we see Fanny again, we need to persuade her to find paying work as a governess, instead of this unpaid nonsense in Wales that Papa has made her do," Mary said.

"She might discover she doesn't like working with children."

"It doesn't really matter," Mary said. "Who would hire her to do anything else? Any sort of work is sweeter if there is money attached. All of Mother's efforts with her pen, and nothing has improved for women."

"Maybe you will write the book that will change things," I suggested.

"I am terribly attracted to romantic tales," she said. "Maybe I will become a philosopher when I am old, thirty or so. For now, I just want to write stories."

"I don't blame you. They are ever so much easier to read."

We turned into the building that housed the Bow Street Runners, the Magistrates' Court, and the lockup. The rooms were filled with men, and not a few women, decidedly down on their luck, the volume of noise representative of the distress they faced.

"I thought we were done with the two of you," growled a Runner, who walked toward us, holding his tipstaff. A hulking man in the prime of life, he created an aura of intimidation around his muscular body. While his words sounded annoyed, I could see that his gaze lingered on Mary's face.

"Mr. Fisher," I said politely.

Mary bobbed a curtsy, scarcely glancing at him. "Could you please take us to the lockup?" she asked.

His wide brow creased into multiple wrinkles. "Whatever for?"

"Mamma had our cook arrested for stealing," she explained.

His baritone voice dropped into the bass range. "Did she steal?"

"Borrowed, at the very least," I confirmed. "But such a matter should not have involved outsiders. Mamma has a temper, and we could not dissuade her from calling a constable."

"She's cruel," Mary said succinctly.

"I remember your mother's temper, but you must consider your own reputations. The lockup is no place for young ladies," he warned.

"We are Godwin's daughters," I reminded him. "We don't follow the ordinary rules."

"You are trouble, is what the pair of you are," he grumbled. "I'd hoped to never see the two of you again."

"That may well be," Mary said pertly. "But we have to visit our cook. It's not right to leave her here alone."

He winced as if not liking what he was about to offer, then gazed intently at her. "I could take her a message and that basket."

"That is very kind," Mary said, "but we missed the start of the catastrophe."

"We need to interview her ourselves," I said in agreement. "It isn't right to leave the poor creature here alone."

"She is half-mad as it is," Mary interjected. "Her family was guillotined in France."

Mr. Fisher's chest deflated as he exhaled. He said nothing, just pointed a meaty hand toward a door set in the wall. We walked that way, and then he unlocked it and went in ahead of us.

I had thought the din of the outer chamber more than irritating, but the low hum of human despair underpinning the activity of the lockup became the preeminent sound here. At least three voices whined, "I didn't do it," in a variety of commonplace accents, along with the sound of retching. That brought its attendant smell of gin, very recognizable from any street alongside a prison, of which there were a multitude near Skinner Street. I heard tears, not the least bit manly, and even some feminine screeches of the most ill-refined sort.

"Dreadful," Mary rasped, but I could see her eyes were shining, even in the dim torchlight. More storing up of places she could put in her books.

"Will Isabella the Penitent from your story end up in a place like this?" I whispered. I could feel my throat closing against the noxious stuff the torches were made of.

"She'd never survive," Mary said. "But there are plenty of other characters to come."

Mr. Fisher had gone to consult with a turnkey, but he returned to us and gestured forward. "Stay in the middle," he said roughly. "Unless you want your clothing torn off."

Mary's eyes went wide, and she stepped very close to Mr. Fisher's back. I followed her, and we walked down the tiled floor, torn between skirting the drains, which had a steady stream of yellowed water dripping into them, and the grasping hands of the unfortunate incarcerated.

Mr. Fisher pointed into the dim recesses of a large cell across the back. "They keep the women here."

"Our basket won't fit through the bars," Mary said.

"There's no point in her having it," Mr. Fisher said. "This isn't the prison, just a temporary holding place."

"Thérèse de Saint-Lary?" Mary said in an unusually quavering sort of voice.

I couldn't see into the cell at all. I peered forward, then startled back as something hit the bar right in front of my nose.

Mr. Fisher shook his fist in the air, then lifted a torch from its bracket on the wall. The face of a grizzled old hag came into view, her nose poking through one of the spaces, broken-veined cheeks pressed against the bars.

The Runner waved the torch a couple of inches from her

eyes, making her rear back, then repeated the name of our cook in an authoritative voice.

Mary gagged and covered her mouth. I suspected the odors were catching up with her. She was used to the hearty, healthful smells of the kitchen already, rather than this human misery.

Finally, Thérèse appeared, impossibly shrunken in Fanny's dress, compared to the old-fashioned peasant's black she normally wore, with multiple petticoats, even in summer's heat. She seemed to have developed a limp.

Mary stayed a cautious length from the bars, but she pulled open the napkin in her basket and held out a yeasty roll. "Polly said these are your favorite."

Thérèse nodded and took it, then closed her eyes as she took a deep breath. Movement flashed next to her, then quick as a wink, the roll went into another mouth. A mountain of a woman chewed, toothless mouth gaping, then vanished into the murky interior of the cell.

Thérèse cried out.

"No matter," Mary said quickly, then handed her another.

This time, the cook didn't hesitate but stuffed it into her mouth. Mary gave her a second one as soon as she had swallowed it down, then opened a bottle of ale.

"*Avez-vous autre chose?*" she started in French, then shook her head and returned to English. "They do not feed us here. Is there more?"

"Yes," Mary said, "but I fear you won't be able to hold onto it."

"I'll stuff myself now," Thérèse said.

I wondered at her complete lack of gratitude. We were her employers, after all. But she had such a wild-eyed look about her that I wondered if she was even more mad than usual.

Mary handed her a slice of ham, then a slice of cheese. Then she pulled out another roll but didn't push it through the bars as before. "Why did you steal the dress?" she asked.

Thérèse licked her lips. "I only had the one."

"What happened to it?"

"Your mother is as evil as Beelzebub, but I didn't expect her to prefer I be unclothed," the cook said.

Mary swallowed down her impatience. "Your dress was destroyed?"

Thérèse hugged herself. "It burned."

"How?"

"In the fireplace. Your mother is very unreasonable. I needed something to wear," she said in a near monotone.

"We shall get it straightened out," Mary soothed.

I was most confused. "How did the dress burn? Were you not wearing it at the time?"

Her eyes bulged in a frightful manner. "I was, you know I was. I'm a decent woman."

I crossed my arms. "The skirt is what burned then?"

"And the sleeve." She pushed up Fanny's sleeve, to show us a sore, puffy rectangle on her arm. "Right through to the skin. And elsewhere as well, where the kettle branded me. I should be in bed with a nurse present to care for me, not here."

"How did it happen?" Mr. Fisher asked. He'd been adjusting the torch to best display Thérèse's wound.

"That Russian family's footman." She touched her nose and winked three times.

"The Naryshkin footman?" Mary asked.

Thérèse nodded with exaggerated movements. "It was he who pushed me into the fire and burned my dress and my poor flesh."

"I don't remember any commotion," Mary said.

"We weren't there," I reminded her. "This all happened while we were walking."

Thérèse's nostrils flared. "He delivered a letter and then must have asked for a drink of water or something, because Polly brought him down to the kitchen."

"Does he have a scar down his face?" I asked, remembering the man in livery who had been smoking outside the warehouse.

"No. He's a squat sort of man but his face, ugly though it is, is not scarred."

"Did you ever hear his name?" Mary asked.

"Fedorov," she said. "I think that is what Polly called him. Alexander Fedorov."

"Princess Maria seems like a nice woman," Mary said. "We'll do our best to get restitution from her for the dress."

"Yes," I agreed. "Mary and I don't think this," I gestured, "is the solution. But it was very bad of you to take the dress without asking."

"If I'd had time to mend my own before the mistress caught me, things would have been different," Thérèse said. All of a sudden, she started crying. I expected she'd exhausted her reserve of sanity for the moment.

The torch Mr. Fisher still held began to splutter.

"Can you eat any more?" Mary asked.

"Cheese?" Thérèse sniffed.

Mary handed another lump through the bars, then we made our goodbyes.

"Why does it not surprise me that the Naryshkins are mixed up in another bit of our recent misery?" she asked, as we followed Mr. Fisher down the center of the passage and back into the cacophonous antechamber.

"Why do you say that?" he asked.

Mary stared at him. I could see her brain calculating what he ought to know. After a moment, she said, "Pavel Naryshkin had made promises to Papa that his murder interrupted. It has made Skinner Street a woeful place."

"Do you know anything about the murder?" he asked, his gaze narrowing.

"Nothing at all," I said, tugging at Mary's arm. "We must return home. We don't have our elder sister or a cook now. We have to help Mamma."

I could feel his suspicious gaze on my back even when we were back in the street.

"What are we going to do?" Mary asked.

"I feel terrible for Thérèse, but she did steal."

"That is the problem," Mary agreed. "And she doesn't have a sister like you do to protect her."

Chapter 4

Mary

"It's time for Mr. Godwin's tea," Polly told Mary an hour later, after she'd returned to the kitchen.

"Do I need to take it up?" Mary asked.

"Yes. He likes a cup at this time of day, when he's in his study."

Mary set down her paring knife. Should she take off her apron as Papa would prefer, or leave it on to look like the kitchen drudge Mamma was turning her into? She felt a hard expression settle down over her lips and left it on.

Polly set a couple of biscuits on the tray, and Mary went up the two flights of steps with it. She knocked on Papa's door, then went in with the tray after she heard his "enter."

He glanced up from a pile of papers.

"What are you working on, Papa?" Mary set the tray on the edge of the desk, feeling better now that she saw his sweet face.

"A few adjustments to *The Pantheon* before it goes back into print." He wiped his pen. "Have you been in the bookshop today?"

"I am in the kitchen now, in place of Thérèse. Shall I pour?" He nodded, so she set to fixing his beverage the way he liked. "Jane and I went to see our cook today."

He startled. "You didn't go to the lockup, I trust?"

Mary bristled, though she remained impassive externally. "We did, Papa. Her side of the story was important."

"I do not agree." He took the cup from her hand.

She persisted. "Thérèse says not to trust Alexander Fedorov."

"Who is that?"

"The Naryshkins' footman." She heard steps on the stair outside the study door. "She said he deliberately pushed her into the fire and that is why she was injured and her dress damaged in multiple places."

Jane appeared and dove into the private conversation before she even reached the desk. "Thérèse had nothing to wear, Papa, and Fanny is out of town. What did it harm?"

"We can't expect her to go about in ripped, burned cloth," Mary added.

"The poor, silly thing was burned!" Jane added.

"She stole it," Papa said, setting down his cup.

"What about your philosophy that it is acceptable for people to take what they need from those who have it?" Mary asked.

His expression went cold. "She stole from her employer, which is different."

"Why?" Jane asked.

"She did not attempt to mend her dress or ask for help."

"She was in pain, Papa. Not thinking straight. You know she's never been quite right. She has terrible, dark moods. And she's your dependent." Mary's ire rose. Where was the charity here?

"Your mamma runs the household as she sees fit," Papa said. "I will not interfere. She is a good woman, and I am sure she had her reasons."

Mary gestured to her apron. "This may be the reason, Papa. She has taken me even lower. Am I to be in service now? And Fanny as well, without so much as a stipend for either of us?"

He pressed his lips together. They formed a white line until he spoke again. He did not look as kindly now. "You are daughters of this household. Do not be shameless, Mary; you owe us a daughter's duty and obedience."

Mary fisted her hands into her apron. "I have not been raised to be dutiful in the face of injustice but to speak out about it. This is—is tyranny, sir."

He stood. "This is an orderly household, is what it is. Now return to the kitchen. The family must eat tonight. You will not wish to make your brothers starve because of your intransigence."

Jane looked aghast, but Papa's gaze had returned to his papers, and he didn't look up again. Mary knew he would not until they had gone. Jane grabbed her sleeve and followed along in her wake, shutting the door behind her.

"Is Thérèse going to hang?" Jane asked.

"Transported, more like." Mary rubbed her temples. "What a house of fools we live in."

"She shouldn't have stolen the dress," Jane ventured.

Mary whirled around. "What makes you think that Mamma was in the house at the time? Was Thérèse supposed to go up to the public floor and humiliate herself by walking across the bookshop with her burned skin exposed? She is gentle born!"

Jane wiped her eyes. "Polly should have done something."

Mary sighed. "She is an underservant. I only wish someone had seen Thérèse before she went fishing through Fanny's things. She had to have gone upstairs to our sister's room to get the dress."

Jane nodded. "It wasn't like she took it off the drying rod in the scullery. Fanny's garments are all put away."

"Such a business." Mary wiped her forehead. "It is back to the kitchen for me, until I can think of some better solution to my woes."

Shelley had said he was coming to dinner. Mary made sure her part of the meal was ready in the dining room before he arrived. She washed up in the scullery, pulled her sleeves down, and removed her apron before attempting to fix her hair without a looking glass. Having the feeling that her efforts were insufficient, she crept upstairs, taking her notebook and her pencil. She'd been too distracted by cooking to work on her book *Isabella, the Penitent*, and entertained herself instead by coming up with a fiction of her own life titled *Mary, the Desperate; or, The Motherless Slave of Skinner Street.*

> *A Romance; in which is depicted the wonderful Adventures of Mary, daughter of Fame, who was diverted from the track of accomplishment by the untimely disgrace of a disturbed cook, who fell in a fire after an act of foreign violence, and, who, despite the safety of her humble home, was forced into service by her dastardly stepmother so she could destroy the person of a most rare beauty; how Mary was discovered despite the cooking smells by a young poet.*

No. Based on her recent experiences, poets had no funds with which to enact rescues. Mary pulled the pins from her hair while revising her outline in her head.

> *How Mary was discovered despite the cooking smells by a young Scotsman, who had been traveling far to rescue the daughter of Fame; and the particulars of the means by which the Scotsman caused the body of Mary to be conveyed in a sleep to the dank*

and mildewed rooms where he accomplished his wicked machinations on the innocent virgin, whom he then falls madly in love with, though attended by a dastardly servant, who afterward betrays him to his judgmental father, in the madhouse of which he is confined, and suffers torture; and how, to escape from thence, he assigns over his soul and body to Mary, who is ever faithful to him, even unto her ignominious death, shortly followed by his own.

Mary smiled to herself and brushed out her hair, then pinned it up again. It still smelled like soup.

When she went to the dining room, Jane pinched her arm. "Why do you look so cheerful?"

Mary shrugged, then blushed as Shelley gazed at her.

"You are in looks this evening," he said, from his position across from Papa at the table.

She sketched a curtsy, then drew Jane to the table. Mamma stared at her angrily as Polly brought in a double armful of serving dishes and set them in the center for *service à la française*, but Mary wasn't about to allow herself to be degraded as a servant in front of Shelley. Shelley wouldn't care if Polly spilled a drop or two of sauce, but he would notice her coming disheveled and overheated directly from the kitchen, still with a soup-stained apron on.

The meal started quietly enough. Papa, revisiting the Greek gods thanks to his editing, lectured on the story of Prometheus in between bites.

Mary listened to the retelling, which she had heard many times, of how Prometheus's clay man was animated into life by a portion of celestial fire from the chariot of the sun. Would the modern equivalent of that godly fire be Galvanism? She remembered reading about the experiments on dead limbs, and how electricity would affect them, causing movement. Musing on this, she didn't notice when the subject of conversation changed until Jane poked her. She pushed quivering frog legs from her thoughts and focused on Shelley.

"One doesn't like to see your bookshop spied upon," Shelley was saying. "My thoughts always return to the village of Tremadoc, and the terrible things that happened there in Wales to me and my family."

"You fear that the assassin who attempted to kill you will come to London," Jane added.

"A realistic fear," Mary added, "since you have been hounded to London by the moneymen."

Shelley picked up his glass and saluted Papa. "I thank you for running Williams, that agent of Tremadoc, off, sir. He will insist on demanding money from me, even if it is his master's fault that I left."

"We cannot have you harmed, Shelley," Papa said agreeably.

"I must return the favor, so I've been looking into that footman who's been hovering about."

Papa frowned. "A footman?"

"With a facial scar that makes him instantly recognizable," Mary said. "Who is he, Shelley? We are all ears."

"His name is Viktor Hesse," Shelley revealed. "I had thought he might have a connection to the Russians, but he is actually attached to the advance party of the king of Prussia."

Jane frowned. "Why is he lurking around Skinner Street?"

"As varied as my correspondence is, I have had no contact with Prussia recently," Papa said. "That is indeed an oddity."

Mamma put her hand on his arm. "It is rather exciting, Mr. Godwin. I hope we will have another visit like the one from the delightful Princess Maria very soon."

Mary noticed that Jane went rather wide-eyed at the notion, for all that the princess had shown no interest in any one but Mamma and her own dead mother. But then, Jane did dream of travel to foreign climes. If they were ever able to get to Russia, she supposed they would be offered hospitality in whatever home the Naryshkins had. What an experience that would be.

She heard the name Fedorov amid her daydream and sank her fingernails into her palm. *Stop daydreaming and listen!*

"I know you girls have been concerned about what our cook claimed had been done to her by Fedorov, the Naryshkins' man," Papa said.

"She said he's dangerous," Jane said.

"It seems that Thérèse was not wrong." Papa wiped his mouth and set his napkin down. "This Alexander Fedorov was arrested for Pavel Naryshkin's murder today."

"His name wasn't mentioned during the inquest. The verdict was 'sudden wrongful death by the hand of another where the offender is not known,'" Shelley said.

"More has been learned since," Papa said. "Let us hope this is an end to the matter."

"How can you say that, Mr. Godwin?" Mamma said. "With the promised diamonds missing."

"Was everything done as it should have been?" Mary asked. "Was the coroner thorough?"

"They took care with the body," Shelley said. "An autopsy was done by a doctor named Nathan Wilson. Otherwise, they might have called it a drowning and not wrongful death at all."

"Dr. Wilson found other wounds," Papa said.

"Signs of strangulation," Shelley added.

Jane put her napkin over her plate and pushed it away.

"How dreadful," Mary said. "Papa, can you agree that this makes it even more clear that Thérèse is not to blame for the damage to her dress? This Fedorov is most evidently a violent character."

"I will only reiterate that the incident turned her into a thief, and she is to blame for that," Papa said calmly. "I will hear no more upon the subject. Such a person has no place in my household."

Mary glanced at Mamma, but she was busy cutting her meat and did not look up. How old they had both grown, and how inflexible. Jane's hand nudged her leg. Mary took the cold fingers and squeezed them gently. If they ever had reason to keep servants, they would be much more liberal with them.

"May we be excused, Mamma?" Jane asked. "I am feeling quite faint."

"Go," Papa said. "Shelley and I will discuss the Greeks."

"Actually, sir, I think the girls need fresh air," Shelley said. "Why don't I take them up to Charterhouse for a bit? I believe the weather will not remain as fine as it is now."

Mary glanced out the window and saw that clouds were indeed coming in. She added her agreement to his proposal. Jane merely smiled wanly.

When Papa gave his irritated assent, the trio leapt into action while Mamma's mouth was still full of meat. Mary suspected she'd be tasked with cleaning up the dinner if she didn't escape instantly.

In truth, it would likely all be waiting for her when she returned. *Tempus fugit.* The three of them ran downstairs as if they were foxes fleeing a host of braying dogs and paused only to grab outerwear. When the door shut behind them, Mary and Jane kicked off their slippers and pulled on shoes, already in the street, then slid their bonnets over their heads and stuffed their slippers into cloak pockets.

"That looks very rehearsed," Shelley said. "I like that for the scene in a play."

Mary laughed. "Mamma will swallow eventually, and I did not want to wait for what she had to say."

"It is an argument for the consumption of meat," Jane said. "That it takes longer to chew and keeps people quieter as a result."

Shelley laughed and stepped between them, taking both of their arms. "Let us go to Charterhouse."

"Is your wife going to be there again?" Mary asked, remembering their previous encounter there in the quiet garden. Shelley had abandoned them as a result.

"I know not. We are not speaking," Shelley said. "Really, girls, I am much too incensed on this matter of your cook to think of anything else."

Jane put her hand over her nose and mouth. They were closing in on the market. Shelley stopped speaking. They hurried north away from the smells of a warm day of animal killings.

Once they reached the quiet grounds, they paused under an elderly mulberry tree that canted in one direction, then another, growing spindly at the top. Untended, its branches were so heavily burdened by serrated leaves that some of the branches trailed to the ground, creating a secret bower. Underneath, the dirt, damp and cold, formed around Mary's shoes.

"Your father knows very well that society cannot always blame the servant class," Shelley said, pacing around the tree, his hands emphasizing his words. "After all, the average poor man has better morals than a rich man."

"My mother would say the cook's character was formed by her job." Mary leaned against the tree. "Our cook couldn't be expected to have sufficient strength of mind to have chosen differently than she did in regard to the dress drama."

"And my mother says she belongs in the Bow Street lockup," Jane said impatiently. She dropped to the ground and spread her skirt over her knees.

Shelley nearly tripped over her foot when he came around the tree. He caught himself, pressing his hand into the deeply ridged bark just next to Mary's shoulder, and laughed. "How dare your mother deny her this fresh air, this beautiful night!"

"There's nothing we can do about it now," Mary said. "We need to be practical."

Shelley pressed his cheek to the bark. His skin brushed against her shoulder as well, and she didn't know which, her shoulder or the bark, he wanted to nuzzle.

She didn't move. His head tipped lower, until his tawny

curls brushed her cheek. She wished she had dressed less warmly. If she had left off the cloak, his lips might be on her flesh just now, in that delicate place between clavicle and neck. She shivered at the decadent thought.

"Mary!" Jane exclaimed. "Why aren't you talking?"

She shook her head, dislodging her sensual thoughts. "As to the matter at hand. Err, leaving the cook aside, Mr. Fedorov has been involved in other doings."

"So your father said," Shelley murmured, not moving.

She straightened slightly. He moved with her. "I suspect someone in a position higher than footman ordered Mr. Fedorov to kill Pavel Naryshkin."

Shelley took a deep breath and straightened, holding her gaze for a heated moment, then turned to lean his body against the bark. His arm brushed hers. "I agree that some contemptible aristocrat ordered Pavel Naryshkin to be killed, probably out of greed."

"Someone who wanted the diamonds for themselves?" Mary suggested.

"Who could order the Naryshkins' footman to do anything, except one of them?" Jane asked. "This means Princess Maria or her husband ordered his brother killed."

"There will be no justice for him," Mary said.

Shelley grunted. "It would indeed be none of our affair, if the diamonds hadn't been promised to your father."

Jane shivered so dramatically that it was evident. "We cannot confront them. They might send Mr. Fedorov after us."

Shelley dropped next to her and put his arm around her. "Don't worry, Jane. Stay away from them. Your father must consider this a lost cause."

A green haze of fury filled Mary's vision as Jane leaned into the poet's embrace. "I like not this scene," she muttered, then stomped over to examine some roses.

After a pause of a minute or two, Jane spoke. "Why did you decide not to go to Wales?"

Mary didn't hear Shelley's answer.

"I am sorry Fanny will not have a visitor," Jane said, then mused, "though given her unacceptable fondness for you, perhaps it is for the best."

Mary stalked back toward them. "Don't be rude, Jane."

"Fanny is my friend, as are both of you," Shelley said. "I am sure I have never given her reason to think otherwise. Your father must know that all of his daughters are safe with me."

"But what about your wife?" Jane persisted.

Shelley dropped his arm from her shoulder and leaned back. Mary slumped against the tree, not willing to stain her cloak by sitting on the ground.

"I am separated from my wife and will no longer abide by any of her wishes," Shelley said, his expression becoming pained. "She wanted to go to Wales, not I, who was nearly murdered there."

Mary clasped her hands against her chest, feeling his distress as if it was her own. "I do hope you can avoid her."

"Completely," added Jane. "Who would be so cruel as to try to get you to venture into Wales again?"

"Her," Shelley said simply, and lay back on the grass.

Chapter 5

Jane

The next day, I climbed the stairs past a gin shop in Hart Street near Covent Garden to go to my singing lesson. The rooms were respectable enough, despite the location, and the teacher still performed in the provinces, though she did not have a career here in London. As always when I made this trip, I wondered if it would be my last time here, given the state of the Skinner Street finances. Today I had felt another burden as I crossed Bow Street. Our cook burned away her hours there, in the lockup, still wearing Fanny's dress.

Once in the upstairs passage, I knocked and went through the door into the apartment there. Mrs. Jones, the singing teacher, had two rooms, but we were generally not allowed into the inner chamber. This meant that I walked into another young lady's lesson.

I had not seen this student before. She appeared to be a couple of years my senior, with flaxen hair of the kind that had likely been near white as a young child. Her eyes were blue of a brightness and clarity visible from several feet away. She wore a dress of the finest muslin, with a Greek design along the bottom, and a lacy trim. I could not imagine the cost of it and wondered how she had come to learn from Mrs. Jones, rather than have a teacher come to her at home as the wealthy normally did.

Mrs. Jones was a fine teacher; perhaps she had more of a reputation than I realized. I hoped this new pupil didn't cause her to raise her prices.

The singer was performing scales. She sang a lovely E, though her voice could not manage a proper F. Our teacher nodded.

I had been staring only at her. When I heard a male cough behind me, I whipped around. In the corner, lounging in an armchair, was none other than that delicious Lord Byron, who I had seen at a party once. He, a poet, and Papa, a philosopher and novelist, had some commonalities in their acquaintance, but the baron had never called on Papa to my knowledge. I hadn't seen him at Skinner Street except in book form.

Lord Byron had hair as dark and nearly as curling as mine, sensually molded lips, a strong nose, and brooding eyes. Sometimes he looked very deep and other times rather snarling. In either mood, he attracted a great deal of interest. His love life was greatly whispered about but was conducted in rooms both above and below my station. He had no air of respectability whatsoever, though power radiated off him, and Papa would be thrilled to have him among his sponsors. Alas that he had no children or need of coin to either shop from the Juvenile Library or write for it.

"Very nice, Miss Sandy," Mrs. Jones praised as she stilled her fingers on the keyboard. "You are a sufficient alto." She turned to look at me. "Just a moment, Miss Clairmont. I will be with you shortly."

"Miss Clairmont?" Miss Sandy inquired.

"Yes, let me make your acquaintance." Miss Jones stood,

careful not to look in the direction of the lord in the corner. "Miss Sandy, may I present Miss Jane Clairmont? Miss Clairmont, this is Miss Eva Sandy."

We inclined our heads to each other and smiled politely. She had small, very white teeth and was overall very pretty, likely as pretty as Mary.

Miss Jones spoke a few words to the girl and gave her a sheet of music, then dismissed her and disappeared into the inner chamber.

I smiled politely, although indeed I was desperate to converse with her. I wanted to be her friend. Another musical girl whom I would have occasion to see every week? She was a prize to be sure. Probably, though, she was a cousin to Lord Byron and much too high socially to be my friend. I did not think he had a sister.

"Is this your first lesson here, Miss Sandy? I am sure you have training."

Miss Sandy's perfect cheeks took on a rosy sheen. "I have sung in provincial productions. I hope to be ready to work here in London, but I need a more advanced teacher."

"Mrs. Jones is very good," I assured her. "Will you take a lesson every week at this time?"

Miss Sandy nodded. "Mrs. Jones has accepted me as her pupil. How long have you been working with her?"

Mrs. Jones returned with a frown. "Are you girls still chattering? Jane should be doing her vocal exercises."

Miss Sandy curtsied. Lord Byron stood and walked out the door, never having said a word since I came in. She departed behind him after a nod at me. I went to the piano and began my vocal exercises, though the teacher didn't play the notes like she normally did. I heard her lock the door, then she came to the piano and rustled some papers around.

When I had finished, I rubbed my hands together to warm my fingers. "Are we going to work on *Armide* today?" I asked.

The difficult monologue in Act II, Scene 5, had kept me challenged for weeks now.

"Yes," Mrs. Jones said. "I am sorry to say, though, Jane, that you can't come anymore without payment in hand."

I pressed my lips together. "How far is Mamma behind?"

"You haven't paid in a month. I cannot let it go any longer than that." She bent her head to the piano and played the opening notes of Lully's glorious piece.

I could see the conversation embarrassed her. I said no more and applied myself to the piece. Tears ran down my face as I acted out Armide's spiral of love with a man she'd meant to kill. Afterward, I sniffed and wiped my eyes.

"Very good," Mrs. Jones said. "That was the first time I felt the despair in your voice."

I hiccupped a laugh and wiped my eyes, but I maintained both of our dignities by not commenting on why I felt despair so keenly. Now that my school had been dismissed for the summer holiday, music was my only opportunity to escape my duties at home. Without this outlet, I'd probably go mad. What would it take to turn the princess's ring into cash to pay for lessons?

I had thought it best not even to think about the ring, hidden in a wool stocking in my bedroom chest, until the Russians were safely out of London, which would not happen for many weeks. But could I survive a summer with no music lessons?

I thanked Mrs. Jones and promised I would find the funds somehow. It wasn't much of an expense for me to stay sane.

I walked down the stairs, pulling my skirts close to avoid a couple of gin-soaked old rascals leaning against the wall. As I swept out the door, I covered my eyes against the brightness of the day.

When they had adjusted, I walked out and started up the street. A jewelry shop was two doors down. I often stopped to admire the gold bracelets sparkling in the window display, wondering if I'd ever be able to afford one. As I took a quick glance at a garnet brooch, the shop door opened. A man came out. I recognized the livery he wore, as well as his scars.

I turned away, hiding my face under my bonnet. What was Viktor Hesse doing here on Hart Street? Was he following me? Were we about to have a confrontation? My heart sped up. I pressed my hands to my stomach. Then another person exited the shop door, even stranger than the first. My mouth dropped open when I recognized Shelley's sister-in-law, Eliza Westbrook. Mr. Hesse bent his head toward her bonneted ear. They were obviously together.

Eliza Westbrook, always conspiring to steal Shelley's family funds, here on Hart Street. How were the Westbrooks involved with the Prussian advance team?

Had they enjoyed calls from the Prussians, as we had from the Russian aristocracy? Pride slowed my heart to a steady rate. The Westbrooks only rated acquaintance with a footman, while we'd had multiple visits from a princess.

But Princess Maria had focused her attentions on Mamma, in terms of the living, at least. Mary Wollstonecraft could only speak to her disciples through books now.

Mary had proven that Mamma and Eliza were in cahoots when she'd seen them at a late-night meeting. I had to wonder if the Prussians and Russians were connected, or if this devilish partnership had broken apart somehow.

I could think of one reason for that. Shelley had refused to return with his wife to Wales, as he'd evidently promised before that fateful night when he'd met Mary. Was the Godwin clan being blamed for Shelley cutting ties with his wife?

I made it home just ahead of Shelley, arriving to take us to observe the royal drawing room arrivals at St. James's Palace. As we walked through the streets, more crowded than usual with a higher class of person, come to see the actual notables, I reported my news to Mary and Shelley.

"A month behind on your music lessons?" Shelley said.

Mary's expression was sour. "I am most surprised, given that money is forever being spent on you."

"School isn't even in session right now," I said, for I could not disagree with her. Mary was half an orphan. Well, I suppose I was as well, but Mamma controlled the household accounts, since that was the normal way of things.

After I felt that Shelley was sufficiently upset on my behalf, I raised the stakes higher just before we walked into the palace.

"My ghastly sister-in-law, wrapped up in mysterious doings again!" Shelley ranted after I shared my news. "I'm sure she got her hands on the missing diamonds somehow."

Mary looked gratifyingly alarmed. "You think the Westbrooks would have killed a Russian diplomat in order to deprive my family of funds?"

He patted her arm. "No, my dear girl, any retaliation would be against me, not the Godwin family. But given my genuine support of your father, this could be a way to beat upon me."

I wasn't sure I understood that logic. Shelley hadn't always been around when the footman had been watching us. I ignored their continuing chatter. I, unlike Mary and Shelley, wanted to appreciate our surroundings, from the fine paintings on the walls to the human parade, all sharing our interest in the upper classes.

But then we were pressed from the back as more ticketholders crowded in to our viewpoint. We fought for footing and for a view of the dignitaries.

Shelley, having more knowledge of society, muttered the names of various English dignitaries as they entered, and made rude remarks about the parentage of most of the young ladies who were being presented.

Queen Charlotte entered on the arm of a courtier. I thought the queen's jewelry was magnificent. She was adorned entirely in pearls, from hairpieces to earrings to a fabulous string wrapped multiple times around her slender neck. While elderly, she had a strong presence.

We did not see any of the Russians, however, much less an errant Prussian footman.

"It is a few days until the main parties arrive," Shelley said to us as we strolled in the courtyard, gasping for fresh air after the crush inside. "It may be that no one in town now is important enough to be presented."

"Not even a princess?" Mary asked, tilting her head to the blue sky and closing her eyes.

Shelley shook his head. "I have asked around. She is the long-time mistress of Tsar Alexander and, as such, is not likely to be respectable enough to be presented. Such fools morality makes."

"Oh," Mary said. "I suppose that is why she is part of the advance team."

I giggled. "It's more about her than her husband."

Mary flung out her arms and nearly slapped a merchant who had been in line in front of us. "It is a pity. These drawing room attendees are missing out. I wonder why her husband is not here?"

I took Mary's arm as the merchant frowned at her. "They are in mourning, you ninny. His brother is dead."

She made a face at me. "Business, young Jane. They haven't much time before the tsar arrives."

Shelley winked. "Their business might be more in the line of ordering new dresses for the princess."

Mary's cheeks went scarlet. A couple of women glanced at us curiously as they passed by. A good number of onlookers had departed, finding the rooms too close as we had.

"Should we go back in?" I asked. "Now that people have left."

Shelley glanced at the guards. "I doubt it would be allowed. No, we have had our fun. Let's get you home before your mamma's temples begin to throb."

When our trio arrived home, we discovered a household in turmoil. Lines of stress were visible on the faces of everyone present. Papa, never very well recently, had gone quite gray in the cheeks. His friend Francis Place was with him, but he looked frantic himself. His eyebrows were very disordered, giving him a shocked appearance matched by the rest of his facial expression. Mamma's eyes were red-rimmed, and her hands were blotchy from the way she was squeezing them together.

"I'll go east, and you go west," Mr. Place said. "There are friends in both directions."

My brother Charles came out of the bookshop as Papa and Mr. Place grabbed their hats and edged around us without speaking.

"Papa?" Mary asked, but he merely shook his head and left.

Charles had a nasty little smirk on his face. I knew Mary thought him a fool for not supporting the family. All the cost of his education in publishing had not made him like it any better. His limited efforts dragged us down far more than Mary's and my reluctance to wait on bookshop customers. At least we worked when we were forced to. Charles merely lounged.

"What is this rushing between houses?" Shelley asked.

Mamma went to him, her arms outstretched so far that they strained the seams of her gown. "We are lost," she moaned.

"Lost?" Mary said, her customary calm expression disordered.

"No money," Mamma said. "They are going to take your papa away."

Shelley swore, then apologized. "If only I had the means to help today."

"You have done your best," Mary assured him.

He sliced his hand across his forehead. His hat went sailing off, and he jammed his fingers into his curls. "Oh, poor Godwin, that your greatness comes to this!"

Mamma shook his arm. "Come, sir, we need practical solutions. Is there anyone you know with ready funds?"

Shelley moaned and fluttered his hands about his person.

"Do you have any coins at all?" Mary asked him.

"Do you have any coins?" I repeated pointedly to Charles. I knew he had a money box hidden in his room.

"How desperate are we?" Mary asked, as Shelley produced a few small coins. "Willy's birthday money is upstairs."

"And what about you, miss?" Mamma asked.

She shrugged. "Why would I have any? I know Fanny took all her paltry coins to Wales."

Mamma's eyes narrowed. "That is not an answer."

"My pockets are to let," Charles said.

"Mamma, he's lying," I cried. "I know he has money."

"Your papa will have to go to the sponging house," Mamma said, very intent on Mary.

"What about the accounts?" she said in return. "Can't we send the porter to beg for payments?"

Just then our porter came through the door wheezing. He dropped six guineas, one by one, into Mamma's hand.

I kicked Charles's shoe. "Get your money box. This is desperate."

"What are you sacrificing?" he asked.

"I'll take that silver plate to the pawn shop," I said.

"You have the list of our accounts in Mayfair," Mamma said to the porter. "Go knock on all the doors. Tell them they may not find the bookshop open to them again if they do not pay something on their accounts."

I dashed into the parlor as the porter left, ready to seize the fine silver plate from the mantelpiece, but it was already gone.

When I returned, Charles was stomping up the steps, going to his room, I hoped.

"I sent Polly to pawn the plate earlier," Mamma said.

Papa came through the door. He handed Mamma a handful of coins, then clapped Shelley on the shoulder. "Let's pay a call at St. Paul's Churchyard. Surely the publishers will help me."

"Papa, what can I do?" Mary asked.

He barely glanced at her. "Take a look at the book of accounts."

She nodded eagerly. "Perhaps we can write to our regular customers and remind them to come in."

"It's much too late for that," Mamma scolded. "Cannon's men were here. We need money today."

Papa pushed Shelley out the door.

Mamma nodded. "It is best that he is not here."

I looked at Mary's back as she walked into the bookshop.

"We could pawn the tea set?" I suggested.

"We need real money, girl," Mamma snapped.

I knew I'd have to do it. I hung my head. "I will check my room, and Fanny's and Willy's."

She gave me a little push. Tears filled my vision by the time I reached my room. I didn't want Papa to go to a sponging house. It was the final step before sending someone to debtors' prison. What shame, for the immortal Godwin to sink to this!

I went through the rooms. Nothing but tuppence in Willy's room. Two shillings were hidden in a stocking in Fanny's room.

Charles appeared in the doorway. "What about us?" he asked, his money box in his hands. "Everything will go to the debt, and we won't even be able to take rooms. I need to keep enough for that, at least."

I scowled at him. "We don't pay rent for Skinner Street. There isn't anyone to kick us out while the ownership of the building is in dispute."

Charles shook his head. "Mamma is proud of how well she manages the business. How can the household be so deranged that even free rent has done no good?"

"I don't know." I slammed down the lid of Fanny's chest, then gestured at him to move. "We cannot afford servants, or our educations, or our travels? I'll check Mary's room next, then mine."

"Give me the money you've found, and I'll take it to Mamma."

I shook my head. "I'll take it myself to prove I hunted. Give her your money, Charles. They won't stop paying you a salary, after all. You're a man."

He tilted his head. "Do you want me to ask for a salary for you, after this crisis is passed?"

I pushed the coins into the pocket pinned to my skirt. "No, it will just bring more abuse from Mamma. She doesn't even want to pay for my singing lessons anymore, and I don't think there will be any more school either, when the fall term resumes. I'm sixteen now."

He frowned at me. "I worry about your future."

"Worry about yourself." I stomped to Mary's room, waiting for him to go downstairs before I could retrieve the ring from its hiding place.

When I came down, Mr. Place was back with a loan of fifty guineas from someone. An hour later, Papa and Shelley were back with two hundred, borrowed from a trio of book businesses around St. Paul's.

They went into the bookshop and wrote everything down, so they'd know what additional loans they had taken on. Mary found a little box to put all the coins in after they were carefully counted. Mr. Place went out again to see what else he could raise.

My heart stopped as someone banged on the front door. I glanced out of the bookshop window and saw three men in the street.

I knew the man in the center had been here before. He wore a blue coat and tan breeches, plus the fine black boots that were practically a London gentleman's uniform. A watch chain stretched across his lean middle, and his top hat was precisely brushed. Dark, straight hair stretched over his skull, flat against his rather pink flesh. He would be the moneyman, and the two much younger ruffians flanking him were his enforcers. Would they hurt Papa? My hand closed around the ring, still in my pocket. I had no idea of its true worth, but handing it over might put my neck in a noose. My lips trembled.

Mary came up next to me as Mamma opened the door. It was unlocked, but any potential customers must have sensed this was an unlucky day, for we'd had no trade since we arrived back from the palace.

"Don't worry," she whispered. "This won't be the end. Find your pride, Jane. Don't let Mr. Cannon see your distress. Such men feed on emotion. They sense a sinking ship."

I nodded and wiped my eyes, then blew my nose before following her into the front hall.

"You will pay, or you will go," Mr. Cannon was saying to Papa. His young men folded their arms across their large chests. What did they do to create such physiques? Carry around barrels filled with nails all day? I doubted that breaking kneecaps could create such bulk.

"I can pay three hundred on account today," Papa said calmly.

"Where is it?" the moneylender demanded.

Mamma held up the box. Mr. Cannon gestured us into the bookshop, as if he were the proprietor here, then took the box and poured it all out onto the counter.

Mary dropped coins she had taken from somewhere into the mix, in just a moment creating disorder where there had been an amount matching Papa's sum. But I appreciated it. Mamma produced some silver spoons, confusing things further. Charles's little stash included a cravat pin. When no one was looking, I added in the little ring with its red stone, along with a few small coins.

Polly, who had returned from pawning the plate, released her coins. They fell right over the ring. Mary glanced at Polly and they both went out, probably to prepare the evening meal. Charles followed, whistling as if he had not a care in the world. I suspected he had kept a few coins back.

As Mr. Cannon counted through everything, estimating the value of the non-money items, I stood rigid, fearing someone would ask where it came from. But no one recognized my sacrifice, perhaps because the ring was valued much lower than I expected. I could hardly speak up and say I didn't think the stone was semiprecious because it had dropped from the hand of a princess.

Papa stood stony-faced, flanked by his own ruffians, Mr. Place and Shelley. Mamma, next to me, kept applying a handkerchief to her eyes. Mr. Cannon didn't even look at her or me. Finally, he announced the total.

"Godwin, you have managed it for now," he said. "This is enough to buy you another two months, but I expect another payment next month, or I will be on your doorstep so early in August that you will not have time to go a-begging."

Papa didn't cower, but he didn't grace the moneylender with an answer, either.

"Do not concern yourself, sir," Shelley said. "There will be more, and the debt will be paid."

"I have not given up on the contribution from the Russians yet," Papa said.

"I do not care where it comes from," Mr. Cannon said. "This is a business matter, and we will handle it as men of business do." He poured the last of the coins into the little box and handed it to one of his men, then readjusted his top hat.

A hint of gray winked at his temples, but he was in his early forties at best. No hope of Papa outliving the debt. We had to repay it somehow.

Shelley nodded at me. I had to put my trust in him, that he could solve Papa's problems with these strange death loans he was working on. At least the ring was gone. If it ever came up again, I could deny it came from me, or that I had ever even seen it. Who was to say different, when it would simply be found in the possession of a moneylender?

No one had noticed. I was safe.

Chapter 6

Mary

"You are not going to wear that," Mamma sniped at Mary the next morning, as she came downstairs in her favorite tartan dress.

Mary straightened her collar and checked her sleeves. "I think it is good to look original. It's a flattering dress."

"Change it right now," Mamma snapped. "We must look like sober and prosperous citizens this morning."

Mary remembered the tale of what it was like to beg from moneylenders that she had heard recently. It didn't sound very respectable to do so, for all that the Prince Regent himself had moneylenders. But she knew Mamma to be a hypocrite long since.

Papa came out of the dining room with a bit of egg on the corner of his lip. Mamma threw up her hands and went at him with a handkerchief.

"Change!" she ordered Mary.

"I'd like a bit of breakfast," Mary whined.

"You should have eaten in the kitchen, stupid girl," Mamma growled.

Jane edged around Papa and handed Mary a slice of toast, then ran downstairs to open the bookshop. Papa nodded at Mary. She sighed but went upstairs to change. After all, she had asked to go to this appointment. It might help her understand the inner workings of masculine lives a bit better, this business of making deals and exchanging money. That might come in handy with her books, and with the financial issues of a writer's life.

She changed into a sober gray dress suitable for the bookshop and ate her toast, then went down so they could leave the house together. Her stomach grumbled as she walked in Mamma's wake deeper into the city, heading to Throgmorton Street where Papa had been invited to call. Great gray clouds scudded across the pale sky. A fine sight for a seashore, but in London the clouds too often blocked the meager sunlight.

"Is this really the wisest solution?" Mamma said as they walked. "I thought all of your communications with Mr. Teasdale would lead to the Stone brothers forming a partnership with us."

"Solicitors move slowly. More documents, more inspections, more meetings," Papa said, nodding at a man who dodged around him.

"Still, that is better than begging for more money from yet another moneylender," Mamma groused.

"We are out of time, Mrs. Godwin. John Cannon has no patience left for us. We have to find another seven hundred pounds." Papa tilted his hat after a gust of wind nearly upset it.

"You never should have promised him those diamonds. It made him greedy." Mamma snapped her skirts to avoid a small child begging along the wall of a bank.

"He called on me demanding a payment. What was I supposed to do?" He glanced back at Mary, then offered her his arm. "Don't worry, my girl, we always figure something out."

"Shelley will come to the rescue in the end," she said, taking his arm. She immediately felt better with her hand on his sleeve.

"He has made several calls on this firm with me," Papa said in an agreeable tone. "They know we will have the money in the end. Shelley has gone to great lengths already in order to secure the loans."

They went into a court and walked up steps alongside a draper's shop. The sign on the door said BALLACHEY AND BRIDGES. The business did not have a sinister air. They could have been solicitors or men of business or private jewelers, for all she knew.

Inside, a pair of clerks sat at tables. A large man, around forty, sat behind a desk in the center of the room. He was the first sign of anything unusual, for he had the look of a dockworker, rather than a banker, all curling dark hair and tanned skin, and arms double the size of an ordinary man's.

"Good day, Mr. Smith," Papa said. "Is Mr. Ballachey available?"

"Has Shelley finished his paperwork?" The voice revealed that he'd been extracted from foreign parts, Germany, perhaps. Was moneylending an international business?

"No." Papa's tone was short.

The foreigner's nostrils flared at the base of a nose that had been damaged a number of times. A thick finger rubbed over the flare, then he stood, his stool falling over. One of the clerks jumped off his stool to right the fallen one. The foreigner stepped to one of the doors in the back, each step looking slow and painful for all its purpose. He knocked on the door and entered without pausing.

When he came back into the room, he waved them forward. Mary felt, oddly, quite awed by the scene. She noted the details of the clerks, rather healthy specimens compared to the men who trudged home through her neighborhood at the ends of days. Their quill pens were fresh, and their desks were free of marks.

When they entered the inner chamber, the moneylender was already standing. His vigorous appearance belied his bald head. He greeted Papa with a hearty handshake and expressed pleasure at meeting Mamma, then he winked at Mary when Papa introduced her. Mamma was seated in one chair, then Mary in the other. Mr. Ballachey ordered a third chair to be brought in.

"What can I do for the Godwins?" he asked, rubbing his hands together. He had ink stains on his right and left index fingers and paper cuffs over his coat. His desk held the evidence of previous spills of iron gall. Happily, his trousers, waistcoat, and tailed coat were all of a dark brown, which hid most of the damage he could do to them. "No Shelley today?"

"No, Mr. Ballachey, but you know we have funds coming from him."

"I heard a rumor about Russian funds?" the moneylender asked.

Papa nodded shortly. "I do not know if they can be recovered given the unfortunate demise of the one who had promised support. Nothing else has changed. We are working on the matter of the business partnership, and I expect good things there. Unfortunately, this matter of the Russians has excited my creditor Mr. Cannon, and I wish to remove my business from him to you, in light of your intimate congress with the Shelley loans. It makes sense to have all of our business in one place."

"I understand that Cannon meant to have you in a sponging house last night."

"A threat without teeth," Papa said. "We are not destitute or without friends or fame."

"No," Mr. Ballachey said. His rather red face stretched in a sickly smile. "As soon as Shelley can get us all the required information, you will have what you need."

"He is not our only option," Mamma said quickly. "The partnership. Our foreign admirers."

The moneylender cleared his throat. "What other options do you have? I already have all the details on the Juvenile Library."

Papa coughed. "I have an idea for a new novel. Three volumes, a historical novel set in the seventeenth century with parallels to our own time, featuring the life of an extraordinary man."

"That sounds like the work of many years, Mr. Godwin."

Mamma gave a little cough. "I have a translation to do—a retranslation, in fact—of an interesting French novel by de Grainville titled *The Last Man*. It depicts the end of the world. The earlier translation has had some success, despite its defects."

Mary thought that sounded rather exciting. She'd never seen it in the shop, but Mamma must have it in her office. "I am going to write a children's book for the Juvenile Library," she announced.

"Mr. Godwin and I are also working on another translation of a Swiss novel that is sure to be most popular," Mamma added. "*De plus*, in terms of our household, we have two fewer mouths to feed and clothe since one daughter and our cook are gone, and Mary here is now doing our cooking."

Mary went cold and hot in turn. "That is most temporary, as I am sure the misunderstanding with our cook will be cleared up soon. My contribution to our current financial crisis is my literary offering."

The moneylender gave her a paternal smile, then quickly wrote some lines on a piece of paper. "This is what I can do for you, Mr. Godwin."

Mary's hands shook until she closed them into fists. No one noticed. No one cared. Would anyone other than Fanny give her the natural due she deserved as Mary Wollstonecraft's literary heiress? They ought to exclaim in delight at her offer.

Shelley. He had made many remarks indicating his understanding of that. She closed her eyes as her father spluttered, bringing the poet's angelic face to mind. Such a distinguished man, Shelley. Sure to be as famed in a literary sense as Lord Byron, some day. He respected her, unlike her conniving stepmother and desperate father.

"Mary."

She opened her eyes as her father called her name. The moneylender was already standing. They must have come to terms. She stood as well and followed Mamma out. Then Papa closed the door, leaving both women in the anteroom.

Mamma put her heavy hand on Mary's shoulder and pressed down purposefully. "This is not the time to be putting on airs, girl. You live in my home, and you will do as I say. We raised you wrong, as I always say to your father."

Mary winced at the pressure but didn't dare give Mamma the satisfaction of moving away. "My mother wrote explicitly on how she believed young ladies should be raised. Any way in which you subvert that directive is an obscenity."

Mamma pressed down harder. The pain intensified. Mary firmed her lips and locked her gaze to Mamma's, not giving way.

"Madam?" The large man, speaking in a harsh tone, stopped in front of them.

Mamma moved her hand away. Mary rotated her arm in its socket. It made a popping noise.

"Yes?" Mamma said acidly.

"No nonsense," the man said. "You all right, miss?" His smile exposed a missing tooth to the right of his front teeth.

Mary realized he was flirting with her. She curtsied to him. "Very well, thank you, sir. My stepmother does not know her own strength."

He started to say something else, but the door opened behind Mary. They all turned as Papa exited. Mr. Ballachey nodded at his enforcer, and they were escorted out of the office to the stairs.

Mary trudged home, careful to remain behind Papa and Mamma, thinking about what the end of the world would be like, and wondering if it would really be all that bad.

When they arrived home, Mary wanted to run down to the kitchen and throw the roast into the fire. She felt tears prickling at the backs of her eyelids from the emotional hurt even more than her aching shoulder. If she couldn't take her revenge, she wanted to fly into Papa's arms like she had as a little child, so he could make her feel better. He always managed to miss Mamma's cruel moments and seemed apart from them.

She removed her bonnet and glanced at him hopefully. He must have some words of kindness to take away the sting of Mamma's cruelty.

"A cold luncheon today." Mamma examined the watch pinned to her bodice. "Ham sandwiches, Mary, and don't stint on the butter. Two for me." She handed her bonnet to Mary and went through the bookshop door.

Mary let the bonnet slide through her fingers and drop to the floor. "Papa?" she whispered. "I want to be a writer. That's what you want, too, isn't it?"

"He that loves reading has everything within his reach," Papa said. "But your mamma needs you to cook for us right now. You wouldn't want your old father to go hungry, correct? I'll take one ham sandwich, but with two pickles."

He walked upstairs, not looking back. Mary let the tears fall freely as she went to the kitchen stairs. She wouldn't need salt on the sandwiches; her tears would be sufficient.

Polly asked her what was wrong when she came into the kitchen.

"I am a child of misfortune," Mary sniffed.

Polly blinked at her. "Then what am I?"

"Not Mary Wollstonecraft's daughter," Mary said. "They want ham sandwiches for lunch."

"That is easy enough. I'll slice the bread and butter."

Mary nodded and went to fetch the ham from the cold storage. She debated destroying it, but Mamma would beat her for sure if she did. How she hated the old witch, with her black dresses and green visor. She took petty revenge by serving Jane first, in the bookshop. Mamma would throw a fit if she noticed Jane had a sandwich in there. She'd expect Mary to forgo her own luncheon and work behind the counter while Jane took her time to eat it.

Forget that. She dropped a double pair of sandwiches, mere slivers of bread containing the toughest edges of ham and fat, on Mamma's desk, then took the last sandwich upstairs.

When she put her hand on the doorknob, she heard voices from within. When had callers come to see Papa? She forgot her ire with him for fear that John Cannon had arrived again.

She turned the knob and opened the door an inch. Shelley stood in front of Papa's desk, his hands underneath his coattails. Her heart skipped a beat at the sight of him, broad-shouldered, young, and strong.

"You must finalize your loans, Shelley," Papa urged. "We are in a most dire situation."

"I am aware of that, sir," Shelley said, his voice respectful though he could snap Papa in two if he liked. "But it will be well into summer before it can be managed. These moneymen only move quickly when they are taking money back, not when they are giving it out."

"You must do better," her father said coldly. He seemed to echo something of Mamma with that tone. "You made certain promises to me and to the Juvenile Library. If I am in prison, my devoted wife will have to tend to me there, and the business will fall apart."

"No one can seize this house while the property is in dispute," Shelley said. "Charles can run it, even if Mrs. Godwin decides to follow you into prison."

"You would allow this, sir?"

"I will do everything in my power to prevent it, as well you know." Shelley began to pace, each long step taking up the length of the desk. "But I cannot raise the money without the post-obit loans processing through, not unless my grandfather suddenly dies and forces my father to come to terms with me."

"That is not good enough."

Shelley's voice lost its warmth. "I have nothing more to offer."

Mary appreciated Shelley's manly tone and earnestness, but she felt nothing but shame for her father's demands. How had he sunk so low? This was philosophy? Her mother would rather have attempted to drown herself from the shame of living, or traveled to Norway in the hopes of restoring her lover's finances, than demand money from others.

Mary's eyes fluttered closed. This could not be her life. Disrespecting her father's conversation, she pushed the door open and dropped her father's sandwich on the desk. A pickle rolled off the plate and slipped wetly onto some papers.

She fled, realizing she still wore an apron. A man like Shelley would not appreciate her looking like a drudge. Although it might make him press the moneymen for the loans, if he saw how low Wollstonecraft's daughter had been brought by the lack of funds.

Except. Her feet stopped on the third stair from the bottom. He knew that was not the cause of it at all. They had sent Fanny away, who loved to cook. They threw their cook in the lockup. This was not poverty but stupidity, and it was all Mamma's fault.

Why would Shelley give funds to support her?

Mary stomped back to the kitchen. Polly sat on a stool in the corner, eating a thick sandwich, a guilty expression on her face.

"No one said you could eat the cook's portion as well as your own," Mary said. "Be careful. They won't be able to afford you either, with gluttony like that."

She wrapped half of Polly's sandwich into her handkerchief and took her notebook off a shelf, then ran up and out the front door, feeling like wolves were chasing her. Who cared that dinner preparations needed to be made? She wasn't Mamma's daughter but Mary Wollstonecraft's.

Outside, the pleasant weather surprised her, given the storms in her head. The sky had turned blue, and the clouds were just candy floss low on the horizon. Sufficient wind blew the animal smells away, if not the flies.

"I cannot continue like this," she muttered aloud. "I am not hardened by this harsh peasant life, like Leonardo, the heir to Loredani, able to throw myself on the ground anywhere and sleep like a cat. What if someone doesn't find me and take me in, recognizing my nobility as they did with Leonardo in *Zofloya*?"

She stomped down the street, ill use making her body feel heavy. Each raised foot demanded more effort than usual. If only Mr. Naryshkin had taken better care. Why had he been transporting diamonds through the street without a guard? Or had his guard killed him? Everyone always blamed servants for everything, and here was a situation where it might be true. Had the footmen and such been properly guarded?

Before she knew it, she found herself in front of St. Sepulchre. Though it abutted the busy street, a stand of trees guarded one corner of the old church. She settled herself under one of them. As her skirts touched the loamy ground, her stomach growled.

She unwrapped her sandwich and took a large bite, then opened her notebook. Jane had been advocating for Diego to be the hero in her book, but he had to be Egyptian since Mary had already decided he knew how to summon mummies. She tapped her pencil on the page. Diego would be the villain, which meant Fernando, at last, would be the hero, though Isabella would have to do most of the work. Her time as an apprentice nun would give her the information to dispel the mummy's curse, saving Fernando's life.

She took another bite of sandwich, then began to describe Fernando. After a few thoughts, she wrote:

> *Isabella cowered against a tree.* Oh, mighty oak, shelter me from the doings of these dastardly men! *In front of her, atop a dashing stallion, a grandee sat proudly. Near to fainting, she pressed her mother's locket to her chest. "Mother, give me strength!"*
>
> *The grandee, black-haired and stern, yet with a good-natured cast to his eyes and mouth, said, "What is this talk of mothers, señorita?"*
>
> *Isabella regained her wits despite her almost overwhelming sense that doom was upon her. "My mother died at my birth, señor."*
>
> *"What accent is this? What country do you hail from, my lady?"*
>
> *She blushed and curtsied. "Scotland, señor."*
>
> *"You are far away from home, and this forest is not safe for the likes of you."*
>
> *"Why not?" Isabella asked. "I have survived a great peril already, señor, in the abandoned keep in the center of this forest."*
>
> *"There are mummies in the caves underneath us," the grandee said darkly. "They come out at night to trap the living and return them to the caves for their unholy pleasures."*
>
> *Isabella trembled with fear. "Mummies? In Tuscany?"*

"I, Don Fernando, will carry you safely from this cursed place," the grandee said, tapping his chest. "Come, señorita." He held out his gloved hand.

Isabella saw dark spots in front of her eyes, but she could not allow herself to faint. How could she trust this man? True, he was noble, but some of the nobility, especially outside of her native Scotland, were deeply depraved.

His eyes glowed blue despite his deeply olive skin as he leaned forward in his saddle.

"You look engrossed in your studies."

Mary startled and looked up. "Shelley!"

Her friend cast himself down next to her, unheeding of the damage the soft soil would do to his clothes. She offered him part of her sandwich, but he refused it.

"Oh." She colored. "Ham. I forgot."

"How you can eat the flesh of such an intelligent creature as the pig I do not know." He rubbed his eyes.

"I eat what we have," Mary said. "I do not have the time or money to prepare complex meals."

"Oh, Mary, the Skinner Street household is indeed a mess."

"It is, and you are Papa's creature. Will you be able to give him funds in time to save him?"

He smiled at her, a sleepy, eyes-half-closed, sensuous look that made her want to fall into his blue orbs as if he were a washtub and she a bather. "I am yours alone, sweet Mary, the best of both of your parents."

She smiled and looked down at her notebook. "Are you going to use those funds to set me up in my own household?"

He chuckled. "My money is pledged to your father, but my heart is now pledged to you."

Her fingers clenched around her pencil. "Shelley, you shouldn't say such things."

He pulled the pencil out of her hand, then lifted her unresisting fingers to his lips. "But I do say them, sweet Mary."

"Ahem."

Mary glanced up and had to blink away the sun. Without her noticing, Reverend Doone, a clergyman attached to the church, had approached. He had a light walk despite his well-known love of the table. The cook at the rectory was excellent.

She tried to pull her hand away from Shelley's, but he didn't loosen his grip. Rather, he tightened it.

The curate, who had gone to school with Shelley, demonstrated his loathing yet again. He stomped on Shelley's sleeve, which tore their hands apart.

"How dare you make love to this young lady?" he barked.

"Calm yourself, Doone, or you'll bring on an apoplexy." Shelley used his other hand to pull his sleeve from under the curate's shoe. It came away dark with damp.

"Do not fuss, Reverend Doone," Mary said, noting that Shelley reacted to the condition of his sleeve with nothing more than mild puzzlement, rather than the rage that another young man might have displayed. He proved himself over and over to be a superior gentleman. "He is merely teasing me, as he does my sisters."

"Regardless of whether it is you or Miss Imlay or Miss Clairmont he thrusts his attention toward, Shelley has a wife," the curate said.

"We are well aware." Mary gave Shelley a quelling glance just in case, as she would have done with her brothers.

The curate inclined his head. "I am sure you are also aware that I do not have a treasured life companion."

Shelley laughed heartily. "I cannot imagine why not."

Mary had seen a better side of the curate than his current harpy-like manners, though she could not possibly be interested. It struck her that he had too much of Austen's Mr.

Collins in him for love. She clasped her hands together. "Alas, as you know, my father is an atheist, sir."

The curate regarded her sourly. "You are not, Miss Godwin. I wonder why you do not break from your household. Your immortal soul is at stake."

She lowered her eyebrows and gave him a direct stare. "I cannot leave my father, sir. It is my duty to care for him."

"He has a wife." Mr. Collins—err, Reverend Doone—adjusted his collar. "I am sure he would see the betterment of his daughter that I could offer, and—"

"All this trouble about wives," Shelley interrupted. "What is important is love, which Mary Godwin has from me." He leapt to his feet. "Do you declare yourself my rival, Doone?"

Mary's heart dropped into her stomach, then rose up again, creating a lump in her throat. How very flattering Shelley was. She adored him, and he her. Even nature's glories were but dim against the wonder of this poet's eyes.

"You cannot have a rival, Shelley," came the curate's sour reply. "When you have a young, blooming wife. I have seen her, you know. What do you want? A seraglio of women like some foreign potentate?"

Shelley burst out laughing. "You have quite the wrong idea, sir. I desire a community of like minds. Women have the right to an education just as a man does, in their own sphere. I do not want our loveliest creatures locked away from the world."

His words reminded her of dire warnings she had heard from better men than the curate. It had been said that Shelley had brief obsessions with women other than his wife. She had even heard a couple of specific names spoken, one of them a connection to a certain disciple of her father and easily verified.

"What would you say, Miss Godwin," the curate said directly to her. "If I paid a call on your father?"

She bowed her head. "It would be better, sir, if you paid a call to him on Fanny's behalf, rather than mine." She wanted a life of study, not good works. Fanny, though, might she feel differently?

"Have you a better offer?" he asked, more gently.

"I still have hopes of my Scottish suitor, young as he is," Mary explained. "He claimed he is coming to see me here in London."

"Your father turned away the first Scotsman," Shelley said.

She licked her lips and tasted the salt left from the ham. "He told me he feared Mr. Booth would not be gentle with me."

"Then he showed himself wise," Shelley said.

"Shelley will never do you aught but ill," the curate prophesied.

"We speak of Mr. Baxter," Mary told him. "He may very well be my future." She heard the lie in her own voice but didn't correct herself. It must be so, whatever force of will that might take.

Chapter 7

Jane

Mamma came into the bookshop, already complaining before she'd even reached the counter. "That dratted Mary is nowhere to be found, and your Uncle Joseph is here."

I frowned and set down the quill with which I was recording my sale of a Rousseau volume. "Uncle Joseph wants to see Mary?"

"No, you stupid girl. I need tea brought and some of those little honey cakes. He has expectations of a better table than your father does."

"I do not know where she is." I picked up the quill again and formed the *eau* of the name.

She plucked the quill from my hand, spilling ink over the top of the page, and shoved the tip back into the stand. "Go make tea, girl."

Sullen, I said, "Polly can do it."

"Tell her to make the cakes. There may be time if it is a long visit." She grabbed my arm and pulled me several inches toward her. I hissed against the pain, then ripped off my shop apron and went out. Mamma could be terrifying when she desired and had a lot of strength for such a middle-aged lady. I rubbed my arm as I went down to the kitchen. It wasn't until my feet left the staircase that I recognized my gesture for one that Mary often made. It made me wonder how often Mamma had hurt her arm over the years. Mary had been distressed by a pins-and-needles sensation in her fingers at times, as well as various skin lesions. If it happened to me, too, I'd know it was Mamma's fault.

"What are you doing, lazybones?" I demanded as I entered the kitchen.

Polly jumped up from her stool, though she looked angry rather than guilty.

"Make some honey cakes," I ordered. "Mamma wants them for Mr. Godwin's visit."

When Polly went toward the flour barrel, I checked the inside of the large teapot we used for breakfast. I wasn't surprised to see this morning's leaves still in the pot, rather than properly dried. Mamma had the key to the tea chest. If she had thought of it, she'd have wanted to serve Uncle Joseph new tea, but I didn't have access to it.

I upended our daily pot into the finer decorated one we used for company. Half-dry leaves plopped into the bottom. Then I took up a rag, poured water from the kettle over the fire into the teapot, and set it on a tray.

I found some flat biscuits in a tin, chose the best half dozen to set on a plate, and then added a pretty spread of marmalade. It wasn't honey cakes, but it would have to do for now. Then I hefted the tray containing all of it and went upstairs.

When I went into the parlor, I heard Uncle Joseph say, "I am sorry that your debt is coming due, brother, but there is no help to be had from the Godwins."

"Is no one in our family in funds?" Papa sat on a wooden chair, leaving the sofa for his younger brother.

"None of us desired the fame you found and have always lived modestly." Uncle Joseph clasped his hands between his knees. "Our quiet lives have not allowed the massing of large fortunes."

"You would think that with thirteen of us, and descended on one side from wealth, that there would be someone to aid me in my time of trouble," Papa said with a genial smile.

"There are only five of us left now, brother." Uncle Joseph smoothed his hand over his graying head. At least he still had more hair than Papa.

"What about Hannah? Or Hull? If I applied to them for funds, would they aid the Juvenile Library?"

I set the tray down. Uncle Joseph glanced at it with lips downturned.

"Hmm," Uncle Joseph said. "You are not the usual girl."

"Uncle Joseph," I said, shocked. "I am Jane."

His lips curved into a slight sneer. "I am not your uncle, girl."

"Brother," Papa chided. "All of my children are equal."

Uncle Joseph snorted. "To return to your point, Hannah is not in the best of health, and Hull may be good for a turkey or ham for your larder, but he has seven children to feed off the bounty of his farm. You know what that is like."

Papa sighed. "I do not like to hear this about Hannah. Perhaps she should go to Hull until she feels better."

Uncle Joseph returned his gaze to me. "What are you still doing here, girl?"

My cheeks burned. "I have instructed our kitchen girl to make honey cakes, sir. I hope you will have a long conversation with Papa so you can have them before you go. Or if you are staying for dinner?"

"I will depart within the hour," Uncle Joseph informed me. "Make me up a basket."

"Would you like me to pour, Papa?" I emphasized his honorific, causing Uncle Joseph's lip to curl anew.

Papa nodded.

"Now." Uncle Joseph folded his fingers together under his chin. "As to your money troubles. I do know a man who owns a rather indelicate business. Very profitable. If you had fifty pounds to give me, he could squeeze twenty or thirty out of it by the middle of June."

I poured the tea for them, then walked out, not at all sorry to have only spent the soggy tea leaves on Uncle Joseph's sour face. Papa must be furious not only to have failed to wheedle funds out of his family but to have had the displeasure of paying for the visit in cake. Knowing what I had heard of how badly Uncle Joseph treated Aunt Mary, his wife, I could only imagine what sort of disreputable nonsense this "businessman" was mixed up in. Nothing even so gentlemanly as smuggling, I expected. Likely one of the skin trades.

I nearly bumped into a taller figure as I stepped into the front hall.

"There you are!" I exclaimed, recognizing Shelley as I closed the parlor door.

Mary came in behind him. She had green stains on the side of her skirt, and encrusted dirt marked one of Shelley's sleeves.

I gestured them to follow me to the top of the rear staircase, out of earshot of both the parlor and the bookshop. "Papa is desperate enough to call on his family for aid, but there is none forthcoming. At least none that he would accept."

"We have a month, don't we?" Mary asked. "Until Mr. Cannon comes again?"

"It might not be more than a week," Shelley contradicted. "He is greedy enough to come again and rattle your father's cage."

"We gave him rather a lot," I said, remembering the ring.

"He will call it interest, only, and come for the principal," Shelley said.

"Surely not!" Mary clapped her hand over her mouth after I gestured at her. "Can Papa be so deeply in debt to one man?"

"Cannon's rates are usurious," Shelley said. "Something must be done to help your Papa before it is too late. If he went to debtors' prison, he might find it to his taste if he were to be left alone in peace to do his work, but if your mamma joined him, it would be a different story."

Mary shuddered. "Mamma could not go, if the bookshop were to keep running."

Shelley tilted his head to her. "Dear girl, once your Papa is gone, the rest of the creditors will descend like wolves. Skinner Street would be stripped. You might not have to leave the building, but there would be nothing in it but a few sticks."

Mary rubbed down her arm. "What are we to do?"

I remembered one thread of the problem of the missing diamonds. "Did you go to see the Westbrooks, Shelley? Since I saw Miss Eliza Westbrook on Hart Street yesterday?"

Shelley's eyes widened. "I did not. What an excellent idea. Let us go see my wife's sister. If she has the diamonds, I will make Harriet hand them over."

"Do you think Miss Westbrook killed Mr. Naryshkin?" Mary asked, curiosity filling her expression.

"Who can say what the black-haired witch might do?" Shelley said. He held out his arm to her.

"She can't go," I said. "Polly is baking cakes for Uncle Joseph. No one is making dinner yet."

"Dung and diamonds," Mary muttered. "Mamma will skin me like a cat if I leave again."

"I'll go," I offered. "Shelley, I'm sure you would do better with a friendly face. It might save you from violence toward the witch."

He brushed at his sleeve absently, which did nothing but smear the dirt, since it was still wet. "Come along, then. We had better hurry so we can be back before Mary's excellent meal."

"You'll have a nice fat turnip on your plate," she said saucily, then sauntered down the back stairs, her hips swinging. And she accused me of having hips. Very impertinent, my sister.

Shelley and I hopped a cart from the cheese monger down the street, which took us half the way to Chapel Street. The Westbrooks were very wealthy, though not aristocratic at all. Mr. Westbrook had started a coffeehouse and other businesses. I knew nothing of him other than his success. If only Mamma had thought to open a tavern or coffeehouse instead of a publishing business. But we were thoroughly in our sort of life now. None of us but her had the cunning to run such a place. Mary and I could scarcely face the customers without the knowledge that we had books to read hidden under the counter, and Charles hated everyone.

At the house, a pretty maid a little younger than I let us in. "Mrs. Shelley is upstairs with your daughter, sir. Would you like to go to the nursery?" She glanced at me curiously. I checked my dress. Did she think I was a new nurserymaid?

"I'd like to see Miss Westbrook," Shelley told her. "Is she at home?"

"I will find out, sir." The maid went up the stairs to the next floor, leaving us there.

Shelley rolled his eyes and took me into a room on the right side. "This is their excuse for a library."

The room held nothing of particular interest for one who had grown up around Papa's ever-growing collection of books, but they did have a couple of bookshelves. "What sort of school did Mr. Westbrook attend?" I asked, picking up a Latin grammar. "He seems to have collected the books of a classical education."

"He fancies himself a gentleman now." Shelley pulled out a book of euclidean geometry. "But mathematics is what made him his fortune. How much to spend to acquire the drinks he served, how much to charge the patrons."

"Your insults toward my father are truly insensitive, given how often you come here looking for money," said an acid-tinged voice.

The black-haired witch—who Mary said conspired with Mamma, no less—walked through the doorway. She had dressed her hair in an elaborate coronet crowning the back of her narrow skull, and stringy ringlets around her sallow face. Her plain muslin dress did not go with the fancy hairdressing.

"You persuaded me to marry your sister to take my money and future title," Shelley said in a surprisingly good-natured tone. "But I am not here to battle you over who went after whose income. Today I am on a more philanthropic mission: to find the missing funds promised to Mr. Godwin."

"We have no connection to the Godwins," Eliza said.

"That is not what I've heard," I snapped at her. "You are very friendly with my mother."

She had a long, thin neck, and when her head swiveled toward me it was as if a snake turned in my direction. "You must be Jane."

I curtsied to her. "We are looking for the diamonds that were stolen from Pavel Naryshkin."

Her nostrils flared. "I have no idea what you are talking about."

"I'm sure you've read about the murder of the Russian in the newspapers," I said. "And I saw you leaving a jewelry shop in Covent Garden in the company of one Viktor Hesse, who has been spying on our house."

"You must be misinformed," she said, pulling her chin back, giving herself a roll of neck fat.

"I am not," I said. "I had no difficulty recognizing you, and Mr. Hesse's appearance is unique."

"I was not in Mr. Hesse's company but merely in proximity. I was shopping for a new bracelet."

Shelley raised his eyebrows in a sardonic expression I had never seen before.

"He is a footman, Shelley," she gasped. "You cannot think I would spend time with a footman."

"Why do you know his name?" Shelley asked.

She glanced up to the ceiling. "The shopkeeper introduced me. He seemed excited that the man worked for royalty. Quite a gossip, that one."

"What did he tell you?" I asked.

"He had the temerity to whisper in my ear that Mr. Hesse is likely Princess Maria's lover." She pressed her lips together, feigning disgust.

"The Princess Maria who is married to Count Naryshkin?" Shelley asked.

Eliza nodded, her expression becoming eager. "He also said Mr. Hesse was more than a footman. He's a spy."

This was a woman who loved to gossip. She likely had a web of associates around town, like this jewelry store shop-keeper, who might tell her useful stories. "I often admire the pieces in the shop window. Which bracelet did you buy? I'd love to see it."

Eliza blinked rapidly. "Oh, I put it into my father's vault for safekeeping."

"While you describe the piece to my friend Miss Clairmont, I believe I will go up and see Ianthe," Shelley said, referring to his young daughter. "Miss Clairmont is an excellent singer. Why don't you show her your sheet music?"

Shelley disappeared in a blink of an eye. I had scarcely seen him move his feet. Miss Westbrook and I were left to stare at each other, equally confused.

"Why are you really here?" she asked, going frosty.

This woman's ever-changing moods were difficult to follow.

"You already are aware we are chasing the missing diamonds. I had hoped you might have some information, due to your association with the Prussian footman."

She sniffed. "I have told you I do not, so you may leave."

I clenched my jaw. "I cannot leave without Shelley."

She went to the unlit fire and toyed with a bit of painted pottery on the mantelpiece. "Why, is he dallying with you, now? Is he done with Harriet Boinville's daughter, that Cornelia?"

"Of course not," I said, offended.

"You are the same age as Harriet was." She picked up a creamware punch pot and inspected it for dust.

"You pushed her into his arms. I cannot listen to you." I turned away, emboldened by Shelley to march over to the piano. The music on the stand was a piece by Joseph Haydn, one that did not have a vocal part.

When I had finished studying the music, I looked up, but Miss Westbrook had left. I shrugged my shoulders and sat at the piano. I did not have much opportunity to play an instrument, but I knew my scales, and I might as well warm up my voice.

Lost in my practice, I did not look up again until Shelley came in, jingling some coins in his fingers.

"Where did those come from?" I asked, not removing my hands from the keys.

"My wife," Shelley, who had clearly dismissed poor Mrs. Shelley from his thoughts as soon as he left her, said.

"Is Ianthe well?"

"Oh yes."

"Is Mrs. Shelley blooming?"

He sat down next to me. "I see no sign of a coming child. I do not know what to think where she is concerned."

"She is a complicated woman, your wife."

"Do you think so?" he returned. "I do not agree. I spent years of my life attempting to educate her. What do we do now?"

"I am confused. I thought Mr. Hesse had something to do with this Naryshkin mess, but I have no insights."

Shelley pushed the coins into his waistcoat pocket. "We know he is watching Skinner Street. We know he has an interest in jewelry shops."

"Yes, it made sense he had some tie to the matter. What will we do now?"

"Leave this house," he said. "Return to yours in time for Mary's dinner to be served."

We both rose from the piano bench and walked out of the house. I rather loathed doing so. It smelled beautifully there of dried lavender and other flowers, with no hint of damp. I imagined those dusty mantelpiece ornaments would feed us at Skinner Street for months.

"It's not that I want money, but they do live in so much comfort, Shelley," I said as we reached the street. "Why do you not come to terms with Harriet and live there with her, instead of in a succession of grubby rooms with your poet friends?"

"If I reconciled with her, we would not live in her father's house but in a grubby room with Ianthe and her sister," Shelley said. "The comforts of that home were never available to me."

"Because you eloped to Scotland."

"It would seem so." He coughed as a street sweeper sent dust floating above the street. "Now we must come to some decision. What does Princess Maria want with your household?"

"You think she instructed Mr. Hesse to watch the house?"

"It stands to reason, if Eliza is right about their relationship."

We dodged a horse-driven cart as we crossed a street, leaving the residential area. "Mary is afraid that her mother's precious portrait will be stolen."

"By Viktor Hesse?"

"Or someone else in the employ of the Naryshkins. They are rather obsessed with anything to do with Mary Wollstonecraft."

"Interesting theory," Shelley said, tilting his head.

I knew he liked it because it was Mary's idea. "I think of even worse possibilities, like it being sold."

"Sold?" Shelley asked, turning to me.

I pulled him toward a bakery door, since he had funds. "Yes. Papa might sell it if they offered enough. To keep him out of the sponging house."

"Oh, he would never sell that. It ought to be Mary's."

"Not Fanny's?"

"She was expecting Mary when she was painted. I think it ought to be hers."

"Papa would sell it," I said. "He would tell us not to be obsessed with possessions."

Shelley started walking again, rapidly, leaving my hope of the bakery behind. "I would not allow that. I would deny him my support if he did such a thing. No, I would not believe it. A portrait of a beloved mother."

I trotted behind him as he raved. I had not known he felt strongly about the portrait, though I knew Mary did. Mary Wollstonecraft was the good angel of us all, and any thought that she might be disrespected was anathema.

Back at the house, Shelley muttered something about remembering other plans and left me at the door. He did not offer me any of the coins he had obtained from his wife. I expected if he had come in with me, Papa would have extricated them from him somehow, which probably explained why he didn't stay.

At dinner, I watched Papa and Mamma for new signs of stress but found none. I looked out the windows many times as the evening passed, but neither Mr. Hesse nor anyone else lurked around our house.

On my way up to bed, I visited the Wollstonecraft portrait. Holding my candle high, I swept my gaze around the frame. Even framed, she was less than four feet by about three feet. I measured the painting with my arm. Two and a half feet by two feet, I thought, if she was cut out of the frame, as I had heard thieves sometimes did. She could easily be carried down the staircase.

When would the danger come? Likely when the Russians were ready to return home. That is when we would have to set up a guard, months from now.

"I will protect you as your avowed disciple," I whispered to that serene face.

"Jane, what are you doing in here?" asked Papa, coming in behind me.

"I wanted to see the painting," I said, thinking quickly. "I thought I might attempt to learn drawing again and make a study of this work."

"You are a very good singer, Jane. Focus on your strengths."

"I'm not asking for you to pay for lessons," I said, turning with the candle. The flame touched the shadows under his cheekbones. How old he had grown, while his first wife remained ever young. "I thought I could draw items around the house."

He regarded me. "It is not a bad occupation for summer, when the light lingers late into the evening. But do not waste candles on it."

I inclined my head. "Yes, Papa."

"How is your singing coming along?"

"Mamma doesn't want to pay for lessons anymore," I blurted. Surely he remembered that, but one couldn't be certain.

"No?" He frowned, casting his chin into full shadow.

"Too expensive, she said."

"I will speak to Mamma." He gestured to me to come toward him.

When I was a foot away from him, he said, "You must not be too hard on your mamma, Jane."

"We were speaking of how she is too hard on me," I said. "I am not attempting to deny her anything."

"It is not too much to ask for you to work in the bookshop."

A number of things crossed my mind, but this was a household that had sent its cook to the lockup and put its brilliant daughter into the kitchen. I did nothing but nod.

He smiled, exposing his worn teeth. "Very well. Goodnight, Jane. Go straight to bed."

"Goodnight, Papa," I said dutifully. Defiant to the last, however, I did not go to my room. I sneaked into Fanny's instead.

I went to her oldest chest—more of a casket, really—that she kept with her most precious things in her bedroom. She must have been sure she'd be allowed to come home from Wales eventually to have left it here.

I pulled it out and wiped away the film of dust forming on the wood. Poor Fanny, such a dutiful housekeeper, had been gone long enough for this deterioration of her private treasures. I opened the box with the candle giving me light.

Gently, I pawed through it, until I found what I was looking for. A collection of clumsily hemmed handkerchiefs, all of white muslin. I knew what these were. The last remains of Mary Wollstonecraft's dress from the portrait, cut down into squares and turned into these little remembrances. I had seen Fanny crying over the contents of this pathetic box many a time. But she wasn't here now, and I was.

I stole one of them, then quickly tucked the rest in the casket and pushed it under the bed.

In my room, I tucked the relic under my pillow, then undressed and got into bed without saying goodnight to anyone.

The next morning, Mary was helping me to pin and tie myself into my apron-front dress when we felt the house shake. Someone had gone in or out of the street door.

"It is much too early for anyone to be about," Mary said crossly. She'd already been up for an hour, with Polly in the kitchen.

I shivered and pulled my shawl over my shoulders. The day had not yet warmed. "Did Papa have an early meeting? Or Mamma?"

Mary went to my door and opened it to listen. Her body straightened at the sound of a certain voice.

"What is Shelley doing here?" I asked.

"There must be some news." Mary turned to me, excitement coloring her cheeks. "Has he found the diamonds?"

Instinctively, I hugged her. "Oh, it must be something good. Let's go down."

We didn't make it all the way to the first floor, for we heard Papa taking Shelley into his study. Following them, we entered the room I'd been dismissed from just a few hours ago.

Papa still wore his dressing gown.

"Papa, go and dress," Mary suggested. "I will bring up coffee, and you can speak to Shelley more comfortably."

Shelley shook his head. I regarded him more closely then. He still wore yesterday's clothes. His cravat had a red wine stain on it, and his beard had come in. The shine had gone from his boots.

"Mary, hush," I said. "Something has gone very wrong."

Mary's hand went out, but then she glanced at Papa and dropped it to her side. Her other hand went to her arm to massage it.

"We have misunderstood everything," Shelley said in a hollow voice.

"What do you mean?" Papa asked.

Shelley took a deep breath, then let it out. His large body swayed.

Mary trotted to Papa's bottle of gin and poured a bit into

a cup, then handed it to Shelley. He drank it down, then coughed. After several blinks, the color came back into his cheeks.

He ran his hands over his face, then said, "I found Pavel Naryshkin's remains in a wine butt in the underground stables by the Bull and Mouth Inn. I recognized the scar you described along his chin."

I watched Mary's mouth drop open in tandem with my own. Papa walked slowly to his desk chair, in the manner of a wooden soldier who had no elbow or knee joints, then collapsed into it.

"Two dead Russians?" Papa asked. "Two dead Russians found in London? What desperate business did they bring with them from their home country to have caused this?"

"What were you doing in the underground stables?" Mary asked Shelley, focused on an entirely different train of thought compared to Papa.

"Were the diamonds in the wine butt as well?" I asked. The words landed rather stupidly from my mouth. A man was dead, and I thought only of our advantage in the discovery. *Such a life we lead in Skinner Street.*

Shelley shook his head. No answer at all. He was a picture of misery. "I went to Bow Street for aid. I ran there, in fact, I was in such shock."

Mary patted his arm as he continued. "Some constables returned with me with a medical man they have in their employ and poured him out of the butt."

Papa winced before Shelley spoke again. "I watched very carefully and saw no sign of the jewels when they searched him. I was alive to the risk of some sleight of hand, though I didn't tell them what I hoped to see, but he had nothing on his person. If I had not been able to identify him, he would have been nothing but an anonymous gentleman."

"Was he dressed like an Englishman?" I asked.

"I do not think the manner of dress of the Russian upper

class is different from ours," Shelley said. "Unless they are in a uniform. How did he dress when he came to dinner here?"

I had no memory at all, since I'd been focused solely on Princess Maria, but Mary said, "A dark costume, with a white collar and cravat. Very high collar, rather like a dandy. A pin that flashed in the light, a diamond most likely."

"Is that how his remains were clothed?" Papa asked.

Shelley put his hands into his curls. "I don't think so. Not quite so formal. No stickpin. A tailcoat. No shoes."

"Interesting," Papa said. "Did they fall out of the barrel?"

"No, we searched the immediate area."

"What made you visit there?" Mary asked, repeating her earlier question. "Did you have some sort of clue to follow? A message?"

Shelley's fingers clenched around his hair again. Strands were pulling from his scalp. His jaw worked. "I watched the place to see if my wife and her lover were visiting there again."

"Oh, Shelley," Mary said. "Why do you care?"

"Stop it, Shelley," I said, working my own fingers together. "You are pulling your hair out!"

He stared at me, then slowly removed his hands. Strands drifted to the floor, wafting through a sunbeam that came in through the window. "She is a deceiver. Says she wants one thing and does another."

"You are done with her," Mary said. "You've said it many times."

"That is not a matter for you," Papa said. "Girls, I want to speak to Shelley in private."

I took Mary's arm. Her steps dragged, and her head swiveled to watch Shelley until I closed the door behind us. Dragging her across the passage, I opened the dining room door.

"There's no food here," Mary said, peering into the room. "Mamma will be cross. I must return to the kitchen."

"She's not down yet," I said. "Mary, focus. Who was the

original dead Russian, then, found in the river? Where are the diamonds?"

Even as she turned to me, she remained lost in her primary question of Shelley. "Why is he wasting time following his wife?"

"He has an inconstant heart," I said, rather harshly. "She's a great beauty, and we were just at her father's house. Who knows what was said? I wasn't invited to go upstairs to see her."

Her eyes were wild when she turned to me. "He saw her?"

"Just yesterday. We went to confront Eliza Westbrook. He went upstairs. I know he saw Mrs. Shelley and Ianthe. He came back with some coins."

Mary drew herself up. Her facial expression lost some of its tension. "I suppose she is his source of income. We must be practical and cannot expect he will quit her entirely while that is the case. Drat his father."

"We need to think about the Russians," I said, impatient. "Why do you care so much about Shelley?"

"I don't want to tell you."

I took both of her upper arms in my hands and shook her, just a little. "If you can't tell me, then there is no one else. Mary, you keep too many secrets." Or at least, I thought she did. Heaven knew I kept plenty of mine.

"He declared himself to be mine," she whispered, so low I could scarcely hear her.

I winced. "Do you trust that from a free love enthusiast like him?"

"Can I trust Shelley's heart?" she asked. "Faith, how could I do that? I don't believe he knows his own heart. I can't depend on it. Papa says, though, that honorable men tell the truth. Shelley must believe his words to be true."

"La, there you go," I said, releasing her. "Words of love, a poem even, he can dash such things off in a heartbeat. His trade is words, Mary. See what he does, not what he says. His actions will reveal the truth. There will be no deception there, upon his honor."

Her gaze met mine. "What he did was spend the night in a stable, in watch for his faithless wife."

"Exactly my point, for all that he means well and respects you as a daughter of fame." I brushed soft hair off her cheek. "Now we need to get breakfast on the table, or I won't be able to eat before I have to open the shop."

Her lips curved. "An army marches on its stomach."

"Exactly," I agreed. "I hope the toast is fresh today."

Chapter 8

Mary

Shelley did not stay for breakfast. He left the house with unexplained reddened eyes as Mary and Polly came up from the kitchens, arms laden with serving dishes. Mary wanted to go to him and gentle those sad eyes, but he left with no more than an anguish-filled glance at her.

The rest of the family thundered up and down the stairs in short order, then gathered around the table to eat.

As soon as Jane ate, she was sent to open the bookshop. Mary returned to the kitchen to help Polly with the dishes and to prepare for roasting the meat they would need for the rest of the day.

At midmorning, Polly poured boiling water into Mamma's favorite teapot. "You'll need to take this up, miss, so I can keep turning the spit."

"I can turn it," Mary said, thinking she could do it with one hand while writing with the other.

Polly made a face. "I can't go up, miss. She'll set me to dusting her office, with Fanny gone, and then I won't have time to peel the potatoes. You go."

Mary had a moment of warring inside herself, what she wanted to be versus what was expected of her. Really, though, Mamma already saw her as a servant. Bringing her tea would not make things any worse. "What about my father?"

Polly shrugged. "If he's here, he'll send for coffee."

Mary nodded and picked up the tray. Papa probably had calls to make.

When she entered the bookshop, Jane said from the counter, "It's midmorning, and the porter has not appeared."

"What does that have to do with me?" Mary asked.

Jane tapped her fingers on the counter. "I persuaded Mamma to let me deliver some books to a fine house with thirteen children near Hyde Park, great customers of ours."

Mary sighed. "Do you need me to watch the counter?"

"I'll run over to the warehouse and tell Charles it's his turn. Take the tea in, and then we can go. Look out the window, Mary. It's lovely today." She turned her head. "Someone is knocking at the door. The mailman, most likely."

Mary took Mamma her tea. When she returned to the counter, Jane had three letters in her hand.

"Mamma was very quiet, bent over a manuscript," Mary reported.

Jane handed her a letter. "It's from Shelley, isn't it? He was only here a couple of hours ago."

Mary bent over the counter and carefully unfolded the note. "Yes, he has news. Fedorov, the footman, has been released in the aftermath of Shelley's discovery."

Jane folded her arms. "He's a violent sort. I don't like to think of him walking the streets."

"It makes no sense to me," Mary agreed. "He still might have killed either man, right? They are both Russians like him."

"I hope Shelley can learn more about Bow Street's reasoning," Jane said.

"What about Princess Maria?" Mary asked. "She doesn't know what the footman did to Thérèse. As his employer, she needs to be warned."

Jane showed her the paper and string-wrapped package. "See, I'm all ready to leave. I'm going near the Pulteney Hotel. Let's stop in. We'll be quick."

Mary and Jane were shown into the fine hotel sitting room where Her Royal Highness sat on a comfortable sofa, draped with a variety of soft textiles that she must have brought from home, due to the reports of London's unusually cold winter and spring. Though the room's appointments were impeccable with creamy walls and deep carpets, the tall, narrow windows let London inside, with a constant din from carriages in the road keeping the ambient noise level high. In this instance, at least, the wealthy did not live any better than the impoverished. Though Mary did note the small fire burning merrily. Few in London would waste coal on such a fine June day.

They curtsied to the Polish princess, who ordered tea from the maid who had brought them to the royal suite.

"May we, Your Royal Highness?" Jane asked, pointing to a couple of chairs too far away for convenient conversation as soon as the maid had departed.

Princess Maria nodded. Mary and Jane pulled the chairs so close that their hostess could have touched them with her slipper-shod feet. She had an album open on her lap, with a shawl underneath to protect her silk skirts from the leather cover.

"Is that one of your children, madam?" Mary asked after she sat down.

Princess Maria turned the album so they could look at the charming watercolor portrait of a little girl. "My little Sophia. Quite a good likeness."

Mary leaned forward and regarded the pink-cheeked cherub. "She has your eyes."

"You are kind to say so." The princess smiled wistfully and turned the page.

"What is that?" Jane asked, when a pen-and-ink sketch of a magnificent columned arch was revealed.

"The Narva Triumphal Arch. I sketched it as it was being constructed. It celebrates the victory over Napoleon."

"It must be very inspiring," Jane said. "I'd like to see it someday."

"Then you must keep working on your French," the princess said. "The upper classes scarcely know Russian at all."

"She has the ear for it, more than I," Mary said. "It must be the music training."

"Your mamma speaks French very well. Why did she not come with you?" the princess asked.

"We used to live in an area full of refugees from the French Revolution," Mary explained. "Mamma is working on a translation today."

"This isn't exactly a social call," Jane admitted. "We heard all the dreadful news about Mr. Naryshkin."

The princess patted her book. "Yes, my husband was notified that the English authorities made a mistake."

"His brother was incorrectly identified at first," Mary said solemnly. "But now he has been found. My sincere condolences."

The princess forced a smile. "We were not very close, but it is a pity. A very capable man has been lost, and just before the senior members of our party are arriving."

Why did the princess deny any closeness to the man who had traveled with her all the way from Russia? Her marriage was of long duration. She had known her husband's brother for many years. It seemed odd to Mary. Maybe it had something to do with the considerable age difference between them.

"Has Alexander Fedorov returned to you?" Jane asked. "We understand he has been released."

"My husband went to deal with the matter," the princess said. "I have not yet seen him. Do you think his health will have been destroyed in just a few days?"

"Not if someone in your party has been caring for him, madam," Mary said. "If you sent food, a blanket."

The princess sighed and set her album next to her. "You bring me gossip, but I am no fool and sense there is more to this visit. What else do you have to say to me?"

"Mr. Fedorov pushed our cook into the fire," Mary said boldly. "He ruined her dress and frightened her."

"We don't exactly know why," Jane added. "But we thought you should know about his violence."

"I know all about his violent ways." The princess folded the shawl on her lap. A large, embroidered red velvet piece with fringe, it was too warm for a June day. "Fedorov is the count's enforcer."

Mary attempted to adjust her opinion of the cultured, wealthy men who had visited Skinner Street with this dazzling princess. "Why does your family need an enforcer?"

The princess smiled faintly. "Imperial courts need such men."

"In London?" Mary asked. "I can understand the need for bodyguards, but you make your footman sound like a hired thug."

The princess stroked her cheek. "Perhaps my English is not so good. It is easier for me to speak to Mrs. Godwin in French."

Mary wasn't ready to let the topic of the footman go. "Do you think he killed your husband's brother? Was he released in error by our authorities here?"

The princess shook her head slightly. "He would not have killed Pavel, though it is possible he did kill the unidentified man. I cannot say why. I am not involved in men's affairs. Do you know who he was?"

"Why would the footman have need to kill anyone in London?" Mary asked.

The princess set the shawl aside. The fringe spread across her black silk, and she played with it. "He was Russian, no? He might have been a threat to the tsar. An assassin come to attack him here on foreign soil. Our Mr. Fedorov may have been doing his job. If indeed he was involved at all."

"We haven't heard anything more about the first victim," Jane told her.

Princess Maria moved her fingers from the fringe and drummed them on her album cover. "Do you have something like this, with sketches of your family?"

The maid reentered the room with a kettle of water. She placed it beside a large, round table with a porcelain tea set on it. Mary had been hoping to see a samovar, but the Russians were taking their tea the English way.

"Nothing so fine," Mary said. "In our family, all sketchbooks tend to be filled with words more than art."

"Have you painted your sister?" the princess asked.

Mary glanced at me. "Not well, just with a pencil, when I was younger."

"I meant your older sister. Do you have a likeness of her?"

Mary tilted her head. "Yes, I suppose so. I ought to have thought of it when you first came to visit. When you call again, I can show you my drawings. Fanny's as well, for I am sure she left her sketchbooks here."

"Is she very like your mother?"

Mary shook her head. "She must take after her father. I never knew Mr. Imlay. Fanny is like Mother in that she cares very much about her family, but unlike her, she is happy to stay at home. She's quiet."

"But she is not at home now."

"That was Papa's decision," Jane said. "Because she's in love with a married poet."

"Jane," Mary chided.

The princess smiled. "Is he very handsome?"

"Very," Mary admitted. "But he is not in love with her."

"He loves his wife?" the princess inquired.

"No," Mary snapped.

Princess Maria's eyebrows went up. "I see you do not like this woman. Tell me, is this poet worthy of your sister's heart?"

Mary found all these questions suspicious, but perhaps some good would come out of the interrogation, if they handled the Naryshkins properly. Maybe the princess would offer Fanny a position. That would be better than serving as an unpaid governess in Wales. She imagined receiving letters all the way from St. Petersburg. How would Fanny manage so far away from the family? Well, they would see how she was when she returned from Wales. She might not want to stay at home after a taste of life away from Mamma.

"Mary would ask if Fanny is worthy of the poet's heart, not the other way around," Jane said with a giggle.

Mary decided to change the subject before the princess started focusing on her. "Papa decided to send her away, so he had some sort of opinion in the matter."

"Would she be sent for if we wanted to meet her?" the princess asked.

"As far as I know, it seems unlikely. She has only just left," Mary said. "At some expense, as you can imagine. Speaking of expenses, our cook is languishing in the Bow Street lockup because of what your footman did to her."

"Lockup?" the princess asked.

"Jail," Jane said prosaically. "Mamma sent her there for stealing a dress from Fanny. But she had nothing else to wear because of what Mr. Fedorov did. It's a terrible mess. We can't leave our cook in jail, but Mamma is very angry."

"I am sorry for your cook's troubles. Is she a truthful woman?" She took the offered teacup from the maid.

"She has worked for us for years without a hint of trouble," Mary said, starting to feel heat in her cheeks.

"That may not be entirely true," Jane said, accepting a cup. "Mary, you were gone to Scotland for a long time."

"What did Thérèse do?" Mary demanded. "I heard nothing."

Jane put her cup to her lips and spoke over it. "She sold half our stew meat for a couple of months, until Mamma started complaining about watery stew and discovered what was going on."

"Why did she do that?"

"To get the money for a new bonnet."

Mary smiled at the maid and took the last cup. "What happened to the old one?"

"It tore on a branch." Jane slurped, then apologized.

"If nothing else, that proves she only goes to extreme measures when her clothing is destroyed," Mary said. She closed her eyes and breathed in the delicate, smoky scent of the tea.

"Is she a comely woman?" the princess asked.

Jane shuddered. "No."

The princess's gaze wandered around the room, then returned to the sofa. She picked up the shawl and tossed it to Mary. "I am sorry that the cook's dress was burned, but I do not have any English money."

Mary stared at the fine velvet in her lap. "You're giving our cook this in recompense?"

"She's in jail over this," Jane said. "Mamma won't have her released until she has the money to pay for a dress."

"Then sell the shawl," the princess said. "It is of the finest quality."

Mary fingered the velvet. The embroidery was excellent, but where would they get full price for such an item? Would someone be willing to trade it for a dress?

Jane nudged her. "What do you think?"

"I think Mamma won't be satisfied unless there is money for two dresses," Mary said, then drank half her tea, as she could see their interview was about to end.

Outside, she heard a crash. Two carts must have collided, for men's voices rose in argument.

The princess set her teacup and saucer on the table next to her. "This is all I can do for you. In the future, there is no need to invite our servants to your kitchens. Make them wait in the street."

Mary had no table nearby for hers, but the maid rushed forward to collect it. Jane looked irritated when she had to hand her still-full cup over, but she received the message. They both curtsied and left, Mary carrying the shawl.

They walked through the hotel to the main hall. The passages were full of uniformed porters moving about, carrying trunks and cases. Excitement was ramping up, and more foreigners were coming into London. The city would be full of festivities in only a few days.

"It would have been better to hold off murdering anyone until all the dignitaries arrived," Mary observed on the staircase. "It might have been less noticeable."

"Maybe the man really was an assassin that they couldn't leave alive," Jane said.

Mary clutched the shawl close to her chest as a porter squeezed by, three valises under his arms. She could hear him puffing as he climbed the stairs.

"He was a man of middle age, in a gentleman's suit. Does that sound like an assassin?"

"Faith, what would you expect?" Jane asked. "Most men look very much the same. It is not as if an assassin would have, oh, I don't know, a telltale set of horns or a tail."

Mary laughed all the way through the front hall and past the street door. Outside, a cart had indeed collided with another, and the various street sellers were nose to nose, close to coming to blows. She linked arms with Jane, and they hurried away to a pavement edge, then dashed across the street and into Green Park.

The street sounds slowly faded as they moved past hedges and through trees, deeper into the park.

"We need to get back," Jane said.

"You still have your package to deliver. I will go home alone and face her wrath, if necessary," Mary responded. Her feet moved instinctively into moon-shaped grass, surrounded by a mix of evergreen and leafy trees. She half expected to find Shelley here, writing in his notebook.

"I could take the shawl over to the seamstress shop I know by my old school," Jane said. "They could tell me a fair value for it."

"You don't have time to go so far. I would wish Fanny home to help, except I still am not sure what the Russians want from her."

"If I take it directly to the pawn shop, admittedly closer, we'll never know what it might really be worth," Jane argued.

Mary let go of her vision of Shelley, writing in the little meadow, and grabbed Jane's arm. "Come, we need to go home. We have a lot to think about. How was the first dead Russian connected to the still missing diamonds, if at all?"

"How did he get misidentified?" Jane asked.

"It happened at the inquest," Mary said.

"Could we speak to the coroner?" Jane asked.

"Papa was at the inquest." Mary worried at her lip. "But I don't know if he was able to stay for all of it. And he was out paying calls today."

"While we are out already, let us pay a call of our own."

"We could speak to that surgeon, Mr. Wilson, who did the autopsy," Mary suggested.

"Is he up on Harley Street?"

"No, Papa said he was at St. Bartholomew's Hospital. A proper physician wouldn't get his hands dirty with an autopsy."

"It's a perfect day to stay out walking. I'd rather he was in Harley Street." Jane allowed Mary to pull her back out to the street.

"I don't like Barts either," Mary agreed. "Going by there is just as bad as walking past the slaughterhouses." They passed the hotel again, delivered Jane's package, and then walked toward Covent Garden. When they reached the market stalls, they were able to find a cart that let them off very close to Barts.

Mary had never been inside the ancient stone building, which was bracketed by two wings, before. They found an inhabited office. A clerk there told them Mr. Nathan Wilson could be found in the post-mortem room.

They hunted it down, though it took some time.

"I don't think I could have done this, if we hadn't become inured to the smells from the market and the prisons," Jane whispered.

Mary shrugged. She found the scene rather energizing and varied. From murals and paintings in the grand front areas, when they went into the real working parts of the hospital, they found whitewashed, bricked walls. She could smell the great age of the hospital and imagined all that had passed in these halls.

Eventually, they found a card posted on a door, indicating they had reached their destination.

"Bodies," Jane said with a shudder. "You know there will be bodies."

"Don't be squeamish," Mary scolded, then opened the door.

Inside were a number of tables, scrubbed clean, around the center of the room. Shelving units crowded the walls, full of specimen jars. Her nostrils filled with copper, meat, and harsh preservatives.

Jane coughed, but Mary pulled her in. At the rear left of the room, three men were conversing over a small, sheet-covered form on the table.

"I hope that isn't a child under there," Mary said, pausing. She gathered her nerves as Jane clasped her hand.

Jane shuddered. "Let's get out of here as soon as possible."

"Err, Mr. Nathan Wilson?" Mary called.

The three men, two middle-aged and one young, all looked up. The light, rather good from the windows, made their faces visible. All of them frowned.

"I'm Wilson," said the oldest man. "Who let you in here?"

"No one," Mary said. "But we were given your location from a clerk. We have a question about the body found in the Thames."

The surgeon snorted. "Which one?" He came toward them, rearranging his cuffs and buttoning his coat.

Had they just finished investigating the remains of that small being under the sheet? Mary could see dark stains on the once white fabric of his shirt, and the surgeon's hands had a reddish tinge, indicating they were freshly washed. At least they hadn't come across the men still in their butcher's aprons, gleaming with fresh blood. She could imagine the scene, however.

"The Russian, sir," Jane said with a little squeak at the end of her words. She hadn't let go of Mary yet, and Mary wasn't sure she wanted her to.

"There have been two Russians," the surgeon said with a frown. Now that he only stood a few feet from them, Mary could see he was a bit younger than she thought and rather attractive, with soft brown eyes and a full lower lip.

"One in the Thames, and one in a wine butt belonging to the Bull and Mouth," Mary said boldly.

His cheek twitched. "Who are you?"

She curtsied, then introduced herself and Jane. It did not satisfy the surgeon. "What do these deaths have to do with you?"

"We are afraid that our household is in some way responsible for these murders," Mary said. "Have you heard of the Juvenile Library?"

"Morally," Jane added quickly. "Morally responsible."

"No, I have not heard of the Juvenile Library." The surgeon's tone had grown increasingly rude. "Make yourself clear, and quickly, miss. This is no place for you."

Behind them, the youngest man lifted the sheet-covered body and placed it on a flat cart.

Jane trembled. Mary squeezed her hand tighter and continued. "My father owns the publishing firm. The Russians promised to give the business a small fortune in diamonds."

"Why?"

"To continue its educational mission," Mary explained, forcing herself to leave out the important parts, about her mother. "We were expecting Mr. Naryshkin to arrive with the diamonds, but he never did. We know that the first body was misidentified, and we wanted to know why, exactly. Was someone impersonating Mr. Naryshkin?"

"Yes, what was used to identify him?" Jane asked.

"The dead man was identified as Pavel Naryshkin because he had a Russian prayerbook and ring with Cyrillic letters on it," the surgeon said. "No one else was known to be missing."

The second man approached, now that the younger man had departed with his burden. "To clarify, Pavel Naryshkin was the only *Russian* known to be missing in London at the time."

"This is my assistant, Watson," Mr. Wilson said.

"Thank you for the information," Mary said. "Do you still have the ring? I'd like to show it to Mr. Naryshkin's family. I assume they haven't seen it."

Mr. Wilson shrugged. "I have been told they are busy with assignments for their tsar."

Or they were avoiding the situation because Dmitry Naryshkin himself had ordered the murder of the first man?

"Wasn't Count Naryshkin at the inquest?" Mary asked.

"A representative only. A Mr. Hesse, I believe," Mr. Wilson said. Next to him, Mr. Watson nodded.

"Yes, we've seen him around," Jane murmured.

"Will showing you the ring bring an end to this business?"

"Yes," Mary said. "If we can jot down the details."

"You can make an etching of the signet," the surgeon said. "Why not? If you can get the Russians to take a look, all the better for us. The dead should be named."

Mr. Watson went to a cabinet and returned with a small box, a sheet of paper, and a pencil. He held the ring up for Mary. A small gold circle, it might fit the smallest finger on a man's hand. One side had been flattened into a disk and etched with three apparent letters, though the middle one was wholly unfamiliar to her. She put the paper over the signet and did a rubbing as best she could.

"I hope this helps us learn the identity of the Thames corpse," Mary said, after examining her effort to make sure the characters weren't too blurry.

"What about the prayer book?" Jane asked.

"Very common," Mr. Watson said. "Nothing identifiable about it."

"Did you check every page?" Mary asked.

The assistant nodded.

"Let us know if you can learn anything about the ring," Mr. Wilson said. "Or at least notify the coroner that you took a rubbing. Good day, ladies."

Mary rolled up the paper and put it in her glove for safekeeping. They curtsied again and left.

Home wasn't far, so they separated to return to their respective duties and didn't speak again until they were around the dinner table at five that evening. Outside, the sun still shone brightly. Mary felt full of energy and ready to learn the identity of the first man. She hoped that learning about him might help uncover the fate of the diamonds. Knowing that they had been given a shawl by the princess because of the burned dress made her think there might be more to come from the Russians if they had additional information to share.

"Did you make calls all day today, Papa?" Mary asked.

He did look gray and weary. Papa was not the sort to be content unless he was actually traveling somewhere of interest or spending a significant portion of his day in his study, books open around him.

"Did you see Count Naryshkin?" Jane asked.

"No, why?" Papa asked.

"We thought you might inquire if there is any reward for finding his brother's body," Jane said.

"Shelley would receive the reward and maybe share the money with us," Mary added.

Papa frowned. "I do not want to bother an important man such as the count with such things. Time is running out before his master arrives in London."

"We have some information to trade," Mary said. "He wasn't at the inquest, we heard. He never saw the ring or the prayer-book on the body."

"I didn't see them myself," Papa said.

"We have an etching of the ring," Mary said. "I think it has initials."

"Really?" Papa asked. "And how did you get that?"

Mary hoped to gloss over that information. "What if we took the etching to the Pulteney Hotel after dinner? We could show it to the count and ask about a reward for Shelley?"

"He's a gentleman, our Shelley. He would never ask," Papa told her.

"That's why we have to do it, Papa," Jane said. "We can't be proud."

Mamma spoke up. "These people won't be here for long, and they've caused us a lot of trouble."

Papa drained his wine. "The stew is quite unappetizing this evening, so I will go."

"We'll come with you," Mary said, ignoring the insult. "You're tired, Papa, and you will get a ride more easily if I am with you."

"From whom?" Jane asked. "The carts are put away at this time in the evening."

"No, they aren't," Mary said. "It's a fine summer's evening. There will be plenty of street sellers about. Please, Papa, we need to speak to Count Naryshkin."

Papa stood. Mary and Jane followed him out while Mamma, Charles, and Willy remained with their dinners.

They hadn't walked half a mile when they did find a fruit seller with a horse-drawn cart who took Papa up next to him. The girls paced the cart.

Mary fretted about her father's health. Normally, she would think nothing of him walking miles in a day, but the health complaints he'd suffered of late seemed to have caught up with him under the load he must be carrying. Few men thrived in prison. It might shorten his magnificent, important life.

Happily, the Naryshkins were at dinner in their suite. They were allowed entry. The count greeted them in quite a jovial manner and had a servant bring chairs.

Mary marveled at the food on offer. Turtle soup, salads, and vegetable dishes, swimming in cream. A beautiful baked fish, and an entire roast, just for the count and his wife. They were dining alone.

The three of them were soon served some of the bounty. Papa kept the conversation light, though he was forced to tell several stories involving Mary's mother rather than indulge in the philosophical conversational matters he preferred, on the political topics of the day. Still, these were foreigners, and not interested in local issues.

Jane gasped with delight when a sponge cake was served at the end, with the first of the season's strawberries and delicate cream. Mary tried hard not to gorge on the treat herself, but she felt unpleasantly full after just a few bites, following the heavy meal.

"If I'd known this was how the meal would end, I'd have been more careful," Jane said gaily to Princess Maria.

"The Pulteney Hotel has taken good care of us," she said.

"The street noise is dreadful, however," the count said. "I think someone stood outside our window half the night, singing about vile women."

"Speaking of vile things, count, my daughters have something of importance to show you." Papa wiped his mouth with a snowy white cloth and set it beside his plate. "It is clear that we were not blessed with a thorough inquest."

The count frowned. "I thought the inquest for my brother would take place on Monday. This is what I was informed."

"I'm speaking about the first inquest," Papa explained. "My daughters, in their unseemly desire to help, interviewed the surgeon who conducted the first autopsy today."

Mary pulled her rubbing from her pocket.

"What is this?" the count asked, taking it.

"The body found in the Thames had a Russian prayerbook and was wearing a ring."

He frowned. "Pavel did wear a signet ring."

Mary nodded at the paper. "Was this the engraving on it?"

He lifted the paper to his eyes and examined it closely. "My brother had our family arms on his ring. This ring is engraved with the initials of Michael Karamzin, one of the tsar's secretaries."

Princess Maria's eyes widened. Her glance at her husband held alarm.

"Did he come with you to London, my lord?" Papa asked. "Have you seen him in the past week?"

"He was tasked with going to Hull, to discuss shipping business," the count said. "He had no reason to be in London at this time."

"Hull is two hundred miles away," Papa said.

"He must have finished his business quickly and taken a private carriage here." The count, his mouth thinned into a tight line, rang a bell on the table next to him.

"At great expense," Papa added.

Mary imagined what the carriage would have cost. These Russians had a great deal of funds at their disposal. Was it in letters of credit, moving money between banks, or were all of them carrying pouches of diamonds?

"He was not expected in London for another week," the count said. When a door to the apartment opened, the count rose.

A footman walked in. He wore a red coat and knee breeches, not the hotel's livery. Mary remembered the cook's description of the man who'd struck her as a "squat plug of a man," and ugly. This footman met that description, though Thérèse's words had left out the impression of the sheer strength of the brute. Mary would well believe this man to be an enforcer, whatever that actually meant.

The count moved toward him, a predator stalking, faster than Mary would have expected, given his age. Before she could even draw breath, the count struck his servant across the face with the back of his hand, catching the footman's flesh with his rings.

Jane jumped up, her chair falling over, cream still coating her lips. Mary realized she'd pushed her own chair away from the table. Papa reached for her hand and gripped it, then pulled Jane to his other side.

The princess set down her teacup and sat in a languid pose, lovely and inscrutable, as her husband shouted angrily at the footman in Russian. The footman put his hand to his face and investigated the blood that came away from his cheek. He said nothing.

The count pushed the footman through the door he'd just entered and slammed it behind him. They could hear his shouts growing fainter as they moved farther away from the parlor.

Mary stared at the princess. Would she not say anything? Was this a normal occurrence? "I expect you were right about Alexander Fedorov having murdered the first man, even though the authorities released him."

The princess's perfect ivory shoulders rose and fell, but she did nothing more than meet Mary's gaze.

"Our friend Shelley went to some trial and expense learning the truth," Mary said boldly and a bit facetiously. Still angry that he had chased after his faithless wife, Mary felt bold. "You owe him a reward for his efforts. He did the work of a Bow Street Runner, and they are paid."

The princess considered her for a moment, then stood. Papa quickly rose, but she paid no attention to him, just left through the same door the others had.

"How big is this suite?" Jane asked. "Will they hide from us for the rest of the night?"

"We weren't invited here," Papa said. He stuck his utensil into a strawberry half and placed it in his mouth. "Who can say?"

"Should we leave?" Jane righted her chair but sank into it.

"I asked for a reward," Mary said, picking up her fork. "Let's wait them out." She stared at her dish. The cake had lost its appeal. The strawberry leaching into the cream now reminded her of blood, and the animal smells of the earlier cooked meats intensified the experience.

"We should go," Papa said. "I don't want to have to testify at another inquest due to these violent people. I am not served well by being under the notice of the authorities. I am sure the Home Office has a great number of extra eyes on London with all the festivities starting soon."

Just as he stood, the count reentered the room. Mary could feel the centuries of breeding in his erect carriage. He was the member of a family that shared blood with the tsars.

Mary stood up next to her father. Jane followed.

The count said nothing but held out his hand to Mary. As he dropped a short shower of gold coins into her palm, he said, "You asked my wife for money earlier, and now this is the result of your meddling. We are done with your nonsense. Take this reward for your troubles and go."

"We have done plenty to earn it," she said, mimicking his tone. "And your brother made promises to us besides."

"We will contact you again if we desire it," he said, looking down his patrician nose. "Leave now."

Papa grasped Mary's sleeve and towed her out the door with nothing more than a curt nod in the Russian's direction. He went directly to the stairs and marched them down to the lobby.

At the foot of the stairs, Mary stopped him and dropped each of the five guineas into his hand individually. "There, Papa. These should save me from having to do the cooking. Between this and the shawl Princess Maria gave me, Thérèse should be released now."

The expression in Papa's eyes was no warmer than the count's. "I appreciate your considerable powers of intellect, but you do not make any decisions in my household, Mary. I will decide what to do about the domestic arrangements."

He shook his arm free of Jane's grasp and started toward the main hotel door.

"I can get more money from these people," Mary said, keeping pace with him. "Her Royal Highness was lying about her lack of funds, I know it. Think of the expense of travel from Hull to London, Papa. Even if the first diamonds are gone, there will be more. You don't have to make me live like this."

Papa stopped abruptly, a few feet from the door. A gentleman brushed past him, swaying drunkenly, and went to the front desk and leaned on the counter in front of a clerk.

"You cannot keep harassing a princess, even a Polish one," Papa said. He walked through the front door as soon as a hotel doorman opened it.

Mary and Jane followed and were surprised to see Papa hailing a hackney. They all squeezed in.

Once they were inside, and Mary was sure that the driver couldn't hear, she said, "Mr. Hesse, the Prussian man, was at the jewelry shop. Jane saw him."

Jane nodded. “It’s concerning, especially since he’s the princess’s lover, we’re told. Was he turning those diamonds into money?”

“They seem entirely cold-blooded,” Mary added. “The count’s behavior was positively indecent. Could he have killed their brother Pavel?”

“Or Mr. Hesse,” Jane suggested. “The princess could have ordered him to do it.”

“I cannot believe these people are really my mother’s followers,” Mary said.

“They are believers in education,” Papa replied. “That does not preclude the violence of their race.”

Chapter 9

Jane

"It is such a beautiful evening," I said tentatively, as Papa paid the hackney driver in front of our house.

Mary nodded vociferously and shook out her skirts.

"Don't you have to make the kitchen ready for morning?" Papa said acidly. He unlocked the front door and walked in, without looking back.

Mary's lips tightened as we loitered on the pavement. "He turns the dagger into my breast as if I were Caesar."

"Five guineas," I offered in an agreeable tone. I felt for her, really I did. She thought of herself as Papa's true heir, but sometimes I thought her hero worship backfired into her being even more hurt when she was treated like any girl would be.

"It would pay a cook's wage for months," Mary growled.

"You did very well to procure the money." I patted her arm. "But Papa's financial difficulties are tremendous."

"He cannot see past the end of his own nose," Mary agreed. "As much as I adore him, I realize that it matters not to him who is cooking, as long as he has food in front of him three times a day."

"Does it matter to Mamma?" I queried.

"She adored having a French cook, but she loves putting me into a menial role even more, as it turns out." She bared her teeth.

"I expect there is much to learn that will be useful," I suggested. "You'll be running your own household soon and are unlikely to have a cook yourself."

She kicked at a large stone that had rolled up to our door from somewhere. "I don't suppose there will be a cook in my future. But I cannot believe we are speaking of such nonsense when we have just learned the identity of the Thames corpse."

"Two dead Russians," I agreed. Across the street, someone poured the contents of a pot out of the front window. "Disgusting." I reached for Mary's hand, and we walked down to St. Sepulchre, where we could hide from the late day sun under the trees.

"I expect the murders are solved," Mary said as we walked. "Fedorov the enforcer killed them both. What a villainous appearance. He looks as if he were born a murderer."

"I disagree," I said. "Princess Maria insisted that Mr. Fedorov would not have killed his master's brother."

We reached the trees. Mary leaned against a broad trunk. The sun, coming through leaves, dappled her face. For once, I did not imagine the glories of Reverend Doone's nearby rectory table since I was full of the Pulteney's glorious strawberry-and-cream cake.

"The proof, you know, will be whoever is proven to have the diamonds."

I shrugged. "If the surviving Naryshkins retrieved them, we'll never know. They will take them back to Russia."

"I wish we could get them out of their rooms by some ruse

and search them." Mary tilted her head, rubbing her bonnet against the wood.

I pulled her away before she ruined the fabric and made her sit with me on the grassy patch. "It is not safe to visit the Russians again. They are dangerous."

"I do not worry about the princess, but we can hardly look for the diamonds if she is there. Besides, there might be a safe. Possibly not in the suite, even."

"Do we let the matter go, then?"

"No." Mary's tone was decisive. "I need something to puzzle over in the kitchen or I shall go mad. It gets as hot as the fires of Hades down there."

"What shall we puzzle over, then?" I asked.

"We can't search the Pulteney. Can you imagine the security, with all the heads of state in residence there? But what about the Bull and Mouth Inn? Shelley has done well there."

"What do you want to learn?"

"We don't really care about the first man. The Naryshkins are aware that he shouldn't have been in London at all. That is their problem. We care about Pavel because he had the diamonds."

I pulled up a stalk of grass and knotted it. "We don't even know when he died."

Mary nodded eagerly. "Let's go to the Bull and Mouth and see what we can learn."

I hadn't considered what it might be like at an inn on a Saturday night. We had no hope of blending in, though people crowded the public spaces. A couple of Italian singers dotted the courtyard, and a hot potato seller did a brisk business, along with a pea soup seller. They worked back-to-back. I drew closer to one of the singers, standing under the protection of an overhanging roof. He had a lovely tenor and was singing a piece I had not heard before.

Mary took my arm and pulled me toward the registration desk inside the hotel. "Good evening," she said to the tired-looking young man who stood behind it.

I could tell she was attempting to make herself seem older. She'd straightened and lowered her speaking voice.

"Our friend Mr. Shelley had the misfortune to find a body in your stables," she said.

"Yes, there was quite a hue and cry about it last night," he agreed, pulling off his spectacles and rubbing his rather indented nose.

"The thing is, the corpse—that is, Count Naryshkin's brother—was expected at our house last Monday. Mr. Shelley was understandably flustered by his finding and didn't ask any questions."

"The inquest is Monday," the clerk said, half turning away from us.

Mary waved an imperious hand. "Of course, of course, but this is Saturday. We would like to trace Mr. Naryshkin's movements. Do you know if he had been at the hotel? He was not in residence here."

"I did hear gossip from the maids. He didn't have rooms here. They saw the body as it was carried out and didn't recognize him." He rubbed the bridge of his nose again, then replaced his glasses.

"Unsurprising," Mary said. "Was he seen in the hotel at all?"

"Not by me." The clerk raised his hand and gestured some travelers forward. I hadn't seen them approaching the desk, no doubt for rooms that we were not wanting ourselves.

I pulled Mary away. "Now what?"

"We've got to go into the public room."

"It's not respectable," I said. "We aren't traveling, and someone might recognize us from the neighborhood."

"We're investigating," Mary said in a patient tone. "It's either that or make Shelley do it, and we're already here."

I let her escort me through the archway into a room full of the smell of spilled ale. Heavy smoke hung along the ceiling from too many cigars. The din of voices bounced off the pillars and walls, echoing back to us. I didn't see how we'd be able to hear anything, and I felt very small in a room full of large men.

Mary, on the other hand, though shorter and more slender than me, forced her way around several knots of men until she reached the bar. We had to wait a few minutes, but she eventually caught the attention of a barman of some forty years, a stained apron tied over his sober clothing.

"You shouldn't be in here," he said, looking us up and down. "Go home to your mothers before something happens to you."

"I want to know about the corpse found in the stable last night," Mary said.

The barman frowned. "What was he to you?"

"He was meant to visit my father on Monday, six days ago, and never arrived. Did you see him here?"

"I don't want you in here," the man said.

"We'll leave as soon as we get an answer," Mary said stoutly.

The man evidently thought her word was good, for he turned and raised his hand toward another barman. He set down a bottle and came over to us.

"You saw that dead Russian in here, right?" the barman said.

His younger colleague nodded. "Yes, Maisy described the corpse, and I know he was in here."

"When was that?" Mary asked.

"Monday, about the noon hour," he said.

I nodded eagerly. "That makes sense."

"Was he alone?"

The younger man shook his head. "No. He was having a drink with a Welshman right here in the public room."

"A Welshman?" I queried.

"Yes, I'd recognize that accent anywhere. My mother's mother was from Montgomeryshire."

I glanced at Mary. A man of business from the village of Tremadoc was in London after Shelley's money a couple of weeks ago. His name was John Williams. "Did you hear his name? The Welshman, I mean."

A dozen men pushed through the crowd and jammed up against the bar. One of them slammed his fist on the polished wood, demanding attention.

The barman shook his head. "Sorry, can't help you there."

"You girls go now," said the older man.

Mary nodded, and we worked our way out of the crowd back into the hotel, not without a few pinches and smacks, some managing to bruise my flesh. She shuddered at one particularly foul suggestion from a man with a missing eye. We didn't stop moving until we reached the safety of the front desk again.

"We had better send Shelley a note to make sure John Williams went back to Tremadoc," she said. She went up to the front desk again and begged a slip of paper and a pencil from the clerk.

After she thanked him, we went over to Newgate Prison, where there were always a few boys available to deliver messages.

"It's getting late," I said, after she paid the lad we'd found.

She nodded. "I'd better make some preparations for tomorrow's meals. But I'm going to insist we buy bread from now on. It's ridiculous to keep making our own."

"Papa won't have the money to pay the bakery," I said. "What do you want to bet those five guineas have already gone to John Cannon?"

"Don't you believe it," she said. "He'll wave it about in order to hook in some new investor. I don't think he'll go anywhere near someone he owes a debt to. Maybe he took it straight to the Ballachey firm."

"It would have been best if he actually took it to someone he owed, to pay a debt. We are daughters of the house. We should not even be aware of the difficulties."

"The Godwins are not the usual sort of family," Mary told me, as we arrived at our front door. "And that is never going to change."

The next morning, Mamma asked us to take Willy to services at St. Paul's. We enjoyed the sun on our faces as we walked there.

I daydreamed through the service. The vicar spoke on God's call to spread good news throughout the world. I wouldn't mind the travel, though it seemed rather dreary just to spread religion. I rather suspected it meant going to the sort of places with no culture or books at all. While I didn't need castles and gowns and banquets, I did want music and learning and entertainment.

Willy poked me. I realized I'd had my eyes closed. "That lady is looking at you."

I craned my head around. To my surprise, Eva Sandy, the girl from my music lessons, sat across the aisle. She wore a cambric dress in an unusual lavender shade, with a spencer in a slightly redder hue, both trimmed with exquisite embroidery. Her impractical bonnet had matching lavender satin fabric, which wouldn't survive a spot of rain. Such visible, flagrant, and careless wealth, while I had not the money to pay for a music lesson. She had a maid with her, dressed in black.

I suppose I had no reason to think Lord Byron and his relations were atheists like Papa. I did not see the lord here.

Mary leaned over Willy and put her finger under my jaw. "Stop drooling, Jane. Such finery would do you no good."

"It would attract notice," I whispered back. "You of all people know the value of that, with your silly tartan dress."

She wrinkled her upper lip at me and smoothed her skirt. I couldn't wait for the silly dress to wear out, so that I could stop having my eyes assaulted by the loud fabric. My gaze returned to Miss Sandy, whose attention had returned to the vicar. The bonnet was ridiculous, but I thought I'd look rather dashing in that spencer. It brought out the color in her cheeks, and I expected it would do the same for me.

After the service ended, we took ourselves outside of the church in a blink, ready to enjoy the sunshine again. Willy spotted a boy his age and sprinted away. Mary went after him at a more sedate pace.

I felt a touch on my arm and turned to find Miss Sandy.

"Good morning," I said, delighted to be singled out. "I don't think I've ever seen you here before."

"We usually sit closer to the front, but some baron had his extended family here today and took up our bench." She fingered the lace that composed the collar of her spencer. It matched her flaxen hair.

I wished I still had the ring I stole, so I could wear it around Miss Sandy. Would it make me seem more equal in her eyes?

"We've been trying to solve some murders," I blurted out.

Her blue eyes went wide. "Whatever for?"

Mary came up to me, hauling Willy away from his playmate. "Please introduce me to your friend."

I made introductions.

"I have my lesson again on Thursday this week. I'm sure I will see you there." My new friend smiled at me, then hurried away, followed by her maid. I watched them walk to a line of carriages waiting out front and get into one.

"Imagine going to all the effort of taking a carriage to St. Paul's, rather than walking," I remarked.

"Maybe they live far away."

"I don't think so, since she is taking lessons at Covent Garden with me," I said. I wanted to keep the gossip about Lord Byron to myself. "But it's not much of a mystery compared to the Naryshkin matter."

Chapter 10

Mary

When Mary returned to the kitchen, Polly, the maid, had been in such obvious pain that she'd felt sympathy pangs. She sent Polly to the scullery to nurse her stomach ache in peace. After Polly had departed, holding a warmed rag to her abdomen, Mary sat on the kitchen stool and turned the roasting meat, lamenting her own fate.

Examining her emotions in the moment, she decided that her character Isabella would feel something similar, while locked into a small cottage in the forest after she'd been kidnapped. Without so much as a maid, she'd have to prepare her own meals and maintain her garments.

How would she access food at all? There must be some villain's trusted henchman who would bring baskets upon occasion. She would have to build her own fire. Or it could be summer, but then she wouldn't be able to cook anything. She could survive on bread, cheese, and wine.

Mary smiled to herself. Add in a few books, some paper, a

pen and ink, and it sounded like a lovely prison. If some handsome caballero burst in, dragged her onto his horse, and rode off, she'd go along with it, as long as she had her notebook with her.

Jane flounced into the kitchen, wearing a navy jacket over her white muslin dress. She turned in a circle. "What do you think?"

Mary frowned, the sound of horse hooves fading into her imagination, and gave the roast a turn. "About what?"

"Look at my spencer. I added ribbon to the collar and cuffs. What do you think?"

Mary looked at the stitching, rather a nice job for Jane. Adding the contrasting half-inch of color around the collar framed her face very nicely. "I didn't know we had any lavender ribbon, but your stitches are nice and small."

"I found them in Fanny's trunk."

"Be careful, or you might end up in the Bow Street lockup." Jane was safe from Mamma's ultimate threat, though Mary wouldn't dare steal herself, even from her own sister.

"Fanny will forgive me if I let her wear it," Jane said, admiring her cuffs. "I made this silly old jacket nice and fresh."

"I think she will resent it, honestly," Mary said. "Your clothes are too large for her, in any case. Don't be thoughtless, Jane. You'd better find a way to buy her some new ribbon."

Jane ignored her warning. "I had to do something with my clothes. Did you see what Miss Sandy was wearing? It looked like something straight out of the pages of a fashion magazine. All that yellow and lace. I felt so drab that it might as well have been autumn, not late spring."

Mary turned the spit again. She did not share Jane's rapture. The garments didn't excite her like Princess Maria's had. Miss Sandy's coloring was all wrong for Isabella the Penitent. "I have to cook dinner. This is no time for gossip."

Footsteps on the first floor made the ceiling of the kitchen rattle. Jane gasped, a haunted expression entering her eyes. "It's Sunday. Surely someone doesn't want the bookshop open!" She dashed out of the kitchen.

Mary stood and stretched. With Polly unable to work, dinner would have to be simpler fare. She hoped no one had been invited to dinner. Papa sometimes forgot to tell anyone he'd offered a spot at his table.

Mamma came into the kitchen sometime later. Mary stood over the sink, pouring out the water from boiled potatoes.

"What is this, miss?" Mamma demanded.

Mary turned at a leisurely pace. "Polly doesn't feel well."

Mamma had a look of outrage on her florid face, but then Mary noticed the shawl around her shoulders.

"You've been in my room," Mary gasped. "How dare you."

"I'll go wherever I like." Mamma took a step forward and slapped Mary across the face. "Stealing, girl? What did you take? Our money? This shawl from a shop?" She closed her grip on Mary's shoulder and squeezed.

Mary tore herself away and put her hand to her cheek.

Polly raced in from the scullery, pale and still holding the towel to her belly.

"Go, girl," Mamma snapped. "This is none of your business."

Polly squeaked and ran out, dropping the towel, probably cooled to uselessness already.

Mary steeled herself, wishing she could throw the hot potatoes at Mamma in self-defense, but there was nothing for it but to accept the attack. It always passed quickly enough.

"Answer me!" Mamma shrieked.

"It was a gift from the princess," Mary cried back. "I'm supposed to sell it to pay for the cook's burned dress."

Mamma tried to cover herself with the shawl, but only the fringe could make the full circumference, given the difference between her shape and Princess Maria's.

"And when were you going to tell me about that?"

"I've been too busy cooking your food to do anything more," Mary said. "What happened to Sunday being a day of rest?"

Mamma leaned forward and grabbed Mary's ear, locking her into place. "You'll do what I tell you, you sly minx. And I'll keep the shawl."

"Will you let Thérèse out of the Bow Street lockup, then? Since you've been paid for the dress."

Mamma sniffed and leaned into Mary. Their noses nearly touched. Mary swallowed hard as nausea from the pain of having her ear tweaked built.

"I'll do what I like. I'm mistress here, not you." Mamma squeezed her ear more tightly, then released it.

Mary tried hard not to sag against the wall, but her face and ear hurt so much she could feel her pulse pounding in her neck.

Mamma strode out, the shawl billowing limply against her back. Mary sank to the floor and turned, leaning her burning cheek against the wall to cool her tormented flesh. She had to escape this place, but the elder generation held all the power, though they had run their household into the ground.

When Mary and Polly brought up the food for dinner—cold meat, sliced potatoes in butter, and a cabbage salad—they found Shelley on the first floor.

"The door was unlocked." He smiled at Mary and took the bowls from her hand.

"I'll take the meat, Polly," Mary said. "Can you fetch the bread?"

The maid, face still strained, nodded. Mary shook her head and followed Shelley up the steps to the dining room. After they set their burdens on the table, he turned to her and put a gentle finger under her chin. "The light is better up here. I can see you've been hurt. What happened?"

"Mamma," she said succinctly. "She found the velvet shawl

that was meant to be payment for Fanny's stolen dress and slapped me for withholding it from her. I meant to sell it, but I didn't have time. Mamma will do nothing for our cook in jail. I think she has no intention of ever bringing her home." She ran out of breath and put her hand across her stomach.

Shelley pressed his lips together. "That woman is a menace. We have to get you out of here."

"You have no power to do that," Mary said. She let her eyelids close. A tear escaped, but feigned it was not. She hurt, and life was utterly unfair and horrid.

"I'll speak to your papa," he offered.

"Do not." She put her hand on his arm. "He will take her side. He always does, Shelley."

Shelley worked his jaw from side to side. "Then what, sweet Mary?"

"Two things. I demanded a reward from Count Naryshkin for your find in the stables. He gave us five guineas, and Papa has them."

"I'll never see them," Shelley said.

"I don't imagine so," Mary said, "but put that blot in your copybook against him."

One of Shelley's hands went into his curls. He hadn't worn a hat, as usual, and his tawny hair flew in every which direction. "What is the second thing?"

"Jane and I went to the Bull and Mouth. We were told that Pavel Naryshkin was seen in a Welshman's company."

"Any clue who he was?"

"I wondered about your enemy John Williams. He has no trouble sticking his nose in other people's business, as we saw when he told Papa that all of your money belonged to Mr. Williams's master for the development at Tremadoc."

"We are surrounded by thieves and fools," Shelley said. "I do not care about money, but nearly everyone else in the world seems to."

"Not me," Mary said. "I don't want your money. I just want a roof over my head, as far away from Mamma as possible."

His hand lifted to her. She captured it and gently placed it against her cheek. "It feels lovely and cool against the bruise."

Polly returned with the platter of bread, causing them to spring apart. The maid didn't notice. "Can you open the wine? Sometimes the corkscrew goes missing."

Mary went to the sideboard and found it in a drawer.

"I'll do it," Shelley said, and took it from her.

The door opened and Mamma walked in, followed directly by Papa. Neither of them looked at Mary, but Papa greeted Shelley jovially.

"I understand you have five guineas for me," Shelley said.

Mary's lips turned up. Would he confront her father for once?

"Oh, sorry," Papa said carelessly, as Jane arrived, without her updated jacket. She must have decided it wise not to allow Mamma a look at it.

"Sorry?" Shelley said.

"I ran into Thomas Turner, and he was in need of a bit of coin."

"You gave him all five of my guineas?" Shelley's tone had a frosty edge.

"Only a couple of them. Mamma took the rest to pay the butcher's bill. Wine, Mary," he ordered, and sat down with a great show of pleased comfort.

Mamma, resplendent in the embroidered shawl that ought to have been sold to free Thérèse, turned to Jane and plunked some shillings into her hand. "For your next singing lesson."

Mary knew the coins had come from whatever was left after paying the butcher's bill. Shelley wouldn't ask for them to be handed to him because he liked Jane too much to disappoint her. Only Mary was left out, with a bruised cheek and no more value than a maid to her own family. Even though she'd acquired the shawl and the money.

Shelley's gaze fixed on the shawl. His brows came together as his head turned to Mary. They stared at each other for a moment, a deep communication passing between them.

"Shelley?" Papa interrupted. "Are you sitting down? Mary, fetch another place setting."

Shelley looked blank. "No, not tonight, Godwin." He brushed past Mary, slow enough that she smelled him, outdoor air with a touch of saltwater, and the male animal underneath.

She didn't move again until Papa barked an order for the wine, just as Shelley's feet reached the landing, each creak of the stair a memory that would never vanish from her thoughts.

"I'm hungry," Willy whined from the doorway. "Do we have to eat Mary's cooking again?"

"Every night," Papa said with a gentle smile for his son. "She will improve."

Hunger clawed at Mary's belly, so she sat in her chair and passed around the food, and even ate it, though she felt like a being entirely apart from her family. Inside, surrounded by a soft glow, she kept the image of Shelley, who, when faced with an intolerable family situation, managed to depart it. He lived betwixt and between a group of like-minded friends now. A peripatetic life, to be sure, but an interesting one, full of books and discussion.

"I have news, Mary," Papa said after they had all eaten their fill.

Even Mary's plate had emptied. She scarcely remembered taking a bite.

"What is the news?" Jane asked.

He smiled at her. "More eager than your sister, I see. I have had a letter from Scotland."

Jane squealed. "Did you get a letter from your friend Isabella Baxter, Mary?"

Mary shook her head. "I've heard nothing. Who wrote me a letter, Papa?"

Papa puffed up his chest. "It wasn't to you, girl. Young Robert Baxter has written to me, to say he is coming to London from Dundee."

Jane's mouth dropped open. "Oh, my goodness."

The glow in Mary's heart faded away. The future came rushing at her.

"What do you think, daughter?" Papa asked. "Do you want to marry him?"

"Are you for it, Papa?" she asked, her mouth moving slowly, as if it was full of honey.

"I am not against it, like with your suitor David Booth. I hope Isabella is happy with her marital choice."

"I hope so, too. She is a good girl," Mary said. "What do you mean, that you are not against it?"

"I do not know this young man, though the family is a good one." He fixed her with a solemn expression. "I warn you that you will leave with nothing but the family's love and regard if you choose to make the marriage."

"What else would she leave with?" Jane asked baldly, buttering a slice of bread.

"The boy has no work," Mamma said. "How will you eat?"

"The living is communal," Mary reminded her. "We will be provided with enough, and I have not been raised to need much."

Mamma sniffed and pulled the shawl tighter around her shoulders. She would spoil the embroidery with constant attempts to keep herself warm with a garment too small for her, and destroy its value. Maybe she even did it on purpose.

"Then you will answer yes?" Papa asked.

Mary stared at Papa—that large, beloved, clueless round head, the wrinkles and age spots. She could not expect him to support her forever. The business would fail. He would go to debtors' prison. She saw no other way out of her kitchen prison. Who was she to be courted by? A muffin seller? Maybe she wouldn't even be working in the bookshop anymore. Mamma may have planned that, to increase Jane's chances of being noticed.

They said they didn't believe in marriage, but they were wed. Did they even think of her future? Was she to be in service, in some distant time? Cultivate a fake French accent and try to get work in some house in a London square? Her mother must be rocking in her grave.

Before she knew it, Mary found herself standing. "Excuse me." She rushed down the stairs, not even holding the railing, and dashed out of the front door. Her intent to go around and into the back garden failed her. She cast up her accounts in the gutter, then leaned her head against the side of the house, her head and stomach whirling like a carousel.

She couldn't stand the smell, so she moved away, thinking to walk up to Charterhouse, or maybe down to the church, but only a few steps in a half circle caused her feet to hurt. The soles of her slippers were too thin for comfort.

Instead, she pushed through the back gate and went into the garden, used for little more than wash day by the houses that ringed it. It didn't smell much better here, but at least there was a patch of grass, always green. She leaned against the washtub, still feeling decidedly ill, and rubbed her arm.

Jane arrived a little while later, a soft breeze tossing her black curls against her cheeks. She carried a shawl, a coarse woolen one, and wrapped it around Mary's shoulders.

"I pulled it out of the winter box," Jane prattled. "La, the wind is picking up. Do you think we'll have a storm?"

"A storm in my heart is quite enough," Mary said. "I am empty, Jane."

"I think the meat had gone off a bit," Jane said. "Odd. Our meat is usually excellent."

"I didn't know how to make a horseradish sauce to hide the taste. But now that the shop bill has been paid, maybe the butcher will give us better cuts."

"Oh, I hadn't thought about that." Jane did a little twirl. "They were probably giving us bad meat as punishment for being behind."

The twirling brought Mary's boiling emotions to a head. "You need to grow up." Mary's words came out sharply.

"Why? I don't have a Scottish suitor. Just a single singing lesson to look forward to." Jane twirled again.

Mary grabbed Jane's arm, forcing her to stop. "Stop it! Or leave me alone!"

"Don't be cruel. I brought you a shawl." Jane pulled her arm away.

"I'm dizzy enough without the twirling," Mary griped, putting her hands to her temples. The shawl rose with her arms, dropping fringe into her mouth. She spat it out, hoping not to be sick again.

"You're upset about what Papa said? About Robert Baxter?"

"Absolutely." Mary gave up on her temples and clutched the shawl. It couldn't warm her fear-iced heart.

"Are you going to follow our family principles?"

"They don't seem to apply in our generation. Papa married twice. And not being married to Gilbert Imlay made my mother want to die."

"Babies make women die."

"They must be worth dying for. Soldiers go to battle while women wage their wars more privately." Mary sighed. "Who is not to say that mothers live on, even while dying, in their children? It is a sort of immortality."

"What do you think your mother would want for you?"

"She went out on her own to make money, at least until her own mother became ill. She always tried to help my aunts make their own way. I still hope they will take Fanny under their wing, though they couldn't possibly take us both on at their school."

"You've never shown an interest in teaching in a small school, but it fascinates Fanny."

Mary put her hand to her forehead. "You're right, Jane. In truth, it seems wise for me to say yes if Robert makes the trip. His family is congenial, and I do love Isabella. We can be married ladies together the way we were girls. I do not like Scottish weather very much, but it is more healthful than London."

"Would your mother have married at sixteen if she'd had a suitor?" Jane asked.

"I'm nearly seventeen," Mary pointed out. "And it's possible she would have. I don't know everything about her. She didn't start philosophizing for years after that. Most anything would be better than being a family drudge, unless one had a sick parent, as she did. But Papa and Mamma are not sick, just terrible with money and very vindictive."

"Did Mamma hit you again?" Jane asked in a low voice. "Your face is all red on one side."

Mary moved her hand to her cheek. "It's still showing?"

"Yes." Jane's hands fluttered in front of her own cheek.

"Is my ear puffy? It hurts worse than my cheek."

Jane's touch was gentle, but Mary winced as she ran her finger up the sore skin. "It looks sore. I'm sorry, Mary. Why did she do it?"

"Accused me of stealing."

"Just like Thérèse?"

"Yes. She is obsessed. I stole nothing. She's the one who did. That shawl was meant to free Thérèse, not be carried about like a—a war prize."

Jane lowered her voice. "You've got to go, Mary. You and Mamma are oil and water."

"I agree."

Jane seemed a little paler than before. "I should come with

you. Would Robert Baxter accept me into the household as well?"

"It would have to be his father's decision. I don't see why not." Mary considered. "Besides, the Godwin household will have to break up if Shelley cannot get his loans processed in time to prevent disaster. Scotland is much better than sharing Papa's cell."

"Fanny may feel less hard-used about being in Wales with all these troubles here." Jane sniffed. "I should have to give up my singing lessons if I went."

"You would," Mary agreed. "And your status as favorite daughter of the house. Mamma has never treated you in the manner she treats me."

As if she'd evoked her stepmother, Mary suddenly heard shrieking from inside the house. "She wants me to clean up the table now."

"Why not Polly?"

"Female troubles. She's probably huddled on her pallet with another hot towel."

"That's not your problem," Jane said.

"It is. Women have to support each other." Mary slid her hand under Jane's arm. They walked through the garden gate and returned to the street.

"I'll help you," Jane said. "But I can't tomorrow. I have my singing lesson."

"Of course you do." Nothing would ever change as long as Mary stayed at Skinner Street.

Chapter 11

Jane

I felt quite bereft during my walk to Covent Garden on Monday morning. A light rain turned everything in the distance to mist, creating a caul over the city. I understood how Mary must feel, being stuck downstairs below street level in the ever-dim light for so many hours each day. To think she had moaned about working in the bookshop, which now seemed rather paradisical.

I kicked rocks through the dirt, lifting brown eddies as I wandered. How could I survive with no Fanny or Mary at Skinner Street? What would become of me when Mary went north with her suitor? I wasn't sure I could predict Mamma's actions anymore.

How nearsighted had Papa become that he hadn't noticed the damage to Mary's face? Pondering on the future, I nearly walked past my destination.

When I entered my teacher's front room, I found Miss Sandy standing next to the piano, quite resplendent in a white muslin dress and another fabulous spencer, this one with military braid. She looked terribly smart.

If only I had a cousin like Lord Byron. He had attended the lesson again. His carefully polished boots stuck out at straight angles on the floor. I made sure not to look directly at his feet, for I had heard he was very sensitive about his club foot. But I could not look at his face instead. Feeling uncomfortable, I took the other chair a few feet from him. He did not address me.

When Miss Sandy's time was up, our voice teacher suggested we work on a duet. "If that is acceptable to you, my lord," she said to Lord Byron. "As you are very much on par, ladies."

I found that quite insulting, but I'm sure she felt the need to butter up her better-heeled pupil.

Lord Byron waved an indolent hand, so she assigned us to Susanna and the Countess Almaviva from *The Marriage of Figaro*. I was not surprised that she gave Miss Sandy the aristocratic role and me the part of the servant, but I did not care since it was such a good singing role.

Before I knew it, a most congenial hour had passed, and I had not thought of our Skinner Street troubles at all. Even the Naryshkins and their diamonds had not drifted into my thoughts. That soon changed when Miss Sandy and I strode up the street, arm in arm after our lesson, Lord Byron bringing up the rear with an air of indulgence.

Who was coming out of the jewelry shop yet again, but that dastardly Mr. Hesse! At least I didn't see Shelley's detestable wife's sister with him this time.

I grabbed Miss Sandy's arm to hold her back until the secretary had vanished into the mist and whispered his identity to her.

"Don't you want to shadow him?" Miss Sandy asked, her cheeks pink with excitement. "We can learn where he is lodged."

"He's probably going to the Pulteney Hotel to visit his mistress," I said.

My new friend's mouth rounded into an innocent bow.

"I am sorry to be so coarse," I said quickly. "My household is run on philosophy, not gentility."

"I know what a—" she lowered her voice, "mistress is."

His lordship barked a laugh.

"Well," I said, bending to her ear. "He is supposedly the lover of a Polish princess married to a Russian count. It's all very despicable, and I see no need to follow him."

"What was he doing at the jewelry shop again?" Lord Byron asked. He had overheard my whispers.

"That I am determined to discover." I still had my hand on Miss Sandy's arm, so I turned her firmly toward the shop door. While I had never been in a jewelry shop before, I would not be surprised to learn that it was Miss Sandy's natural habitat. She wore lovely little gold drop earrings that dangled fetchingly in and out of her blond ringlets. No one would ever hire her to play Countess Almaviva with her youthful looks, but she did manage the role of jewelry shop customer very nicely. Especially with a baron in tow.

I opened the door and ushered her in, feeling like her lady's maid as she walked directly toward the counter, not demure at all despite her tender years. A man stood behind a polished wood counter with a pale marble top. Behind him were pegged racks with various bracelets, necklaces, and rings for fingers and ears. I shouldn't have dared enter if not for my companions.

"May I help you, sir?" asked the clerk to Lord Byron.

He lifted his hand and pointed an elegant finger at Miss Sandy. She clapped her gloved hands with delight and expressed the opinion that "Mamma would be delighted to receive that necklace behind the clerk for her natal day."

If she had a mother in town, I wondered why that lady was not at church with her. Perhaps she was ailing.

I did not take any time perusing the tempting wares behind the clerk. I did see on the counter, on a velvet pillow, the reason why Mr. Hesse had been in the shop. Had he come in the first time to see if they would make the purchase? Or made such finery available to be borrowed?

I stared at the earrings Princess Maria had worn the night she had first come to Skinner Street, some ten days before. A perfect round of pearls, with a tiny gold bow just above, hanging from a short gold chain and topped with a large, teardrop pearl, behind which was the earring back.

I did not believe in coincidence. Nor did I doubt my memory. In my guilt over the ring, I had catalogued what she had worn that night over and over again in my head while I lay in bed, to the extent that I likely had developed Mary's normal recall of detail in the matter.

The clerk went quickly to the opening in the wall behind him and said something into a rear chamber, then returned with another velvet pillow and a gold necklace. He displayed the piece on the pillow in front of Miss Sandy.

"What do you think?" he asked Lord Byron.

Before he could say anything, I asked, "Are these earrings for sale? I think they might be even better than the necklace, Eva dear."

She had not given me permission to use her name yet, but I hoped she would understand why I had been so bold. Wouldn't it be nice if this caper built a friendship between us?

"They are quite stunning, Jane dear," said Miss Sandy, taking my familiarity in stride. "But they are not to Mamma's taste."

A man came up behind the clerk. A familial appearance hinted that this personage was a senior member of the family. He swept the pearl earrings and their pillow away with nothing more than an irritated glance at the clerk and vanished back into the rear chamber.

"My apologies, ladies, those are not for sale."

"Are they for hire?" I asked baldly. "They would be just the thing for the opera."

The clerk drew himself up. His Adam's apple worked with outrage. "For hire? The mere idea."

"Some shops offer such amenities," Miss Sandy suggested. What a game girl she was.

"We would be overrun with unsuitable requests in this part of town." He sniffed.

Lord Byron chuckled darkly.

"Do you have other locations?" I inquired.

"We have private rooms in Mayfair, available by appointment only. Perhaps Lord Byron would like to call on us there?" He stared down his thin nose at me, making it clear that I, in my undecorated dress, would not be suitable for gaining such an appointment.

Miss Sandy sighed over the gold necklace. I began to think she really did believe her Mamma would like it. "Could you please make a note that this is the necklace for Lord Byron to inspect?" she asked.

He pulled out a large black notebook and opened it, then read a tiny tag on the necklace and scribbled down something on the page. "Very good, miss. I thank you in advance for your business."

She smiled at him and took my arm. We strolled away, then I, feigning memory, turned back around.

"Do you purchase items?" I asked.

"From private jewelry makers?" he asked. "No, we do our own work."

"I am glad to hear it, for the workmanship of that necklace is excellent," Miss Sandy said.

"Very much so," I said agreeably, "but I did think, you know, with all of the international royals and other such distinguished people descending on London, if they were to bring in a piece to turn into English money, if you would do that for them?"

His eyes narrowed and his head half turned toward the archway, as if he wanted to call for his superior.

"My family has already been receiving such guests," I added. "If they asked me if there was such a place, I would like to be able to tell them."

His gaze swept my gown, full of judgment, but he nodded reluctantly. "In certain special cases, we might be willing to do such a thing. It is understandable that foreign notables would travel with jewelry instead of money."

"Indeed." I inclined my head and went out. When we reached the street, I hissed, "Mr. Hesse is selling Princess Maria's earrings."

"How do you know?" Miss Sandy asked, pulling me against the shop window as three large men barreled past as if we hadn't been standing there.

"I recognized the pearls from her first call at Skinner Street. She wore those earrings that night."

"You are most observant," Lord Byron said with a hint of a sneer at the corner of his mouth.

"She is a very beautiful lady," I explained. "I took careful notice of her jewels and garments."

Miss Sandy shivered. "Have you catalogued everything about me?"

"Only with the utmost admiration," I assured her. "You have the most sumptuous wardrobe."

She giggled. "Well, Jane dear, if I may keep calling you that?"

"Most certainly." My heart leapt in my breast. I'd made a friend.

"I am very curious to see you when we can speak about more than just music. And I most desperately want to meet your Mary Wollstonecraft Godwin. Would you come to me for tea on Wednesday?"

That sensation of leaping in my breast turned into a lump in my stomach. She wanted to meet Mary. Oh, why had I ever even spoken of my sister? Drat her for being fascinating. "How kind," I said. "I will have to ask my mother's permission for us both to come, but I will tell her how very improving your conversation is."

Eva trilled. "How droll. I do hope you can come. Is Miss Godwin very busy?"

"Our oldest sister is traveling, which means Mary has a great deal to do, as you can imagine."

"There is the trap," Lord Byron said.

I gaped at him as Eva said, "I must fly."

I smiled as she moved past me. Lord Byron helped her up into the seat next to the driver and then climbed in himself without a backward glance at me. What luxury. I had nothing to look forward to but a long walk, but at least the sun had conquered the rain for now. I lifted my face to the sun and tried not to think bitterly of the ring I had given to John Cannon the moneylender.

At tea, we were joined by our artistic friend Amelia Curran, who listened calmly to Papa's chatter about the French translation he was reading of a book called *Le Robinson Suisse*. While the rest of us held teacups and ate Mary's indifferent cake, Miss Curran took out a piece of charcoal and sketched Papa. She was quite the best artist I knew personally.

When he excused himself for a minute, Mary sidled closer to me. "He went to see the moneylenders again today."

"His mood is rather good," I whispered back. "I hope he had good news."

Her lips pursed. "How could it be?" She glanced down at the plate on my knee, littered with caraway seeds that had fallen out. "What did you think of my cake?"

"You didn't put any spices in it, and I don't think you beat the eggs for long enough. I remember Thérèse's face being sopping wet as she toiled over this cake."

She sniffed. "It's more of a nursery recipe. The other one

takes too long and uses too much sugar. I'm trying to economize."

"Mamma will be even angrier with you than she already is," I predicted. "She doesn't believe in denying herself the pleasures of the flesh."

Though I knew she couldn't hear me from her position by the fire, Mamma raised her head from the periodical she perused.

"She's going to scorch that shawl," Mary predicted. "And why do we have a fire? It's June."

"We had a guest."

"It's only Amelia. She wouldn't expect it."

"What?" Amelia asked, looking up from her sketch with an abstracted air common to artists and poets.

"I said you were used to chilly rooms."

She nodded. "I just wear gloves." Her gaze drifted back to her drawing, and the charcoal touched it again.

Papa came back in. Before he could settle himself, Mary asked, "Any more word from Robert Baxter?"

"Nothing in the post today. Why would he write more than once?"

"Was the postmark on the letter from yesterday any closer than Dundee?" she asked.

"It was Dundee," he said. "I expect we could see him any day. He'll take the boat."

Mary returned to her chair and ate a bite of her cake slice. She made a face. She'd better not make the cake that way for Robert or she might not get a marriage proposal after all.

"Papa," I said. "Did you have any luck with the moneylenders today?"

"That is nothing for you to worry about," he said.

I set my plate aside. "The thing is, Papa, I don't think you should expect money from any of the Russians, even if they did decide to make Pavel Naryshkin's promise right."

"You don't think accepting the diamonds is a good idea?" His eyes twinkled at me.

"I mean you should assume they are gone forever. I've seen Viktor Hesse, Princess Maria's particular friend, at a jewelry shop in Covent Garden, twice now after my music lessons."

"What does that matter?" Mamma spoke up sharply.

"I went into the shop out of curiosity," I explained. "My fellow student has the sort of money that would allow her to purchase their wares, and she was with me."

"Go on, Jane," Papa encouraged.

"I saw the princess's earrings on a pillow. And they said they don't rent jewelry, so Mr. Hesse must have been selling them."

"The princess's earrings?" Mamma repeated.

"The fancy pearl earrings she wore the first night at Skinner Street," I confirmed. "The Naryshkins are selling their personal items, which is never a good sign."

Papa took a sip of tea and coughed. "I have already taken them out of the equation of Juvenile Library finances in any case. Once Pavel Naryshkin was deceased, it was clear that he was the only member of the family willing to offer any support. Their strained finances are not of our concern."

"Do you think they are strained because of the diamonds?" Mary asked. "Was Pavel Naryshkin giving us their traveling money or something like that?"

"It is not our concern," he said. "That is a problem for the Pulteney Hotel, and I don't care to think upon the matter anymore."

I glanced at Mamma. I didn't believe only Pavel Naryshkin had an interest in us. What about Princess Maria? Mary met my gaze when I glanced in her direction. I could see she thought as I did.

Chapter 12

Mary

Mary woke up on Tuesday with a sore belly. Nothing would set it right faster than a decent slice of caraway cake, not the kind she had served the day before. Though she hadn't let her embarrassment show, she'd felt it keenly. As long as Polly took her turn beating the eggs, she thought she could do a better job next time. Mamma wanted a French kitchen, so they had a good collection of spices to work with.

For a moment, Mary considered this. How much was the household stock worth? Could she sell it and give the money to Papa? He had nothing to do with the running of the house.

Her insides contracted, robbing her momentarily of the power of thought. She hoped Polly felt better, for today she needed the hot towel and rest for herself.

Jane burst into her room, slamming the door into the wall.

"Why are you up so early?" Mary groaned. "You don't have to prepare breakfast."

"Shelley is in the street," Jane reported. "I hoped you were dressed and could go down."

Jane had her dressing gown on. In such a situation, Mary would happily have raced down, but her pains made her indolent.

"Go down," she said. "At this time of morning I doubt he intends to stay long. I will be along when I can."

Jane peered at her, then went and opened the curtains. She came back and looked again. "Do you have what you need?"

Mary nodded. "I just need a little time."

"I'll go down." Jane patted her shoulder and went out.

Mary moved to a sitting position, imagining how it would be with a lady's maid to look after her needs. Princess Maria probably had hot chocolate and biscuits brought to her on a bed tray on days like these. She distracted herself by thinking of her book as she rose and dressed in her loosest garments.

When Diego had Isabella in his clutches, she didn't have any niceties, but there would have to be an interlude in her book somewhere so that her heroine could have such delicious treatment. Mary imagined the scene and how to incorporate it as she slowly dressed, mindful of the extra arrangements for feminine limitations.

When she went downstairs, she found Polly no better than the day before. Nothing had been started. So much for cake. The family would have to do with sausages and yesterday's bread, toasted.

When she and Polly struggled up the stairs with their trays later that morning, they found Jane already in the dining room, warbling something in Italian as she looked out the window.

"Jane, help Polly with her tray. She needs to go back down for the tea."

Jane complied. As soon as Polly had left, Mary closed the door and leaned against it.

"Are you feeling any better?" Jane asked.

Mary shrugged. "What did Shelley have to say?"

"He had a report. John Williams is still in London."

"Really?" Mary said. "Why?"

Jane continued. "Shelley said we should confront Mr. Williams. What if the Tremadoc problems he had were somehow tied to the Russians?"

"You think Mr. Williams, a Welsh man of business, killed a Russian nobleman for the diamonds?" Mary found that hard to believe.

"Why not? They need the money they thought to extort from Shelley somehow. For their model village or whatever it is that risks not being completed."

Mary could see the sense of that, though the connection was tenuous. Still, a collection of adventurers in search of foreign coin had likely descended on London, given the festivities. "Very well. Are we supposed to meet Shelley somewhere?"

"Yes, at ten. Can you get away?"

"For an hour. Not much more. What about the bookshop?"

"Charles has an important client coming in from a big school. He hopes he can sell a lot of copies of some of our titles to him. I'd just be in the way, or at least," Jane grinned, "that is my story."

Papa came in, looking very distracted, with Mamma behind him. She looked at the table, with its trays of buttered toast, oatmeal, and sausages. "This is it?"

"Polly went back for the tea," Mary said.

"Coffee, too, Mary. I need it today," Papa said.

At least she could hold her belly on the way down the stairs. Jane prattled about all the boxes Charles had brought from the warehouse next door into the bookshop, in hopes of selling the volumes. Would selling the stock they had on hand save them from their financial problems? Mary nodded at Jane and left.

Jane was standing in the street with Shelley by the time Mary snuck out. When she surveyed the poet, she noticed he had dressed with more care today. Someone had polished his boots, and he wore a top hat she'd never seen before.

"You must be staying with a new friend," she commented.

He inclined his head to her. "Much nicer digs than usual. An old friend came into town with a surfeit of luggage."

"Is it to our advantage if the Welshman finds you looking prosperous?" Mary wondered.

He shrugged. "I look like anyone else. You won't be surprised to know that John Williams is at the Bull and Mouth."

"It is quite a coincidence that he is staying where Pavel Naryshkin's body was found," Mary said. "As if there aren't dozens and dozens of other inns in London."

"That is why we need to speak to him. Come." Shelley held out his arms, and each girl took a side.

Mary found it hard to relax, even next to the fascinating poet. She had much to do in the kitchen, and her belly pains distracted her.

"These Russians are tiresome," she opined. "So much effort and little reward for us."

"Such novelty, though," Shelley pointed out. "We haven't much known a world without war. I look forward to traveling, now that Napoleon is licked."

"Mary Wollstonecraft went right into the war," Jane said.

"Not really," Mary disagreed. "Right into the Revolution, yes, but not the bloodiest part. And I'm not sure she didn't regret it."

"Fanny would not exist if she hadn't," Jane said. "Though I suppose your mother didn't care, not really, since she tried to kill herself twice."

"I think some essential part of her character must have been very similar to Fanny's," Mary said. "Fanny has those long periods of being very quiet. Maybe our mother had even bluer moods than that."

"The evidence would prove that out," Shelley said. "It is difficult to be a genius, and so impressive that your mother could make a living by her pen, despite her sex."

They reached the Bull and Mouth and went into the coffee room. "Did you make an appointment to see John Williams?" Mary asked.

Jane released his arm and dashed toward a table before a couple of men could claim it. She dropped onto the bench on one side and smirked at the men. They kept walking, unperturbed, for the room was not full and another table was available.

"No, by Jove," Shelley exclaimed as he and Mary went to Jane. "I would not meet with that devil unless circumstances forced it."

"Yet isn't that him right now?" Jane asked, rudely pointing.

Shelley did a double take as he followed Jane's finger to the door. He sighed and marched toward the man.

John Williams, some dozen years older than Shelley, had one hand on his hat and the other above his ear. Not a bad-looking fellow, he nonetheless didn't hold a candle to the radiant Shelley.

Mary couldn't see his facial expressions in the dimly lit coffee room. Though sun came in through the windows, which looked clean enough, the ever-present cigar smoke clouded the air inside, making it perpetually twilight indoors.

Shelley said some words to the Welshman, then took him by the elbow and steered him toward the table. Shelley remained standing after he pulled back a chair for Mr. Williams. "Why are you still in London? I thought we were rid of you some three weeks ago?"

"I've been traveling locally, trying to drum up support for Tremadoc's building mission," the Welshman said. "I returned when I heard about the dignitaries arriving." He raised his hand in a serving maid's direction.

"I thought as much," Shelley said. "Did you happen to come across any Russians in your investigations?"

Mr. Williams ignored him and stood, waving. The maid finally noticed him and took his order for coffee. "I can't live without it. Sleep is hard to come by with all the noise in this neighborhood. Carriages all hours of day and night."

"Very different from Tremadoc," Shelley said. "My soul cries out for nature when I am in town."

"Have you had any luck raising money?" Mary asked.

"Some promises made." He sneered in Shelley's direction. "Even some coin directly offered."

Mary raised her eyebrows. "Any diamonds?"

"Bank drafts," he said.

"How dull," Shelley said. "One cannot help but dream that a highwayman comes upon you and departs smiling."

"I am not the villain in this piece, Shelley, whatever you might think," said the man of business. "You aristocrats have a way of making promises you never intend to keep."

The maid set down a tray of coffee and poured the thick, oily brew into four cups. "Cream is extra, sirs."

Shelley held up his cup, and the rest followed suit. Mary didn't think it would be drinkable otherwise. "Back to the matter of Russians," she said. "Or possibly Hessians. Have you spoken to any of those sorts of visitors?"

"Are you curious about that dead body found in the stables?" Mr. Williams asked.

"I found that body myself," Shelley said baldly, then drank off half his mug.

Mary winced, for it was quite hot, even with the cream.

"Did you burn your tongue?" Jane wanted to know.

Shelley stuck his tongue out at her.

"Shelley," Mary reprimanded. "I cannot be here all day."

"Very well," Shelley said. "I recognized Pavel Naryshkin, and he, like me, had dealings with Godwin. Did you attempt to extort from him, since he was connected to me as well?"

Mary frowned. Was that what he thought, that all roads led back to his family funds?

"I don't know anything about any Hessians, but yes, I met

with the deceased Russian," John Williams said. He blew on the dark brown contents of his cup.

Mary took a cautious sip. For coffee she hadn't made herself, it tasted well enough. "Did he offer you diamonds for your project like he did my father?"

Mr. Williams snorted. "Your father is in deeper than he knows. I find him to be a naïve, amiable sort despite his philosophizing."

"What do you mean?" Mary said. She could not deny her father was amiable, but naïve? Ridiculous.

"I don't think your father would have received any diamonds unless he was willing to do what the Naryshkins wanted. He'd probably have had them dangled in front of him at a meeting, and then the truth of the matter shared."

The Welshman's musical accent made the words seem sunny, but Mary knew what he meant was very bad indeed. "The diamonds were real, but they weren't simply going to be handed to my father as Mary Wollstonecraft's widower?"

"I thought they should have been given to Mary," Jane said. "If they are supporters of Wollstonecraft, the diamonds could go to the support of her two daughters."

"They seemed very interested in Fanny," Mary said.

"You are no fool," Mr. Williams said, then drained his cup and poured more from the vessel the maid had left.

Shelley leaned forward, his expression stern. "What are you saying, Williams?"

"Mr. Naryshkin wanted Fanny Imlay." His musical voice did not sweeten the words.

"No," Mary whispered.

"Be specific," Shelley said, leaning in.

"He wanted to kidnap Fanny to be a Russian prince's mistress," Mr. Williams said, then got up abruptly and went toward the counter.

"They hoped to get the Welsh moneymen involved." Shelley's face contorted with stormy emotion. "Damn them. They've been watching your household, watching me."

"What would the Russians know about you?" Mary asked. His mental derangement made no sense. This was about her mother.

Mr. Williams returned with a fresh pitcher of cream.

Mary watched him top off his cup, seemingly unconcerned about any of this, including Shelley, who looked near to tears. "How do you know about this? Did you overhear a conversation?"

"Mr. Naryshkin found me. His brother has some business dealings with a bank that holds funds for Mr. Madocks, my employer."

"Why?" Mary asked.

"We had a meeting about it the day after Mr. Naryshkin learned that your sister was in Wales," he told her.

"What was your response?" Mary asked.

"Mr. Naryshkin offered me money to kidnap her." He spread his hands, which had been scarred by years of hard, outdoor pursuits. "I am a man of business, not a criminal. I refused to get involved and left the public room without the Russian."

Shelley dropped his head into his hands. Mary patted his shoulder. "This is not your fault."

"He learned about Fanny being in Wales on a Saturday night," Jane said. "Papa told a moneylender about the promise on Monday. We were expecting Mr. Naryshkin that morning, but he never came."

"We thought he was dead by Tuesday morning, when the wrong body was pulled from the river," Mary said. "But now we don't really know when he died."

"I never saw him after Sunday afternoon," Mr. Williams confirmed. "I don't know who killed the Russian."

Shelley raised his head. "Really, Williams? Did you kill him?"

The Welshman winced. "Look, Shelley, I know you like to

demonize me, but I'm a gardener by trade, who had the luck to become Mr. Madocks's assistant and rose to my current position. I know how to grow plants and towns and businesses. I am no destroyer, and certainly no kidnapper of young ladies or murderer of foreigners, no matter how vile."

"What is your theory, sir?" Mary asked.

"He asked the wrong man for help," Mr. Williams said, after a contemplative sip of coffee. "Insulted him or some such. Maybe died by accident after being punched or pushed, and then was shoved into that wine butt."

"Did he show you the diamonds?" she asked.

Mr. Williams smiled. "No, Miss Godwin, but he referred to them. I cannot say if they are real or fiction."

"What is real? What is fiction?" Shelley asked.

"What is real is that he is dead," Mary said. "Most permanently."

"The diamonds are likely real enough, but not necessarily Pavel Naryshkin's," the Welshman said reflectively. "They would belong to whoever wanted to kidnap your sister."

"Did he offer a portion of them to you to secure your involvement?"

"No. He said he'd pay when Fanny was delivered to the Pulteney Hotel."

"What was the plan, then?" Jane asked.

"To get her on a boat, smuggle her out of England." He considered her. "These are bad people. I don't think you need to worry yourself about the man's death."

"His brother is still alive," Shelley said. "They could still try to capture Fanny."

"She's far from here." Mary stared into her coffee.

"I have a coach to catch," Mr. Williams said. "I can take her a letter, since I'm returning to Wales."

Mary looked up at him. He didn't have a mean or calculating look on his face, but they couldn't afford to make a mistake.

"That would tell you where she is. You've been here for days since Mr. Naryshkin was murdered. You could be working with his brother now."

He stood, shaking his head. "In this life, Miss Godwin, you have to learn who your friends are. You have nothing to fear from me, but I would stay far away from the Russians." After a hard stare at Shelley, he walked away.

Shelley rubbed his clean-shaven face. "I think Williams told us the truth. He's not bred for deception."

"We only met him once, unlike you," Mary said. "Do you think we should have had him take a letter?"

Shelley pulled out his ever-present notebook. "The mail will be good enough. What should the letter say?"

Mary drank the last of her coffee. "We need to warn Fanny about the plot and tell her to stay hidden among the community in Wales."

"Would it be so terrible?" Jane asked. "To live in luxury as a prince's mistress?"

"Can you imagine it making my mother happy?" Mary asked. "To be caged?"

"Fanny is a sparrow, though. It might not be bad," Jane said. "For her."

"No creature should live in captivity." Mary pointed to Shelley's pencil. "Can you borrow ink?"

"Let's return to Skinner Street. Your father needs to know what is going on."

"Did his greed bring danger to my sister?" Mary asked.

Shelley dug deep into a pocket and pulled out small coins for the coffee. "He misunderstood what the money was for. I don't imagine they attempted a clear bargain for Fanny."

"Not in the least," Mary said. "But he must have overlooked something."

"That man who was watching," Jane said, popping up from the bench. "They've been waiting for Fanny to come home."

Shelley tucked away his notebook. "I worry that if the Naryshkins can't get Fanny, they might come after Mary."

Jane's eyes went wide. "Is she in danger?"

Shelley jumped to his feet and shook his head. "I will protect her, even if I have to die in the attempt."

Shelley's curls flew around his face wildly as he postured, his expression stern and unyielding. Mary stared up at him with her hands clasped to her chest. This magnificent man had offered to die for her. Her heart seemed to soar up her throat and float out of the top of her head.

I pledge myself to you, as well.

Chapter 13

Jane

"I know that we've been distracted by this matter with Fanny," I said to Mary as soon as Shelley had finished his note and left for the post office. I paced back and forth in front of the bookshop counter. Right when we returned from seeing Mr. Williams, Charles had muttered something about a letter he had to take to Mr. Ballachey and stormed out, leaving the book crates he'd brought from the warehouse behind. At least some of the books were gone, sold to his client.

One of the pins in my dress poked my shoulder. I winced and continued. "As I was saying about Fanny, Mr. Williams successfully distracted us from learning who killed Mr. Naryshkin."

"Oh, who cares who killed that old kidnapper, anyway?" Mary asked.

I frowned at her. "The diamonds, remember? The saviors of the Juvenile Library?"

She glanced up from the pen she was cleaning. "We will never obtain the diamonds. We need to keep Fanny and me safe from the kidnappers, that is all. I cannot wait until this season of foreign dignitaries in London is over."

I paused in my pacing. "Do you think they will kidnap me if they can't get you or Fanny?"

"Why would they? You aren't a Wollstonecraft."

I touched one of my dark curls. "How would they know? They wouldn't have had a description of either of you. I'm a girl of the right age, living in the right house."

"If you see strange men watching the house, don't go outside to confront them." Mary stuck her tongue in her cheek and pulled out her own notebook. "Now, hush, Jane, I want to get down my thoughts before Mamma reappears."

"You have cooking to do."

"Pishposh." She waved a hand, the sharp point of her pencil passing close to her eye. "I can spare a few minutes. Isabella, unlike Fanny, was successfully kidnapped in my story."

Shelley returned, his friend Thomas Hogg in tow. They had been at Oxford together, and we had heard much about him.

"I have news for your father," Shelley said, leaning over the bookshop counter.

I eyed the pair of them. Mr. Hogg, hook-nosed and dark-haired, had the same broad shoulders as Shelley, and looked healthy enough despite being a law student. "Would you please take those crates down the street to the warehouse?"

"Is your father there?" Shelley asked.

"He's not in the house." I heard the outer door open.

Shelley nodded at Hogg. They each picked up a crate and went into the hall. The greeting I heard was not from Papa. Instead, I had a customer, who kept me busy until dinner, inspecting our wares.

Mary paled a bit when she walked into the dining room, holding a bowl with turnips and potatoes. Shelley didn't notice the domesticity, though he smiled at her. Somehow he'd sent off his friend yet remained for dinner. Polly bumped into Mary in the doorway. Mary nearly lost the bowl but stumbled forward.

"Stupid girl," Mamma sneered. She'd already downed half a glass of wine.

Mary grimaced but managed to set down her bowl without further incident. Polly dropped her platter of steaming meat in front of Mamma and walked out, hunched over.

"What is her problem?" Mamma demanded.

"She's not feeling well," Mary said. "She didn't want to climb the stairs."

"Never mind that," I said impatiently. "Shelley, did you tell Papa about what Mr. Williams said?"

"Williams?" Papa frowned. "Didn't he go back to Wales?"

"No, he did not," Shelley said. "And no, I did not, Jane. I spoke to your father about literary business earlier."

Mary stared at him adoringly, instead of criticizing as I thought she might. Fanny in danger, and Shelley seemed to have forgotten the issue already.

"What could be more important than Fanny's safety?" I asked.

Papa stopped in the act of pouring wine into his glass. "What?"

"Williams had a meeting with Pavel Naryshkin before he died." Shelley related what we had learned to Papa.

He stood, holding the wine bottle. Red wine dribbled down the side of the glass, as he gesticulated with it. "How dare they? Those miscreants. This is what comes of hereditary aristocrats throwing their weight around."

"We'll keep Fanny safe, Godwin," Shelley said. "I've already posted a letter to warn her not to leave the farm with strangers."

"You speak of how the poor do desperate things," Charles said from the sideboard, where he was opening a fresh bottle.

"We know the Naryshkins do not seem to have much in the way of funds, or at least Princess Maria doesn't," I said.

Papa closed his eyes for a long moment. "No one who stays at the Pulteney Hotel is poor."

"Did they have a letter of invitation from someone you know?" I asked Papa.

He clasped his hands over his stomach. "No, they wrote a letter of great admiration regarding the first Mrs. Godwin. It was no different from a hundred letters I have received."

"I did not see correspondence praising the first Mrs. Godwin," Mamma said sulkily.

I would not be surprised if there was little, given how Papa had destroyed Mary Wollstonecraft's reputation more than a decade before. Yet freethinkers did exist. She did still matter to some.

"What about Mary?" Papa asked, ignoring Mamma. "Do not go anywhere alone, my girl. These Russians will not get to Wales. They have to stay in London and wait their master's arrival. But you are here," Papa said.

"I cannot stay locked in the house all the time. With Thérèse gone, who will do the shopping?" Mary clenched her fingers into her palms. "I'll die without the sun on my face."

"I will take walks with the girls every evening so that they can have fresh air but stay safe," Shelley offered. "Your maid can shop."

"Oh, Shelley, you are very kind," Mary said, a beatific smile filling her face with the sunshine she claimed she'd die without.

I thought Mary a little too grateful for the offer, since any gentleman would have offered the same.

"Then it's settled," Papa said with a nod, then emptied the rest of his bottle into Shelley's glass. "No more visits are to be allowed from Princess Maria, Mrs. Godwin. Am I understood?"

"My love," Mamma said. "She has nothing we want."

But as Papa's attention turned to the sliced lamb on the platter, Mamma stroked her fingers down the fringe of the embroidered shawl she still wore. I knew she'd happily take another, if she could acquire it.

On Wednesday morning, when my mattress depressed, I woke. Popping up like a child's toy, I waved my arms around wildly. "Get away from me!"

"Bad dream?" Mary said.

I recognized her voice and immediately calmed. The mattress moved again, then footsteps went toward the streetside window. She opened the curtain, sending a stream of light into my sleepy eyes.

I rubbed them and blinked hard. "I thought you were a kidnapper."

"I see you cannot help making this about you, somehow," she said acerbically.

Stubborn irritation flared. She needed to face the truth. "No one knows what you look like, Mary, or Fanny, for that matter."

She returned from the window and seated herself next to me again. "Attempting to claim to be Miss Jane Clairmont may not save you from a kidnapper?"

"Anyone might claim to be anyone else, in a crisis," I agreed.

She sighed. "I expect you ought to join me in Scotland when I marry Robert."

"Really?"

"You won't like it there, what with the damp and such, but it is for the best."

"Why?" I wanted her to admit I was at risk, too.

"It is too dangerous for any young woman of this household to remain in London."

With the light coming in, I could see her resolved, composed expression. Where was my lovely, flyaway Mary? This stepsister of mine remained a quiet girl, but when her features animated, beauty sparkled from her. I knew the cause of those moments. I had seen it too many times. She had the same depressive affliction as Fanny, though she hadn't created the same drama Fanny had about it or demonstrated the same assurance. She played a deeper game than the desperation Fanny exuded.

"About Shelley," I said tentatively.

"What about him?" Her expression remained closed.

"What are your feelings? I think you have a rather special sort of friendship with him." Frankly, the evidence showed she adored him.

She snorted. "I cannot trust Shelley's emotions."

"Because he's a poet?" I ventured, pushing back the covers.

"Because he is married, and had a flirtation with Cornelia Turner, and then there is the Fanny situation. He pledges himself to me in one moment, then spies on his wife the next." She threw up her hands.

I wiped sleep from my eyes. "That is a bit odd. I expect he still wants to know for sure if there is a child coming."

"You don't need to hide out overnight in a stable to learn that," Mary pointed out.

"There is a fair bit of madness in poets." I pushed my curls behind my ears and began to unbraid my hair.

"Robert Baxter is no poet," she said flatly.

"You'll be safe from Russian kidnappers in Scotland," I agreed. "But you'll be sentencing yourself to that life, instead of any other."

"I know it well." She looked down at her hands, folded in her lap. "I shall have Isabella to comfort me, and you, if you'll come."

"The next thing you know you'll be trying to marry me off," I said.

"There aren't a lot of men, because of the wars, you know."

I sniffed. "Maybe, since that business is concluded, I shall wait a bit and have a younger man."

We both laughed.

"I sincerely appreciate the offer of a home in Scotland, especially since I'm probably not as much in danger myself," I admitted. "The Russians will have to hire new henchmen if they want to take either of us. We already know those that came with them."

"True."

"But you know, you can't offer me that home. Only Robert Baxter can do that. You won't have the right to make your own decisions as a married lady. Look at the damage it did to Shelley's marriage when his sister-in-law moved in."

She patted my leg, then stood and went to fetch hairpins from the little bowl I kept them in. Returning with my hairbrush, she gestured me to move into the center of the bed so she could style my hair for the day.

"All this is why it would be better not to marry, if we could avoid it." She stroked the brush through the remains of my braid. "But better a husband than being Mamma's cook. That is what it is coming to, my life. I don't want to give into the blackness of depression like my mother did. I need to take some kind of action, and this is the best idea I have."

I worried, sitting quietly in front of her as she did my hair. I suspected Mary's feelings for Shelley were stronger than she admitted. What if she wouldn't really want to go to Scotland if the moment came? Where would that leave us?

Charles came in, whistling, with the post just after I entered the dining room fifteen minutes later. Mary and Polly were at the sideboard, arranging food. I could smell the sausages and coffee, but a big bowl of oatmeal took center stage.

Charles handed me a letter. "Who is wasting their time writing you?"

I took it. "Don't be rude. I know people."

"Anything for me?" Mary asked, removing her apron.

"No." Charles dropped a small pile of letters next to Papa's spot, then poured coffee for himself.

I rolled my eyes at his back, then sat to open my letter. "Oh!" I exclaimed as soon as I'd perused it.

"What?" Mary asked, taking her seat with a plate of food as Polly went out.

"This is a reminder from Miss Sandy that we are to be at her house at eleven today for tea."

"Who is Miss Sandy?" Charles asked.

"My new friend from music lessons." I smiled at Mary. She might have Robert Baxter coming, but at least I had an invitation to a nice young lady's house.

I wanted to help Mary in the kitchen so that it would be easier for her to get away, but Polly seemed to be feeling better. It wasn't necessary for me to incur Mamma's ire by leaving the bookshop unattended.

Mary didn't look particularly smart when she met me in the front hall, but I was happy that she hadn't donned her tartan dress for the call. I had pinned a lace collar and cuffs to my dress, borrowed from Mamma, and I felt I'd made sufficient effort.

The Sandy family lived in Maiden Lane in Covent Garden, much closer to our singing teacher than I'd realized. The narrowness of the street made it quieter than many of the surrounding areas.

"This isn't so nice," Mary whispered as we went up the steps behind a barber shop. The flat-fronted brick building had three stories above the street with apartments over the shop.

"I'd be happy with a smaller home if it wasn't decaying from the inside out," I whispered back. "We live above a shop as well."

Mary laughed quietly as I knocked on the door. A maid answered, and I gave Mary a significant glance as we walked in. We didn't have a proper maid answering our door, even with Mamma's lack of economy where servants were concerned.

We stepped into a spacious apartment complete with a tidy

front hall. I noticed the parlor contained both of the two windows that faced into windows across the street. The room had a certain stiffness to it. The sofas and armchairs looked overstuffed and new. A duo of portraits hung above the fireplace, of some very severe elderly people. One frame had severe scrapes along one side, exposing the raw wood. Were they secondhand frames on the portraits?

"This is charming," Mary said, plopping down on the sofa in front of the fire and pointing to an album with mounted pressed flowers pasted to the cover.

"You have discovered someone's hobby." My gaze went to a corner bookshelf. It held ferns on two shelves and a few books on the bottom, where the light wouldn't penetrate. But they appeared to be bound music, given the musical notes engraved into the leather binding. My fingers were hovering over the first of them when we were interrupted.

"Miss Clairmont!"

I turned to see Miss Sandy in the doorway. What a picture she made. She skipped in, carrying a French fashion magazine. A white lace overlay topped her muslin dress, making her look like an angel. Over that, she'd covered her shoulders with a blue shawl, in the most perfectly stylish arrangement.

"How sweet you look," I exclaimed, bounding toward her.

She took my hands and sang a couple of bars of Mozart. I laughed and sang the bars that came next. "Come and allow me to make my sister known to you."

Holding hands, we approached Mary, who had the album open in her lap to a beautiful arrangement of pressed roses. She set it aside as I made the introductions and curtsied very politely.

Miss Sandy dropped her magazine onto the table and took one of Mary's hands, so that we stood on either side of her. My chest bubbled with joy at the sight of us, and I took mental notes of Miss Sandy's dress to tell Fanny when I wrote her.

Before we could speak again, an older woman, perhaps fifty, dark of skin and with rouged lips and cheeks, came into the room, followed by the maid from church, with a lovely tea service on a tray. The teacups were decorated in a stunning geometric pattern in gold and brown.

"Here is my companion," Miss Sandy said gaily, and went to take her arm. "Girls, meet Mrs. Jackson."

We exchanged compliments, then Mrs. Jackson invited us to sit. The maid put the tea service on the table. I could immediately see the benefit of befriending the lady of the house instead of a governess or companion. How could she afford to live alone? Or was her mother out on a call? We were offered fresh cream and sugar in our tea, along with a selection of biscuits, some dipped in icing and decorated with purple flowers. Very cunning.

"Are you related?" I asked artlessly. "The last companion I knew was cousin to her mistress."

"No, miss," Mrs. Jackson said. She had an unusual sort of accent, rather like Aaron Burr's. The American vice president had visited us many times when he lived in London.

Mary smiled. "You're American."

"Yes, miss. My father was a sailor, and he smuggled me aboard his ship after Mamma died. We stayed here because he took work on the docks, and I've been here ever since."

"The voyage must have been exciting," I exclaimed. "My sister does not like to travel by water, but I quite enjoy it."

"Mrs. Jackson is a dresser at the opera house," Miss Sandy explained. "Lord Byron thought I would do well to have an older lady living with me."

Mary's expression remained impassive. Her gaze flicked to mine. *There, Mary, don't I have interesting friends?* How kind Lord Byron was to advise his cousin, or whatever their connection was.

The conversation consisted primarily of a discussion of our

musical studies, with Mrs. Jackson inquiring anxiously of the quality of our teacher, given that I was the senior student. She took a very maternal interest in her employer. I prattled along, praising the educational opportunity. Indeed, our teacher was rather good, and the last thing I needed to do was start cruel gossip that might get back to her.

"I understand your family has a bookshop?" Mrs. Jackson inquired after we had exhausted the topic of music.

"A publishing business," Mary corrected. "We own the Juvenile Library."

"Is your family literary?" she asked next.

Mary smiled. "I am the daughter of Mary Wollstonecraft and William Godwin."

Miss Sandy's eyes went wide. "Oh, goodness. I remember my mother reading me *Mary* when I was a girl. Such a sad tale. Such love to give, and yet everyone died, leading to her own despair."

"It is very sentimental," Mary agreed. "My mother did not like the work later in life, considering it less than her true flowering of genius. I am so happy you have read her. Have you ever looked into her philosophical work?"

"I have not," Miss Sandy said. "I do not even think I have my mother's copy of *Mary* anymore. I would like to read it again now."

"I could fetch a copy for you," I said eagerly. "We have it in the bookshop. Most of the books are for children's education, but we do keep a few shelves of other titles."

"How very kind," Miss Sandy said.

Mary opened the flower album on her lap again. *A bit rude*, I thought, but Miss Sandy immediately started to tell her about the *Rosa gallica* pressing on the first page. Mrs. Jackson crowded in. Mary had uncovered their favorite topic, it seemed.

"I'll just run to the bookshop and be back?" I said, my words soft.

"Oh, yes, dear," Mrs. Jackson said. "I'll get Miss Sandy's reticule."

She disappeared from the room for a few minutes. Mary and Miss Sandy finished with the roses and moved onto the *Paeonia*, which I was quite fond of myself.

Mrs. Jackson came back in with the maid. "Goodness, I can't find it. Where is my head, Alice?"

"You often leave it in the hall," the maid said, and opened the teapot. She clucked and said, "I'll bring more water."

"Do you want me to check the hall?" I asked, since Mrs. Jackson had already seated herself next to Mary, and I didn't want to lose the sale. Mary seemed unconcerned, surprising since it was her mother's book we were speaking of. Each sale might lead to exhausting the stock, and Papa was very good at making financially sound deals for new editions when possible.

"Very kind of you, dear," Mrs. Jackson said. "It's black net with a pink silk underlay and hides everywhere."

I went out of the door. The hall didn't have much in it. Clarity dawned. Mrs. Jackson had poor sight. That was why the companion was hunched over Mary and couldn't find her reticule. Smiling, I went directly to the long table in the hall and looked it over carefully. Cards waited in a tray, along with a Chinese vase holding spring flowers. I checked the shelf underneath, then knelt and felt under the shelf but touched nothing, not even dust bunnies.

Alice passed me in the hall, holding a plainer teapot. "If you're looking for your wrap, miss, it's behind that door." She tilted her chin at a doorknob hidden in the paneling.

I smiled at her and went to it. Inside, a complete cupboard was hidden. I took my shawl, wrapped it over my shoulders, and found Miss Sandy's reticule just behind it on the left.

When I opened it, I discovered several guinea coins in it by feel, among smaller denominations. Why did she have so much money in her reticule? A pickpocket could easily slice the bottom and all the coins would drop into his waiting hand. Besides, she didn't even know where it was.

I heard the door open. Alice, coming out again. Quickly, I hid the purse under my shawl.

These coins might keep Papa from being arrested, and Mrs. Jackson had no idea where the purse was. I didn't want Papa to go to the sponging house, even if Mary and I were going to Dundee.

I shut the cupboard door and turned around to smile at Alice, feeling sweat tickle the curls on my temples. Again, I found myself a thief from the purest of motives.

It wasn't the maid this time, however; it was Lord Byron himself, just a few feet away. Why was he in the apartment? He limped toward me. I made sure to keep my gaze on his handsome face, though my knees trembled.

"Cold, isn't it?" the lord said in a laconic way. "I never feel warm until July."

I nodded with enthusiasm, clutching my shawl. "I was just looking for Miss Sandy's reticule. There is a book she wants me to buy her from our family's shop, but we can't find it."

Lord Byron patted down his jacket. "No coins here, I'm afraid, but I'm sure Godwin will let me have whatever Miss Sandy desires on credit. You tell him I'm good for the debt."

"Yes, my lord," I said with a curtsy. "You are a good cousin."

"Cousin?" he queried.

"To Miss Sandy, to take such good care of her."

His lips turned up in a saturnine smile. "I assure you, there is no connection of anything other than a carnal nature."

I blushed furiously and didn't look up again until he went out the apartment door. How had I been so stupid? All the signs had been there, that Lord Byron was keeping this girl I liked. I pushed my thoughts aside to focus on more important matters. I needed to worry about the matter of my own exploits. After I secured the reticule under my skirts, I went back into the parlor.

"I'm sure Papa will be happy to give you *Mary* on Lord Byron's credit as he suggested," I said. "I'll bring it over in a day or two. Is he staying with you?"

Miss Sandy glanced at Mary, who stared serenely at the flower album. "Bring the book to our music lesson," Miss Sandy suggested. "I do hope we can sing together again."

I smiled as she started talking about Mozart, forgetting the flower album. The paintings of her redoubtable forebears frowned down at me, but the living relic of the Sandys considered me a friend, and that was good enough for me.

Chapter 14

Mary

"Why aren't you speaking?" Mary asked Jane as they walked past St. Paul's, heading north for home after their tea with Miss Sandy. "I thought you'd be dashing ahead of me, excited to get my mother's work into your friend's hand."

"Why would that excite me?" Jane asked.

She seemed listless. Perhaps she'd eaten too many biscuits. Mary continued, increasing her sarcasm. "Because it positions you as my mother's heir is why. Your friends reading Wollstonecraft. What a triumph."

"Everyone should read Wollstonecraft," Jane said, entirely reasonably. "The treatises, the novels, and everything else."

"Indeed, they should." Mary checked Jane's complexion. "Do you have a headache? I can see that something is wrong."

Jane clutched her shawl close with one arm and rubbed her other hand down her skirt. Maybe she had cramps plaguing her, which Mary well understood.

"What are we going to have for dinner?" Jane asked abruptly.

"We bought cockles from a seller this morning. I'll make some kind of stew with it. I try not to waste too much time thinking about it."

"What if Shelley comes? What will he eat?"

Mary darted around a girl selling small posies of wildflowers, her shoes stuffed with rags. "I still have some turnips laid by, and I'll toast the rest of yesterday's bread."

"What would you be eating if you were in Scotland?"

"This is a good month for fruit and vegetables. Maybe sausage rolls with asparagus and a bowl of berries and cream." Mary smacked her lips. "Tomorrow, Polly and I will have to do some marketing."

"A bowl of cherries sounds nice," Jane said. "And cherry jam on toast."

"You can help me make it," Mary said. "It will be a hot business."

Jane nodded. As they went past the prison and then came in sight of their house, she stopped dead on the street. Mary pulled her out of the way of a costermonger pushing a cart.

"What is wrong with you?" Mary demanded.

"Look." Jane pointed.

Mary saw a youth walking into Skinner Street. "Will Mamma be angry that you aren't in the bookshop to wait on him?"

"He had a valise, Mary." Jane let go of her shawl and reached for Mary's arm. "Is that Robert Baxter? Is it time to pack for Dundee?"

Mary took a quick breath, then forced her nerves down deep into her stomach, where the moths could not flutter up again. When she refocused on the door, it had closed. She had not seen the young man clearly. "I don't know. We will soon find out."

"Everything will change," Jane said above the street noise.

Mary stepped up to the house. She could see shadowy figures behind the two wavy glass panels in the door. Was it true? Had Robert Baxter come to London?

A wave of dizziness rocked the invisible world behind her eyes. As her vision darkened, she wondered if she would faint.

She felt a squeeze, and it reoriented her slightly. Jane still had her arm.

"Mamma will soon be losing another cook," Jane said softly.

"I'm not sure if I can go inside," Mary admitted. "What will happen next? How can I leave Papa?"

"You have to, but Mamma will be in such a temper when she realizes you are slipping the noose."

"Do you really think you can leave her?" Mary asked.

"Your Robert Baxter will have to agree to support me if I am to leave. It's not as if they can send me anything to live on from here."

Mary turned to Jane, matching their bonnet sides so that they could look into each other's eyes. "If Shelley can't bring a conclusion to his financial issues, there will be nothing left here. You don't want to have to live in a debtors' prison."

"Or go into service," Jane added.

Mary shook her head emphatically. "I'll be seventeen soon, but even so, neither of us is old enough to be a governess. You'd wind up in a kitchen like Polly. Or worse, a parlor maid, subject to the pinches of the gentleman in the household."

"Or worse," Jane repeated dully.

"It doesn't matter what Robert thinks. We have to persuade him that you coming is a benefit, not a burden. Four hands in the kitchen. Four hands with the laundry. It's quite communal there. We won't have to do very much alone."

"Different from here."

Black dots danced in Mary's vision, then formed into a watery human form. "Yes, but there are books. And Isabella."

Jane took a deep breath, but her face still held that odd expression. "When we walk into the house, everything changes."

Mary felt herself mimicking Jane's hard breathing. "It must. I am sure it must." Hard tears pricked at her eyes. She put her gloves over them and cleared her throat. "It's dusty today."

Jane leaned her forehead into Mary's, crushing their bonnets against each other. "Very dusty."

Mary accepted the touch and set her hand on Jane's waist. She heard something clink in Jane's skirt. Before she could ask why, the front door opened. Mamma grabbed each of them by the arm and hauled them apart.

"What in blue blazes is going on out here?" she screeched. "Get inside."

Shaken from her odd mood, Mary gave Mamma her best look of bored indifference and stretched her shoulders back, then walked inside, imagining how her mother might have walked away from Lady Kingsborough when she was dismissed as governess, looking forward into her own futurity.

Mary had thought that some new maturity would have suffused the countenance of a young man who had decided to wed, but Robert, from the neck up at least, looked much the same as ever—solid, quiet, but with an intensity that hid itself most of the time. From the throat down, he had made changes for his first trip to London.

He had taken great care with his dress, even though he had arrived straight from the boat. His snowy white cravat was tied in a complicated manner that would have impressed Beau Brummell himself. The blue coat he wore had shiny buttons and tails that stretched nearly to the backs of his knees. She couldn't discern if his shoulders had broadened in the past few months, or if the tailoring and padding had created that illusion. His breeches were tight enough to leave nothing to the imagination, and his boots nearly sparkled with fresh polish. Where had a young man from Dundee obtained such clothing?

He had such high color in his cheeks, and pride in the tilt of his upstretched chin, that she did not think it wise to ask, much less tease him. Likely he wanted to fit in here in the city, especially since he had come courting.

They discussed his sisters and parents, sitting in the parlor with Mamma, who had sent Jane to the kitchen for once instead of Mary. Mamma looked Robert up and down several times and seemed to approve of him. They ate a light luncheon of ham sandwiches that Polly conjured from somewhere.

Something felt wrong about it all. Mary, foolishly, would have liked him to pay more attention to her, to prove he had really come to express his love and devotion to her. He looked at Mamma, and around the room, much more than at Mary. She didn't remember him being shy, though he had always kept close counsel with himself. Her focus had mostly been on Isabella back then.

After the sandwiches, she showed Robert to Willy's room, which he was to share. Mamma didn't leave them alone but climbed slowly enough that she was a few steps behind.

"Will this suit?" Mary asked, pointing to the pallet. "It is good to see you, Robert, but I do have to return to my duties."

"Thank you," he said, looking doubtfully at the pallet.

She left, not knowing how to react to his less-than-enthusiastic reaction to his lodging, but then Mamma was in earshot. She nodded curtly to Mary and entered her bedchamber.

Mary went upstairs to her room and poured the remaining water from her jug into her basin, then washed the street dust from her face and hands before going down to ready the dining room for dinner. Mamma had suggested that Robert would like to rest after the many-day boat journey, thereby freeing Mary to work on the evening meal.

She was so focused on the coming of Robert that it was rather a shock to see Shelley entering the dining room behind her father a few hours later. Her gaze moved instinctively to the slender boy already at the table, compared to the full manly bloom of Shelley, with all the advantages of birth and diet.

Even his hair had a carefree, assured manner, while Robert's lank locks needed a good wash after a week aboard ship. Still, though his skin might not be clear and he might not be quite eighteen yet, they were all privileged to have the opportunity to grow older if they were lucky. He'd come a long way in order to find himself at this table, and if he was willing to offer her and Jane safe harbor, she knew accepting his proposal would be the right decision.

She spent dinner feeling like a mouse between two cats, however. Shelley would say something to her, like a request for her to pass the mashed turnips, then Robert would suddenly want the same bowl, so she would have to hold it for Shelley, then pass it to Robert.

"Shall we sit in the parlor after dinner, like we do in Dundee, and tell stories and read to each other?" Robert asked eagerly as the plates emptied, his gaze turning to Mary's as, indeed, it had done throughout most of the dinner.

"We will walk after dinner," Shelley said, fixing his own orbs on her.

"It's nice to go out when it isn't raining," Jane babbled.

Mary could feel her heart beating. Her palms prickled. Her futurity was upon her. She had never once thought, when she went to Scotland originally, that there would be a time when she'd return there for good. But better that than bound as a Russian slave in the bottom of a boat. Still, why did both options suddenly seem like imprisonments, and only staying here felt free?

Her gaze went to Shelley, whose curls were tumbling about like he had some kind of internal breeze blowing through him. She followed the movement and realized one of the windows had been raised. Jumping up from the table, she pulled out the stick that had wedged up the sash. It crashed down like a guillotine.

"I'm sure you have matters to discuss with Mr. Godwin,"

Robert said to Shelley, who had been introduced as a student of Mary's father rather than a friend of the entire family.

Shelley's gaze went unerringly to Mary where she stood. He pushed curls out of his eyes. His warm smile lit her up from the inside. How could he create this glow in her heart, all that warmhearted spirit that he possessed, illuminating the dark recesses of her? She often felt bleak, except when he was around.

"I promised to walk with Jane and Mary in the evenings, because of the threat certain foreign nationals present to Mary, in particular," Shelley said. "They deserve a stroll."

"I will guard them," Robert promised. "With Jane's help. You needn't trouble yourself."

He looked very sure of himself. Robert did seem a bit older, more mature, than when she'd last seen him late in the wintertime. He'd never been poetic, but that did not mean he lacked fine qualities. His general reserve made it hard for her to know him well, and she'd always had Isabella to talk to, or even his other sister Christy. One didn't spend time talking to boys. They were out of the house following their pursuits while the work of a household was done.

"Yes, Shelley," Mamma said, a hint of warning in her voice. "You can go home to your wife."

He bristled immediately. "You know perfectly well, Mrs. Godwin, that my wife and I are separated."

"If you went home, you might be able to remedy that," she said, all false sweetness.

"She lives in her father's house, not mine," he said, then pushed back from the table. "Come Jane, Mary. Let us take the air. I will keep my commitment."

Jane immediately stood, as if Shelley were her puppet master. Mary knew her loyalties had to change if she wanted to make this work. She smiled at Robert and gestured to him. "Come, we'll take you to a garden nearby."

His brow furrowed as he took Shelley's measure, but he smiled sweetly enough at Mary and stood to follow her out. "Is it safe for you to leave the house?"

"You know I'd die if I couldn't be out in nature. I am my mother's child," she said. "All sensibility and in need of the soothing that only trees and flowers can provide."

He hesitated. "We have much better natural offerings in Scotland."

"Let us have the pleasure of showing you our insubstantial London spring," she suggested, a bit irritated by his posturing. "We are not completely without flora, though it is often around graveyards."

"Nasty places," Robert said.

She didn't answer him as they followed Jane and Shelley out, until they were in the front hall. "You are blessed to have both of your parents living. You may find burying grounds a peaceful place if you have people you love interred there."

"They are peaceful in any case, with everyone slumbering underneath," Shelley said.

Mary gave him a quelling glance. Robert needed a chance to express his opinions as well.

"Disease," Robert said, pulling on a greatcoat he must have borrowed from his father, for the sleeves hung down over his hands and seemed too wide across the shoulders. "Sheltering under the soil."

> *"It is found easier, by the short-sighted victims of disease, to palliate their torments by medicine, than to prevent them by regimen,"* Jane said, quoting Shelley himself.

The poet grinned at her.

"Short-sighted indeed. It led to the deaths that Robert is concerned are polluting the soil underneath," Mary said. "For me, though, I fear disease most for the fear that it will create a death that is not absolute, rather than the sort caused by the destruction of the body."

"What a grisly thought!" Robert exclaimed.

"London is a city of natural philosophers," Mary said, buttoning up a pelisse and handing Jane a shawl. "Who worry us about the difference between true and false death, restoration, and dissolution of the mortal frame. One cannot help but think of these things. We are not so distant from those poor corpses under the earth. The only difference is well, electricity or some other vital fluid."

Mary gestured to Robert, but he inclined his head to have her go first. She went out and saw that Shelley had a severe expression on his mobile face.

"What is wrong, Shelley?" How long would Papa want her engagement to last? The sooner they had an agreement, the better. She didn't like this tension among the four of them. Robert attempting to be solicitous while not instantly falling into everyone's philosophy; Jane bouncing around like an eager, overstimulated puppy; Shelley pouting; and her with a pounding heart and terror running through her veins.

"Nothing is wrong. I am checking the street to make sure you are safe." He made a show of scanning up and down.

Her heart melted a little. "Thank you for your good offices, sir knight."

He harrumphed but offered her a wink. "None of you may care about dead Russians, but we need to take care of the living ones."

Jane took Mary's arm. "We've never seen any of the Russians in the evenings since they came to dinner."

"They are probably at card parties and such with the English nobility," Shelley said. "Making contacts while they wait for their masters."

"I have no idea what any of this is about," Robert said, his eager, narrow face jutting forward on his neck.

"Where should we go?" Shelley asked, ignoring him.

"I want Robert to see St. Pancras," Mary said. No matter what Robert thought of such places, he needed to pay his respects.

"Your mother's grave, you mean?" Jane asked.

Robert shuddered. "No graves."

Mary stared at him. How very young Robert was. "It's the most sacred place in the world for me."

He tightened his lips into a mulish expression.

Shelley put his hands on his hips. "Then where do you want to walk, stripling? This is an old city like Edinburgh. Bones under every foot."

"How about the area around the law courts? I thought I might become a solicitor one day." Robert folded his arms across his scrawny chest.

"We can walk over to Middle Court," Shelley suggested.

"Yes," Mary agreed. "We can stroll in Fountain Court."

They started in that direction, walking alongside prisons that, in Mary's opinion, were probably a better legal education than anything found at one of the courts of law.

"How do you plan to go about your education?" Jane asked.

"We haven't the money to have me become a reader. It costs hundreds of pounds. I shall have to be a law clerk and learn while working."

"Not a lucrative position, law clerking," Shelley observed. "Can you support a wife on that sort of pay?"

Robert scowled at him. Mary poked Shelley. She didn't have a proposal yet. Scaring Robert off was not in her best interests.

The truth was, she might very well have to support her future husband with her writing during his years of apprenticeship to the law. Or at least, add support to the household, like Mamma did. At least Robert evidenced some sort of ambition. Otherwise, he didn't seem to have a profession, and he was too well born to labor. Such a life aged a man so quickly, in any case. Shelley had no idea what most people had to deal with. He lived hand-to-mouth but always on his future expectations as a baronet. Someone would always give him a few coins for simply being who he was, rather than for work he provided.

By the time they reached Fountain Court, a large open area surrounded by somewhat updated Elizabethan buildings, she had a stomachache from the stress of the decision she had to make when Robert proposed, which had nothing to do with the reason why she might say yes.

On a fine June evening, the court had a surfeit of other Londoners, out to enjoy the water cascading from the fountain. Light still gilded the tree canopy above, sending drops of gold to the stone pavement and giving the old buildings a relaxed, lived-in appeal. Safety might lie in crowds, but danger did, too. Who might be lurking behind that knot of clerks, talking over something intently? Or who might use the distraction offered by a courting couple boldly kissing in the shadow of an old chimney and leap out from the gloomy recess?

"What's wrong?" Jane asked. "You're shivering, Mary."

"There are so many people here," she said, hugging herself.

A gust audibly rustled the branches far overhead. "I wonder if these trees fall in storms," Jane said. "They seem rather stunted."

"You've nothing to worry about this evening." Shelley put his arm around Jane. "Not from a falling tree, at any rate. Nothing bad of that sort happens in June."

"Do you want to live in London, Mary?" Robert asked.

"I thought you didn't have to go abroad to get a Scottish legal education in this century," Mary said. "Of course, with work on my novel, my head is often in the past. Please explain the current procedure to me."

"To be an advocate in Scotland, one has to pass the Civil Law trial and the Scots Law trial." Robert struck a pose. "There are universities in Edinburgh and Glasgow with the studies one needs, but I thought you were happy here in London. Your letters to Isabella have been full of adventures."

"Full of murder," Mary said. "Can you not be a law clerk in Dundee?"

"It's not a very large place," Robert said. "My sister Christy said your father's house was enormous. I thought I might clerk here for a time." Color bloomed in his cheeks. "Then I might have a question for your father, if everything works in my favor."

Mary swallowed hard. Her moths had transformed her stomach into an aching, dark pit. None of this was as she had expected it to be. He didn't want to marry her and return to Dundee? She had no place to run for herself and Jane? Faith, his plan reeked of good sense for a young man of seventeen. Too young to wed. Her family had misunderstood him, she could see that now. His plan was better than hers.

Shelley rubbed his hand down her arm. She relaxed it, discovering how tightly she'd been cradling her ribs. "There now," he said gently. "I said I'd keep you safe and I will."

She let out a long breath, forcing her shoulders down. Her neck instantly loosened. "How can you in this crush?"

"As long as I stay close, no one can grab you," Shelley said. "You'll let me stay close, won't you, Mary?"

She took a long look at him. His eyes, so clear and reflecting the blue sky, seemed in their purity almost to be dazzling her with a light beaming right up to heaven. "Yes, Shelley. I don't want to be stolen away to Russia."

His lips quirked. "No, your French isn't good enough. But Jane, on the other hand—"

Mary giggled. "Yes, her French is infinitely superior. I don't know why. I don't have her musical talent either."

"Nor do I. Our gift is for words, and hers is for sound. She is not the same as us."

"No," she agreed. "But we are the same, you and I."

His smile broadened. "Never forget that, Miss Mary Wollstonecraft Godwin. We are the same."

On Thursday morning, Polly had charge of the dirty breakfast dishes in the scullery while Mary peeled potatoes in the kitchen. She snatched her hand away when her knife slipped, then put her injured finger in her mouth before examining it.

Thankfully, she realized she'd only scratched it. Idly she wondered how long it would take to die if she'd chopped off her finger. The body could not survive without blood. Was it the vital substance the natural philosophers spoke about that was necessary for life? But people died all the time full of blood. She could smell it in the trimmings of tough mutton waiting next to the potatoes, ready to be chopped into smaller pieces and fried with butter, wine, and vegetables before they were added to her shepherd's pie, a recipe she'd learned in Scotland. Robert would appreciate the effort.

She caught the sound of her own breath. Oxygen, another vital substance, one that animal nature could not live without, based on the way they hanged people outside Newgate Prison. No one was building gibbets for hanging days for anything less than judicial murder.

What was a kiss but an exchange of vital substance? She licked her lips as she thought of kisses. She ran her tongue over her lower lip, soft and supple now that the winter was over, with its chapping winds and coal fires that ate at the back of her throat and dried her flesh.

Did Shelley want to kiss her? What of Robert, with plans that seemed to include an education before the marriage proposal she had expected? Tingles raced up her spine, making her shoulders twitch. Even she had noticed the fullness of the poet's pillowy mouth, compared to Robert's firm, well-colored line. Did it matter, the shape of a mouth, when it came time to bestow a kiss?

She put a hand to her mouth. Her lips were none too full either. Why would either of them want to kiss her?

With that horrid thought, she returned to her potatoes.

An hour later, she left Polly to finish the cookery and went up to the bookshop.

"Here to give me a break?" Jane asked, not looking up as she idly turned the page of Lord Byron's *The Corsair*, a dish of cherries at her elbow.

Mary snatched them away. "Where did you get these? Don't you dare get stains on *The Corsair*. That book, unlike many of our others, will sell."

Jane's lips were stained red by the fruit. "Mamma gave them to me. She walked by with a bag of them when she came in from a morning call."

"I hope it was about translation work. Papa is still poring over that Swiss book."

"I think she went to advance some money against the loan to that moneylender Mr. Hogan." Jane turned a page. "The money from Charles's big sale."

"I hoped she could pay it off."

Jane snorted, and they both laughed. "No dowry for you, Mary dear."

"I don't think Robert's aim was quite as Papa thought," Mary said carefully. "Where is Robert this morning?"

"He probably went out to look for a place with some solicitor or other," Jane said. "When he left, he said he'd be back for tea."

"I expect you are right." Idly Mary picked up one of the fat, glossy red cherries and took a bite.

"Are you just going to stand there?" Jane asked. "You could dust, at least. Or straighten the pencils."

Mary shrugged and finished the fruit around the seed. "You

do it. It is hot in the kitchen. I need to cool down. Maybe I'll go into the garden for a few minutes before I return to my pie."

The front door opened with a bang. Heavy footsteps sounded on the floor. Jane frowned and turned toward the bookshop door. "Someone sounds angry."

"More than one someone." Mary set down the cherries and went to the door. In the front hall, three men stood. She recognized the trio from their previous visit. John Cannon and his lackeys.

Before she could back up and report to Jane, Cannon strode toward her. "Where is your father?"

"Up in his study, I assume," she said. "What are you doing back here? It's only been a week."

"Yes, a week without any further word from Godwin. What happened to my dinner invitations?"

One of the large-bodied younger men snickered, then froze when Mr. Cannon glared at him.

"The table is not as fine as it once was," Mary said boldly. "Now that we no longer have a French cook. You should be happy that the household is spared the expense."

"There are many, many foreign dignitaries in London now," Mr. Cannon said. "I expect your father must have some news."

Mary froze. "Is he feeding you names of people you might be able to lend money to?"

The moneylender snorted. "As if I would lend money to anyone but an Englishman I could find to pay his debts. No, but I can find money for such people, if they give me proper inducement. Your father was supposed to send word of any good candidates, in return for a bit of patience on my part."

"It's been very quiet here," Mary said. "Just a visitor from Dundee, but he's young and poor."

"Then I'll need another installment on the loan," Mr. Cannon said. "If your father isn't going to be any use to my business, I have no patience for him."

Why had Mamma chosen today to give money to Mr. Hogan, who'd always been far more lenient than Mr. Cannon?

Jane came out of the bookshop and marched up to them with an odd sort of look on her face. "How much will it take to make you go away?"

"Why, miss?" Mr. Cannon asked, a bit of spittle appearing at the corner of his mouth. "Do you have friends in high places?"

"Will five guineas buy us another week?" she asked, her eyes bulging a bit in their sockets.

Mary gasped. Had she made some good sales in the bookshop this morning? She didn't hear much upstairs noise when she was by the kitchen fire.

"Fifty," Mr. Cannon said, pursing his overfed lips.

"I have five to make you leave right now," Jane said, pointing to the door. "Look, you are blocking our trade."

The door opened. A young boy, around Willy's age, stared at the two large guards, then reached for his younger sister.

Mary stepped through the guards. "Come in, please. I'm sorry the doorway is blocked."

"I-I'll come another time," said the girl, just a little older than Fanny, who was probably their governess. She put her hands on the pair of children's shoulders and marched them away.

"Take this five," Jane said, thrusting a twist of paper into Mr. Cannon's hand. "Before you destroy our business for the day."

Mary blinked at the clink of coins. How easily Jane handed over money she had no right to command, in order to make Mr. Cannon leave.

The moneylender regarded Jane coldly even as his fist closed around the coins. "How about I run upstairs and talk to your father? If you are good for five, what might he have weighting down a pocket?"

Mary pushed in front of Jane. "Please don't disturb him.

He's working on a translation. He needs to make money to pay you."

"You protest rather too much, my dear." The moneylender smiled nastily at her, exposing a blackened incisor.

"Jane emptied the cash box belonging to the bookshop for that money. It's the morning take. *The Corsair* has been selling well," Mary said, grabbing fictions from the air.

"Maybe we'll stop by every morning, and pick up the next five guineas," Mr. Cannon said.

"I can come by," one of his lackeys said, speaking for the first time. "I don't live far out."

"Not bloody going to happen," the moneylender shouted. "I'd never see all the coins." He shoved the bookshop money into the inside of his shirt and stretched out his neck until he seemed to hang over Mary like a vulture. "How about this? Your father has twenty-four hours to give me five hundred pounds or he is going to debtors' prison."

Mary shuddered back, stumbling into Jane as Papa came onto the landing. Had he been listening before he decided to come down?

"Do not threaten my daughters, Mr. Cannon," he said calmly, his natural nature undisturbed. "They were merely trying to help me."

"I hope you have a quick turnaround on that translation, Godwin." Mr. Cannon set his thumb and forefinger alongside each of his nostrils and blew. "I'll be back tomorrow for my five hundred pounds." He made a circle with his forefinger and his men opened the door for him, then departed behind him, rattling the house as they slammed the door again.

"He blocked a governess and two children from coming in," Mary reported.

"Did we have a good morning in the shop, child?" Papa asked, only looking at Jane. "Did you sell a few volumes?"

Jane shook her head. Papa frowned but didn't ask questions.

"I need to go back down to finish the meal," Mary said, inching away.

"Listen, girls," Papa said. He ran one hand over his balding pate. "You've developed a good rapport with Princess Maria. You are going to have to ask the Russians for help despite their violent behavior."

"Why?" Mary gasped over Jane's shocked squeak.

"Because," Papa said. "Jane saw them selling jewelry, showing they will have funds at this moment. Their master has come to town now, you know. We need to get them to help us before they have to spend the money or even turn it over to the tsar's men."

"Are we that desperate?" Mary asked. She twisted her hands over her apron. "What if they don't let me leave?"

"I'll bring a knife and poke them if they try," Jane said fiercely.

"Oh, you, you have the heart of a rabbit," Mary said. "I'd like to see you commit an act of violence."

"Don't even dream of such a thing," Papa said. "Take Mamma with you. They won't dare try anything with her there."

Mary had to agree that Mamma was more fearsome than any knife. "They might be too busy to let us in."

"What if the tsar is there?" Jane asked.

"At the hotel? Nonsense," Papa said. "You go over there this afternoon and beg them for help. Any amount will do, but try to get the five hundred. I'll see you at lunch." He climbed the stairs, holding onto the banister.

Mary detected weariness in his steps. "He has no intention of paying any calls himself."

"Not until we've done what he wants with the Russians," Jane agreed.

Mary regarded Jane. What had she been up to? She lifted her chin and spoke into her stepsister's ear. "Where did the money come from, Jane? Have you been stealing from the bookshop again or doing something else underhanded?"

Jane pulled her back into the bookshop. "The bookshop is not involved."

"If you didn't raid the cash box, where did the guineas come from?"

Jane pulled the box from under the counter and opened it. When she shook the contents, the dull glint of shillings showed in among smaller coins, but no guineas appeared. "Not here."

"Then what?"

Jane shook her head.

"I wish you wouldn't refuse to explain."

"What does it matter?" Jane asked. "It only bought us one more day."

Mary crossed her arms. "I'm terrified to go anywhere near the Russians, for fear of being kidnapped. I don't want to spend my life in some prince's harem, or whatever they keep their women in. It all sounds very well in books, but that's because someone is on their way to rescue one."

"I promise to protect you with my very life," Jane said solemnly.

"That's all well and good where you are concerned," Mary snapped, "But what about Mamma? She'd probably be happy to sell me for five hundred pounds."

"I doubt it." Jane's lips quivering with laughter. "Polly can't manage the entire kitchen by herself."

Chapter 15

Jane

"I cannot believe that we are returning to the Pulteney Hotel," I groused as I trailed behind Mary and Robert after luncheon that afternoon.

Charles had thrown a minor fit when Mamma told him he'd have to man the counter at the bookshop that afternoon. I didn't have to wonder why. I'd seen the sticks and small bones on the floor in the warehouse. He spent much of his time gambling back there with the clerk and the porter instead of working.

I wore my newest white muslin. Mary had on her ghastly tartan dress, which admittedly was her newest and one that Robert might appreciate. Over that she had donned a gray pelisse which at least broke up the loud pattern. Robert looked very nice for a provincial Scotsman, his hair damp from a quick washing.

"We don't have much choice, for Papa's sake," Mary said.

I shuddered as we came to the end of the last street. "Don't forget that we could be kidnapped at any moment, Robert."

"I won't let anything happen to either of ye," he said, grinning at Mary.

Somehow, I doubted he'd fight to the death for my honor, for he hadn't even glanced in my direction. He led us across the street, weaving between two carts and a carriage as if he was city-born. We scraped the road detritus off our shoes as best we could at the edge of the pavement, and then a footman was opening the door of the hotel for us.

We went to the front desk and asked a clerk, who wore such fine clothing that I wondered how he could afford it, to have a note brought upstairs to see if we could be received. Now that the tsar and others were in town, according to the papers, we didn't know if any Naryshkins would be available to us. Although they wanted something from us, if they hoped to take Mary to be the Russian prince's concubine instead of Fanny.

He passed our note to a porter, then told us we could wait in the lobby. A hum filled the space, imbuing the large room with an energy it hadn't had during our last visit. Dozens of people were moving around. I heard French and German, easily recognizable, along with other tongues. We English were outnumbered.

Did Papa really think Robert a sufficient guard for us in a place this full of foreigners? Or was he being as careless with us as he was with money? Worried for Mary's safety, I took her arm and led her to a bench along the wall, then sat with her, trying to be inconspicuous while Robert stood in front of us.

"Look at that coat," Mary whispered a minute later as a woman passed by, covered in green silk and sable.

"She must be another princess," I said back, marveling at the luxurious high-collared coat, which was admittedly all the beauty the older woman possessed. She had a sharp-cut, cruel sort of face peeking out of her bonnet, like you'd expect on one of those Roman emperors' wives of yore.

"A member of one of the traveling parties, surely," Mary agreed. "That coat is much too warm for June. She must be damp to the bone underneath."

"It's probably too valuable to leave in her room," Robert said, turning toward us.

The uniformed hotel employee who had been sent with our note arrived through an archway, accompanied by the sallow-faced woman I recognized as the princess's maid.

"Come with me, please," the maid said in a heavy accent.

We thanked her and followed her upstairs to the suite. The stairs and passages were busy with travelers. We had to press ourselves to the walls a couple of times, to let the more self-important through.

"You stay here," the maid told Robert, pointing to the wall.

"Nae, I'm here to protect them," he protested.

"Stay here." She pointed again.

"Nothing will happen with you outside on guard," Mary assured him. "The walls are not thick."

"Are ye sure?" he asked, anxiety furrowing his brow. My opinion of him improved.

She nodded. "Knock if we haven't come out in fifteen minutes."

"I'll count it out," he assured us, then leaned against the wall, arms crossed over his bantam chest.

We discovered the suite's energy had changed, as it had downstairs. The count passed in front of us as we stepped in, talking to another man as they disappeared into the secret recesses of their inner chambers.

The maid led us into the parlor. The princess sat with a little toy spaniel in her lap. A modiste stood in front of her, along with an assistant who held fabrics.

"What do you think of this, Miss Godwin?" the princess asked, pointing to a swatch of evening primrose-colored silk, with a cherry hand-painted in the center.

"So beautiful," I said, instead of Mary. The princess must be planning her post-mourning wardrobe. My sister smiled at the assistant and lifted the swatch with her gloved hand, exposing another underneath. "But look at this stunning Pomona Green fabric. What a lovely shawl it would make."

"Ah, but I wanted a new evening gown for autumn," the princess said.

"You will stand out in the veritable sea of white muslin," I said. "What a lovely idea to have something made up in this silk."

"It will be warm," Mary said.

"Then I won't need a shawl at all," the princess said. "I am afraid we are having a rather busy day today."

Mary bobbed a curtsy. "I am sorry we are disturbing you, Your Royal Highness. We will only steal a minute of your time."

"Very well." Princess Maria lifted her chin and addressed the modiste. "The yellow silk, in the pattern we agreed upon. Can you have it done within the week?"

The modiste nodded and curtsied, then made a notation in the book she held, before leading the assistant out of the room, still holding her swatches. I hoped the princess intended to pay her bills. I felt sorry for everyone, like us at the bookshop, having to offer credit to get business from the upper classes.

"What is this one minute for?" the princess asked. The dog turned in her lap and barked. I winced, wondering what damage its claws were doing to the fragile material of her dress.

"Shhh," the princess crooned, stroking the little dog in her lap.

"Papa is desperate, Your Royal Highness," Mary said, when the dog had calmed.

"Why?" Her dog lifted its head and looked at me, then licked its lips and settled back down.

"He had counted on the diamonds Mr. Naryshkin had promised, you see." Mary glanced at a chair, but we weren't invited to take seats.

Princess Maria's eyelids fluttered closed for a moment. The heavy lids stayed half-closed when she reopened them, giving her a sensuous look. "He should not have made any decisions based on these diamonds, which may not have been any more than a figment of Mr. Naryshkin's imagination."

"But the diamonds had to have been real." Mary clasped her hands behind her back. "Papa is not a fool. He had reason to trust your family."

"And what did he do then?" the princess queried. "Buy more possessions for that overstuffed, groaning house you live in?"

I bristled. "I doubt Papa took out more debt in the short time between Mr. Naryshkin's promise and his murder."

"I agree." Mary took a step toward me. "No new financial decisions were made. But word got out about the diamonds, and his creditors have rushed our house."

"Why so many creditors?" the princess asked, stroking her dog.

"This is old debt to keep the Juvenile Library running, which my mother, Mary Wollstonecraft, surely would have supported with her work in education."

I put my hand on Mary's arm as she spoke, impressed that she thought to remind the princess of her heroine and mine. *A masterstroke*, I thought, but the princess's expression went sour.

"Your father," she began, then rose. The dog scrambled, then slid to the floor, unnoticed. "Such damage he has done."

Mary frowned. "Whatever can you mean, Your Royal Highness?"

"Such bitterness I have toward him," the princess said, gesticulating. "I come here to England, to the home of your mother. But her name holds only shame now."

"That isn't true," Mary cried, stepping away from me. "How can you say such a thing to her daughter?"

The princess shook her index finger in the air. "Your father made disastrous decisions after his wife died. He is a poor caretaker of Wollstonecraft's memory."

I could feel the centuries of regal privilege in her gestures. I felt I should fall to my face on the floor like an ancient peasant and beg for mercy. Instead, I reached for Mary's waist and clasped her tightly.

"We hold my mother, as we always have, in high regard," Mary said, stiff before the onslaught.

"You, her daughters," the princess added, her rant continuing. "What are your prospects, Miss Mary Godwin? You come here asking for money for a thieving cook? Begging for funds you claim Pavel promised your incompetent father? What is he doing to secure your future?"

"He allowed a family friend to visit, one who may have an intention of a marital sort toward me," Mary said in a tight voice. "He is outside. Your maid would not let him enter."

"He is a good man, with land and money?" the princess asked.

Mary hesitated. "He is from a good family. They took excellent care of me and allowed me to regain my health, which had sadly faltered in London."

"It is a bad neighborhood you live in," the princess said.

Mary nodded and swallowed. What more could she say? Robert had shown no sign that he wanted to return her to Scotland. Rather, he wanted to remain here. He did not look like a solution to anything, though that might change if he did find a job as a legal clerk with prospects for studying. So much had gone wrong.

"You need a dowry," the princess said, fiddling with her rings. Had she noticed the missing one? Her fingers were full of them, as if she'd never lost one at all.

Mary lifted her chin. "There is none. My father does not much believe in marriage."

The princess snorted. "Because he is very bad at it? I wonder. You need a dowry, to marry such a young man. There, you see? I was told you were with a young man. Do you want my blessing?"

Mary curtsied. "Please, Your Royal Highness."

The princess gestured impatiently at her maid, then said something in Russian. When the woman trotted away, she reseated herself, then picked up her dog and fed him a bit of odiferous meat from a tray.

Soon Robert entered behind the maid.

"Come," the princess commanded. "Let me look at you."

He stood calmly in front of her.

"Do you wish to marry Miss Godwin?" the princess asked.

"If we c-can make it work. I came a long way to see her again, but I cannot afford to wed just now," he stammered.

The princess made a noise that wasn't quite a word. "I have no English money, but I see the wisdom of a husband for Miss Godwin. You must promise me not to reside under her father's roof."

"Me?" Robert asked.

"Either of you, after you are wed. Promise me you will form your own household."

"When I can afford it," he said, doubtfully.

She stared at him, but he didn't move or break the stare. After a moment, she nodded and pulled one of her necklaces, a long, plain gold chain, from her neck.

"Come, child." She gestured at Mary.

Mary moved away from me and approached. The princess handed her the gold chain.

"This is an engagement present and is not to go to your father," the princess said.

"We won't tell him about it," Robert said. I couldn't see his expression due to the light coming from the window and shading his face in white, but he had no particular reason to pay allegiance to Papa rather than Mary.

"I won't, either," I added, not that the princess cared about my promise.

Mary curtsied and lifted the chain over her head, then settled it out of sight under her dress.

"So graceful," the princess praised. "One of the ladies of the tsar's court could not have curtsied more prettily."

Jealousy stabbed through me. I might not want a husband, but I craved the praise Mary had received.

"You must think us very brave," I prattled. "To come here again, when your husband's man attacked our cook and is now returned to his service."

The princess's lids closed even further. "Our Fedorov has been sent out of town."

Had he gone to Wales after Fanny? Mary and I shared an alarmed glance.

"Do you need staff, madam?" I asked. "Mr. Baxter here is looking for a position. I'm sure a character from the count would work wonders for his future after a temporary place with you."

Robert stepped out of the light. A flash of irritation crossed his face.

"You are very kind, child, but no. We are not in need of another footman." She gestured behind her.

Her maid curtsied and tilted her head toward the exit. Our audience was over before I could suggest Robert for something better.

It wasn't until we had reached the passage that I realized that we had not accomplished our mission. Quite the opposite. We all walked to the top of the staircase, lost in our own thoughts.

Mary stopped in the stairwell a few minutes later and leaned against the wall. "What are we going to do now?"

"There's no point in giving Mamma the chain. She'll adorn herself with it, just like the shawl," I said.

Mary's mouth firmed before she spoke. "I have no plan to tell her about the existence of the chain."

"What about Papa?" I asked.

"One small gold chain will not hold off Mr. Cannon."

"What do ye think it is worth?" Robert asked.

"It's rather heavy," Mary admitted. "Maybe three or four pounds?"

"We could ask at the jewelry shop in Covent Garden," I said. "They are used to these Russian items by now."

"I did want to check on Thérèse." Mary sighed.

"There is no need to go to the jeweler's," Robert opined. "Even if the chain was worth double what ye think, it will not save your family. My family will accept ye, whether or not your father is in debtors' prison."

"It is sometimes the fate of literary men," Mary said sadly. "The world does not respect great minds."

"You could pay the baker's bill with it," I suggested.

"If the household is about to be broken up, I do not see the point." She started down the stairs again. "I'll tuck it in my trunk to save for the future."

Outside, the blue, cloud-scudded sky instantly lifted my mood. Could I believe, under this sunny sky, that Papa would be hauled off to a sponging house tomorrow? No. He would bring a partner into the business. Perhaps he could even persuade Mamma to make concessions on how the house was run, even if Mary and I did manage to leave.

I smiled at her, but she did not respond in kind. Instead, her gaze went uneasily to Robert. I understood. She'd been nervous enough about accepting his suit when she thought he'd been about to offer. How could one little gold chain change his mind?

I felt for her; really, I did. The Baxters were a community-oriented family who cared no more for material things than we did, but Robert was simply too young. If only the first member of this community to offer marriage—David Booth, the Baxters' former son-in-law—had been a better candidate, someone Papa could have accepted for her.

We had no way out, not at sixteen. Governessing or working at a school, the only genteel options open to us, were years away from being possible. Mamma and Papa were supposed to be caring for us still. But instead, they did not even pay me a salary.

The blue sky had lost its power to keep my mood up. I stared through the window of a cheese monger's shop as we passed by. A girl worked behind the counter, cutting into a large wheel of cheese. I preferred selling books, though selling cheese would be better than working in a basement kitchen as Mary was doing.

We were all lost in our thoughts as we walked up King Street to make our way through the market to the Bow Street lockup. Mary had pulled ahead, followed by myself and Robert. A street seller called out to us, offering the last of the previous autumn's apples. Mary stopped to ask about the prices.

I turned to Robert to see if he had any small coins that would allow Mary to purchase the bargain fruit.

He lifted his hands, displaying his palms. "Not a coin, Jane. Will there be another seller closer tae Skinner Street?"

"I'm sure she has something else planned for today's meals," I assured him.

The vista of the public square opened in front of me, full of people out shopping and enjoying the fine weather. A juggler caught my attention at the edge of the crowd, throwing pins high into the air. Men stood around a deal table, operated by a narrow-faced youth. Three cups were lip-down, and the men were pointing to cups and putting pennies in the youth's hand as they bet on which one contained a prize. A child crouched a few feet from me, with a crate full of mewling kittens. "Mousers!" he yelled in his high-pitched voice.

"How sweet," I said, tugging at Mary's sleeve. "Come see the kittens."

Robert had already walked toward the juggler, who added a fifth pin into his aerial rotation. I watched the juggler as Mary and I went toward the kittens.

"Do you think Mamma would let us have one for the scullery?" I asked. Behind us, men shouted. The street magician must have successfully protected his prize.

"We do have mice," Mary said. "A pair would be even better." She stopped and looked over the box. "Oh, they are darling!"

The ragged child stood, though even at their full height, they only reached my rib cage. Boy or girl, I couldn't tell through the dust. "They ain't free, me cats."

Mary made a gurgling sound next to me and abruptly pulled her sleeve from my hand.

"We don't have any money," I told the child, turning to Mary. But she wasn't there.

Confused, I whipped around, to see horror. Three men, in identical red Mr. Punch masks, had their beaky faces turned toward Mary. And worse. One of them had his arm around her waist, and the second man was tying a rope around her neck, already covered with a burlap bag. That was why I hadn't heard her properly.

My mouth dropped open, but otherwise, I felt paralyzed, as if time had stopped. How could I help her?

Before I could force my limbs to move, the third man threw her over his shoulder. The sight of her kicking legs, stockings exposed to her garters, broke through my immobility.

"Help!" I screamed, turning behind me, to where the juggler was, looking for Robert.

The ragged child had disappeared, leaving the kittens in the box. Had they been paid to distract us? Several feet away, Robert was speaking to the juggler.

The market player met my eyes, then spurred into action. He ran in the opposite direction, toward the north side of the market. Had he been paid, too?

"Robert!" I yelled, then dashed, lifting my skirts, moving toward the man hauling away my sister. The kidnappers were heading toward James Street. I could see a waiting cabriolet, identifiable as theirs because another masked man stood next to it.

I ran out of the square, my shoes crunching over rocks. My bonnet came untied, and one of the ribbons hit me in one eye. I didn't care that I'd started crying. Tears streaming, throat hoarse from shouting, I reached the man holding Mary and pummeled him with my fists, remembering, oh, how that man had trapped me into a dusty curtain last month and exposed my legs like Mary's were now, and I couldn't stop him alone, but Shelley saved me, and—

I pulled his coat with both hands full of the worn fabric. His shoulder seam tore. Another of the demonic masked figures came at me and slapped my face. I stumbled back a step, shook my head, and charged again, screaming nonsense. My hands found purchase on his dirty ivory shirtsleeve and I ripped that seam, too, then clawed at his flesh with my fingernails. Mary kicked feebly against his back, like a bug flipped over in the dirt.

We were both losing strength. She was probably choking on the bag, and I had so much snot and tear moisture on my face that I kept coughing. I fell back a step, then bent forward and slammed my head into the demon's side.

He bounced off the cabriolet. Mary tumbled off his shoulder and was half caught by another of the kidnappers. She turned under his arm in a macabre dance move, then fell to her hands and knees. My head spinning, I tried to punch Mary's dance partner, but my swing missed.

I heard shouts as I looked from side to side for where my next blow should aim. The fiendish masks were weapons in themselves, with huge noses and chins that created a dangerous pincer in the face. Mary was trying to crawl away, her head still in the bag.

Then more men appeared. I wiped at my eyes with my sleeve because I'd lost my shawl somewhere along the way. Two men, neither with masks. And one of them was Shelley!

Our savior grabbed Mary around the waist and hauled her upright to stand against him, while the other man, young like our friend, in an orange coat and buff breeches, put up his fists and started laying about. He had a boxer's skills, unlike me, and flattened one Mr. Punch. The driver, unseen behind the upright hood of the cabriolet, called to his black horse. He drove off. Another of the Mr. Punches jumped on the rear rumble seat and soon disappeared around the corner, the last Mr. Punch running behind like a seasoned groomsman.

The odds had changed in our favor. Robert arrived at last, reached for the fallen failed kidnapper, and hauled him up by the shirt front, his shirtsleeve halfway down his arm from where I had ripped it. But instead of being cowed, he head-butted Robert and ran straight into the market.

Robert, meanwhile, fell over backward. Shelley shoved Mary into my arms and ran down James Street in the direction of Hart Street after the cabriolet. I didn't see how he thought he could catch up, but his friend followed him.

I untied the rope around Mary's neck. We both tangled our hands in the bulky bag, trying to remove it from her head. Underneath, her face was red, filthy, and streaked in tears, not to mention scratched in places from the rough burlap. I didn't realize how much I was crying until we hugged each other, cheeks colliding between crushed bonnets, both damp with each other's tears.

As I came back to my senses, the street noise returned to a hum. I heard coughing, and a grunt, then Robert ran to us. Mary lifted her head and threw her arms around Robert.

"You saved me!" she cried.

I felt a strange sort of sorrow. "Shelley saved you. He came out of nowhere with a friend. That juggler and the mite with the kittens, they were all distracting us so you could be stolen away."

Mary turned to me. "S-Shelley?"

I nodded. "That foolish man. He ran after the kidnappers."

Her eyes went wide, swollen though they were with dust and tears. "We have to follow them!"

"No, we don't," Robert said in manly fashion. "We need to report this to the authorities."

"No one will care." Mary puffed out her cheeks and sighed loudly. "We aren't wealthy. We can't afford to hire guards."

"Robert has a point," I told her. "Who is behind this? Foreign dignitaries, that is who. And it's tied to two murders. I think we should tell Bow Street."

Mary's arms dropped from Robert. She spun around slowly, taking her measure of the surroundings. In Covent Garden, it was as if nothing had happened. No one had even noticed, perhaps because the juggler had held the crowd's attention. Along the street, old Jacobean buildings crowded us, down to the intersection. With the cunning born of city living, a London street managed to be empty in the middle of the day only during a crisis. "Can we catch up with Shelley?"

"No," I said. "But he will find us. He is always there when we need him."

"I lost my hat," Robert said.

I looked past him, then pointed my finger. "It's there in the street."

He scrunched up his nose, looking very young, and went to snatch it up. After batting off the brown muck on the crown of the beaver top hat as best he could, he stuck it back on his head. I noticed for the first time that it slid down over his eyebrows. Was it his father's?

We straggled off toward Bow Street, Mary holding my hand but walking in my wake, and Robert behind her. I was furious—for Mary but also for myself. The Mr. Punch gang had the indecency to know who was Mary and who was me.

"They had a description of you," I muttered indignantly. "I was right next to you, but they knew who to grab."

Mary sped up to walk alongside me. "You are right. It was very targeted."

"And planned," I added. "The masks, the carriage, the kittens, and the juggler. An expensive attempt with all those players."

"Ye will have to stay indoors from now on," Robert said from behind us.

"I will not," Mary said indignantly. "We get little enough sun as it is."

"Don't go anywhere with fewer than two of us," I urged. "Even that might not be enough, but now we know we cannot be distracted by anything."

"No more markets," Robert added. "Nowhere crowded."

"I can agree to that." Mary rubbed her lips dry. "Only St. Pancras, to visit my mother's grave, or other such peaceful places."

"Even the burying ground has loads of places to hide," I said. "Why, if someone was tucked back in that stand of willows, I wouldn't be able to see them."

"Or crouched behind monuments," Mary said. "Still, though, we know the place well, and I shan't ever be alone."

We crossed the street, then walked into the Bow Street Runners' chambers, and reported the attempted kidnapping to the man at the desk.

"Wot do you want me to do about that?" he asked rudely.

"Don't ye care what the foreigners are doing?" Robert demanded.

The clerk shrugged. "That's not an English accent I hear."

"I'm English," Mary said. "London-born, no less. Isn't it someone's duty to keep me safe from slavery?"

"Have your family hire a guard until the foreigners are gone back to where they came from," he said. "I can give you some names."

A hulking figure I recognized came out of the doorway. Mr. Fisher ignored us and disappeared out of the door to the street.

I sighed. "Can we see Thérèse de Saint-Lary, please? She is in the lockup."

He assented with a grunt and called out to a turnkey to take us in.

"We'll be safe as the Bank of England in here," I said gloomily as we walked behind the turnkey through the barred door to the cells.

"Ha." Mary sniffed and wiped at her face. "I think that sack they threw over me had straw in it at one point. I feel scratchy."

"Maybe we should leave," Robert said. He'd been sulking since the clerk insulted his accent.

"Not until we see Thérèse," I said.

Mary clutched my sleeve, reminding me that my shawl was gone. I hoped Mamma wouldn't notice. "I'm worried about Shelley. Do you think he's all right?"

"He had his friend with him. I'm sure they lost track of the carriage eventually. They couldn't possibly keep up with a horse."

"What about that kidnapper who ran as well?" she asked.

"He had the easy lope of a man used to service," I opined. "He'll have more stamina than a poet."

The turnkey stopped at the cell and pointed. Our cook hadn't been moved. She sat on a bench at the back, not speaking with the three other women locked in with her. They crowded the bars and attempted to get our attention.

"Coins?" one asked, thrusting her hand through the bars. Her wrists were all bones.

"Food?" asked another, displaying blackened teeth.

The third crone merely growled at us, in the manner of a guard dog.

"Thérèse," I said wearily. "Come speak to us, please. We have had a very trying day."

She stood and came toward us, pushing her way between the growler and the hungry woman without a glance at either of them. Her own bulk had reduced. She looked rather old and sunk-in. "What do you have for me?"

"Nothing." I shrugged. "I lost my shawl coming here. Some men tried to kidnap Mary."

"White slavers," Thérèse says. "Liked the look of her hair, I suspect."

She sounded less French now, as if she was picking up the accents of those she was spending time around.

"We think the Russians are after her," I said.

The cook lifted her chin toward our companion. "Who is that?"

I introduced Robert, but Mary broke in. "We are rather desperate, dear Thérèse. That moneylender, John Cannon, is coming to take Papa tomorrow, and we can't think of anywhere to go to raise money. Do you keep any contacts at the Polygon? Have any of the émigrés come up in the world?"

She sniffed. "John Cannon loves to ruin people. I hear all kinds of gossip from the door-to-door sellers."

"I am sure he does love his work," I said. "But names, Thérèse. Do you have any suggestions?"

She regarded me with dull eyes. "Why do you think I could help you? The Godwin family will be destroyed, and you will leave me here to rot and die. That Cannon is greedy."

"We did try to help you." I wrapped my hands around two of the bars.

"Yes," Mary said. "The princess, Maria Naryshkina, gave us a lovely shawl in recompense for what her footman did to you."

"Where is it?" Thérèse asked.

I shrugged. "Mamma took it, I'm afraid."

"We hope Mamma will forgive you in time," Mary added.

"I should have the shawl," Thérèse groused, "but your mamma will never give it up now."

"It wouldn't do you much good in here," I said. "We were meant to sell it, but Mamma got it away from us."

"That woman has no more mercy than Robespierre," Thérèse said. "You girls need to get away from her, before you suffer the same fate as me."

"Have you no hope?" I asked.

"Of everlasting bliss in the arms of my lord and savior?" she asked. "Yes. Of my neck not being cut in two by the swift blade of a guillotine? Yes."

"We hang people here," Mary said darkly.

"Yes, and dissect them later, like a poor sweet lamb for stew," Thérèse said. "I have lived more years than expected, given my poor parents' fates."

"You're a respectable woman," I insisted. "We'll free you somehow, but I really wish you could remind us of some of the richer people around the Polygon. We were too young to know the circumstances of our neighbors."

"France is open now," Mary said. "Possibly some of our former neighbors have access to money that they did not before?"

The cook sniffed and stepped back. The crones took over, banging on the cell bars until we were forced to move away.

"She won't help us," I said sadly.

"Why would we have thought any different? Our efforts to help her have come to nothing," Mary said philosophically, then scratched at her cheek. Her fair skin was quite blotchy.

We walked out into the clerk's room again. I found myself leaning against the wall by the door to the lockup instead of escaping to the better air of the street.

"Yer Thérèse has a verra low opinion of this John Cannon fellow," Robert said, standing protectively in front of Mary as she leaned against my shoulder.

"Do you think he killed Pavel Naryshkin?" Mary asked me.

"Papa told Mr. Cannon about the diamonds," I said slowly, thinking it through. "What if Mr. Cannon, being greedy, wanted them for himself? He might have wanted the diamonds *and* more money from Papa."

"What diamonds?" Robert asked.

Mary scratched her chin and explained the story. "Mr. Cannon could have met with the Russian after Mr. Williams did."

"Is there anyone who might have witnessed such a meeting?" Robert asked us. Two men gave us a sidelong glance, but our male companion stared them down and they continued out the street door.

"Mr. Naryshkin was found in a stable. He probably went there to have a private conversation with whoever killed him," Mary said.

"How can we learn the truth?" I asked.

Mary shook her head. "I don't know. My head is sorely full of fear for myself, and for Papa. I can't think straight."

"What would Isabella the Penitent do?" I asked.

Robert frowned. "Who? My sister?"

Mary smiled faintly. "I named my story's heroine after your sister."

Robert nodded but still looked confused.

I poked at Mary. "Well?"

"She would find her hero, and he would help her," Mary said.

Robert looked rather pleased with himself at that, but I suspected that my sister hoped Shelley would be the one with a solution.

Chapter 16

Mary

Jane and Robert looked like thirsty, drooping flowers on either side of Mary as they entered the house. She didn't want to be home. Worry for Shelley had kept her scanning the streets all the way back from the Bow Street lockup. They'd avoided Covent Garden and had seen no evidence of any sort of altercation in the area around the market, but it hadn't lessened her concern.

"I hope Shelley has turned up," Jane said, as if reading Mary's thoughts. "I don't suppose you even caught sight of his friend under the circumstances. I didn't recognize him."

"I was covered up," Mary reminded her. "There's no hope of me knowing who he or any of them was."

"If they'd captured one of the Mr. Punches, they'd have hauled him to Bow Street," Jane said. "I expect they didn't get so lucky."

Robert pulled off his hat and carefully placed it over a peg, then looked at Mary. "Why don't ye wash your face, Mary? I can tell your skin is still troubling you. I want to rinse my hands, and then, if ye would, I'd like to speak to you in the parlor?"

Instinctively, Mary moved close to Jane.

He glanced between them. "Privately?" he added.

"D-don't you need to speak to Papa?" Jane asked the question Mary might have asked herself, if she'd dared to.

Upstairs, male voices floated down. Mary tensed, hoping not to hear the voices of any of Papa's creditors, but then a strong, young voice spoke and she relaxed. *Shelley*. He was safe, and nothing else mattered.

"Mary?" Robert asked, interrupting her happiness and ignoring Jane. "Would ye rather talk now, before we tidy ourselves?"

Jane's eyes slid from side to side in their sockets, watching both of them anxiously.

Mary's heart skipped a beat, then pounded in her chest. It made a drumbeat that thundered, *Run, run*. She closed her hands into fists. "Can't you see?" she asked. "This is not a good time."

"Why not?" Robert asked.

Jane coughed theatrically, an especially kind gesture since she tried never to cough in order to protect her voice.

"We are parched." She put her hand to her throat. "I can hardly speak for the pain, and I itch like the devil is scratching me." She reached for Jane's arm, then towed her toward the kitchen stairs.

"We'll bring you some ale," Jane called behind her, as Mary opened the door.

"What is wrong?" Jane asked, when they reached the kitchen.

Mary stared at the fire. Something was wrong. What was it? She realized that it had nearly gone out. "Polly!" she called. "Where is that dratted girl?" She rushed forward and stirred the coals, slowly coaxing them to life.

Jane offered her bits of kindling, then coal, until it had fully returned to life. Only then did Polly enter from the scullery, looking pale and holding a rag to her mouth.

"You cannot let the fire go out," Mary scolded. "Whatever is the matter with you?"

"Pains in my belly, miss. I'll be better soon." Polly took the poker from Mary. A foul scent emanated from her.

"Fetch Robert that ale you promised, if you please," Mary snapped at Jane.

"You cannot avoid him forever," Jane said.

"Why does he want to marry me now?" Mary threw up her hands. "I thought he was going to look for a position."

"He was frightened into worry that he might lose you," Jane said. "The kidnapping was certainly enough to make a man propose, if indeed that is his plan. You have to give him a chance."

"Kidnapping?" Polly repeated, her rag dropping to her side.

"Throw that in the wash bucket," Mary demanded, pointing at the rag.

"A bag over her head. A waiting carriage." Jane gestured.

"*Mon Dieu*," Polly said, no doubt aping Thérèse, and picked up her rag.

"Everything is fine now." Mary went into the cold storage and fetched fresh meat. She took a moment in the cool space to gather her thoughts. Shelley was well. Robert was her future.

When she returned, she handed the meat to Polly and gave her instructions. "We have to return upstairs."

She went to the water butt and drank deeply from the dipper before splashing all of the exposed skin of her face and hands.

Jane dispensed ale from a cask into a cup and drank some water as well, then they went back up. In the parlor, they found Papa, Shelley, and Robert standing around the unlit fireplace.

Jane handed Robert the cup of ale. When he thanked her, Papa said, "None for the rest of us, child?"

"I'll fetch more, Papa. I didn't know you were coming down." Jane hurried away.

Shelley's boots had lost any hint of polish. They showed clear signs of scuffing. His buff breeches were dotted with dust, and even his coat had a streak down one arm. Mary searched his face anxiously but saw no signs of a fight.

"You and your friend?" she asked. "You are not hurt?"

He shook his head. "I am sorry to say we failed in the pursuit of the would-be kidnappers."

Papa swallowed hard. "Foolish of you to chase them."

"Any gentleman would have done the same," Shelley said.

Mary clasped her hands under her chin. "You were outnumbered, Shelley. I am grateful for your rescue. I would like to thank your friend as well."

"He was winded enough to stay in a tavern while I came here to make sure you had arrived safely," Shelley said gravely.

Jane's quick steps sounded on the creaking floorboards. Her curls were dancing in and out of her eyes as she rushed in with the additional cups of ale. Droplets slid down the sides as she handed them to Shelley and Papa.

After Papa drank, he said, "Young Robert has been telling us that you had no luck with Princess Maria."

Mary's gaze sank to her dusty shoes. "No, Papa." Her fingers itched to hand over the chain, but it would not make a difference. She would not ease her father's burden with three or four pounds worth of gold.

"Well." Papa sighed. "We are not without friends. I will make myself busy with letters this afternoon. Perhaps Ballachey will yet come through with what we need."

"Papa," Jane said, with a violent tremble.

"What is it, child?"

"Do you remember when John Cannon came that day, while you were waiting for Pavel Naryshkin to arrive?"

Papa hesitated. "Yes."

Jane nodded eagerly, sounding as innocent of knowledge as

possible as she asked. "Did you tell him about the diamonds or simply that you had a supporter who had promised funds?"

Papa considered. "The diamonds. They would have needed to be weighed and valued before I could decide if I would hand them straight over to Cannon or turn them into guineas first. I could not risk trusting him with their valuation."

Shelley's face had taken on that hardened aristocratic look Mary had seen before when money matters came up. "What are you thinking, Jane?"

Jane blinked. "Papa, quite reasonably, told Mr. Cannon about the diamonds."

Mary could see her point. "And we thought Mr. Naryshkin died sooner than he did, because of the first body."

Jane put an index finger in front of her mouth. "What if Mr. Cannon killed for the diamonds himself? Or one of his henchmen?"

"He is a hard man, but surely not a killer," Papa protested. He lifted his mug and drained it.

"Moneylenders become inured to violence," Shelley said.

"We could see if Mr. Williams recognized him," Mary suggested. "Find a way for them to meet?"

"Would the diamonds be worth enough that Mr. Cannon would boast about winning them?" Jane mused.

"I do not want to go anywhere near Mr. Williams myself, for fear that I will punch him in the nose," Shelley declared.

"You cannot accuse Cannon of having the diamonds," Papa said. "That is tantamount to calling him a murderer."

"What if he is?" Mary asked.

Robert shook his head violently. "He should be turned in tae the local constabulary, Mr. Godwin. He cannae demand money from you then."

"We cannot persecute an innocent man," Papa said.

"He is anything but that," declared Shelley, humor in his voice.

"Mr. Williams was at the Bull and Mouth just two days ago," Mary said. "Let us see if he is still there, then persuade him to come to Mr. Cannon's house with us. That is wisdom, is it not?"

"If Mr. Williams recognizes him, then we can go to the magistrates?" Jane asked.

"I will take you to the inn," Shelley said, nodding at her. "Though I like it not. Baxter, will you come with us?"

Robert glanced at Papa. "I would like tae speak tae Mr. Godwin first. He ought to know the details of what happened in Covent Garden today."

Mary gave him a quelling look. "Once we are gone." Papa would not allow her to leave again once he'd heard the entire story. She'd be trapped in the kitchen all summer, dying by inches.

"You should join us," Jane said, glancing nervously at Mary.

Mary put her arm on Jane's arm. "Let him stay. I'm sure he and Papa have much to discuss." Her entire future was at stake.

Robert nodded solemnly.

"Very well. Come, girls," Shelley nodded at Papa and walked out of the parlor. The girls followed behind him.

"Do you think they will attack Mary again?" Jane asked while Mary rubbed the dust off her shoes with a rag.

"We need to keep our wits about us," Shelley said. "It is impossible to tell, in this city, who might be paid to follow us. There are so many people about."

"I wish we didn't have to wear bonnets but could wear hats like men," Jane fretted. "Bonnets do not allow us to see anything that isn't straight ahead."

"I will watch from side to side," Shelley promised, opening the front door. "Let's go to the Bull and Mouth quickly, shall we?"

They made quick work of the streets, with Mary in the center. Shelley's boots raised dust to knee height in the inn's yard. She coughed and, blinded by dusty eddies, nearly walked into the side of a dog cart. Jane pulled her out of the way just in time.

They went in the main entrance. The front hall was busy with travelers coming and going. Shelley went straight to the counter and asked for John Williams.

Mary stood stoically while Shelley bantered with the counter attendant, trying to get his point across that they wanted to see a man they knew, a Mr. Williams from Wales. The inn apparently had three in residence by that name. It had been much easier to find him when they had come before.

Jane swayed from side to side, alternatively wringing her hands and covering her mouth, then pressing her bonnet sides back to have a better range of view. Mary dragged her to a wall, so they could protect their backsides. Jane calmed then, though she took her bonnet off completely.

Eventually, Shelley came to them. "Let's sit in the public room. I think they are sending a porter to fetch Mr. Williams. I don't know where that clerk is from, but his English was impossible to understand."

"We are lucky Mr. Williams is here," Mary said.

"If he is." Shelley huffed out a breath and directed them into the public room, then called for wine.

They were enjoying a decadent glass when Mr. Williams appeared in the doorway, dressed in a black coat and tan breeches. He caught sight of Shelley and frowned, then came toward them.

"Are you ready to come to terms with us at Tremadoc, Mr. Shelley?" Mr. Williams asked, taking the end of the bench that Mary indicated. "Ladies."

"We want you to take a look at a man," Shelley said, pouring wine and pushing a glass toward Williams. "To see if you recognize him as the person who was speaking to Pavel Naryshkin when you saw him."

"Where is this man now?" Mr. Williams asked, taking the glass.

"He lives in Bedford Street."

Mary blanched. "But that is just off Covent Garden. We don't want to go back there."

"Why not?" Williams asked, drinking off half his glass.

Jane launched into a dramatic telling of their horrifying adventure on the opposite side of Covent Garden. It took a good ten minutes, and all four of them had drained their glasses by the end of the story.

Mary felt quite merry, in fact, and not a little reckless as the wine reached her belly. "We cannot be d-distracted," she warned. "If you see Mr. Punch nearby, we n-need to run."

Jane shuddered. "I will never watch a puppet show again."

"Do not blame Mr. Punch," Shelley declared. "It is not his fault that masks of his face are easy to come by."

Mary giggled, finding that uproarious. She stopped and put her hand to her mouth when she hiccupped.

Shelley set the bottle to his glass and found it empty. He frowned and stood to take it to the bar.

"I have an engagement this afternoon," Mr. Williams called, a look of concern in his eyes after he cast his glance toward Mary. "I will go with you, but only if we leave now."

Shelley waved a hand and spoke to the bartender, then returned to their table. "Now, let us hie to Bedford Street."

"I must know if Mr. Cannon is a thief and a murderer. He'll take my father away tomorrow, you know," Mary said.

Mr. Williams frowned. "Take him away?"

"He is going to take Papa to a sponging house tomorrow," Jane explained. "But Papa would have had the repayment if Mr. Naryshkin hadn't died."

"That's why we think he stole the diamonds," Mary added.

"You cannot frame an innocent man to protect your father, Miss Godwin," the moneyman said.

"I doubt he's innocent," Shelley told him. "We are doing the right thing by taking you to get a look at him."

"What if he is the murderer?" Mr. Williams asked. "What then?"

"We will come up with some story," Shelley said. "I will say I am there to offer him twenty guineas on account to hold off on his arrest of Godwin until next week. While he is arguing with me, you can get a good look at him."

"Very well, then." Mr. Williams patted his chest.

They made their wary way through the streets, Shelley no less cautious than Mary and Jane. Only Mr. Williams seemed to be enjoying himself, occasionally whistling a couple of bars of a song Mary didn't recognize.

Any time they heard a bit of bird call, he would imitate it.

"You have a good ear," Jane praised.

Mr. Williams grinned at her. "When I was a gardener, I amused myself by putting out seed to attract birds. I became rather good at imitating them."

"Here is Bedford Street," Shelley said, when they came to a broad street, built up on either side with flat-fronted gray buildings. The ground floors contained shops and tradesmen, with housing above.

"Which one is Mr. Cannon's house?" Mary said, feeling more sober after the fresh air.

Shelley pointed. "That one, with the door open."

Mary looked to her left, where indeed, one of the shops stood open. They crossed the street and found a small sign with Mr. Cannon's name on it. He must keep the ground floor as his moneylending headquarters.

"No guard out front," Mr. Williams noted.

"It is a warm day," Shelley suggested, ushering them in. "The guard is out of the sun, perhaps."

Inside, the light immediately dimmed. The front of the shop

contained a couple of chairs and one tall desk with a stool but no people.

"That door is open as well." Shelley pointed to the wall that stretched across the back of the interior, some eight feet from the front door. It had a single door in it. "The staircase to the living quarters must be behind it."

"Mr. Cannon must rent the entire building." Mr. Williams knocked on the wall. "This isn't a permanent structure."

Shelley went through the interior door. Not thirty seconds later, Mary heard him retch.

"Shelley?" she called and, forgetting caution, ran through the door after him, followed by Jane and Mr. Williams.

The space had lighting from windows at the back, facing onto a mews. It was enough to find Shelley, standing behind a large desk, his coat sleeve over his mouth. Mary went to him instantly.

"What is it?" She followed his line of vision and saw a crumpled form behind the desk.

John Cannon still wore the highly polished black boots she'd seen on him before. The watch chain that had stretched across his waistcoat was gone. He didn't wear a hat, and his black hair clung to his scalp with some kind of pomade. His eyes were half-open, gazing into eternity.

Tight around his neck, a scarf—unseasonable, hand-knit wool dyed green but faded in parts—had been secured, and above it, his face, never the healthiest color, had taken upon it the hues of death.

She backed away, bumping the desk, grateful to the wine for dulling her response. Her pulse sounded in her ears. Jane caught her around the waist. Mr. Williams walked around them, moving toward the body.

"Strangled," he said, edging around Shelley and crouching down. He lifted one of the corpse's eyelids to expose the eyeball completely. "You can tell from the eyes."

Jane shuddered, but Shelley leaned forward to see what Mr. Williams pointed at.

"We should go," Jane said. "This is a most dreadful business."

"Where are his guards?" Mary asked, patting Jane's hands. Mary glanced around everywhere but at the body, now that she'd seen the worst of it. "We expected them to be here. The room doesn't look ransacked either."

Jane lifted her head and pushed Mary's bonnet aside. "Where are the diamonds?"

Mr. Williams knelt on the floor, scraping his boots, and did a cursory check of the corpse's body, patting down his chest, arms, and flanks. He flipped open the coat and checked it as well. "Nothing on his person."

Mary blew out a breath. This wasn't all disaster. "He can't take Papa to the sponging house if he's dead."

Shelley clenched his fists. "Godwin still needs the diamonds. Someone will take over this business eventually."

"Do we know if Mr. Cannon had a family?" Mary asked. "Or a partner?"

"I think he would have kept them exceedingly private if he did," Shelley said. "But I never caught a whiff of matrimony off him."

"Someone will fill the gap," Mr. Williams advised. "One of his guards, perhaps. Whoever has access to his most private files and the money will take over. This is hardly a legal enterprise."

"He is an extortionist," Shelley declared. "Godwin never should have had dealings with him. He is the only person I know who ever risked such a foolish thing."

Mary bristled at the characterization of her father as foolish. "Mamma probably found him."

Jane glanced at her, wild-eyed, and began investigating the desk. None of the drawers were locked, and little was in them.

Mary watched Jane for a moment, then inspected the rest of the room. Behind them on one side, a staircase went up to the next level, but other than that, the room contained nothing but the desk and chairs.

"Someone might see the open door and call the watch," Mr. Williams said.

Shelley nodded and went to the outer chamber to close it, then returned. "He has another study upstairs, with a safe in it. If the diamonds weren't stolen, they would be up there."

"How do you know that?" Mary asked.

"It stands to reason. Besides, I came here once with a friend and managed to talk him out of doing business in this house," Shelley explained. "Cannon had a sly and hungry look to him."

"We won't be able to get into a safe," Mr. Williams commented.

"We might be able to find something," Shelley said over his words.

"You can't be thinking to steal from the dead man," Mr. Williams said, aghast.

"This was a crooked man," Shelley said. "He did not act in good faith and has paid the price."

"I cannot see retrieving anything but the diamonds," Mary said. "If they are here. Although if we could find the ledgers, and rip out anything pertaining to Papa, I would not think that a bad thing. He's had plenty of money from us—quite enough, I'm sure."

"Does the murder have anything to do with us?" Jane asked. She'd stopped investigating. Her breath had started to come in little pants, and Mary feared she would descend into one of her horrors or the shrieks she had uttered the first time they had found a murder victim. They couldn't risk Jane's drama here. The walls were thin between buildings.

She wrapped her arms around Jane's waist and pulled her close. "We can't know that, Jane. Let's go out to the front room and let the men go upstairs. We can't help them." Though she wanted to, desperately. Jane could tear down the entire enterprise, however, and bring those who might think they had killed the moneylender.

"It's not safe to be apart from Shelley," Jane protested.

"There is a lock on the door. Come now." Mary tried to pull Jane along, but her feet were firmly planted around one leg of the desk.

"Let's go up, shall we?" Mr. Williams said to Shelley. "It might give us more information to share with the constabulary."

Shelley nodded, his expression grim. "Lead the way."

Mr. Williams walked to the staircase. It had a fancy appearance, with carved, twisted balustrades and wood that matched the half paneling on the walls. He put his boot on the first step and started to go up.

Shelley glanced back at Mary, nodded at her, then followed the Welshman. His foot had just touched the third step when Mary heard sounds overheard.

"Someone is up there," she cried.

Mr. Williams took one more step up, but before he reached the next step, a concussive burst sounded in the room. Something hit the wall.

Jane screamed. Mary pulled her away from the desk and started towing them both toward the door to the front room.

Mr. Williams fell back, whether under his own power or not, Mary couldn't say. Shelley leapt backward, then turned and ran at the girls.

He pushed hard at them both, screaming, "Wales, Wales!"

The breath left Mary's midsection. She crumpled to the floor next to Jane. He'd knocked them both over.

"Are you well?" she cried.

Jane flipped over and began to crawl away. Mary slid behind her, staying on her belly. She heard the sound of another something hitting wood. Was someone shooting at them? What was going on? While she pushed at Jane's backside, they both sped up and went through the door.

"It's not a real wall," Mary panted. "It won't protect us."

Mr. Williams stumbled over them as he ran through the door. He slammed the door in the false wall shut, then turned to pull Jane to her feet. Mary crawled until she reached the tall desk, then scuttled out the front door, followed by Shelley.

She looked at him up and down. "Are you hurt?"

He shook his head. "I just was remembering what happened that horrible night at Tremadoc. What are we going to do?"

Mr. Williams, his arm around Jane, helped her through the street door, then closed it. He bent forward, panting.

"Bow Street," Mary said. It's not far."

"He'll get away," Shelley gasped.

Mr. Williams stared at the street. "He has a gun. We can't stay here and attract attention to ourselves."

"The market?" Jane asked.

Mary shook her head. "We'll go up the street and turn east before the market, but we need to run for the constables before anyone else complains about gunfire."

Shelley stared at the Welshman, wild-eyed. "The Home Office had its eye on me before, for my pamphleteering. I cannot be in the middle of this as well."

"I am your witness," John Williams said. "Come, Shelley, you were in the room. No one can say you fired a gun from the first floor."

"Was he warm? Mr. Cannon, I mean?" Jane asked.

"An excellent point, Miss Clairmont," Mr. Williams said. "Yes, the body was still warm. Therefore, Shelley cannot possibly be the murderer because he was with us."

Shelley breathed shakily and held out his arm to Mary. "Let us go to Bow Street."

Mary took his arm, a nightmarish sense of unreality filling her thoughts as they walked toward the market, then turned right before they reached the central area to go toward Bow Street.

Shelley could not possibly have killed the moneylender, but what about her father? They had dallied some time at the Bull and Mouth before they came in this direction.

Her lips trembled. She wiped tears away with her free hand. It didn't matter what she knew, if she didn't tell anyone. Jane hadn't seemed to notice. She was intent on looking for the diamonds, not examining the body.

But Mary had looked Mr. Cannon over closely. She hadn't known enough to be as certain as Mr. Williams that the scarf had been the instrument of murder, but she had fixated on that scarf nonetheless.

Fanny had knitted that item for Papa as a gift. Mary recognized it as unique. Fanny had bought the wool from a street seller, and after Papa had received it, he'd dribbled red wine on it when he was out somewhere. When Fanny washed it, the dye leached out of the wool, leaving the color patchy. The color hadn't been set properly, and Fanny fretted that her gift was ruined, but Papa said he liked it anyway.

"I think you should let me talk," Mr. Williams said, when they reached the door of the magistrate's court.

"Shall I take the girls home?" Shelley asked, pulling Jane from Mr. Williams.

The Welshman shook his head. "You have to come in with me. I do not want to say I was alone when plenty of people might have seen us."

"We are each other's alibi," Jane said.

Mr. Williams squinted at her, then opened the door. They followed him in, and he began the long process of explaining to the men there what they had seen.

After they had made sense of the matter, Shelley took the girls back to Skinner Street while Mr. Williams led a quartet of constables to Bedford Street.

Mary and Jane were both shaky with tears as they entered the front door. Mamma came out of the bookshop, her face red with rage, but when she saw Jane, her expression went slack.

"Where is Papa?" Mary asked, through panting breaths. "We must speak to him. The moneylender is dead."

"Murdered." Despite Shelley's hand under her arm, Jane collapsed to the floor in a dead faint.

Mary, feeling none too steady herself, went to her knees and tried to rouse Jane.

"What is this?" Mamma cried.

"Where is your husband, madam?" Shelley said in an emotionless way over the girls' voices.

"He went out with young Robert Baxter." Mamma wrung her hands. "Jane?"

Mary patted Jane's cheeks. She didn't rouse, but Mary wasn't sure she was really unconscious. Her cheeks still had color. Honestly, she wished she'd thought of fainting to get out of answering questions. Fear for her father pounded in her chest. "Smelling salts, Mamma. Please find some. Shelley, go find Papa, please."

Chapter 17

Jane

I had been unwilling to let Mary out of my sight after I regained consciousness from my faint the previous afternoon. I did not want her or me to be alone and vulnerable after finding another corpse. We shared her bed that night.

I felt strange waking in her small chamber on Friday morning. We had expected to spend the day among our acquaintance, begging for money in the hopes of keeping Mr. Cannon from taking Papa away. What would happen now? Maybe nothing would change, even if his henchmen arrived to collect on the loan. Would Mr. Cannon's favorite sponging house do business with his underlings?

As we helped each other dress, Mary and I stayed silent, haunted by yesterday's events and the specter of what might come this day. Finally, I couldn't stand the quiet anymore.

"Mamma will be outraged that you did not prepare a breakfast this morning for us." Perhaps I should not have started the conversation with an attack, but I desperately wished for normality.

Mary shrugged. "I am more concerned about Papa. I stayed awake until the watch called one in the morning, and I never heard him come in."

I pinned the back of her skirt closed. "He is with Robert."

She tied her neckline together and slid her arms into her apron. "Where? Robert is not the sort to spend the night at taverns, or worse."

"You hadn't seen him for more than three months, and young men change fast." I knotted her apron strings behind her slim waist. "Maybe he does like taverns now. And besides, I am sure Papa and Robert came home at some point, after we were asleep."

The entire house rattled. We shared a glance of concern, then ran to the window.

"Did Papa forget his key?" Mary asked.

"I cannot say, but that is a constable in the street." I pointed my finger down against the glass. A man in a long gray coat stood in the street. "I think it's Constable Wharton."

I realized how agitated Mary was by the way she ran her hands down her apron, fingers trembling.

"We should go down," she said. "At least we have the benefit of being dressed."

"What do you think is happening?" I asked, my voice as trembly as her fingers.

"I am sore afraid for Papa," she admitted.

"And Robert?" I asked.

She stared at me, or rather through me, and moved quickly to the door.

We went downstairs, not troubling to stay off the most rattling stairs. No one else seemed to be about. Perhaps Mary had not lain in bed much too late after all, if our brothers and Mamma were not yet stirring. She might have time to get the tea made, at least.

At the foot of the stairs, she gathered herself visibly and set her hands, one folded over the other, along her waist. At her nod, I unlocked and opened the door as she stood behind it, as solemn as a queen.

"Constable Wharton?" she asked, with just a hint of a wobble in the word. "How may I help you?"

The constable lifted a paper. "There is to be a coroner's inquest this morning in regard to the death of John Cannon."

"Are Miss Godwin and I being called to testify?" I asked.

Constable Wharton glanced at me, not unkindly. "You are children still, both of you."

"Are you calling Robert Baxter, then?" Mary asked. "He is just seventeen."

The constable rubbed his knuckles over his day-old growth of ruddy beard. "No, I am looking for Percy Shelley and a Mr. Williams. Are they here this morning?"

I shook my head. "No. He doesn't lodge here. Shelley, I mean."

"You should be able to find Mr. Williams at the Bull and Mouth," Mary said. "He's been staying there."

"How about Mr. Shelley?" the constable asked.

"Do you know the booksellers and circulating library at 15 Old Bond Street?" Mary asked. "Thomas Hookham and Sons?"

"I can find it," the constable said.

She continued. "Mr. Shelley is a friend of Mr. Thomas Hookham, Junior. You might find him in that household."

The constable nodded. "Thank you for both directions, ladies." He saluted us and walked away.

Mary shut the door and leaned against it. "I hope we can trust both men to say the right things."

I frowned at her. "How do you know where Shelley lives?"

"I don't," she admitted. "But Papa introduced Shelley to the Hookhams in the first place. It's a reasonable assumption."

We were both nervous all throughout the morning. I helped Mary and Polly make breakfast. I was surprised to find Papa and Robert drawn down by the smell of bacon and potatoes when the door hadn't roused them. Papa had reddened eyes. Robert's youthful face held no similar signs of exhaustion. Mamma ignored us, fluttering about Papa. I really thought she was afraid he'd make himself ill. No concern came in our youthful direction, though we'd been the ones to be shot at and to find a corpse.

After the men ate, Charles took Robert with him to the warehouse, and Papa went up to his study. I left Mary and Polly to the cleanup and let Willy's tutor in, then Mamma told me to open the bookshop.

"Do you need to work on the books, Mamma?" I asked.

"I am going to work on that Swiss book," Mamma said. "Papa has a list of sentences he wants me to translate for him."

I nodded and went downstairs to unlock the doors, then checked the post for delivery requests. There were, happily, a couple of small orders for schools. Mamma came down a few minutes later and went into the office. When the porter arrived, I sent him out with the orders and settled in to wait for street traffic.

After the church bells rang with the incessant toll for noon, Mamma came out of the office, her hand to her forehead. "I am going to lie down until lunch is ready. I need a new French dictionary with bigger print."

"Perhaps some spectacles might help?" I suggested. "Or a magnifying glass."

She glared at me and swept out. I wanted to run downstairs and tell Mary to hurry up with food, but she wouldn't listen, even to the growls of my stomach.

About half an hour later, I was near starvation, but I hadn't heard anyone come up from the kitchen. I'd had two customers, fifteen minutes apart, so I didn't dare close the bookshop. One of them had purchased a copy of Papa's *St. Leon*, and the other had bought a selection of Lamb-authored titles, and a copy of William Hazlitt's *A New and Improved Gram-*

mar of the English Tongue, which I had not sold for a while. I appreciated each and every clink into the money box, as well as these moments when I wasn't in solitude.

I was surprised to hear banging on the front door as I rubbed my empty stomach. The door was not locked.

When I went out, I found Mary coming toward me, followed by Polly, holding a tray of cold meats and another of cheese and pickles. They stared at me, confused, while I opened the front door.

Constable Wharton had reappeared. He had two more men with him this time, and I recognized neither of them.

He held up a piece of paper. "I have a signed warrant here, Miss Clairmont—by a magistrate, you understand."

Mary and I glanced at each other.

Mary quickly handed Polly the second tray and shooed her upstairs. She went up the steps, ungainly with her double burden. "For what purpose? Is the inquest complete?"

Constable Wharton nodded solemnly. "Yes, Miss Godwin. I am here to make an arrest in the name of the king."

Spots of high color appeared on Mary's cheeks. "Whom do you want to arrest?"

"And why?" I added.

He glanced down at the paper. "Mary Jane Godwin. Is she in the house?"

"Mamma?" I asked, confused.

"Is she in the house?" he asked again, the question focused on Mary.

She stared at him. "I do not know. I was in the kitchen."

"She is in her bedchamber," I said. "She has a headache."

"Can you fetch her, please?" Constable Wharton asked as the other two men shuffled behind him. "I do not want to pull the woman from her bed."

Another of the men cleared his throat. "How many doors are there?"

"Just this one," Mary said. "It is the only way to leave Skinner Street."

"Mamma is not trying to escape anything," I said. "She translated this morning, and it gave her a headache, that is all."

He nodded. "In the name of the king, miss. Go quickly and fetch her, now."

"I'll go," I said, and ran upstairs before Mary could say different. Mary's voice drifted up the staircase, offering to make tea or coffee for the men. I hoped they said no, for I didn't like the idea of them having access to the parlor and even the bookshop while she went into the kitchen.

I knocked on Mamma and Papa's door, a bit out of breath, then opened it. Mamma must have closed the shutters, for there was little light. Once inside the room, I heard the nasal breathing of Papa. He must have joined Mamma. Maybe she'd wanted him to have a nap after his mysteriously long night.

"Mamma?" I whispered, going to her side of the bed. I felt around in the dark and found her shoulder. Shaking it slightly, I called her again, then went to open the shutter into the back garden.

When I turned, she was sitting up, her lightly gray-dusted braid dangling over one shoulder. She was only wearing her nightgown.

"Why are you waking me, girl? I had a late night, what with Papa and that Robert Baxter out of doors all hours. I cannot wait until he jumps back on that boat, I can tell you."

I went to stand next to her, mimicking Mary's closed posture with my hands folded. "Mamma, there are constables downstairs. You had better dress, quickly and warmly."

She picked at her front tooth. "Why, child?"

My voice came out as a squeak. "Mamma, I am sorry to say, they are here to arrest you."

She snorted. "Arrest me? For what?"

I thought about that. In all the horror of it, and indeed, excitement, Mary and I had not thought to ask. "I don't know, Mamma, but the constable has a signed warrant."

"Did you read it?" she demanded. "Did they come from the inquest?"

"I think so, but I'm not certain." The thought struck me that Princess Maria had finally discovered her missing ring. But why would she have Mamma arrested? And then Eva Sandy, and the money I'd stolen. Had Lord Byron decided to get his revenge on me? Oh, I had so many sins. Why was Mamma the one they had come for?

She climbed out of bed and shook my arm. A sour smell emanated from her flesh. "Think, Jane."

I wriggled my shoulders. "Wash and dress, Mamma. You don't want to go on the street like this."

She stared at me, her face half illuminated. "You aren't joking."

I shook my head, mutely. In the bed, Papa let out a snore and rolled over. "Should I wake him?"

"Help me dress first." She went to the jug and basin and began her ablutions.

I removed Mamma's day dress from its peg, then opened the trunk to pull out a wool shawl she had just put away for the season. The embroidered shawl had no place in the lockup.

"I'll bet that Thérèse has cooked up something to have her revenge on me," she muttered, switching out her nightgown for a shift. "It is the continental way."

I could not imagine that our cook had the power to have her estranged mistress arrested, but I kept my thoughts to myself as she muttered about aristocrats. I helped Mamma with a petticoat, then handed her stockings, then worked on her stays, before we pinned her into her dress. She coiled up her hair while I pinned her shawl around her bodice for warmth.

"No tea, no coffee?" she asked.

"Mary is keeping an eye on the constables, Mamma. There are three of them."

Mamma bit her lip, then went and shook Papa's shoulder. "Wake up, man. There are bad tidings!" Then she turned to me. "Fetch me something to eat, Jane."

"They will wonder why I am running about. They already seemed concerned that you might flee. But Polly just put lunch in the dining room, and maybe you can stop there on the way down?"

She glared at me, then went to her shelf, pulled a covered dish of shortbread from it, and reached for a piece, biting into it savagely. "Is there any water left in the jug?"

I fetched it for her. She washed down the shortbread with a gulp.

Papa looked old and gray in the early afternoon light, whiskers catching bits of sun and glinting up from his face. "What is wrong?"

"Mamma is to be arrested," I told him. "The constables are downstairs."

"Arrested, Jane? Whatever for?" Papa rubbed his eyes.

"I don't know," I whined.

He sighed. "It must be for debt, because her name is on the business."

Mamma turned to him, wiping a water droplet from her chin. "Do you think some moneylender has moved on us because of Cannon's death?"

I handed Papa his breeches. "No one came but the constables."

"Not everyone enjoys seeing their dark deeds carried out," Papa said. "Is there a warrant?"

"Yes, but I didn't read it. This might be because of the inquest. I wish Shelley had called to give us an update. I had better return to Mary."

"What about Willy and Charles?" Mamma asked, worry starting to come into her voice.

"Do you want them to see this?" Papa asked.

She sniffed. "I want to see them. What if this is the end for me?"

"I'll get Willy," I promised and went to fetch my brother from his lessons. His tutor was teaching him boxing instead of Latin, but I had him in his coat and downstairs not too long after the others.

We came down the stairs as Papa argued with the constables, shaking the warrant.

"My wife is no murderer," he said. "Mr. Cannon had dozens of clients. This is absurd."

I put my hand to my chest. Mamma was being arrested for murder?

"You'll have to take it up with the magistrate, sir," the head constable said.

Behind the constables, Robert and Charles came in from the warehouse for the meal. They both looked confused at the sight of Constable Wharton and the others.

"Mamma?" Willy asked, breaking away from me. He flew down the stairs and threw himself against Mamma.

I put my hands over my mouth as my little brother burst into tears. His emotions seemed to spur the constables into motion. One of them opened the front door while the other two whirled Mamma around, away from Willy.

Mary grabbed for his shoulders as the constables ushered Mamma out the door.

"We'll fight this absurdity," Papa called to her. "You'll be home soon, Mrs. Godwin."

I started to come down, wanting to be a comfort like Mary, but instead, my knees gave way and I collapsed onto a stair. My vision fogged with tears.

Mamma was no saint, but I wasn't any better. Had I just seen my future? Would any of us in this cursed household avoid the gibbet?

"Your buttons are all wrong," Mary said, bending over Willy to fix his coat.

Charles paced back and forth in front of the door, slapping one fist into an open palm. "Unacceptable," he muttered.

Robert stepped into the front hall and patted Mary's arm, ignoring my tears. "What will you do, Mr. Godwin?"

Mary looked up and sniffed. The sheen of tears added luster to her eyes. The sight of them through my own blurred vision made me feel even worse. I dropped my head into my hands.

Papa pulled on his coat lapels. "I can do nothing with this dreadful ringing in my ears. I need coffee. Mary, get a luncheon on the table for us all. After I dine, I will need to start paying calls."

"Lunch is already there. You know a great number of important people," Mary said. "Surely this is persecution."

Papa nodded. "You are correct, and I will get to the bottom of this. I need to spread the word. Letters. There are many letters I must write."

Robert bowed his head. "I have a good hand, sir. Please dictate to me as soon as you've dined."

"An excellent suggestion," Papa allowed. "We can get them into the next post."

They went up the stairs, ignoring me.

"What will you do, Charles?" Mary asked.

He shrugged. "There is nothing to do but continue the business of the day. We need the income."

"Shouldn't someone write Fanny?" Mary asked.

Charles rolled his eyes and took Willy's arm. "Come on, Willy, let's fetch some food for you. Then you can help me in the warehouse after your tutor leaves." They went up the stairs.

I stared through the outer door, where I half expected to find a crowd on the cobblestones outside, staring at us and waiting for the gossip. But most people who lived in this neighborhood were incarcerated, and it wasn't as if there had been any of the sort of shouting to bring people from their work. Instead, a herd of cows plodded by, and not a few sheep, the only humans their herders.

Mary shuddered at the smell and closed the door behind her brothers. "I need coffee."

"How can you think of t-that," I gasped. "My stomach is all in knots."

"I am too cold to think," Mary said. She came to the stairs and held out her hand. "Come with me to the fire. If Polly isn't working through all this commotion, I swear I will box her ears."

Her violent outburst sent a fresh flood of tears down my face. I didn't seem to be able to stop them. I lurched to my feet like an uncoordinated child. Mary put her hands to my waist before I could fall.

"Whatever is the matter with you?" she demanded. "You have to pull yourself together. We have a business to run, and Papa will be of no use at all. His only thought will be to help Mamma."

I sniffed hard. "We can't manage the accounts. We aren't trained." My breath came out in short pants. My chest hurt. It wouldn't allow me to draw a deep breath. I passed my hand over my eyes. Dark spots drifted behind my eyelids.

Mary pulled me down the last two stairs, then supported me into the passage leading to the kitchen stairs. "I don't have time for your hysterics, Jane. Compose yourself."

She opened the door leading down to the kitchen. I danced back, feeling like my insides were about to flow out of every orifice I possessed. I put my hands over my ears.

Mary shook her head at me. "What is wrong? This is some misunderstanding. I don't trust Mamma one bit, but I cannot imagine she strangled John Cannon with Papa's scarf."

"What?" I asked, the word coming out in a high keen.

"I think Papa may have done this," she said. "When I recognized the scarf, I knew we were involved somehow. He seems so ill, though. Do you think Charles did it? Or Shelley defended us, with his hero about to enter a sponging house?"

I reared back, accidentally cracking my head against the wall. The shock was enough to drop me to my knees.

Mary crouched next to me. "Sweet heavens. Did you kill him? I didn't know you had the strength, but well done if you did."

I closed my hands around Mary's apron. "Are you mad? I am no killer."

"You're acting like a hysteric. Perhaps you don't remember?" She stared hard at me, then relaxed her face. "No, the killer shot at us from upstairs."

"We don't have any guns in the house," I muttered, fighting a sudden lassitude that meant I was likely to swoon.

"Papa's scarf, yet a gun," Mary mused. "It is quite a puzzle, with pieces that don't fit together."

"Do you believe in hell?" I asked.

"I'm sure Mamma will spend eternity there," she said in a cool tone.

"So will I." I put my hands over my face and sobbed.

"Come, Jane, you are not so bad as that."

"You don't know," I moaned.

"Know what? You didn't kill the Russians, or have our cook arrested, or strangle Mr. Cannon." She wiped her nose. "We don't have time for this, Jane. Pull yourself together."

I hiccupped, bringing the taste of foul bile into my mouth. "I'm a thief."

"I know that," she said patiently. "But I thought we agreed to be done with that. You said you wouldn't do it again."

"I did worse," I said. I crossed my arms over my bodice and let my head fall against the wall. I scarcely felt the pain. Did I have a fever? I couldn't stop shaking.

"Did you steal from the money box?" Mary asked, kneeling in front of me.

I swallowed hard. It didn't help the taste to go away. "I stole from Princess Maria."

She said nothing for a moment. "How?"

I told her about the ring I found. "And then I stole from Miss Sandy." Somehow, admitting it calmed me. "Not that it did any good in either case. The ring went in the cache of things we gave to Mr. Cannon the first time he threatened to take Papa to the sponging house."

"What did you take from Miss Sandy?"

I gathered myself. "Her purse that had enough money to live on for a month. I will be caught, and the whole family will be hanged together."

Her eyelids fluttered as she took in my confession. "Were those the coins you so brazenly gave Mr. Cannon to make him go away?"

I nodded. "But I still have the purse. It's a lovely bit of hand-worked lace over a silk lining."

"Burn it, Jane," Mary said. She stood, looking impatient. "The ring and money are no longer in our possession. That's the last tie to this nonsense of yours. I'm not about to be hanged with you. I did nothing wrong."

"Lusting after a married man is a sin too, I'm quite sure," I snapped.

"Fanny and I will be hanged for that?" Mary inquired, not denying my accusation. "It matters not in either case. I will wed Robert, and Shelley thinks of Fanny in a most sisterly way."

"I don't want to burn it." I sniffed. "I am such a sinful creature. I will never make a friend. The purse is all I will have to remember her by."

Mary clenched her teeth, then suddenly, before I could react, she set her hands to my neck. Her throat worked. "How does this feel, Jane Clairmont? Is this the last sensation you want to feel? Not a soft breeze caressing your face, or a soft sheet under your hand, but tight, squeezing, rough-hewn pressure, and then the drop?" She let go of my neck and pushed hard on my shoulders.

Despite her slight stature, kitchen work was already toughening her up. My knees buckled. I let myself fall against the wall and slid down, sobbing into my hands. She was right, I knew it. Though she hadn't hurt me, the skin of my neck tingled from the sandpaper feeling of her hands.

Mary growled and whirled around, then left the kitchen. I stayed on the floor. I deserved no better spot. Marinating in my misery, I had no urge to move. I heard footsteps a couple of minutes later, but it was only Polly.

"You had better stoke the fire," I said between sniffs. "Mary will want it hot."

"Mrs. Godwin won't like the coal bill."

My hands shook as I lifted my face. "She's in the lockup, Polly. Her orders won't matter. Throw on some bloody coal!"

She hurried to adjust the fire, then left the room. I was too poisonous for even a servant's company. The heat burnished my face. Sweat coated my hairline and dripped under my arms. After the drop Mary had brought to life for me, this was my fate. If I believed in religion, that was.

I wiped my eyes. I didn't believe. Earthly punishment, tangible and full of pain, was bad enough. But when life ended, I'd be asleep, nothing more. I rubbed the moisture from my face and turned around. I'd been a fool. I needed to protect myself. Mary had the sense of it, as usual.

Chapter 18

Jane

When Mary came back into the kitchen, she had the little purse I had stolen from Miss Sandy tucked under her arm. I took it from her and set it on the table, then realized this wasn't Miss Sandy's purse at all but one Fanny had made. Mary hadn't recognized it, since Fanny had constructed it last autumn while Mary was away in Scotland.

With Fanny gone, there was no one to correct Mary's mistake. Miss Sandy's purse was much nicer, anyway. I sliced up all the tidy seams Fanny had sewn and cut the handmade lace into strips. I hesitated over the pink silk lining, fabric that had, I believed, once belonged to Mary and Fanny's mother. It could be turned into a handkerchief, but my hesitance might betray Mary's mistake. I destroyed the pink silk, too, and then we fed it into the fire, piece by piece.

As it disintegrated into ash, my breath caught and shuddered with each flare of the flames hiding my shame, doubled now. I had destroyed something of Mary Wollstonecraft's to hide my own theft. I coughed at times, between the smoke catching at my throat and my shame-filled internal workings.

"Do you think people like Lord Byron are ever troubled by their choices?" I asked. "Or is it only us poor girls who think ill of ourselves?"

"We all have our troubles," Mary said sharply. "High- or lowborn. You only have to recall Lord Byron's poetry to know he feels deeply." She quoted:

And now Childe Harold was sore sick at heart,
And from his fellow bacchanals would flee;
'Tis said, at times the sullen tear would start,
But pride congealed the drop within his e'e:
Apart he stalked in joyless reverie,
And from his native land resolved to go,
And visit scorching climes beyond the sea;
With pleasure drugged, he almost longed for woe,
And e'en for change of scene would seek the shades below.

I rubbed my eyes and shivered a little as she quoted, the words sinking in. "Childe Harold would die in the poem, just to change his place."

"Is that what you want?" Mary asked, setting down her pencil. "Would you die to be gone from here?"

I put my hands to my neck. I could not deny she'd made an impression on my thoughts. "No. My reputation is one thing, but my life?"

Mary paced in front of me, ruminating. "I can't take an admitted thief to the religious and proper Baxters in Scotland." She stopped and stared at me, then began to move again. "But then, will Robert propose at all, given our household turmoil?"

"I hope so," I said. My hands dropped. I was not the only one in despair. I was being selfish. We had to do something.

She whirled around. "He is my only hope of escape."

"I am sorry to say it, but I don't know what your chances are to become his bride," I admitted. "He frightened you with talks of legal clerking and such."

Now both her hands flew into my face. "But then he wanted to speak to Papa last night and before that, me. Do you think, in advance of all of this horror with John Cannon, that they were speaking upon marriage?"

I reached for her hands. When I felt the icy chill of them, despite the fire, some of my fear leached out of me with this evidence of her distress. "They must have been. All will be well. I will finish burning the purse and never, ever, admit what I've done to anyone but you. Only you know what I've done."

She squeezed my hands. "Do you promise?"

I nodded, and proved myself by letting her go and snatching up the last of the scraps. I fed them into the fire, calm enough to lament as each pretty piece of lace or pink silk transformed into ash. I told myself to hear each little pop of disintegrating thread as a bit of my sin disappearing forever, however falsely, beyond the reach of man, into the void. The void could forgive me, if humanity would not.

When it was all gone, Mary nodded at me. "Fetch some writing paper. We need to send word to Fanny. Surely Papa will fetch her home now, with Mamma gone."

"Don't you want to do it?" Breathing in the fire had left my eyes so burning tired that I wanted to lie down.

"I need to prepare some hot food. Bannocks, I think." She forced a smile. "It's a domestic life for me."

I pushed my fists into my belly. "Please hurry. I need something to fill this hole inside me. I will go write Fanny."

I felt I had to do penance, even with Mamma imprisoned. Not only that, I continued to be unwilling to be alone. I woke at the sounds of Mary's steps on the floorboards on Saturday morning and leapt out of my bed to join her. After helping her fasten the bits of her clothing that Polly usually helped with, we dressed me, then went downstairs together.

When we were bringing up the pot of tea, the leftover bannocks from the afternoon before, and the last of the sausages to the dining room, we heard a knock on the door. Shelley was visible through the window. I set my tray on the table and let him in.

"Come up to the dining room," Mary invited, smiling.

"Is there any news?" he asked soberly.

"I think Papa was in a kind of daze," she said as I went on ahead.

Shelley picked up my tray and followed us up, then went through the dining room door after I opened it.

Mary shrugged and set her tray directly on the table, then went to the sideboard to gather teacups and plates for us there. By the time we filled our bellies, all of the bannocks were gone and half of the sausages.

"It should be fine." Mary set her fork down. "Only Charles is likely to be down to eat this early. He can have what is left."

"Your father?" Shelley inquired.

Mary's expression was sour. "I doubt he'll be up early. I don't believe he has a conscience as guilty as Jane's, whatever he may have done."

"You bring up two important points of interest," Shelley said. "First, what is it that you think Godwin has done?"

Mary bared her teeth before subsiding into a gentler expression. "The scarf around Mr. Cannon's neck belonged to my father. You know what that suggests. What else could I believe?"

Shelley's eyebrows winged as he spoke for both of us. "This is discouraging news. Why didn't you remove it when we could have?"

Mary's hands fluttered over her plate. "It all happened too fast, Shelley. The shots started coming at us. If you think about it, we were there such a short period of time."

He pushed his fingers into the curls at his temples. "I do not like this at all. We must forget that scarf, Mary. Who else would recognize it but you?"

"Fanny, who is gone," she said. "Mamma, probably, though she may have thought it was thrown out."

"It is too late to forget the scarf, for they arrested Mamma," I pointed out. "Someone must have identified it."

He fixed me with those brilliant blue eyes. "I doubt they know about the scarf. Unless your Papa wore such a loathsome thing in public."

"It was fine before the dye leached from the wool," Mary said. "I hope he has not worn it since."

"But its earlier incarnation would not be recognizable," Shelley suggested.

Mary nodded. "I do see what you are saying. We don't really know why Mamma was arrested and not Papa."

"They are fishing for answers," Shelley said. "They suspect her, or Godwin, and hope one might accuse the other or some such."

I gasped. "Can they do that?"

"It seems reasonable to me," Shelley said. "They may have thought your mother would tell the full tale of Mr. Cannon's death out of fear."

I realized something important. "She doesn't know about the scarf. She never saw the body."

"Unless she put it around Mr. Cannon's neck in the first place," Mary said. "But I don't believe it. She's a violent creature, but I cannot see her having the strength to kill Mr. Cannon."

Shelley swallowed his last bite and followed that with coffee. He wiped his mouth. "For now then, onto the second point. What does Jane have to be guilty about? Is this something new?"

I bit into the inside of my cheek, then spoke indignantly before Mary could say anything more. "Mary has betrayed my confidence."

"Shelley must know all, if he is to help us," Mary said. "I'm sorry, Jane. But the truth will not leave this room."

I stared at her, struck by with the realization that she already saw the poet as a part of the family, of herself even, despite her theoretical commitment to Robert.

"What is it, Jane?" Shelley asked in the mildest of tones.

"I stole from Lord Byron's mistress," I said quickly.

Shelley frowned, as did my sister.

"That is not all," Mary said, her words trailing off to make me reveal the full truth.

"I stole from Princess Maria before that," I added, feeling sulky.

Shelley made a little growling noise. "The mistress is one thing, but Princess Maria? Those that surround her are inclined to violence, Jane. I am most disappointed in you."

"But the circumstance will explain all," I cried, and told him about the ring being left in our parlor the first night we'd met the visitors.

"Your behavior is terrible," Shelley said inexorably. Light streamed through the windows, wreathing him in angelic sunbeams, his fresh-shaven cheeks and purity of expression giving him the look of a youth no more than Robert's age. "I cannot imagine why your impulses lead you down these dark paths."

"You are purer than I am," I said with a sniffle. "Forgive me, Shelley. We have so little, and when I saw, both times, an easy way to acquire something for myself, I took it. It did no good. Both results of my thefts went to Mr. Cannon in an attempt to save Papa. You cannot deny that the moneylender was the biggest thief of us all."

"You might think yourself a new Robin Hood, but look at how the universe has repaid Mr. Cannon for his crimes," Shelley said. "Do you want to die by human hand as well?"

My lips trembled. I had every intention of living a full life despite my despair the day before. "I will try to learn a lesson from this."

"The lesson you have learned so far was to stop stealing from your own household and to steal from outsiders instead," Mary snapped.

I tightened my lips. "I see that this is how it looks, but the ring was here in the house. Tell me, Mary, would you have taken it to the Pulteney Hotel?"

"Yes," she said, very earnestly. "I'd have used it to curry favor with Princess Maria, before we learned about their dastardly plans. She could have been a literary patron for the Juvenile Library, or even my future works. We didn't know back then that they weren't exactly in funds."

I hung my head over my plate, my dark curls obscuring my vision. "I see why your approach would have been sensible."

"We cannot let any of this get out," Shelley said. "Lord Byron is much too important a person, even if his mistress is not."

"We aren't going to be able to retrieve the money or ring from greedy Mr. Cannon's house, if the items are still there." Mary set her plate on top of mine.

"There is no way to connect them to Jane," Shelley said. "As long as the three of us never admit anything. Is there any other evidence?"

"Destroyed last night," Mary said, adding utensils to her pile. "There is nothing else we can do."

"I'm not worried," Shelley said. "We can't admit her thieving ways or Jane will be arrested and hanged or transported. Jane's secret must be kept at all costs."

"We agreed about that." I looked between them, both with deep resolution in their expressions. I felt guilty but knew we had to hide the truth. Instinctively, I jumped up and hugged Mary, then ran around the table to do the same to Shelley.

The door opened, hitting Mamma's precious Greek-inspired wallpaper with a bang. Charles entered, dispelling the mood.

"Is this all there is to eat?" he said with a frown as he looked at the limited spread on the table.

"You are lucky to get that, with the house in an uproar," Mary said, then stood up, gathered the pile of empty dishes, and walked out, leaving us to stare after her.

"It's a good thing Mamma isn't here to see you hugging a married man," Charles said, pulling the remaining platters toward himself. "Get me a cup of tea, Jane."

"Shelley is a better brother to me than you are," I said, feeling better for the comfort of those hugs, even though I had offered them. I released Shelley.

"Any thoughts on what is to be done about your mother?" Shelley asked, winking at me before directing his attention to Charles.

"She has the wit to think of someone else to hang the crime on," Charles said carelessly, sliding the rest of the food onto the sausage platter. "They'll probably arrest Polly next, leaving Mary and Jane to do all the work around here. Will do them good. Keep them out of trouble."

"I can well believe that, though I think Polly is a difficult case to make," Shelley said. "She's a rather slim creature, is she not?"

"She's strong," I said. "Have you ever noticed her forearms? Turning spits and the housework has developed her musculature. She's better at carrying buckets than Mary or me."

"Do you think she's involved?" Shelley asked me.

I tossed my head and laughed. "I'm just trying to think like Mamma would. I cannot imagine she will accept her unearned fate lightly."

"Then let us go to the coroner," Shelley said. "I want to suggest he attempt to tie Mr. Cannon's death to the Naryshkin murder. We can explain the Godwin connections to both situations and Mr. Cannon's greed, along with the missing diamonds."

"It's Saturday," I said. "The inquest happened yesterday. Why didn't you testify to all this?"

"I don't think the coroner understood the points I attempted to make," Shelley said. "There was a great deal of noise, and he might have been half-sprung, anyway. Focus, Jane. We have to free your mother."

"There he is. Finally!" Shelley exclaimed later that morning. He pointed out George Hodgson, the coroner for Middlesex, seated at a table with several cronies, in the third Covent Garden-area tavern Shelley had looked into.

An unexceptional middle-aged man clutched a tankard. Mary looked expectantly at our poet companion.

"I hope that this early in the day, he isn't too deep into his cups," Shelley said. "Wait here, ladies."

We left the doorway as he entered and leaned against the wall to protect our backs.

Down the street, a street singer warbled a ballad about a country murder. A companion attempted to hawk song sheets, but the verses were nothing exceptional. A strawberry seller walked past us, pushing a wheelbarrow, shouting out the prices of his wares. I could smell the sweet, herbal notes of the fruit. If Mamma had been with us, coins would have been produced from somewhere in an instant, and Thérèse would have been baking her famous strawberry tart for dinner tonight.

"Do you think Mamma and Thérèse will receive the same fate?" I asked, my voice trembling.

"The innocent can be set free," Mary said. "If we can sort out this mess, Mamma will be fine. Perhaps her experience will give her a change of heart about our cook."

I snorted. "Mamma? I cannot imagine anything changing her opinions."

Mary shrugged. "You asked."

Shelley came through the door, his hand tucked under the arm of the coroner. Mr. Hodgson stumbled a bit, but it might have been the unevenness of the floor. Shelley looked both ways, then spotted Mary and towed his companion toward us.

"What is all this?" the coroner spluttered. "I have nothing to say to any of you."

"We are trying to aid you, sir," Shelley said. "So that you can close this Russian business before the festivities are fully underway."

"The dignitaries are going to the opera tonight," Mr. Hodgson said. "You are leaving it a bit late."

"Events occur on their own timeline," Shelley said.

"Well, man, tell me your news." The coroner's tone was testy. Probably because he'd been pulled from his porter.

"The Naryshkin family made contact with my father as soon as they came to London," Mary said. "He is William Godwin, the celebrated author."

"I know him. He's infamous, in any case. He was part of the Pavel Naryshkin matter, and another recently, if I recall."

Mary nodded, ignoring the insult. "The very same. We have remained in close communication with the Russians since that first meeting, visiting them both at the Pulteney Hotel and at our house in Skinner Street."

"What of it?"

"The Naryshkins all but admitted that their footman, Fedorov, killed the secretary found in the Thames. You know, the man who was thought to be Pavel Naryshkin at first."

"Until Mr. Shelley here found the real corpse," the coroner said.

"Exactly," I said earnestly. "But now, this dreadful footman, Mr. Fedorov, who attacked our cook in our own kitchen, has disappeared."

"He shouldn't have been released from the lockup, unlike some other people," Mary added.

The coroner glanced at each of us in turn. "You are telling me that we had the right man all along?"

Shelley nodded. "The right killer, the wrong name for the victim, Mr. Hodgson, yes. I don't know that you could pull a foreign count into your coroner's court, but there you go."

"Disappeared, eh?" The coroner's eyelids fluttered. "Well, we can put out a flyer describing him. See if he can be picked up anywhere in the kingdom."

"I'll go with you and describe him for your secretary," Shelley said. "To expedite the matter."

"What about us?" I asked.

"Go along home," the coroner instructed.

Mary turned without a word and marched off. I stayed close to her, holding her arm. I could feel how upset she was from the contracted muscles of her upper arm. She didn't want to be out here without protection any more than I did, in this neighborhood where we'd been attacked before.

Chapter 19

Mary

Mary felt so perfectly dreadful that by the time they reached Skinner Street, her nerves permitted her to do nothing but make a pot of tea when she returned to the kitchen.

"We need bread," she told Polly, who was stirring the fire. "And sausages. I'm sure Willy needs more food than we've been providing. I think he's grown an inch in the past month. And there is Mr. Baxter to feed as well. Is there anyone left who will give us credit?"

"Mrs. Godwin always gave us the week's shopping money on Saturday," Polly said.

Mary's stomach gurgled. "I think we paid our account with the butcher across from Smithfield recently."

"I'll try there," Polly said. "I do fancy some fresh air." She plucked her bonnet off a nail and went upstairs, still in her apron.

What were they going to do? Papa would not tolerate any change to the household routine, but they couldn't possibly handle the laundry with two fewer pairs of hands. How could they keep the bookshop open? Who would manage the bookstore accounts with Mamma gone? As much as she disliked her stepmother, she could not deny the woman did a great deal of work. They would be in difficult circumstances indeed if she could not be extricated from the lockup.

Mary drank her tea with her feet propped up in front of the fireplace. Settled in with a rare moment to herself, she had queer thoughts about the members of her own household.

Did Papa frame Mamma for Mr. Cannon's murder? Though he was the best of men, he tolerated no changes to the order of his life. As a result, would he allow Mamma's suffering to continue in the same manner they had treated their cook? Would he consider the sacrifice of his wife acceptable to end John Cannon's very real threat of debtors' prison for himself? His political linchpins included the end of government, which should naturally give way before reasonable men. What would he do to stay out of the clutches of the prison system? He would never believe he deserved to go to debtors' prison. He had a right to take money he needed from those who had it, he'd said.

Mary dropped her head into her hands. Would her father sacrifice a woman for his own freedom?

Footsteps sounded behind her.

Mary whipped around, tucking down her skirts, but it was only Jane. "I thought you were going to open the bookshop."

"I'm freezing," Jane whined.

Mary pointed to the teapot. "Me, too, at least in my heart."

"What are we going to do?" Jane asked, taking a cup from the shelf.

"We cannot free Mamma if Papa is guilty," Mary said. "This is what plagues me."

"We need someone else to pin Mr. Cannon's murder on." Jane bumped the table, making Mary's chair rattle.

"Someone who is guilty of bad things, even if not specifically this death?" Mary suggested.

Jane poured her tea. "Is there any cream?"

"Who would have time to fetch it?"

"Where is Polly?"

Mary drained her cup. "I sent her to try to get food on credit. Mamma always handed out the kitchen money on Saturdays, but I don't know where the household money is."

"Locked into the office, maybe?"

Mary worried at her lip. "Will Papa know? When I returned home in March, I went into training for the bookshop, not the household. That was Fanny's department."

"You have to ask him."

"Ask Papa for money? Now?" Mary's blood ran cold at the idea.

"We have to eat." Jane wiped a stray tea leaf from the lip of her cup.

"Now I begin to wish you'd kept Miss Sandy's stolen money for yourself," Mary said. She had a small coin stash of her own but wasn't ready to dip into it, not yet. The day might soon come, however.

The house shook as the front door opened and closed.

"Blast," Jane muttered, then tossed back her tea. She went upstairs, leaving the kitchen blissfully quiet again.

Mary didn't like any of her thoughts. She'd have to face Papa. A scolding from him would send her spirits plummeting even lower than they were, but Jane was right. They had to eat.

Polly came back with a paltry package of day-old newsprint. Inside were sausages, slightly brown instead of a healthy pink, the same vintage or worse than the newspaper. Trading sighs, they fried them up with some eggs they habitually traded with neighbors who had a small garden, who were allowed to borrow volumes from Papa's library.

Mary carried the food up and Polly followed with the refreshed teapot, on its third use of the leaves. In the dining room, Papa sat with Jane and Shelley. Thankfully, Charles was out on business, and Willy, accompanied by Robert, had gone walking with his tutor.

Polly boldly curtsied next to Papa and said, "Sir, I ordered these sausages on credit, but I need the coins to pay for them and tomorrow's roast or there won't be meat for Sunday dinner."

"Go back to the kitchen, Polly," Papa said, not even bothering to look in her direction.

Polly's lips pursed alarmingly. She whirled around and left the dining room.

Mary and Jane shared a glance. How long would it be until their kitchen maid fled? Mary hoped her wages weren't in arrears. She knew nothing about the household accounts.

Even worse, not knowing Shelley would be present, she had provided nothing for him to eat. Tears welled up in her eyes. She bowed her head, begging God to have mercy on her and allow her to remain calm through all of these troubles. How much was she to bear?

The lines of exhaustion were evident on Papa's face. Even Shelley had dark circles under his eyes. A real gentleman, though, he knew when it was time to take charge.

"Godwin," he said, the instant Papa had cleared his plate. Shelley himself had taken nothing but wine. "You must find proof to present to Mr. Hodgson the coroner in order to save Mrs. Godwin. He is willing to listen to us. We saw him just this morning."

Mary watched closely. Would Papa show any sign of guilt? His expression retained its customary air of mild attention, however.

"If you have any suggestions, I am ready to hear them," Papa said, gesturing to Jane to pour him another cup of tea.

She tipped the spout over his cup, but only dribbles came out. Emblematic of the day, really.

Mary pushed her half-finished sausage to Papa. "I have sufficiently lined my stomach. I will refill the pot."

"Wait a moment, daughter," Papa said. "Shelley?"

"We need to return to Mr. Cannon's house," Shelley said. "We could not get upstairs yesterday due to the gunman."

"Can we enter?" Papa forked up the rest of Mary's sausage.

"Unless he had family that is securing the place, I do not see why not."

Papa took a bit and chewed thoughtfully. "Very well."

After they all walked to Bedford Street, the foursome discovered that even a moneylender's home became unguarded when there was no one living to pay the security bills.

The door had an old-fashioned key plate. Shelley rattled the doorknob. "Locked," he informed them, "but it is very similar to those at Field Place. Could you lend me a hairpin, Jane?"

Jane pulled a securing pin from one of her curls, then moved to block Shelley from passersby.

"A little to the left, Jane," Shelley said. "I need the light."

She shuffled until he could see. Mary linked her arm with Jane's to further shield him. Not sixty seconds later, she heard a click. Shelley snickered in satisfaction, and the door swung open.

"Make haste," he said, and stretched out a hand to Papa, who stepped in, not commenting on Shelley's chicanery.

The trio followed, shutting the door behind them.

"It's dark in here with the shades drawn," Papa commented, moving to the back wall.

"We won't find anything down here," Shelley said as Papa opened the inner door, which wasn't locked. "Let's go upstairs."

Mary sniffed the air, wondering if the scent of death still lingered in the closed space. It smelled of nothing but dust in the antechamber, though when they went into the office, where Mr. Cannon had lain, Jane recoiled against her.

"Come, Mary," Jane whined, tugging at her. "It smells even worse than the Bow Street lockup in here."

They all hesitated at the foot of the steps, but no shot rained down on them this time. Brave Shelley set his boot to the first step. Mary and Jane followed, with Papa bringing up the rear.

The stairs opened to a long passage above. On the left they found a bedroom with a luxurious coverlet and hangings in a fashionable shade of green. The bed had been torn apart, however. The mattress was half off the frame, and sheets were crumpled on the floor. A painting of a boy in Elizabethan clothes holding a lute rested on the floor, its frame broken.

Shelley walked around the bed. "Overturned tables, broken ewer."

Papa went to the fireplace. "Ashes all over the place. I don't know if it was the gunman or the constables who did it, but I'd say the room has been searched."

Mary regarded the painting. The boy's watchful eyes stared into eternity. "If it was the killer, he must have been looking for a hidden safe."

"That's what I would do," Shelley agreed. "I wonder where Mr. Cannon came from, that no heirs have arrived. He had a London accent. South of the river, I'd say."

"Surrey, probably," Papa said. "I remember him telling me he had no sons, or brothers either."

"Regardless, people could come at any time," Mary said. "We should hurry."

"Can we find something the killer didn't?" Jane asked.

Mary didn't like her skeptical tone. "We interrupted him, so why not?" She marched out of the room.

Across the passage, instead of the parlor one might expect to find in the home of one who entertained, was another study. A large iron safe covered half of the rear wall. Was it for show, possibly hiding the fact that a smaller hidden safe still remained in the house?

Mary went to it and tugged at the knob, but the safe kept its secrets secure. She could not begin to imagine where the key might be, and opening it would, in any case, turn her into a thief. They were looking for something to tie Cannon to Pavel Naryshkin's murder, not money, after all.

Shelley came through the doorway. "As I thought, the real office."

"The desk chair is overturned," Mary observed.

"But the drawers are unopened." Shelley offered her that sweet smile she adored. "This must be where the killer was interrupted by us."

He opened the first drawer on the left. Mary saw there were drawers on each side, along with one in the middle. She opened the three drawers on the right. They held ink, spare quills, pieces of cheap notepaper, and a selection of ledgers.

Mary dropped the ledgers on the desk and looked at the notation. "Ha!" she said, when she deciphered the first page. Mr. Cannon had kept them in some order.

"Come here, Papa," she called.

"What is it, child?" Papa asked, stepping in.

She poked one of the ledgers with her finger. "This one has G-H-I in it. Find your name."

While he looked through, she opened a bottle of ink and prepared a quill pen.

"Here I am," he said.

Jane looked over his shoulder. "That is an old debt. See?" She put her finger to the line. "You paid it in full last year."

Shelley chuckled. "Canceling your debt?"

"If we can find it," Papa said, his voice going grim. "I owe the dead nothing, and their legal successor even less."

Mary handed her loaded quill to Jane and went to the center drawer. "It's locked," she said, after unsuccessfully tugging at it.

Shelley produced Jane's hairpin from a pocket and knelt down to fiddle with the lock. As usual unrestrained by a hat, his springy light brown curls begged Mary's fingers to smooth them. She clenched her fingers and turned away.

"Found the new figure," Papa said. "Jane, what date shall we write?"

"Wednesday," she said decisively. "A day before he died, but too late for him to have been thought to have commented about it to anyone."

"Done," Papa said.

"I'll make the writing look as much like his as I can." Jane poked her tongue inside her cheek and carefully wrote on the line.

"What about his enforcers?" Papa asked. "They might know what happened that day."

"Make the date Thursday, Jane," Mary said. "If Papa paid the morning before Mr. Cannon died, that would be good."

"No," Papa said. "That makes me look guilty of the murder."

"I disagree, sir," Shelley said. "It makes you look innocent."

"Hurry, Jane." Mary pulled blotting paper from the drawer.

When Jane had completed her forgery, she and Mary surveyed the rest of the room while Papa tidied away the drawers. Eventually, Shelley popped open the center drawer, after Jane had taken up a stance behind the curtains, keeping an eye on the street.

"What is in there?" Mary asked, returning to the desk.

Shelley started lifting out small boxes. "He seems to have used this drawer as a sort of safe." He opened one and found monogrammed cufflinks. Another held a necklace of carnelian beads. A third held a cameo.

"Nothing of great value," Papa observed. "Maybe this was Cannon's version of a pawnshop."

"Only for the best customers," Shelley drawled. He held out another set of cufflinks. "Recognize the initials?"

Papa chuckled. "Only the best customers indeed."

Mary reached into the drawer and pulled out another box. This one was a treasure in itself, of black lacquer with a painted top. A talented artisan had painted a golden nest with creamy eggs. Two birds sat vigil on either side, and the edges were painted with vivid blue, red, and yellow flowers.

"That's Russian," Shelley said. "The workmanship is unmistakable."

Mary nodded. "Evidence of the Naryshkins?" She opened the box. Inside, it seemed empty, but when she held it up, something slid across the box. Shelley reached in, then displayed what he pulled out between his thumb and forefinger.

"A diamond," Papa said bleakly. He put out his hand as if to touch it, then hastily put it behind his back.

"In a Russian lacquer box," Mary added. "It would be too much of a coincidence for it to belong to anyone but the Naryshkins."

"At least we now know," Shelley said. "The diamonds were real, and Mr. Cannon was indeed involved in their theft. Where are the rest?"

Jane, leaving the window, came toward them. "Who took the rest?"

They glanced between each other.

"There is no guarantee that the rest ever existed," Papa said. "No one ever saw them. Pavel Naryshkin may have intended to show me this one, or give it to me, and the rest was an empty promise, as many are."

"We know the princess doesn't have them, or she wouldn't be selling her jewels," Mary said. "We know you don't have them, Papa, nor Mamma."

"We can't say Mr. Cannon never had them, for he was a dreadful man," Jane declared.

Mary's gaze went to the safe. "What if the rest are in that safe, and he just kept this one in his locked drawer for some reason?"

"The drawer holds his talismans?" Shelley suggested. "And the safe holds the main treasure?"

Mary smiled. He understood her perfectly.

Papa cleared his throat. "They will need a skilled man to get in, whoever the heirs are. For now, we at least have a bit of evidence to tie these strange events together."

Shelley nodded. "I suggest we revisit the coroner. He has had more time with his porter, but hopefully he can still focus on the events at hand." He tucked the box into his coat.

They finished with a cursory look around the office. Mary caught Jane sidling toward the desk and gave her a steely stare.

Jane blushed. "What if the safe combination is written somewhere. The locked drawer is a likely spot."

Shelley pulled out the last couple of boxes. One held a watch and the other, a signet ring. "Sadly, no. I'm sure Cannon kept it in his head. Probably never even let his men up here."

"Let's find Mr. Hodgson," Papa said. "The sooner this business is sorted, the sooner we can extricate Mrs. Godwin from her predicament."

The phrase *the sooner* echoed in Mary's thoughts with each footstep she took. Mamma needed to return home, and she needed to find a different place for herself.

Once on the street, it did not take them long to reach Mr. Hodgson's favorite tavern. The coroner's table held a different group of cronies and empty tankards of porter, but his gaze still seemed clear enough.

"A word with you?" Shelley asked politely.

The coroner frowned but inclined his head respectfully to Papa. "Gentlemen, I must have my office." His friends picked up their tankards and drifted off.

When they were gone, he asked, "What is this?"

Shelley produced the lacquer box. "As you know, sir, Mr. Cannon seems not to have any heirs available presently, and his servants have disappeared. We took it upon ourselves to check the upstairs of his house, where we were prevented from egressing on the day of the murder due to the gunman upstairs."

"A gunman who was surely the murderer," Papa added. "My wife, sir, has never fired a weapon in her life, besides."

"What is this about?" Mr. Hodgson asked wearily.

Mary could smell spilled porter on his cravat. It mixed with the starch of his shirt and the smell of his pomaded hair, making her head swim a bit after the breathtaking circumstances of their search.

"We knew Mr. Cannon had an office upstairs," Shelley explained, setting the box in front of the coroner. "Look. A Russian box, with a diamond in it."

The coroner opened the box, rattled it around, then closed the box and examined it closely. "Russian, to be sure. But you said they promised you diamonds worth a thousand guineas. Did your wife take the rest?"

"I assure you that Mrs. Godwin does not have any money. She'd have used it to stave off imminent disaster with our finances," Papa said in his stiffest voice. "John Cannon was not our only creditor, just the pushiest. I am glad I was able to clear my loan that final morning of his life. My conscience is clean."

"Where did you find this box?" the coroner asked, not commenting on Papa's lie.

"In the desk in his upstairs office," Shelley said.

"We searched that room. Did you break into the safe?"

"How would we do that?" Shelley asked. "No, good sir, only the center drawer in the desk."

"You had better not have broken it," the coroner said sharply.

"Definitely not, merely fiddled with the lock a bit. No harm done," Shelley stated in his most winning manner. "I assure you, on my word, that only one diamond was in the box."

The coroner sighed and tucked the box inside his coat. Papa's head jutted forward, and Mary could see his fingers working, as if he wanted to snatch it away from the coroner.

"It is proof of our good intentions," Papa said, "that we brought it to you. You could ask people on the street who saw us coming from Mr. Cannon's residence."

"Mr. Cannon killed Mr. Naryshkin," Jane blurted. "Don't you see that this is proof? He knew about the diamonds and went to get them himself, so he could have them and make Papa find more money for his debt."

"I am sorry, child," Hodgson said. "But this is no evidence to free your mother."

"Why not?" Jane said, leaving her mouth hanging slightly open like a petulant child.

"My men did not break into any safes, nor drawers," said the coroner pointedly. "But we did have a look at the files in the desk. We took them with us, in fact."

Papa lifted his chin. "You found a file with my name on it?"

The coroner nodded. "It contained only a letter in John Cannon's hand."

"What did it say?"

"It seemed to be an analysis of the members of your household. It called Mrs. Godwin a dangerous woman. Evidence, you see." Mr. Hodgson struck his open palm with his fist.

"What did it call the rest of us?" Papa asked.

Mary stood very still. She knew he would not welcome any defense from her.

The coroner waved his hand. "When we searched the records, Mrs. Godwin was the only personage who seemed to concern him."

"Stuff and nonsense," Shelley declared. "You cannot tell me that Cannon was afraid of anyone."

The coroner smirked. "And yet he is the deceased party." He raised a finger, and a barmaid appeared as if summoned out of the fire, with a fresh tankard. She placed it in front of him, then whirled away. "I'd like to return to my meeting now."

"What are you going to do with the diamond?" Shelley asked.

"I hope you will verify its origin with Count Naryshkin," Mary said, unable to help herself.

"Indeed, child," the coroner murmured. "You can always count on me to do my duty." He lifted his tankard.

Papa took Mary's arm in one grip and Jane's in the other, then marched them out of the tavern. "We have done all we can here," he said when they reached the street.

Mary felt dizzy with rage. "Now what, Papa? This is unspeakable."

"Poor Mamma," Jane said.

"I am sure he will take the diamond to the count," Shelley said. "If only to curry favor. But if that solves the question of who killed Pavel Naryshkin, it does not answer who killed Cannon."

"I should think that is obvious," Papa said. "Count Naryshkin killed Mr. Cannon to revenge his brother's murder. Very Russian, that sort of thing. Mr. Hodgson will not want to go to the Pulteney Hotel unarmed or without constables. I cannot imagine the delicacy of the matter."

"Oh," Mary breathed. "The count did it. Of course." She felt her eyes twitch in their sockets as she took in the notion. Jane stole the princess's ring. Had Count Naryshkin stolen Papa's scarf off the peg in the front hall, perhaps blaming the Godwins for what had transpired? She could see how he or his men might.

Shelley nodded thoughtfully. "As always, your wisdom is evident, dear Godwin. I will ponder the matter further, but I expect you are correct."

"Come back to Skinner Street," Papa invited. "The girls need to return to their duties."

"Very well," Shelley agreed, "but I think the girls could use a bit of a treat tonight."

"I think not," Papa said.

"It might be to our benefit. The dignitaries are going out en masse to the opera house tonight. I thought I might walk over there with Mary and Jane after the evening meal. Who knows what we might see, safely in the crowd?"

"Oh, very well," Papa said. "But I do hope you will not see the Russians there. If only the coroner will do his duty between now and then."

Chapter 20

Jane

I closed the bookshop at five, then ran upstairs, holding a slim volume of Mary Wollstonecraft's *Mary* in my hand.

It had been a long day with a lot of walking back and forth to Covent Garden because of Mr. Cannon's murder already, but I needed to act. I couldn't risk being caught with the evidence of my choice, and the only path forward that I could see necessitated a trip to Maiden Lane.

Burning what Mary thought was Miss Sandy's purse might solve a problem, but I wanted to throw suspicion entirely off myself. No one—other than Mary and Shelley, who would never betray me—would ever know the truth.

I pulled the empty purse from its hiding place in a stretched-out wool stocking in my trunk and tucked it into my pocket. Down the stairs I went, hugging the wall to prevent the stairs from squeaking. I grabbed my bonnet and ran into the street, not taking the time to tell anyone I was leaving. If I wanted to go to the opera house with Shelley and Mary later, I needed to come and go quickly.

Since Lord Byron was keeping Miss Sandy, I wondered if she was already a singer at the Covent Garden Opera. It seemed unlikely, though. Maybe she was an apprentice. I suppose she could have met Lord Byron just about anywhere, though she clearly had ties to the opera, to have an acquaintance with Mrs. Jackson.

Hopefully, Alice, the maid, would be there in the Maiden Lane apartment, so I could let myself in and be alone long enough to tuck the purse behind a cushion or something.

I didn't really have a plan. But desperation makes for bravery, and I went up the steps to the apartment without having a clear notion of what to say to Alice.

I knocked smartly on the door, then paced in front of it with my hands in my pockets, my heart racing from the exertion of my fast travel and the heat of the day, which had not yet begun to dissipate. Bakeshops all along the way had been preparing evening meals, sending hot smoke into the air and making my stomach rumble.

I was thinking longingly of eel pie when the door opened. Miss Sandy herself stood there, looking cool in white muslin with blue ribbons and lace details.

I pulled my hands out of my pockets. She glanced down, a confused expression crossing her face.

I followed her gaze and found the little netted purse in my left hand. I blushed scarlet. If only I knew how to swoon. I thought fast.

"It is the strangest thing," I said, then started coughing from the dust in the streets.

"You had better come in," she said, tugging at my arm.

But she didn't invite me into the parlor this time. I was in trouble. Thinking fast, I claimed, "I can see you recognize this. I found it in a bush on the walk here."

"A bush?" she repeated.

"An ornamental one," I explained. "In a pot?"

"Oh." Her expression cleared. "On the corner."

I had no idea what she meant, but I was glad she had filled in my lies. I handed her the purse. She opened it, but it was empty.

"The thief who tossed it in the bush would have taken the money," she said sadly.

I nodded, a perfect thief myself, as little as I had profited from it. "Indeed, I am sure of it." I stared at my right hand, which oddly enough, I scarcely felt, as if it were detached from my body. I handed her the little volume of *Mary*. "Here is the book. I hope it brings memories of your mother."

"Oh, thank you." She smiled, and I knew she had not a shred of suspicion of me. Thank goodness I had thought to bring *Mary*. What a silly tale my fate rested on, but I had never thought she would open the door herself.

She went to the mantelpiece and opened a little box there. "I do not have the price of a book, but here are five shillings. A reward, I suppose."

"Lord Byron said to put the book on his account," I ventured.

"That was kind of him," she said, handing the money to me.

"He doesn't have an account with the Juvenile Library," I prattled. "He would have no use for children's books. But I am sure Papa would be honored to give him credit."

She smiled wanly.

I stared at the coins in my hand. "Me without a reticule," I said. She would never have offered me a reward if she had thought me a young lady of quality, rather than a shopgirl. My cheeks flushed. I was torn between being the thief I was and the girl I wanted to be.

I shook my head. "Are you singing at the Covent Garden Opera tonight?"

"Me, no. I've never been on the stage at all."

"Oh." I stared at my dusty shoes. "You are very good. I'm sure you could do it."

"You could as well."

I forced a smile. "Perhaps I will consult Lord Byron on the subject someday, when our teacher deems me ready."

She inclined her head.

"Well." I kept the false, humiliated smile on my face. "I wanted you to have the book I promised, and what good luck that I saw the purse on the way here. I will leave you to your evening."

"Please remember me to Miss Godwin," she said.

I curtsied and walked straight out of the apartment and down to the street. Terrible as I felt, I thought I was in the clear as to the theft.

Once again, though, I did not think I would return to Maiden Lane. My dreadful instincts had made me strange, and I had lost the chance to make a friend. Though the very shillings she had given me were enough to continue with my lessons, I must give them to Papa, given the dire state of our lives. Or better, use them to make Mamma more comfortable in prison for a few days.

This family was all I had, and I needed to stop fighting against that essential truth. If Mamma never came home from prison, I, like Fanny and Mary before me, would know the tender loss of a mother.

"My feet hurt dreadfully," I complained over the hum of the crowd, hours later, standing in the street outside the Covent Garden Opera House. We had come early enough to stand under an oil lamp. The light wasn't bad yet in any case, though evening was coming on. Mary and I had played at making shapes with a long piece of string I had knotted into a circle for a while, but I had grown bored of it. Fanny made the best shapes, in any case. I gave up and looped it half around my wrist and half around hers.

"Where are the dignitaries?" I further complained, but no one heard me. Mary's attention had turned entirely to Shelley, who whispered in her ear. I wished our friend would pay as much attention to me. Mary should have made Robert join us, but he and Willy had not yet returned.

The wide street felt as narrow as any three-hundred-year-old alley, with all the people crowded into it. Costermongers shouted out their wares, exhilarated by the unusual amount of trade, ignoring the men employed to keep the crowds away from the entrance as they darted around, so the carriages of the wealthy and important could arrive. A man with a violin and an enormous black mustache passed by us and winked at me. I turned away and licked a crumb off my glove.

Feeling guilty, I had paid for the eel pie I'd been craving earlier out of Miss Sandy's money. Mary had put an early dinner on the table at four, but it had been a sad affair of carefully portioned out cold ham from a street seller and potatoes.

I shared my pie with Mary, and she did not refuse a share. We had done a lot today on our pathetic rations. Even Shelley had a bit of crust, before he'd gone into a tavern for a refreshing glass of porter. When he returned, he had two friends with him. I never did hear their names because of the noise. They had enjoyed far more beverages than Shelley, and I could guess they were poets, because even if I couldn't hear much of what they said, I could tell the ends of their sentences rhymed.

"What is taking so long?" I said in Mary's ear, after another half hour had passed. The sun had sunk a little lower, and clouds were starting to cover the bright summer blue of the sky.

She stood on tiptoe to ask Shelley the question and he conferred with his friends. Eventually, the answer was passed down to me. "The Prince Regent, the emperor of Russia, and many others are dining at Fife House."

I knew enough to understand that it was the prime minister's house, which meant a great deal of speechifying and posturing in front of the foreign visitors.

Finally, as church bells struck six, a little after the theater doors normally opened, a few carriages arrived in front of the theater, moving slowly enough that a phalanx of liveried footmen could keep pace on foot. Even the transports were dwarfed by the large building, and the elegant people exiting them seemed tiny.

The crowd surged forward to see the upper classes arrive. I kept hold of Mary, the yarn encircling my wrist cutting into the skin above my glove. Shelley had his arm around her—in case she lost her balance, I supposed. Did he worry the kidnappers could carry her off in such a crush?

The line of guards broke at the announcement of a notorious earl's name. I lost sight of Shelley's friends. All I could do was hold tightly to Mary's hand and be swept along in the crowd's wake. We climbed the shallow steps, and before I knew it, we'd gone through the columns and into the theater—without paying, no less.

People were out in their multitudes, streaming in every direction to claim spots in the pit and gallery before anyone could remove them from their free entertainment. The guards were shouting, "Make way," but only managing to clear a narrow passage through the crowd.

"Come," I heard Shelley say. "It will be safer on the Grand Staircase."

Mary's hand jerked and I was led off, along the front of the crowd. One of the guards shouted at me, close enough to my face that I could see the dead tooth centered in his lower gum, but I would not let go of Mary for anything. Besides, we were doing nothing different from anyone else. We passed by people dressed in finery and the plainest garb. All the classes were intermingled, as always happened at the theater, though generally people were not so crowded together as they were on this June night. And they usually had paid.

The theater was very grand, with columns everywhere and

arched ceilings. After a while, I ignored the human parade and focused on the architecture, wondering how my voice might sound in such a grand space. I gathered up myself and sang a middle C. I thought I kept my volume low, but Mary gave me a curious glance, then turned to Shelley as he spoke into her ear. The way she smiled at him made me nervous.

I had just lost my chance to have Miss Sandy as a friend. I did not want Mary putting anyone before me. Except Robert, of course, our ticket out of London, if he would have her now.

I nearly let go of her hand, but regained my purpose and gained another step with them, following in Shelley's wake.

Eventually, we jerked to a stop. We had made it up less than ten steps before our progress was stopped by people ahead of us, but it gave us a vantage point down into the crowd.

There must have been five hundred people below us, not to mention those who had entered earlier. I knew the theater was vast, but still. How could we all breathe? I did not think we'd be able to enjoy any of the actual opera, for we wouldn't be able to get near the stage.

The orchestra flared to life as they tuned their instruments. This didn't silence the crowd but instead made the sound of voices increase. We were pushed up the stairs, moving backward, for there was no way to turn around. But even then, we didn't make it into the room, though we were close enough to hear the music begin. It must have been seven, the usual starting time. I balanced myself against the balustrade and settled myself to listen.

An unusual way to spend an evening, to be sure, but the display of rank and fashion surrounding us, along with the stunning music, kept me happy enough. So much so, that I was lulled into forgetfulness about the real purpose of the night.

The music stopped. I was dizzy from the heat of thousands of bodies. We must have been there for hours. Had the performances finished? I tried to get Mary's attention, but then shouts resounded. The guards below us seemed to be passing along a message. The acoustics made the sounds bounce off the wall, losing meaning if not intensity. They started clearing the hall, forcing a stream of people out of one door before opening another. Hundreds of people were removed from the theater. They even opened a path on the staircase. It was wide enough on the edge that we were not sent away.

A phalanx of men came through the doors, liveried. I watched as if this was in itself a performance.

Jewels glittered on tiaras as the dignitaries and their hosts came through. I instantly recognized the Prince Regent by his bulk. His dark curls were plastered along his cheeks below his top hat.

"That will be the emperor of Russia," Mary said in my ear. He had lighter hair and long sideburns that curved almost to his mouth.

"That's Princess Maria next to him!" I squealed. To think we knew an actual royal. She wore green silk with an abundance of lace and was closer to the emperor than her husband.

I knew from the papers who some of the others must be. The duchess of Oldenburg, who was rumored to be difficult; the king of Prussia, a man of middle years; and his two sons, who were likely just a little older than I was.

I nudged Mary. "I wonder if they are looking for wives. The oldest has such beautiful blond curls."

"We'll have to ask the princess," she said archly. "I prefer the golden waves of the younger prince, however."

I laughed, for the princes' hairstyles looked very silly by London standards.

The royals were followed by many people, who I assumed were of similar rank as Count Naryshkin, who stood a few rows behind his wife. He looked disgruntled, and no surprise. The poor man had likely expected to endure all these festivities with his brother by his side, and look what had happened.

"I wonder why the princess is walking with the tsar," I said. "She's even ahead of his sister."

"Look at those earrings," Shelley said from behind me.

When the royals began to climb the steps, I caught sight of one of the princess's ears. From it dangled a long, gold scroll-work oval, which danced along her elegant neck. The gold seemed to reflect back into her dark hair, giving it a lively sheen.

"That necklace," Mary gasped.

I looked more closely. Princess Maria sported a gorgeous rivière necklace with perfectly cut amethysts set in gold. Her gown had a square-cut bodice, revealing a great deal of creamy skin and a bountiful stage for the necklace to shine.

"She has to be the tsar's mistress," Mary whispered in my ear. "That is the only explanation for her precedence."

Just then, the tsar glanced into the princess's cleavage, proving her point.

With unspoken consent, Mary and I pushed sideways on the stairs. When the princess came alongside us, we curtsied, then walked up next to her, followed by Shelley.

We were not dressed in a way that would have allowed us to fit into such glittering company, but no one stopped us. Even the princess didn't frown, though her mouth tightened.

The door to the Prince Regent's box opened. We followed in his wake. Looking out from the box as the view opened, a sea of pea green, rose, and gilt sparkled under the lights. All five tiers of boxes around the theater were crowded with the better classes, and the main floor was stuffed with humanity in all its London varieties.

Thunderous applause began around the gallery as the unmistakable figure of the Prince Regent came into view. Shelley grabbed us from behind and pulled us into the gloom along the wall, out of sight of the revelers around us. Many minutes went by as those assembled applauded. I expected that Tsar Alexander was more responsible for the applause than Prinny, as he embodied the courageous Cossacks who had chased the French out of Russia.

Eventually, the orchestra began again, a hymn this time. A choir came onto the stage and sang admirably. When the hymn finished, the Prince Regent waved to the crowd. The tsar did the same, and the crowd went wild for a few minutes longer before the opera resumed.

The princess spoke in the tsar's ear, then came toward us. I felt Mary stiffen against me. Shelley came out from behind us to block us.

"Did you attempt to have Miss Godwin kidnapped, Your Royal Highness?" he asked her.

"Whatever can you mean?" she asked, most charmingly.

"Just after we left you, two days ago," Shelley said. "An attempt was made to capture our Mary in Covent Garden."

She tilted her head. "How dreadful."

"I hear you are not denying it, madam."

She fingered one stone of her necklace. A gold bracelet slid up her arm. "Indeed, I do deny it."

"And your husband? Might he have been behind it?" Shelley asked with no courtesy.

She licked her upper and lower lip in turn. "What use would he have for Miss Godwin?"

I let go of Mary and stepped next to Shelley. "Have you heard of the moneylender John Cannon, Your Royal Highness?"

"Is he the man who was strangled in his office?" the princess asked. "The count read the story out to me from the newspapers. I cannot read English very well."

"Yes." I described the lacquered box with the diamond that we had found in his desk.

"The box is familiar," she said. "Do you think he was involved in Mr. Naryshkin's murder?"

"He must have killed Pavel himself," Mary said, coming to

stand on Shelley's other side. "All but one of the diamonds is missing, though."

"You do not know any of the diamonds ever existed," she said.

Something in her eyes made me doubt she was quite so innocent as I had previously believed. Both she and Miss Sandy were not who I thought them to be.

"Had you been to his office?" I asked. "On Bedford Street, across the square from where the men tried to take Mary?"

"Why would I go there?" she asked.

"Why would Mr. Cannon kill your husband's brother?" I countered. "I know our papa told him the diamonds were coming, but what would have made a rich moneylender decide he needed those diamonds badly enough to murder? And what did the first dead man have to do with any of this?"

She sighed. "A lovers' spat between my husband's footman and Michael Karamzin led to his murder. It had nothing to do with any diamonds."

"Oh," I said, taken aback. I didn't know about Russia, but that sort of activity between men was a crime punishable by death here.

"Where is Fedorov now?" Shelley asked.

"My husband has sent him home."

"The coroner will try to arrest him again," Shelley said. "We will pass this information to him."

The princess smiled thinly. "Fedorov is a valuable asset to my husband. He is sure to be safely in France already."

"I'm sure he knows too many Naryshkin secrets to be arrested," Mary said.

The princess flinched. "I have nothing more to say to you, except this advice from a mother. Stay indoors, Miss Godwin, where you belong. A woman's place is in the home." She turned around and went back to the emperor.

Shelley took Mary and me by the arm, and we left the box

before the princess could have us kicked out. I found it hard to keep from laughing. Had the tsar's mistress just told my sister that a woman's place was in the home? Really? How droll.

Shelley formed us into a sort of V-shape, using his body as the point to push us through the crowd, with Mary and me trailing behind. A creature of nature, he had no interest in the pressing and odiferous human drama around us and walked through the crowd as if cutting through butter.

I forged on, stumbling behind him. Mary, placid as always, had to take two steps to each of Shelley's, but she kept up, and soon we were out of the theater. With all of the exalted personages inside, the streets were as full as if a parade was about to come through.

Street sellers were out in force, which meant pickpockets and other miscreants would also be lurking. Girls younger than me, with the beautifully pale complexions that probably indicated they had consumption, solicited men in the crowd. Their embrace could be a deadly one, but then who could say that their customers didn't have equally deadly scourges lurking on their flesh?

Shelley moved us steadily through the crowds, keeping up a kindly stream of apologies as he made his way, applying his broad shoulders as needed. Mary and I stayed close together behind him, each holding one of his hands. Mamma would have been scandalized to see it, but given the only view I had was of Shelley's back, I was shocked by how quickly we exited the theater area. We broke into our V-shape again, and it was then I realized we were back in front of John Cannon's house.

I stopped, which jerked Shelley back. He let go of my hand and turned to me.

"What is it, Jane?"

I gestured at the house. "We have to sort this out, Shelley. Princess Maria didn't seem to know how Mr. Cannon had ended up with the diamond and the lacquer box."

"She confirmed it belonged to them, however," Mary said. "Maybe her husband learned what had happened and killed Mr. Cannon because of it."

"It was that footman, Alexander Fedorov," Shelley said calmly. "We know he killed the first man. He killed Cannon as well, then fled."

"That doesn't help us at all," I cried. "How do we free Mamma if the killer has left London and will never confess?"

Mary let go of Shelley's hand and patted my shoulder. "We have to look out for ourselves now, Jane. Mamma's downfall will ruin the entire family, even if Papa stays out of debtors' prison."

I sniffed. "She's my mother. I cannot let her hang."

Shelley folded his arms over his chest. "While I do not think she killed Mr. Cannon, I cannot prove she did not. If only we knew that one of the Russians stole Godwin's scarf. With the murder weapon having come from your own home, the situation is dire."

I rubbed my eyes. "Mamma is a good Englishwoman. Surely, the authorities understand that foreigners are behind most of any violence in London. They must know that the Russian footman was the killer and not my mother."

"We have done our best," Shelley said gently.

"I'll take her to Scotland," Mary told him. "I will persuade Robert to take us there and give up this idea of legal clerking in England."

"You cannot," Shelley said, distress taking over his mobile features. "Your life is here."

She shook her head. "Our life here is over. Jane is going down a terribly dark path, and Papa can't seem to sort out his finances. We have to go. I'll make Robert see that I will be a good helpmeet to him, and that he doesn't want to delay our marriage."

"Marriage?" Shelley said.

Even under the streetlight, I could see he had gone as pale as one of those street girls. "You knew this had to be coming, Shelley. Robert Baxter didn't travel all the way here for a little visit."

"You will be wasted on that boy." Shelley's jaw worked. "Don't throw yourself away, Mary."

She tightened her lips, then stalked off without responding. I followed, as I forever must. It didn't matter what Shelley did now. He couldn't save Mamma, and we knew our way home.

Chapter 21

Mary

Mary felt Shelley's gaze on the back of her head as she walked through the late-night streets with Jane. Gratitude was the only appropriate response to a man who still felt the need to shadow two young ladies for their own protection on these dangerous streets, when they had left him behind.

Still, she couldn't help wishing that somehow, he could find a way to let her go. If he freed her from her place in his heart, could she let him go as well? Entering into a marriage with one man while longing for another surely violated every principle she had. She believed in following love, and he had made it very difficult to love Robert.

Despite these troubling thoughts, she liked peace, craved order. The Baxters' communal style of living in Dundee had suited her fine for the years they had been there. She and Isabella had enjoyed their friendship together, and Christy and Robert were also a pleasure to be around. Now she and Isabella could be young wives together, supporting each other through the birth of children and the other joys and pains of life. The chaos of Skinner Street rarely had a parallel with the Baxters in Scotland. Or at least, it had been hidden from her.

Dear Papa. Hopeless with money and not very good with romantic interchanges, but so congenial and intellectually generous. As kind as Mr. Baxter was, Papa was the better father. She would hate to say goodbye to him, but he couldn't afford to support her, or Fanny, or Jane. Maybe with all of his women gone, he could take a smaller establishment with Willie. Let the expense of the tutor go and educate his son himself. Charles could run away to the continent as he wished.

Everyone would benefit by Mary's marriage. She could see that. Yes, the decision had been made.

"I have to tell you something," Jane said, interrupting her thoughts.

Mary sighed. "Can I not have a minute's peace?"

"I don't want to lie to you," Jane said with a little whimper.

"What have you lied about now?" Mary asked. How much would her ungovernable stepsister do to destroy the peace of Dundee? She had to know all now, so she could learn the simple secrets of Jane's mind and be ready to outwit her.

"When you went to fetch the purse I stole, you found the wrong one," Jane said, her footfalls the only street sound.

"I did?" Mary asked. How could that be?

"Yes. We burned an old one of Fanny's that I had taken upstairs by accident."

"Blast it, Jane," Mary exploded. They had reached the neighborhood around the prisons, where no one would mark a woman yelling like a banshee. They had just passed a tavern, and across the street, the windows of a gin shop blazed with the light of oil lamps.

People stumbled in and out. Even in the night air the door stayed open, for too many people passed through for it to have a moment to close.

"How are we to make a new purse?" Mary asked. "I can do the netting, but we haven't the money for a new silk lining, not to mention Fanny's stitches are tinier than ours."

"Don't be distracted." Jane sounded far more reasonable than Mary felt. "I'm telling you I still had Miss Sandy's purse."

"You need to get rid of it," she snapped.

"Steady," Shelley said behind her.

Mary stopped walking and let him caress her shoulders. She leaned against him, finding herself quite out of breath. The hour was near midnight, and she had to be up with the dawn to start the morning meal. Was there any food in the house? Hot tears pricked her eyes.

A door opened behind them, and a group of men came out of the tavern. One of them brushed Mary's arm as he passed. "Be done with her, man. It's my turn." He whistled at Mary, then walked away, laughing.

Mary bristled, but no wonder she was mistaken for a prostitute, being out at this time of night.

"What did you do with Miss Sandy's purse, Jane?" Shelley asked, in the kind tones one might use to calm an animal.

"I returned it to Maiden Lane. Miss Sandy wanted one of Mary's mother's books. I brought it to her, and I claimed I'd found the purse in a potted plant." Jane cleared her throat. "I truly think she believed me. She even embellished the story herself."

"It is good that you told us. Mary might have had trouble schooling her face if she'd seen this young lady with the purse she thought had burned," Shelley said. "But you must stop lying to us, Jane."

"I know," Jane said in a small voice.

"You cannot ever return to voice lessons," Mary said. Whether it was punishment or good sense, Jane needed to avoid Lord Byron's current mistress in the future. "You do not want your neck in a noose, right?"

"I agree that is wise," Jane said meekly, but then her tone firmed. She stamped her foot. "It's a good thing I'm an atheist, because I wouldn't want to go to hell for stealing."

"Whether hell exists or not," Shelley responded, "you want to die quietly in your old age in your bed, and not as part of a show outside Newgate Prison."

"How will I survive without my voice lessons?" Jane's tone had gone petulant. So many different poses she had, in such a few short moments. Mary quite despaired of her. "Singing is about all I am good at."

"That is patently untrue," Shelley said. "You do well in the shop, and I know you can be a writer like Mary. You are good with Willy. I am sure you will make a fine mother someday."

"What if I am caught stealing again?" Jane whined.

"Don't steal anything," Mary warned.

Across the street, two men started arguing loudly over someone named Peg.

"Transportation to Australia might be just as bad as hell, and you need never do such a thing again," Shelley said, still with the patience of a saint.

"How are we to get money for Papa?" Jane asked.

"Cannon is dead, so Papa will have a respite from that creditor until his heir catches wind of the loans," Mary pointed out. "My hope is there is no heir, and the loans die with Cannon. I don't know if the changes to the ledger will hold up, or if we caught all of Papa's outstanding loan."

"Don't forget, I will have my post-obit loans soon and I will take care of the rest of the Godwin financial problems," Shelley promised.

"That would reduce the pressure on the household," Mary agreed.

"Exactly," Shelley said. "We have to give it all time to play out."

More men came out of the tavern. As they walked past, singing an old ballad about a hanging tree, gin fumes made

Mary's stomach roil. She leaned against Shelley, enjoying his warmth. They shared a moment of quiet communion. How she wished she could take Shelley to Scotland and not Jane.

"You have often said you wanted to make a community of like-minded people," she ventured. "What if you moved to Scotland? Perhaps Mrs. Shelley would come with your little daughter to keep house."

"It is a religious community," Jane said. "Shelley wouldn't like that."

"He's not an atheist," Mary reminded her. "You never know. Maybe the answers you seek are in Scotland, Shelley."

"Are the answers you seek there?" he countered.

"As long as they let me write a little, I will be content," she said.

"And you'll still have me," Jane said.

"And Isabella, and even Christy," Mary added. "You would like them, Shelley. And if your wife leaves her London influences behind, it might go better between you."

"You want me to be a husband now, because you've decided to be a wife?" Shelley asked. "After what I've said to you?"

Mary felt the hurt in his voice, though she couldn't see him clearly. She hated to hear his pain, especially through her own growing grief.

Screams scattered the intermittent peace of the street as two women were pushed out of the gin shop. One of them fell into the street. The other began kicking at her. One of the men along the wall outside grabbed the kicker's waist and hauled her back, and another man lifted her skirts.

"Time to depart," Shelley said, giving Mary a little push.

She grabbed Jane's hand, and they went up the street at a trot, eager to escape the drunken violence. London had its wonders but also many miseries. Mary knew she would miss it.

"Ah London, that great sea," Shelley murmured from behind her, expressing her thoughts better than she could. She had much to learn from his brilliant mind.

"Why are there so many lights on at this hour?" Jane asked, as they walked northwest up Snow Hill.

As they went past St. Sepulchre, Mary wondered what Reverend Doone would think to see them out and about at this hour. He would call them decadent revelers, probably, as he stuffed his mouth with a huge hunk of cake.

"With so many wealthy people in town, the criminal element is out," Shelley opined. "The less darkness, the less opportunity they have to strike."

"The lights are on at home, too," Jane observed. "What does Papa fear?"

"Not the expense of lamps and candles," Mary said. "I am disgusted at the lack of parsimony. How are we to find a replacement for what he has burned tonight? No one will give me credit when I try to do the shopping."

"Fanny would have her ways if she was in town," Jane said. "Don't fret, Mary. We'll soon be gone."

"The windows are lit in the parlor, the dining room, and Papa's library," Mary said. "Look. Even Charles's room isn't dim. Is he having a party?"

In her irritation, Mary sped up. She flung open the door and walked in. No people were in the front hall, but her carpetbag, and another she recognized as Robert's, were bulging full and on the rug they used to wipe muddy boots.

"What on earth?" she said.

Jane came up behind her, breathing on her neck. "Why is your bag packed?" she asked. "Look, your tartan dress is sticking out a bit."

Mary marched over and undid the buckle, then stared at the contents. Her beloved tartan, her black silk evening dress. Evening slippers tossed on top of what had been a clean shift. Polly had been the only woman in the house while they were gone. Who had pawed through her things?

Her pulse leapt. Was she to be banished? Why? Even now,

was there a broker's man on the premises, valuing up Papa's possessions to be sold off?

Panic filled her. She flew down the passage to the kitchen and threw open the door, then took the stairs to the basement two at a time. Polly was fast asleep on her pallet in front of the fire. The light from it flickered on the walls in time with her steady breathing. Who had packed her carpetbag if Polly had not?

Mary pressed her lips together and stepped around the sleeping maid, then reached behind the salt canister to fetch her notebook. Even if she was being banished, for good or ill, surely Papa wouldn't expect her to go without her private writings. This notebook contained the most recent. Now she had to go up and fetch her box.

It contained letters to her from Papa and others, not to mention ink and pens. She was loath to leave the human inhabitants, but if she left her writings and letters as well, it would be an equal blow. Fanny had a similar box, which included letters from their mother, and even a couple from Gilbert Imlay, her father. It had gone to Wales with her, as indeed it ought.

When Mary came upstairs, hugging her notebook, the stairs up to her box were blocked by Papa and Robert, looking very solemn. Jane and Shelley, confusion evident, were behind them.

Mary lifted her chin. "I will be an obedient daughter, Papa, but please do not ask me to go before I've packed some small personal items. Surely the bailiffs won't be so cruel as to sell my letters and notebooks."

Papa tilted his head. "No one is taking your notebooks away, child." He took her book from her and set it inside her carpetbag. "Jane, please fetch Mary's box from her room."

"I need to pack, too," Jane whispered, then dashed upstairs, keening softly.

Papa ignored the start of Jane's histrionics. He guided Mary into the parlor with a gentle touch. She tried to catch Shelley's gaze, but Robert followed them in, blocking her view of the poet.

As suspected, they had built a fire here, despite the hour, the summer night, and the expense. Three candles burned above the fireplace, and an oil lamp made shadows on the wall from a table in front of the window. It might have been the winter holidays, from all the expense of the light.

She turned to look at Robert and found he held his carpetbag but not hers. Frowning, she started to ask him what he was doing with it. Papa kissed her on the forehead, then walked out of the room, leaving them alone.

"It is dreadfully hot," Mary said, undoing her bonnet string. "Really, Robert, what was Papa thinking? Are there men upstairs? Polly seemed content enough in the kitchen."

He set his carpetbag on the sofa. "No, only the family is here. Your father and I had a great deal of business tae discuss tonight."

"Did you find a clerkship with a lawyer?" Mary asked.

"I am returning to Dundee." Robert placed his hands behind his back and went to stand by the fire. "It is obvious that the irregularities here will prevent me from being a boarder and starting my career in London as I had hoped."

"It is very irregular here, to be sure," Mary murmured.

"Instead, I will clerk with an uncle in Edinburgh," Robert said. "This would be my family's preference in any case."

"That sounds like an excellent idea," Mary said. "I wish you the greatest success." Was she finally going to hear what the plan was for her?

Robert stretched out one leg, then turned to face her in an awkward parody of a military man's movement in a drill. "I would hope so, since your future happiness is so closely tied tae mine. My father has long considered your father a friend, and the ties between our families were only tightened by your two long visits to Dundee and my sister Christy's visit here in between."

"My visits to your father's home were indeed a happy time." The words came out as a whisper. She attempted to clear her throat, but her racing thoughts had elevated her nerves to the breaking point.

His brows drew together. "I would like to make our connection formal. Mary, would ye be my wife?"

Mary's teeth clacked together as she opened and closed her mouth without responding at first. Her mind was unable to send words through to her lips, likely because the forefront of those thoughts was *no* even though practicality and duty insisted the answer should be *yes*. Eventually, she pushed past a sense of looming dread. She wrung her fingers together and looked down demurely, feeling it as an act of theater. "I believe it is customary to act shy at first, then say yes at a later date."

He rubbed his nose, then set his fist over his mouth. "I think we both know that there isn't time for that. Ye want to leave Skinner Street."

"I am only sixteen," she ventured.

"Ye are nearly seventeen," he rasped, "and we both know it is time for ye tae leave London."

"With Jane," Mary whispered. "Oh, Robert, I promised she could come with me if I left."

He nodded as if he expected this. "She can come to Dundee. I'm sure she'd be welcome. Ye will go there at first as well, until I can take suitable rooms in Edinburgh."

She tilted her head. Did she have both an escape and a stay of execution, given that her father had said back in the spring that she was done with Dundee? "But will we be wed?"

"Yes, just over the border. That is good enough, is it not?"

Soon, then. The wedding would come first. Though she could feel the pulse pound in her throat and belly, she forced her voice to remain steady. "It has been for many a person."

"Do these plans meet with your favor?" he asked.

She swallowed. Her throat ached like the desert. "It is very romantic. You asking me to elope." If only he was the right person. She wanted desperately to refuse, but this chance might not come again.

He took a step toward her and held out his hands. She took them automatically. The cloth of her gloves skritched over his skin. "Well, will ye, Mary?"

"Y-yes." It was obvious her father wanted her to marry this stripling. What other choice did she have? If only Shelley had been free to love her. But she had to add him to the list of people she could not have, just under her long-lost mother. She had to lock sweet Shelley deep within her heart, then throw away the key. The pain dug so deeply that she couldn't meet Robert's eyes. She stared at his reddened nose instead.

He nodded, still in a very solemn frame of mind. "I have your well-being in mind. I know this is irregular."

She squeezed his hands. "I don't expect anything conventional. I don't need much. We will be fine, running a little household."

He tilted his head down, a small smile she'd never seen before on his lips. "I have managed something better for us. Ye will be pleased."

An alarm bell rang. What did he know of her desires? Had he found her a position? Was she to be married and also be farmed out to support her husband?

"Did you contact your uncle in Edinburgh already? But you've been in London. I assumed you didn't want to work in Scotland."

His smile grew broader, the angles it created hinting at the shapes under his skin still covered by the roundness of youth. "I secured something much more useful. Look."

He pulled her over to the sofa, still holding both her hands. She stumbled on the edge of the rug, then caught her shins against the sofa. A hiss of pain fell from her lips, but he didn't notice. Dropping her hands, he reached for his carpetbag and undid the latch.

He pulled it open, then pulled out a knotted-up cream linen handkerchief. After setting it on the sofa cushion, he undid the knots, then spread out the square of fabric, revealing a vast number of glittering pebbles.

She blinked at the sight. Diamonds. Her hands went to her mouth as she recognized the significance. These were the missing diamonds, the ones that should have been in the lacquered box they found in John Cannon's desk.

Robert had missed one, if indeed they had ever made it to the desk. But Robert hadn't been with them in Bedford Street. Where had he been? With Charles, she thought.

He hadn't been in London long enough to meet Count Naryshkin's brother, who had been dead for well over a week. Or had he? How could a humble Scottish boy be mixed up in any of this?

The sound of gunshots flared in her memory. Someone had been upstairs at the Cannon house when they had found the moneylender's body. The killer. The diamond thief, or at least the second one, after Cannon himself.

Had John Cannon killed Pavel Naryshkin, only to be murdered by Robert?

She drew in an audible breath. For the first time in her life, she desperately wanted to speak to her half brother Charles about his whereabouts. Hadn't he been squiring their visitor about London? Had Robert deceived them all?

Robert looked at her, his determined expression piercing through her. "Ye have a choice, of course; it is up to ye. I know how much my own father reveres yours, and that he is in financial difficulty. I know he has many creditors. The choice is yours, Mary mine. Ye can give them to your Papa or have me keep them to start our new life together."

He reached for her hands, but she quickly twisted her fingers together before he could touch her. Surely, she had more than just a choice about the deposition of the diamonds? Papa would never make her do this.

"What about half to us and half to Papa?" she asked, temporizing while she tried to think.

"I don't think half will help either of us. Someone will have to take the diamonds far away from here to sell them. That is best done by one person, don't ye think?" He raised his brows. "A wedding trip to Amsterdam, perhaps? Or Antwerp?"

"Is it better to sell them all in one lot?" she asked, to feed his ego. What would this boy possibly know? He wanted her to have no choice at all.

"Maybe not, but it is better to sell them far away from the Russians who seek them, don't ye think? We should leave tonight." He caressed her shoulder.

She took a step back. Her calves hit the sofa, and she collapsed into the seat. "What if I want Papa to have them?"

His mouth tightened. "I'm sure ye want me tae be comfortable, after everything I went through to obtain them, don't ye, sweetheart?"

She clenched her hands into fists, growing too angry to be careful. "You gave me the choice. I thought I was to decide."

His chin tilted down. "I expected ye to make the right choice. I didn't kill a man to have the proceeds given away tae someone undeserving. I've earned a comfortable life, with my wife and her sister tae keep house for me."

He thought Papa was undeserving? What kind of man was Robert? Not like his father, to be sure. "You brought a gun with you from Scotland?" Mary's mouth trembled. "I don't understand any of this."

"No, but the severity of your father's problems made it impossible for me to live here and start my career in London as I wished. The diamonds will allow me to have a good life elsewhere." He pulled his shoulders back. "I knew the moneylender must have taken them. Charles told me the entire story at length. I knew exactly what sort of man Cannon was. A greedy, grasping bloke, just like a lawyer. I know the type well."

"Then why do you want to become one?" Mary asked. "You are not from the sort of family that creates lawyers."

"I disagree. What is an education for, but church or the law? And being a professional man of God was not for your father. Nor is it for me. No, I want the ease of a large income. I am tired of congenial poverty. It does not suit me."

She remembered how finely he'd been clothed when he arrived, though he'd relaxed his dress since. "I see that it does not. You are a fine figure of a man." Given his sartorial standards, she was genuinely shocked to hear what he had to say next.

He lifted his chin, as if that finely tied, elaborate cravat was back around his neck instead of a simple stock. "I borrowed your father's scarf. It was a better choice to blend intae this working-class neighborhood."

"I had wondered how it came to be around Mr. Cannon's neck," Mary said, fighting the urge to flee. Why did he have to be so proud of his actions? She would have wished the moneylender dead as much as anyone in the Godwin household might, but to destroy the life another creature in this manner?

"I used it to kill him." He flexed his shoulders. "I am very strong, you know."

She cleared her throat. "I had noticed your shoulders seemed different, broader."

He grinned. "Boxing. I have put on a lot of muscle. I enjoy the sport of it." He made fists and jabbed toward her nose.

She leaned back with a squeal, then put her hand to her chest. He had gone mad, or had always been so.

He laughed. "Don't worry, Mary. I would never hurt ye. But it was easy to kill that despicable murderer. So much of our future happiness depended on it. I knew your father had told Cannon about the diamonds. When I realized Cannon had murdered the Russian for them, it became clear that the path forward could only be retrieving them."

"You went to Bedford Street?"

"Exactly so. I told Cannon I wanted them. Roughed him up a little."

"He usually has guards. I'm surprised you could get anywhere near him," Mary said.

"It doesn't take long to kill a man, particularly when ye are angry that he has refused a reasonable request. Only a minute's search told me that the diamonds were not on the first floor, so I went up to look for them."

"They were in the desk in the second-floor office," she said.

He nodded. "The gun was upstairs, too, above one of the doors, probably for a guard if someone came to steal Cannon's riches. But I outsmarted all of them. I thought your party was the guards returning. I started firing down the stairwell to scare ye off." He regarded her seriously. "I really did think ye were the guards. I'd never have shot at ye, Mary."

"Of course not," she said automatically.

"You're safe with me," he insisted. "I'm not a violent man, just a protective one."

She nodded, though she aggressively disagreed with his claim. At such a young age, he had only begun to discover himself, and she did not like what he had found thus far. For herself, she had uncovered fear. Her hands had started to shake, so she folded them together. It wasn't safe to act like prey in front of a predator. She had to act like none of this was of importance.

Or was that the correct approach? Perhaps acting the part of a feeble woman would rescue her sooner. She needed help. She needed to free herself from him. Marrying a killer, even one who had thought to benefit her family, was not possible. And what about Mamma in the lockup? How did her imprisonment benefit the Godwins?

She gave a little cough, thinking fast.

"What is it, Mary? Are ye ready to go? The boat will need tae leave with the tide. I've spent all day arranging it."

"Who packed my luggage?" she ventured. "There are certain things a woman needs."

"Your servant did," he said impatiently. "Come, Dundee is not the end of the universe. Isabella will have everything ye need."

She did not think Polly had packed for her. "Jane needs a bag of her own. Go out and instruct her to pack, will you?"

He grunted. "She can follow us on the next boat. They only had two berths available."

She didn't believe him. "I am so sick on the water," she said. "If I had her to help me, it would go better."

He pushed out his lips. "There are only two berths, Mary."

She put her hand to her forehead, attempting to mimic Jane's dramatics. The gesture felt wooden.

"What is it?"

She put a hand to her midsection. "My stays, they feel tight."

She felt like a fool, but she could see from Robert's solicitous expression that he believed her distress. What might Jane do next, to get what she wanted?

"Water," she said feebly, letting her eyelashes flutter and her face go slack.

"Mary!" Robert cried.

She swayed, then collapsed sideways, boneless, onto the sofa. Eyes closed, she stayed in a slump, even when Robert roughly shook her.

He snarled out a curse when she didn't respond. After a moment of pacing in front of her, she heard him go out of the room.

She sat up, listening intently, then crept to the door. Good, he had gone toward the kitchen. Quick as a cat, she ran upstairs, hugging the wall, then flew into Papa's library. She shut the door behind her and turned the key in the lock.

Papa stood in an irritated posture behind his desk, arms crossed over his chest, while Jane entreated him about something. Shelley had disconnected from the conversation and gazed thoughtfully at the portrait of Mary's mother.

"Jane, stop, please," Mary begged.

Her stepsister turned to her, teary-eyed. "Papa says I can't go with you."

"There aren't any berths," Mary said, vibrating with her distasteful and frightening knowledge. "Listen, Jane. I can't go either. Papa, Robert murdered Mr. Cannon, and in cold blood, too. I don't know if he was trying to get you or Mamma blamed for it. I didn't quite understand why he used your scarf."

Papa's face went slack as Jane's eyes rounded in shock. "Are you sure?"

Mary nodded. "I pretended to faint to get away from him, but he's still in the house. What am I going to do?"

Shelley turned, alarm spread across his handsome face. Jane ran to him. He hugged her close and patted her back.

"I have harbored a killer under my roof?" Papa asked, an unusually blank expression in his eyes.

"He could have us all arrested," Jane exclaimed, muffled by Shelley's coat. "He could say you asked him to kill the man!"

"He needs to be arrested," Mary told them. "That is what is most important. He's a murderer."

Papa looked at Mary, then Jane. He blinked several times, then shook his head. "The most difficult part will be to save your mamma. She is already in custody."

Mary gritted her teeth. He had a murderer in his parlor, but his main focus was his wife? Now that troubled him? She tried very hard to follow his line of thought, then realized the point.

"He might claim Mamma was his accomplice. How do we fix this?"

"We bargain," Papa said. "We will have to endeavor to keep Robert from the noose since he could easily, however unfairly, claim we put him up to it. Our priority must be Mamma's safety."

"How do we appeal to him, to find a bargain? He has the diamonds." Mary shook her head. "He is selfish and greedy, so unlike the Baxters. A changeling, a fox in the henhouse."

Jane let go of Shelley and wrapped her arms around Mary from behind. "Stop, dear. Control yourself. We cannot give in to emotion now."

Mary choked out a laugh. Of all the people to give that particular counsel. But it was Jane's example that had taught her how to escape Robert's clutches in the first place. "What is the bargain, Papa? Shelley?"

Chapter 22

Jane

"There has to be a lie involved," Shelley said, clapping his fist into his palm. "If we can get the diamonds away from him, I can concoct a story the magistrate will believe, on my word as a gentleman."

I nodded. Shelley, as nearly always, showed such good sense. What a wonder it was to expect to be believed, simply because of one's station in life.

"What good will that do?" Mary asked, loosening my tight grip around her midsection.

"We can trade the diamonds for Mrs. Godwin." Shelley raised his fist into the air. "I can take care of that, Godwin, but only you can wrest the diamonds from Robert."

"He is no disciple of mine," Papa said, steepling his fingers. "Mary makes it clear that he is no believer in my *Political Justice*. I wish I had found the time to educate him to reason before he committed this crime, but we must adapt to the changing situation."

"We don't have much time before the boat comes," Mary said.

"You are correct, child." Papa let out a deep breath. He picked up a pewter candleholder. "These are doings for the dark of night, are they not?"

He went to his desk and opened a drawer, then tucked his bottle of gin under his arm before unlocking the door and going out of the room. Shelley held out his hand to Mary. She took it and squeezed.

"To think, only ten minutes ago I thought I might never see you again, and now my very flesh is pressed against yours," she said.

I winced at the words, which bordered on the erotic. It was time to change the subject before Mary became careless. I was worried about her vulnerability. "What do we do now?" I demanded.

Shelley turned, still holding fast to Mary. "I think we should move to the top of the stairs to be ready for Godwin's word."

"Where are Charles and Willy?" I asked. The lamp flared to life as I lit the wick.

"They must have gone to bed hours ago." Mary glanced up at the ceiling. Shelley let go of her hand and went through the door to the passage. Mary stepped to Papa's desk and picked up his letter opener. I took the oil lamp, then we both followed Shelley.

At the top of the staircase, I could hear the low murmur of voices. I had been afraid that Robert would be angry that Mary had escaped him, but I could not uncover the workings of his devious mind.

I strained to hear the discussion, but the parlor was too far away from the stairs for actual words to be discerned. Eventually, footsteps sounded in the hall.

"Shelley," Papa called.

Shelley nodded at Mary.

"Good luck," she whispered.

He took the lamp from Mary and went down, leaving the second floor dark.

I found Mary's hand and squeezed. "Now what?" I asked.

"Wait and be ready for anything," Mary said.

A couple of minutes later, we heard Shelley's voice in the front hall. "I'll be back as soon as I can."

He went out into the street, closing the front door behind him.

"I'm desperate to know what is happening," I whispered. "Your fate is being decided tonight, Mary."

"Not anymore," Mary said. "I'm not going anywhere. I hope Papa is safe." Her fingers were slick with sweat as she clutched the letter opener.

"We can't hear anything," I whispered.

Mary squeezed my hand, then pulled me to the steps. We went down achingly slowly, then sat at the base of the stairs, the lamp next to them. The parlor door was closed.

"Is Papa keeping Robert prisoner in there?" Mary asked. "I wonder how long it is before the boat leaves."

Shapes moved behind the glass of the front door. The wind had picked up, and I heard at first a faint pitter-patter, then a clattering as rain began to hit the cobblestones. I hoped Shelley had found shelter, wherever he had gone.

An endless amount of time later, Papa came out into the hall, shutting the door behind him. "Mary?" he called.

"Right here, Papa."

"I thought I heard Shelley. Has he come?"

"No, Papa, it is just the rain. What is going on?" she asked.

"Robert recognizes that he has confessed to murder, and as a result I cannot in good conscience allow my daughter to be his bride."

Mary put her hands to her chest. "That is good news, but what about Mamma?"

"We will rely on Shelley," Papa said, thrusting a piece of cloth at her.

She took it, judging its weight with a little shake. "The diamonds?"

"Yes."

"How did you get them away from him?" I asked.

"I explained that he'd never be able to sell them without being murdered himself. Those Russians are killers, as we well know."

Mary tucked the handkerchief deep into the pocket pinned into her dress.

I had a feeling there were dozens of ways to manage selling the diamonds without the Russians finding out, but Robert seemed to be an impulsive creature, who changed his mind with the direction of the wind. He had little experience of the world in any case.

I felt the weight of the stones in Mary's pocket. Did having them on her person make her feel as if some of the guilt of the murder had transferred to herself? I couldn't wait for her to hand them over to Shelley.

"I am sorry this matter of the diamonds went so wrong, Papa," Mary said. "You must have seen them as deliverance at first."

"Such wealth brings out the worst greed in all of us," he said, passing a hand over his face. His fingers trembled. I keenly felt his exhaustion.

The sound of hooves striking cobblestones came up the street, then slowed to a stop outside the door.

"I hope that is Shelley," Papa said. "I've managed to get Robert drunk on gin to distract him, but we emptied the bottle already. I don't know how long the amount I got into him will affect him. He is quite upset about the loss of his marriage."

"Just days ago, I don't think he intended to wed me at all, at least not for years," Mary said.

"Yes, but he didn't consider himself to be wealthy then." Papa shook his head. "As if a thousand pounds worth of diamonds would go far in Edinburgh."

A couple of minutes later, the door opened. Shelley came in, dripping with rain, his hair plastered to his skull. Behind him followed a bent-over creature.

Mary snatched the lamp from the hall table and held it high. "Thérèse?" she gasped.

I beheld our cook, much diminished in size, smelling foul, and with new wrinkles around her eyes. Poor lamb. She had suffered in the lockup. Why was she here?

"Your father sent me with a note to drop the charges against her and bring her back to Skinner Street," Shelley said, wiping his face with his sleeve. "Quick, Mary, go pack her some provisions so we can get them to the boat."

"Jane, pack her some garments," Papa said.

Mary ran for the kitchen, holding her pocket close to her hip for safety. I went up.

A few minutes later, we returned in tandem. I had ransacked Fanny's room, judging that our cook had reduced to Fanny's slim figure. They had always been the same height. Mary had cheese, ham, and a couple of hard rolls wrapped in a kitchen rag.

Their cook still stood in the front hall, looking forlorn. "I'd like to wash the prison off of me," she said in the sad remainder of her French accent.

Papa and Shelley came out of the parlor with Robert, his head lolling, between them. Mary thrust her bundle of food into Thérèse's arms, then ran into the parlor and grabbed the carpetbags. She dumped the contents of hers onto the floor, then held it open for me to set in Fanny's bundle, before adding the food.

"I'm sorry, Thérèse, but you have to go now," Papa said.

"Come," Shelley said, jerking his head at her.

Papa and Shelley supported Robert into the dark street. I could smell dust turned to mud by the changed weather, and an herbal smell that meant summer. Mary ran to the open door behind Thérèse's forlorn, odiferous form, and we watched the men push the boneless boy into the cart Shelley had commandeered from somewhere.

"It's better than prison," Mary said.

Thérèse shrugged. "It is better to be a jailer than a prisoner, I suppose. I will keep an eye on him, if your friend sends me the money he promised."

"I will do my best to hold him to it," Mary said. "I am truly sorry for what you have suffered."

Thérèse sniffed. "It did my soul good to see Mrs. Godwin join me. I hope she is forced to remain in the lockup for at least as long as I did. I never want to see that dreadful woman again."

"Then you will have to find a position in Scotland, so you never have to return to Skinner Street." Mary gave her a little push. "I wish you the best of luck, and to be well rid of this place. Climb up now." She helped their cook into the cart. Shelley ran around to the front and climbed onto the bench next to the driver, another young man who must be one of Shelley's endless store of friends.

Mary and I stood, shivering in the rain, as the cart disappeared, heading toward the docks. Papa took us by the arm and towed us back into the house.

"What clothing did you send her with?" Mary asked me.

Jane shrugged. "Thérèse is quite thin now. And we don't know when Fanny is returning, so I just pulled her winter things out of her trunk and sent them along."

"Fanny is a good soul. I'm sure it is what she would have wanted," Papa said. "Jane is much taller than Thérèse, and Mary is too slim."

"What will Mamma think about all this?" I asked. I could

hear the bellows of her rage now, and she had not been in the lockup long enough to suffer as Thérèse had.

"She will think Thérèse was a tool to get her home safely," Papa said. "I will instruct her to consider the matter no further."

"I believe I shall resolve to avoid Scotland in the future," Mary declared.

"Me, too," I said. "Now what do we do?"

"Wait for Shelley to return," Papa said. "Girls, why don't you tidy up the parlor? I have letters to write."

He went upstairs, leaving a trail of wet footprints behind him. Mary touched her hair. Instead of its flyaway red-gold glory, it looked dark brown and flat, as soaked as if she'd been trying to wash it.

She sighed. "Well, we must have some way to occupy our time. I will fetch a towel."

I glanced at the pile of belongings on the floor. "I'll get one and take your clothes back to your room." She bent down to gather them up, then I left Mary to survey what had transpired in the parlor.

My steps slowed as I reached the upper floors. How much would the events of this night change our future? There had been much doubt of Robert's intentions, then in an instant, all had changed. I had not thought him a killer, but then, who would see me as a thief? At least the discovery meant that Mary would still be here. I would not be the only girl in the Skinner Street house. If Robert had kept the truth from us, even now they'd have been on the boat heading north, the promise to take me with her broken.

I was glad she hadn't left me. Smiling, I found her dressing gown, then went back downstairs.

My mood changed when I reached the front hall. I shuddered when I entered the parlor, the scene of such near disaster.

I handed the dressing gown to Mary.

"This night has been full of loss," she said in dolorous tones. "The end of a somewhat reasonable marital option. The end of the notion of living in Scotland. The loss of any hope that we would see our cook return to Skinner Street."

It seemed that she'd been standing there doing nothing but dripping. "Fix your hair," I said brusquely, then turned to straightening the sofa and banking the fire in case we needed the room to be warm for Shelley later.

We were curled up on the sofa, dozing to the storm-swept music of the steady rain on the cobbles, when I was roused by a sharp rap on the door.

I rose blearily and shook Mary, then lit a candle and teased the fire back to life. "Run downstairs and fetch hot water," I said. "Shelley will need a hot drink."

She sat up, rubbing her eyes and licking her lips. "You're right, Jane."

We both went out. I watched until she had disappeared down the passage, then opened the front door.

I had no idea of the hour, but Shelley was not alone.

"You remember George Hodgson, the coroner," Shelley said. He'd acquired a tricorne from somewhere, and water dripped off it in all three directions. "Let us in and fetch your father, Jane."

I stepped back. "Go into the parlor, please."

They came in. I helped the coroner with his greatcoat and hat, then went upstairs and knocked on the library door. There wasn't any answer, so I went in.

Papa had his head on his hands on the table under the portrait of Mary's mother. I was concerned for a moment. Was he in despair? But then I heard the gentle snore. I shook him.

"Papa, dear, Shelley is downstairs with the coroner," I reported.

Papa snorted, then shook his head and sat up. "Just resting my eyes."

"Mary and I were completely asleep. I've sent her for hot water, and the gentlemen are in the library."

He rose, slowly, a bit unsteady on his feet. I took his arm, glad for my youth and strength. Slowly, we went downstairs, the stairs squeaking like a discordant symphony.

Shelley had Mary's damp handkerchief and was rubbing it through his hair. The tricorne had not kept him dry. Mr. Hodgon had taken Mary's place on the sofa, which was probably still warm from her body's heat. He held a glass of sherry, which Shelley must have taken from the cabinet.

Some silent discourse seemed to pass between Papa and Shelley, who forced a smile and excused himself, the kerchief still in his hands.

I poured Papa a sherry and went back to work on the fire until I had it in a merry little blaze, using coal we probably could not afford, but the walls radiated chill.

A couple of minutes later, Mary entered, looking composed, with a tea tray in her hands. She set it on the table in front of the sofa, then took a seat in a straight-backed chair that I loathed.

Papa cleared his throat, then set the knotted handkerchief that Mary had hidden in her pocket earlier, onto the table next to the tea tray. Some sleight of hand had transferred it to him. He undid the knots.

Mr. Hodgson gasped as the diamonds inside glittered in the firelight. "They did exist."

"Yes, sir," Shelley said. "I had a merry time tonight in the river."

"That is where you found them?"

"That is where John Cannon's killer went," Shelley said, very imposingly.

My eyes widened as he began to spin a tale of death-defying drama on the edge of the river. I remembered he was a novelist.

"I can't swim," he said. "But of course, I had no idea that we would end up in the drink after I trailed the man from a low tavern in Wapping."

"Where is he now?" Mr. Hodgson asked, accepting a cup of tea from Mary.

"In the river, I'm afraid. A rowboat was coming right at us in the dark. I fell back, but it went right over the killer. He didn't come up."

"Dead?" Papa asked, increasing the reality of the spun tale.

Shelley nodded decisively. "He was a sailor from India. I saw him skulking around Cannon's house and confronted him. He had a debt owed to Cannon that he couldn't pay. I knocked the confession out of him."

"What was his name?" Mr. Hodgson asked.

Shelley shrugged. "Eventually his corpse will float up downstream. Perhaps you can find someone who knew him."

"There won't be enough left of him by then, especially if a boat hit him," Mr. Hodgson said philosophically.

Mary handed out the rest of the cups. I didn't get one, but Shelley's fictional tale had woken me up as completely as if I'd been drinking rich coffee.

Shelley tied up the handkerchief and held it out to Hodgson. "On my word as a gentleman, the matter is clear. Mrs. Godwin does not sport with low foreign sailors. She is entirely innocent of this matter."

The coroner hesitated, then tucked the bundle into his coat. I ached to see the diamonds disappear forever. I hoped Shelley had seen sense and tucked a few away for our own use. "What do you think, Mr. Godwin?"

"John Cannon was not above violence. This sailor must have known he was about to lose his kneecaps and struck first. If he couldn't work, there was nothing for him here. He'd have starved in the street." Papa nodded to emphasize his point, then drained his cup. "I believe my daughter told me she'd seen a sailor hovering around Bedford Street on Friday when they investigated."

"There are houses of ill repute in the area," Mary said softly. "It all makes sense now. A foreign sailor would have stayed in Wapping for his amusement, not come to Covent Garden for it."

Mr. Hodgson's cheeks had reddened with the unsavory turn of the conversation. "It is very late, or rather, it is likely early. I will return home for a few hours of sleep, then I will talk to Bow Street and have Mrs. Godwin released."

"Let us go now," Papa said, the tea having woken him up completely. "The magistrates work all night."

"The cart is waiting outside," Shelley urged. "My friend will need sleep himself soon, so let us use it."

Mr. Hodgson sighed. "I don't like being on the streets with the diamonds on my person."

"I will guard you with my life," Shelley promised, though he was looking at Mary when he said it.

She smiled at him. "Mamma deserves to come home as soon as possible. It is dreadful what happens to a person in the lockup."

Shelley offered his hand to Papa. He grunted as he rose to his feet. Mr. Hodgson rubbed his jaw, but he followed them out of the room.

In moments, it was as it had been, just Mary and me. The Skinner Street door opened and closed. I shut the parlor door to keep in the heat, then collapsed onto the sofa.

"Mamma will be home soon," I said. "Everything will return to a state of normality."

"Without Fanny, without Thérèse," she said, dropping next to me. "And no hope of Robert ever again."

I nodded, holding her gaze. "We've lost the diamonds, too. I don't suppose Shelley kept any."

"Money isn't important to him. I have decisions to make," Mary said softly. "I cannot be Mamma's cook."

I'd have kept a few diamonds for myself, even if I'd had to tuck them under my tongue. "I am surprised Papa didn't send me to Scotland instead of Thérèse, but then he doesn't know that I behaved much worse than our cook." I clutched Mary's hand as the horror of that possible fate crept over me.

"He knew Mamma would be freed eventually. He would never separate Mamma from her daughter." Mary smacked her lips.

"That is a great deal of hoping. Shelley came up with a brilliant story. I honestly doubted we could free Mamma."

"I had my moments of thinking Papa must have killed John Cannon, for all that it made no sense to me."

"Poor Papa," I sighed. "He is exhausted."

Mary leaned forward, squeezing my hand tightly. "Listen. If you want to leave Skinner Street, you will have to make that decision for yourself. I don't know what is left for either of us here."

"Willy? Charles?"

Mary shrugged. "I have no prospects left."

"Your aunts might take you as a junior teacher."

"They cannot make up their minds to take Fanny. I do not think that is an option. What can we do together, Jane?"

"I am afraid for you," I admitted. "And afraid for myself. It was good that you tried to fit your life to Robert's. I don't know who else there might be but Reverend Doone."

She shuddered. "That would keep me in this neighborhood. I want to go far away from here."

"I'll work hard on my singing and get work in the great theaters of Europe," I said in a flight of fancy.

"Good luck, now that you can't attend lessons," Mary said. "We are all out of options. We shall have to make our own way." She smiled suddenly. "Shelley is forever full of ideas, is he not? We will consult him in the morning."

I squeezed her hand one last time. "I trust that he will give us good counsel. He has indeed saved our family this night." I released her and stood, then kissed the crown of her head, still a little damp. "Sweet dreams, Mary."

"I will have nightmares," Mary said. "Shelley painted such a scene, with his fiction of wrestling with a doomed sailor."

"You like nightmares. They feed your stories." I winked at her, then went up to my bed.

Acknowledgments

I want to thank you, dear reader, for picking up *Death and the Visitors*. We authors live and die by our book reviews, so thank you for reviewing *Death and the Visitors* and anything else I've written, especially *Death and the Sisters*, the first book in this series.

Thank you to my beta readers—Judy DiCanio, Paula Martinac, Cheryl Schy, and Mary Keliikoa—and I appreciate the emotional support provided by the Columbia River Sisters in Crime chapter. Thank you to my agent, Laurie McLean, at Fuse Literary. Thank you to my Kensington editor, Elizabeth May; my copyeditor, Carolyn Pouncy; and my communications managers, Larissa Ackerman and Jesse Cruz, along with many unsung heroes at Kensington.

While the Godwin family, the larger Shelley circle, and the Baxters are real people, my plot is entirely fictitious. I know little about Robert Baxter in particular and freely admit everything but his name and age are author fantasy. Dmitry and Maria Naryshkin are real as well, but Dmitry's real siblings and staff did not include my fictional Pavel or any of the other members of his household in this book. I worked from old maps to make the movements and locations in the book as accurate as possible. I also used William Godwin's journal to move real people in and out and around the story. A tremendous amount of material is available about this period in London, and I encourage readers to pick up some nonfiction on the topic.

While we cannot truly know what motivated Mary, Jane, and Shelley to do what they did in the summer of 1814, the consequences of their actions affected every one of the people in their lives, and I cannot wait to keep telling their story. Until the third one!

BOOK CLUB READING GUIDE for Death and the Visitors

1. Mary Shelley is an icon for events that occurred later in her life. What new things have you learned about her in this book?
2. Given the fame of Mary Shelley's parents, discuss the pressure she must have felt to find literary success in her own right.
3. Though we don't know for sure, it is assumed that David Booth and Robert Baxter really did offer proposals for Mary. Do you think she would have become the literary superstar she did if she had married an obscure Scotsman and gone north?
4. Mary had multiple suitors in this novel. Do you think she made the right choices in her dealings with them? Do you think her father made the right choices?
5. The female characters were afraid of being kidnapped. White slavery was much feared in the nineteenth century. What do you think is at the heart of that fear?
6. What is your opinion of Percy Bysshe Shelley based on his characterization in this novel?
7. Do you enjoy snippets of contemporary writings in historical fiction, such as the bits of poetry featured in this text?
8. Did it enhance the novel for you to see a glimpse of Lord Byron, arguably the most enduringly famous literary figure of his age?
9. When reading historical fiction, do you prefer most of the characters to have been real people, even if their actions are fictionalized, or do you prefer just a few real people behaving within the absolute parameters of their life and the rest made up?
10. Do you think this story could have been told in a contemporary setting?